A Sexual Watergate!

It was unimaginable that a President of the United States could ever become entangled in a political intrigue as scandalous and, yes, as *stupid* as Watergate. But it happened.

In this story we meet a First Lady whose highly sophisticated sense of politics *and* incredible capacity for erotic adventure brings our nation to the brink of revolt. Watergate, by comparison, was a juvenile escapade.

Carla Callahan had a lust for life that knew no bounds. She enjoyed every power-packed, sex-drenched moment of it. Her mind, her face, her incredible eyes, her body, were all perfectly designed to achieve exactly what she wanted. And no one was immune to her attractiveness . . . especially the one man who would be totally trapped by it!

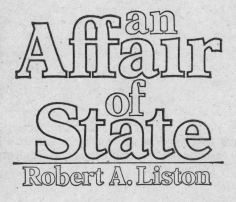

an Affair of State

Robert A. Liston

PINNACLE BOOKS   LOS ANGELES

AN AFFAIR OF STATE

Copyright © 1978 by Robert A. Liston

An original Pinnacle Books edition, published for the first time anywhere.

First printing, July 1978

ISBN: 0-523-40241-4

Cover illustration by Norm Eastman

Printed in the United States of America

PINNACLE BOOKS, INC.
2029 Century Park East
Los Angeles, California 90067

For Jean

Who long ago in the moonlight
believed . . .

AN AFFAIR OF STATE

* * *

It came in the second post, a parcel roughly the shape of an outsized shoebox. I realize now it was a package of historical importance. I should have taken precise measurements and photographed it. I should have been careful opening it so as to preserve it for the Smithsonian. But I had no way of knowing. The box, if it could have been called that, is now long gone. It fell apart in the process of opening it. The sender obviously didn't have a box of the correct size to hold his tapes, so he made one. He cut a heavy cardboard carton—from the label I could tell that it had once held whiskey—and fashioned a container of the proper size. He had used a great deal of heavy plastic tape to hold the box together. To open the parcel, it was necessary to cut the tape. The cardboard fell into its component pieces, and I threw them into the fire.

The makeshift box for the tapes had been wrapped in heavy brown paper. I regrettably did not save it either, but I did examine it thoroughly for clues as to the source of this incredible packet of tapes. Again, the sender had improvised. The brown paper was an ordinary supermarket shopping bag turned inside out. The printing on the paper revealed that he shopped at a Food Fair store. The wrapping had been fairly neat—at least it was intact after its long journey from America. The heavy nylon cord with which it was tied obviously aided that process.

The package was addressed to me, C. Walter Grayson. There was no Mr. or Professor or Dr., appellations that are sometimes used. Just my name. The address of my home here in the Cotswolds was correct. To use the term so popular back home, I am not giving the address for "reasons of security." It is a matter of considerable importance that I safeguard these tapes as proof of the sensational charges they contain. I can hardly do so if squads of CIA, FBI, and other minions of President Lampton are breaking down the doors of my English cottage.

The package was decorated with a large quantity of American stamps, far more than I would guess were required. The stamps were all of a small denomination used on first class letters in the States. A great many of them were affixed to the front of the box, filled most of one side and even part of the bottom. It was as if whoever mailed the package lacked the time or did not want to risk going to the post office to have the package weighed and the correct postage affixed with a postage meter. It is not hard to figure that he simply put on whatever letter stamps he had at hand and dropped the package into a mail chute. Because of all the stamps on the package, it was difficult to make out the postmark. I could read "Washington, D.C.," but I was unable to make out the date. I am certain, however, that the parcel came by sea mail, and from the elapsed time and the events that have transpired, I gather the parcel must have languished in the bowels of some freighter for an extended period. Or perhaps the package was simply caught up in the monstrous inefficiencies of the American postal system. The new American regime is no more able to operate a postal service than its elected predecessors.

I have learned a great deal about the mind of the sender, but I am uncertain whether his entrusting these tapes to the vagaries of the postal system was by clever design or the accidental good fortune of a desperate man. Through discreet inquiries among some friends in the British Foreign Office, I have learned that there has been a massive search for these tapes in Washington. Indeed, the search continues as I write. Every storage locker in the city of Washington and environs was opened and inspected. Hundreds of people have been interrogated and their premises thoroughly searched. To repeat, I do not know whether it was by design or fortunate accident, but it seems dia-

3

bolically clever to me, some sort of perverse justice, that while this massive energy was being expended in a search for these tapes, they were safely ensconced in the postal system, wending their way slowly across the Atlantic by boat in a box bearing a lot of stamps and a green custom slip declaring the parcel to be a "gift under ten dollars." I perhaps carry on too much, but I simply adore the thought of all those FBI agents and police turning the country upside down in a search for these tapes while some obscure postal clerk is dutifully wielding his rubber stamp and sending them out of the country.

But I am getting ahead of the story. I cannot possibly relate how mysterious the package was when it arrived at my doorstep. There was no return address on the outside. I had no idea who it was from or what it contained. When I opened the parcel in the manner I have described, I found that it contained a large number of reels of recording tape, with some facial tissues wedged around them to prevent their rattling. Although I examined every shred of paper, cardboard, and tissue several times, there was no note, no word, drawing, or symbol to explain what these tapes were and why they had been sent to me. Indeed, there was no way of knowing if these tapes contained any sound. There were no numbers or labels or identifying marks on them. They could have been new, unused tapes for all I knew. Of course, I hardly thought they were that. My impatience with mechanical gadgets is well known to my friends. I rarely look at television. I play a radio only for an occasional newscast. I do all my writing in longhand rather than brave that monstrosity known as a typewriter. I will use a telephone only under duress. Tapes for a tape recorder must rank among the last things I would need. It occurred to me that someone might have sent me tapes as a practical joke, a useless present on the order of sending a load of coal to a person living in an all electric home. But all the way from Washington? And so many tapes? No, there had to be something recorded on those tapes which I was intended to hear.

I rang up a friend of mine who I knew owned a tape-recording device. It is of no importance who he was. There is no point in involving anyone unnecessarily into this somewhat dangerous enterprise. Just say I knew him to have a fetish about mechanical gadgets. His house is wired for what must be everything. I suspect he pushes a button to raise and lower his toilet seat, although I've never visited the loo in his digs. At his invitation, I took one of the tapes for him to play. He couldn't. He explained that I was now in possession of tapes that could be played only on some sort of exotic apparatus available at an exclusive shop in London. He looked up the name and address for me. I went up to London the following day, visited the shop, and, yes, they had the necessary machine. It was dreadfully expensive, and I wasn't about to buy one. I arranged to rent the infernal recording machine. Even then I had to make a deposit of one hundred quid, if such mercantile greed can be imagined.

When the store manager demonstrated how to operate the machine, I discovered for the first time that the tape I'd taken to London did contain a voice, a male voice. But I'd had no chance to listen to it because of the droning instructions of the store manager. He consistently assumed that I was extraordinarily interested in the various fascinations and capabilities of his device.

It is possible, therefore, to imagine my impatience to return to my place and at last solve the mystery of the tapes. The train ride from London never seemed so long or the ten-minute walk from the station to my cottage so far. With difficulty, I restrained my impatience, entered my home, and set up the machine on the kitchen table. I had predictable difficulties in remembering the instructions on how to operate the device, but in due course the sound of that masculine voice again emitted from the machine.

My disappointment was boundless. I don't remember what I expected, but it certainly was not an unrecognized voice droning on in a sort of remembrance of singularly uninteresting things past. I guess it would have been too much to expect the voice to say, "Professor Grayson, you won't remember me, but I'd like to confess my part in the overthrow of American democracy." But, dammit, the voice could have identified itself. It could have mentioned a name or date. It could have said what the tape was about or why it was sent to me. Nothing.

I listened for half an hour. I simply did not know the voice. That's all there was to it, and there was no use in kidding myself that I would ever recognize it. It was clearly an American voice. The grammar and vocabulary bespoke someone of education, but not particular erudition. The accent was not pronounced, but I had the impression that the speaker was from the Northeast, although not Boston or New York. I am hardly an expert in linguistics, however.

There were many, many hours of conversations in those tapes. I never counted them, but I would estimate scores of hours, no, hundreds of hours. It was predominantly his voice, but occasionally there were recorded conversations with others. One was called "Mother" and another "Uncle Richard." You'll just have to imagine the number of hours I had to listen to tapes to stumble on those conversations. I know now that I had bad luck. You see, the tapes were out of order. If I had, with luck, picked up and played the right tape, I would have solved my mystery much sooner. But in accordance with a law of nature—is it Murphy's Law that everything that can go wrong will?—it was not among the early tapes I played. It was several days after receiving the package and beginning the listening process that I learned the identity of the speaker.

David Callahan. I then knew who he was and the urgent importance of what I had been hearing. David Callahan. I am certain this book will never be published in the United States. Merrill Lampton's infamous censorship law—euphemistically known (what else in this crazy world?) as the Freedom of Information Act—bars the publication of any materials derogatory to the government, threatening to the peace and stability of the American people, or giving aid and comfort to domestic or foreign enemies of the nation. Since stock market quotations have been suppressed from time to time, it is hard to imagine the circumstances under which David Callahan's shocking revelations would see the light of print in the new America. In fact, I suspect I am herein engaged in an exercise in folly, for it will be a very brave publisher in the United Kingdom who will print what David Callahan has to say. Yet I suspect such brave men still exist in England. I know one or two, although I will not speak to them about this project until the manuscript is finished. Even in Britain, the publisher of this will risk great danger from the CIA. I'm sure the American State Department will bring great pressure on the British government to suppress this book. But perhaps a few copies can be put in circulation before Lampton can react. Still, Americans will never see it, unless a copy, masked in a plain brown wrapper, is smuggled in from Canada. It will give the American border patrol and customs agents something else to search for.

Because this book will be published, if at all, in the United Kingdom, it is perhaps wise to recount here for British readers just who David Callahan is, or was. David Callahan was the stepson of Merrill Lampton, president of the United States of America, the son of his new wife, Carla Callahan Lampton, the ubiquitous First Lady, or, as the London tabloids would have her, the "beauteous queen of America." David Callahan was her son and only child by her first marriage to the late Brendan Callahan.

It is hard to imagine that there is anyone in the world who has not heard of Carla Callahan Lampton. She has received the most massive publicity build up. At this very moment, a magazine kiosk in London, Paris, Rome, and, I suppose, Moscow and Peking, or even Ouagadougou, contains a dozen periodicals with her likeness on the cover. In America, *all* magazines would have her on the cover. She is a daily fixture on television at home and is frequently seen on BBC. There is no doubt that she is a beautiful woman and does photograph well.

The build-up of Carla Callahan Lampton has

been carefully and deliberately orchestrated. She is depicted as a glamor queen, elegantly attired in the height of whatever the fashion is. Her diet and program of exercises that keep her svelte figure at age forty are exhaustively reported in the women's magazines, along with her "beauty secrets" that keep her so young-looking and gorgeous. I suspect her plastic surgeon ought to be interviewed, or at least her cameraman, but I am perhaps being excessively negative and catty. Again, she is a beautiful woman who takes care of herself, no doubt of that. We are treated to Carla Callahan Lampton opening orphanages, visiting newly opened schools, calling upon the wounded, and appealing for peace and an end to violence in America. Perhaps her greatest worldwide publicity attended the funeral of her son, David Callahan. As these tapes make unmistakable, David Callahan was murdered by Lampton's men. He knew too much and was disaffecting. The discovery that he was making secret tape recordings clinched his death. He had only a few, frantic days as a fugitive. Yet his death was trumpeted by Lampton as a case of martyrdom. He had been assassinated, just as so many others had, by the violent, terrorist minority that had laid waste America's great cities. The funeral was a triumph of pageantry and publicity. The world was treated to the vision of the beautiful Carla, her blonde loveliness draped in black, walking stoically behind the catafalque while the drums beat their mournful cadence. She was dry-eyed, her head held high and proud, marching behind her "martyred" son's body up Pennsylvania Avenue, braving snipers' bullets to accompany the procession from the sandbagged White House, past the rubble of the government buildings to the Capitol, with its dome now crumpled by blasts from recoilless rifles. No matter that David Callahan didn't rate a state funeral. Lampton gave him one anyway. Carla Lampton was trumpeted on television and in the press as a symbol of America's courage and determination to survive this internal holocaust and build a new and better America—and other such rubbish. In the months since that funeral, Carla Lampton has restricted her mourning to a black armband while continuing an apparently incessant round of ceremonial and public functions. At least once a week, it would seem, she opens some new school, park, street, or playground named for David Callahan.

There can be no doubt that Merrill Lampton and his cronies find his attractive wife very useful in the subjugation of America. Instead of civil liberties, open elections, and other manifestations of democracy, or even instead of jobs, food, prosperity, and peace, the American people are given Carla Callahan. She is, in essence, a diversion, an elegantly gowned, beautiful, sexy-looking queen of America who mouths an incredible array of banalities and half-truths to make Americans either forget what they have

lost or believe what they now have is an improve-
ment. Quite incredibly, in view of these tapes,
David Callahan plays as important a role in death
as he did as a revolutionary in life. I suppose
every successful revolution needs a martyr, and
so Merrill Lampton would have us believe David
Callahan is his.

Knowing that this was David Callahan's
voice on these tapes and knowing who David
Callahan was or had been did not explain why
I had come to possess his taped confession. I
had to assume that he, not someone else, had sent
these tapes to me and that it was a deliberate
act. Why me? I didn't know David Callahan,
except as a name in the newspaper. I had never
met him or even seen him in person. Nor did I
know anyone who had. Yet he had clearly sent
these tapes to me. He had hardly picked my
name out of the Washington phone directory.
He had quite consciously chosen me. Therefore,
he must have known me. Since I am an extremely obscure academician of whom hardly
anyone has heard—indeed, I don't even social-
ize much anymore—that seemed extremely unlikely.

Faced with still another puzzle concerning
these tapes, I visited the local library to peruse
back issues of newspapers and magazines until
I found several photographs of David Callahan,
most of them associated with his obituary. He
was a handsome young man with blond, or even

reddish blond, hair worn to medium length and expertly trimmed. He had blue eyes, a prominent brow, and a rather squarish face. A strong chin and firm mouth suggested determination and strength of character; yet the overall effect of the face, perhaps because of the long eyelashes or the delicate, much-too-small nose, suggested weakness or softness or even effeminacy. He looked vaguely familiar. Or maybe it was all in my mind from all I had learned about him from the tapes. What can you tell from a photograph anyway? I couldn't really say I'd ever laid eyes on the man.

I decided the answer to why David Callahan had sent these tapes to me would lie, as the question of his identity had, in the tapes themselves. I made up my mind to begin the awesome task of listening to all these tapes very closely and organizing them into some kind of coherent order. Perhaps in so doing I would find the answer to my puzzle.

And so I did. I now believe that David Callahan began these tapes almost two years ago, probably soon after the death of his father. I suspect he talked into a microphone, much as others write in a diary or blab to their psychiatrist, in an effort to try to understand his own tortured relationships with his father and mother. There is a great deal of this in the tapes. As he became embroiled in the conspiracy to overthrow the Constitution, he also began to secretly record conversations with others.

His apartment in Washington was obviously wired for sound. I don't know why he did this, at least in the beginning. But he soon came to believe he was acquiring a measure of protection. He knew he was in a most vulnerable position in the conspiracy, the one person taking the greatest risks. He hoped the tapes would protect him in the event his activities were ever discovered. In short, he hoped to use the tapes as blackmail if Lampton and the others ever tried to throw him to the wolves. David was dead wrong, of course. In the end, the tapes caused his death.

When David realized he was in a trap from which there was no escape, he decided to expose the whole Lampton conspiracy by sending these tapes to someone who would understand what they contained and would publish them. He underwent a change of convictions—if indeed he ever had any real convictions—and hoped to prevent or destroy the great evil he had done to his country.

To whom would he send his tapes? It was an almost unsolvable problem. He could not send them to anyone in the United States. His confession would simply never be published there. He would have to send it abroad to an English-speaking country where publishers were knowledgeable about what was happening in the United States and concerned about the preservation of liberty. That pretty much restricted him to a person in Canada or the United Kingdom. Of even greater importance, the recipient of the tapes had to be unknown to him or so tenuously connected to him that even the most thorough investigation would not discover the link. David Callahan was correct in this. In their search for the tapes, federal agents have sought to trace every person who had ever known or come in contact with him. Finally, I think David hoped to send the tapes to someone who had a familiarity with what was happening in America, disapproved of it, and also had the ability to publish a book based upon his revelations.

That, I submit, posed a most difficult set of criteria for David. It is fascinating to me, first, that he even thought of me, and, second, how he signalled to me in the tapes that I was deliberately selected. Moreover, he did so in such a subtle way that only I would know. If, as seemed likely to him, the tapes fell into government hands, I would not be implicated. A very thoughtful act, I must say.

In what turned out to be the very last tape, David inserted two cryptic words—"Bonnie Bluebell." When I first heard them, I paid no attention to them. It was not until much later as I was laboriously transcribing these tapes that I realized their meaning. I remembered that Bonnie Bluebell is the name of an inn associated with Hinsdale College, a small liberal arts institution in Ohio. Suddenly I realized why the

David Callahan of his photographs looked familiar. He had been one of my students.

Almost precisely five years ago, I taught a course at Hinsdale for a brief period. At that time, Hinsdale operated on what it called the "intensive system." A single course would be taught at a time with a whole year's work being crammed into a seven-week period. It was an interesting educational experiment, and I rather liked the system. A member of the political science faculty had become ill, and I was asked to teach a course for the spring term. This was no great honor to me. I knew the chairman of the department slightly. Since the course was on federal-state relationships and I had written a greatly unread book on the subject and was unemployed at the time, I was invited as a visiting lecturer.

When I say David Callahan was one of my students, that is a guess on my part. I have tried mightily to reconstruct that classroom in my mind. There were only fifteen or twenty students. I had them several hours a day for seven weeks. I ought to be able to remember all of them. Yet, I cannot remember a single face, a single name. I've tried to tell myself that David Callahan sat near the rear or some such place, but I honestly cannot remember.

Yet he signalled to me and me alone on those tapes with a reference that is both humorous and embarrassing. I give lectures that are very orderly, meticulously prepared, and, as a consequence, as dry as dust to all but me. This undoubtedly accounts for my lack of success on the college-lecture circuit. I like to work from a careful outline, ticking off the points I wish to make—one, two, three, four, or A, B, C, D, etc. Thus, in discussing something like revenue sharing, I'll say, "There are five factors affecting the amount of federal funds available. The first factor is . . . The second factor . . ." and so on. Or I might list a number of aspects to state police powers. I'm afraid this, however dull, is the way I think. I really can't help myself. I fear I didn't make a very good impression at Hinsdale. I heard at the end of the term that students kept count in class of how many times I used the words "factor" and "aspect" and got to some ignobly large numbers. David Callahan remembered this and signalled to me by uttering, along with the reference to the Bonnie Bluebell Inn, a strange sentence using the words "factor" and "aspect." It was a clear signal that he intended for me to have his tapes.

The success of David's scheme lies in the fact I have never been contacted by any American agents. My friend in the Foreign Office tells me that agents descended on Hinsdale College like the proverbial locusts. He was a known graduate and apparently a generous alumnus. Apparently the college was turned inside out in a search for the tapes. Anyone ever connected with the college, however remotely, was questioned. Obviously, the FBI didn't look remotely enough. I was there so briefly. And I wasn't supposed to be there and made such a nonimpression while there. My name would not appear on any faculty lists. I wasn't in the yearbook, which had already gone to press. I never made any mailing lists. I didn't even live on campus but at the Bonnie Bluebell Inn. Any pay vouchers and cancelled checks that might have recorded my stay there were long ago destroyed. I feel certain David Callahan calculated all that in selecting me as the recipient of his tapes.

I have wondered how David obtained my address here. It would not have been difficult, but he would have had to go to some pains. Shortly after my experience at Hinsdale, I came into a small inheritance from my mother's estate. It wasn't much, but it forced me to decide what to do with my life. I accepted the fact I was monumentally unsuccessful at university teaching, no matter how much the life appealed to me. So, I took the money, came to England, where I had always wanted to live, and invested it. The income is pitifully small by American standards, but it is enough for me to live frugally here in the Cotswolds as a "man of independent means," as the British put it. I supplement my income by writing an occasional scholarly article for American publications, as well as a piece from time to time for British journals. Obviously, I write on British affairs for American publications and vice versa. Most of my effort is—or was, before these tapes came into my possession—devoted to a lengthy history of British-American relations. I chose that subject because it is so vast I'm sure I'll never finish it and be forced to publish it. I make all these references to my activities as a way of suggesting that I am hardly a household word in the United States. I haven't been home in five years and have very little contact with anyone there.

So how did David get my exact address here? He could possibly have done it through the Passport Office and the State Department, but I'm far from certain they would have an exact address. I still file an American income tax form, so the IRS would have my address. David could have located me through either agency. But it seems to me that in so doing he would have attracted a lot of attention. I think he wanted to protect my anonymity too much to have taken either course.

My guess is that he went to the library and looked me up in some of the dustier editions of the *Periodical Index* or some such. If he got the name of some publications where I have been published, he could have gotten my address by an anonymous phone call. Certainly a mildly fraudulent story about a long lost relative or some such would have produced my address without causing him to reveal his own identity.

All machinations such as this seem absurd in a way. It is still hard for me to believe that an

19

American citizen would have to go to such lengths. Yet so much more that has happened in the United States is also unbelievable. Who would have believed cannonading in the streets, sentries on every street corner, armored personnel carriers, and the rest? Who would have believed cancelled elections, kangaroo courts, censorship, and the heavy knock on the door in the dead of night? And who would have believed that it was all done, as David Callahan's tapes reveal, so willfully by a small group of people? I, for one, would have said it was impossible. As a student of American political science, I believed wholeheartedly that the system designed by the founders, our greatest legacy as Americans, was a method to prevent just the sort of tyranny that has happened. Not very long ago, I was bragging to my British friends how the American Constitution functioned as a safeguard during the Watergate affair. Now David Callahan instructs me in how wrong I was, although I still find it hard to believe that something so good could be turned against itself.

His is an intensely personal story. Much of what is on these tapes is a tale, a singularly erotic one, of a tortured, truly pitiful individual. He became part of probably the greatest conspiracy in history; yet his motives were always personal. He was, I believe, an essentially apolitical person. Yet he played a key role. It seems to me that there must have been others who could have done what he did; yet the fact remains that he did.

And David Callahan's confession also reveals that the conspiracy was so damnably simple. They made it look so accursedly easy. And it was easy. And I could weep for that. As Richard Morrison, whom David Callahan reveals to be the real power behind Lampton, says in these tapes, "Watergate was just a warm up, a mock-up to show how it really could be done."

David Callahan has made it extremely difficult for me to simply tell his story. As I have indicated, the tapes were in no particular order. I have had to guess at the chronology, and that has not always been easy. Although some of the time David has a clear, logical, incisive mind, he also engages in a great deal of rambling reminiscenses, much of it erotic in nature. A confirmed bachelor such as myself would never have dreamed how prominent a role good old sex would play in ending American democracy. I'm sure that was the great mistake of the founding fathers. They didn't figure it either. In editing these tapes, I have tried to report that which is essential to understanding David Callahan and his role in the conspiracy while eliminating the trivial and extraneous. We don't have to know *everything* that ever happened to David Callahan.

What follows is not an exact transcription of the tapes. In the interest of readability, I have eliminated some of his extraneous mental meanderings, cleaned up his language, and tried to help him get on with his story. I have tried to keep such editing to a minimum, but there is a necessity for some of it. Again for the sake of readability, I have presented his third person account of conversations in dialogue form so as to reduce the intrusions of expressions such as "he said" and "she said" and "I replied." David truly did have an amazing recall of conversations. I believe he would have wanted me to present these in dialogue form with quotation marks and so forth to spare the eyes of the reader. Believe me, after months of playing these tapes, I have become an expert in the difference between the written and the spoken word.

The beginning of David Callahan's story lies somewhere near the middle of his narrative, when he describes an important luncheon he attended. It was at this point that David's involvement in the conspiracy began. He was enlisted to the cause of fascism. As David told his story, this meeting occurred shortly before he set up his apartment in Washington, less than two years before his death. Thus, this important luncheon is reported only after prolonged descriptions of his childhood, prep school, and college days, and the year or so that he lived at home prior to his father's death. I have lifted David's description of his luncheon from its natural position in the narrative and used it as a beginning. If historians are offended by this, so be it. I am more concerned that people understand what is transpiring in all that follows.

To set the stage, Brendan Callahan, David's father, has been dead for a short time. My guess is about a month or six weeks. Again, no dates. David and his mother have been invited to lunch at "Uncle Richard's" apartment on Fifth Avenue in Manhattan. "Uncle Richard" is Richard Sinclair Morrison, Wall Street investment banker, power broker of the Republican Party, friend and confidant of presidents, and, as we shall see, the kingpin of Merrill Lampton's seizure of power. He is also an old friend of the Callahan family, so close he was the only person ever invited to stay overnight in their home. He handles the finances for the whole family and has done so for three generations. David grew up calling him "Uncle Richard," although he is no blood relative. Photographs and his rare television appearances show Morrison to be a tall man in his middle to late sixties. His white hair and cherubic face make him look like everyone's kindly old grandfather. Evil does have its disguises.

This is how David Callahan described the luncheon at Morrison's apartment:

* * *

Mother announced that she and I had been invited to lunch at Uncle Richard's Fifth Avenue apartment. There was someone he wanted us to meet. We dressed hurriedly. At least she rushed me, for we weren't supposed to be late.

She was ready ahead of me, mostly because she suggested I change my tie. She waited in the doorway of my room, tapping her foot impatiently, urging me to hurry up. I remember taking my time and making a particular production of tying the knot.

I asked her if she knew whom we were meeting.

"Yes."

"Who?"

"I promised not to tell. It's supposed to be a surprise."

Looking back on it, I realize my perversity was childish. I just didn't feel like a stuffy lunch with Uncle Richard. I undid the knot and started over.

I heard her sigh in exasperation. "You'll be sorry if we're late," she said.

"Who're we meeting? God?"

"You're warm."

She came over to appraise herself in the mirror. "How do I look?"

Mother was wearing widow's weeds, but her soft wool dress was a flower garden on her. She looked particularly stunning. Perhaps it was the undercurrent of excitement she seemed to feel. I felt like teasing her. "If you have to ask if you look good, then you don't."

She made a face at me. "C'mon. We're late."

She snatched up her purse and headed for the stairs. As I followed, I saw her slip into her mink coat. It had to be a special occasion all right. She rarely wore furs.

She seemed impatient on the drive in, fretting over traffic snarls and checking her watch much too frequently.

I noticed a number of extra men on the street outside Uncle Richard's apartment building and in the private parking garage behind it. I remarked about it but still didn't catch on, even when two men stood outside Uncle Richard's door. So I was appropriately and genuinely flabbergasted when we entered Uncle Richard's ornate, antique-filled apartment and I was introduced to his luncheon guest, the President of the United States.

Merrill Lampton was even handsomer than his photographs, and I understood why he was considered one of the more distinguished-looking chief executives in history. His complexion was a pinkish tan, as though he had just come from the sun or used a daily sun-lamp treatment. His hair was snow white and wavy, his eyes a vivid blue, his chin and mouth firm. He seemed very fit, very vigorous, both in shaking hands and in speaking. My only disappointment was that he seemed shorter than I expected. About five-nine, maybe less, I guessed. When he was introduced to Mother, he held her hand in both of his and expressed condolences on the death of my father.

"As you perhaps know," he said, "I lost my own dear wife just over three years ago. I know how lonely you must be."

"Thank you, Mr. President. You are most thoughtful."

She seemed dazzled by him, a feeling I could share.

"My son is a great comfort to me."

"Yes, yes, children are such a help. I don't know what I'd do without my daughter." He spoke of how well Judith Lampton had done as his official hostess, but unfortunately she had her own life and family. He didn't know what he was going to do.

Uncle Richard said he hoped we didn't mind going right to lunch. The President had only a brief time to spend.

The President laughed. "Too many people have the notion it is bad for the country if the President relaxes with his friends."

Only the four of us sat down to the light lunch—soup and shrimp as I recall. I thought it strange that he had no aide with him and decided it must be a supreme compliment to Uncle Richard that he felt no need for one. He was very charming and urbane at lunch, regaling Mother and me with tales of a lecherous Arab oil sheik on a recent state visit. I was extremely impressed with him, even awestruck, by the sense of command he conveyed. The easy way he wore his clothes, his sonorous voice, his natural gestures, and effortless laugh revealed a man in full charge of himself and every situation. He was very attentive to Mother, who sat on his right. She loved it. Her eyes shone, and there was a slight flush to her complexion. I had never seen her so, but then I'd never seen her at a private lunch with the President of the United States.

When lunch was nearly over—we were having coffee—the President became serious and addressed himself to me. I recall precisely what he said.

"David, Dick speaks very highly of you, and that is why I came here—to meet *you*. You are just the sort of young man I'd like to have on my team. Are you willing?"

I was stunned. I mumbled that I was very flattered and would do anything he wished.

"Good. I hoped you'd say that. I'm looking for someone with your background, your qualifications to do—well, call it troubleshooting for me."

I said of course, but asked what sort of troubleshooting.

"I'm not going into that now. I'm going to leave all that to Dick. All I can tell you is that I don't want you to work in the White House. In fact, I don't want you near the place or any other government department. From time to time Dick will have some little jobs for you. Just follow his instructions. Can you do that?"

I said of course and added that it sounded very mysterious.

"Not really. It's just that it would be useful to me to have someone I can trust—totally trust—someone who is in no way officially linked to the government or anyone in it. Dick thinks you're that person. I do too."

I again said I was flattered.

"What I want you to realize, David, is that although you may not see me again for a long time and although I will never speak of our little conversation here again, you are working for *me*. What Dick asks you to do is what *I* want you to do. You are working for me and me alone. Do you understand?"

I was unable to speak. My mouth was dry. All I could do was nod. I felt I was being annointed by God.

"Now, David, I would like to have your solemn assurance that you will never speak a word to anyone of our conversation here. Only the four of us will ever know."

"I swear. I won't say a word."

"Good. And I'm sure, Mrs. Callahan, you won't either."

Mother said, "You have my word, Mr. President."

"And now I really must go," he said and arose. After a gracious farewell to Mother, he left.

Mother and I sat there in stunned silence until Uncle Richard returned from seeing the President to the door.

"He's something, isn't he?" he said. "A real

man, a great leader, a truly magnetic personality."

Mother said something in agreement. I don't recall what. I said, "I believe he could get a person to do anything. But what does he want me to do?"

"It's very simple, David. You are in a unique position. You are someone we can trust, explicitly thrust. I've known you all your life. I've watched you grow up, a fine young man, healthy, strong, with a good head on your shoulders. You've never engaged in any sort of foolishness or wild behavior. To put it bluntly, you have good moral character. That's important to me and to the President. We want no taint or scandal. There hasn't been any in this administration, and there isn't going to be any. That's why we want you."

I glanced at Mother. Her face, her eyes, were expressionless.

"I hope I'm not blushing too much," I said.

"Blush all you want. You're a fine young man. I told the President exactly that. Carla should be proud of you. I know your father was. I certainly am. That's why I want you and the President wants you."

"To do what?"

He laughed. "I did digress."

"And you did pour it on a little thick."

"Okay, but I wanted you to know how we feel. As I was saying, you are in a unique position. Your father maintained a close liaison with these so-called revolutionary groups, the Liberty Party. He was known and trusted by them. Ephraim Squires, the alleged leader, was a particular friend of his. He gave them money and I don't know what all. Through him, you are known. If you'll remember, I encouraged you to go along with your father's wishes and get to know these people. I didn't know why I encouraged you at the time. I just thought it might be useful some day. Now it is. I want you, the President wants you, to continue the sort of activities your father did. Visit these people. Keep up the contact. Gain their trust. Give them money. Do anything they want just so they learn to trust you."

I groaned. "You don't know what you ask. I hate these people. I loathe Ephram Squires as I've never loathed anyone in my life. He's a creep, a queer, a pervert. I can't. I detest them."

"Oh, yes, you can. Just don't let them know how you feel."

"Why me? You've got the FBI to infiltrate them."

"We've already done that. But that isn't what we want from you. I'm not asking you to infiltrate Squires's organization. In fact, I most definitely don't want you to do that. I don't want you to join them and go around carrying signs and blowing up buildings or whatever else they're up to. I want you to maintain the sort of contact your father had. Remain outside. Remain apart.

But just help them, talk to them, encourage them, make them trust you."

"I'll never be able to do that. Father was a much older man. He had spent his whole life in liberal causes. He was well-known. Squires just won't believe me."

"Perhaps, but you are your father's son. He introduced you to Squires and the rest of them. So, you aren't your father. I can understand that. Maybe they won't trust you. But they can be made to need you, and need may serve as well as trust for our purposes."

"And what are those purposes?"

He laughed. "I'm not sure there are any at the moment. But there may be. We'll just have to see what develops. All I can tell you is that it is important that your conversation with the President never become known. You are never to have any official government connection. Nothing must ever be traceable to the White House or even to me. Understand?"

"Yes."

"You are going to have to live a double life, keeping secret forever what you are really doing and for whom you are really working."

I smiled. "That won't be hard. I haven't the slightest notion what I'm really doing."

"Then you're game to help us?"

I wondered what the "us" and "we" meant. I assumed it was he and the President, but I didn't know and I didn't ask. Instead I said, "One question. How long does this go on? It's

31

very important to me. I can't see myself doing this for the rest of my life." I glanced at Mother. There seemed to be a worried expression in her eyes.

"Of course not. I'm talking about a few months or so, perhaps not even that long. And you won't be living with them. You'll be able to carry on a normal life between visits to their meetings and such. Much as your father did."

I nodded.

"Are you game?"

I smiled. "I regret I have only one life to give for my country—or something like that."

He laughed. "I'm sure it won't come to that. Look, David, relax. You might even become very fond of Ephraim Squires."

"And I might love a pet monkey, too."

He reached in his coat pocket and extracted a large white envelope. He handed it to me. "You'll need money—for expenses."

I took it and glanced inside. There was a half inch or more of bills, all used. I saw several hundreds. They were all hundreds.

"I think you should get started on this right away. Try to call Squires. Show up at some meetings around the country. That sort of thing. Meanwhile, we'll move you to Washington as soon as we can."

"Washington!" I was surprised by that.

"Why, yes. You can't do this sort of thing from Westport. Squires has set up a headquarters in Washington. You've got to be near him.

You've got to have a secure place where I can visit you and you can maintain contact with them."

"But Washington . . ."

"I thought you wanted a place of your own."

"I did, but now . . . Mother'll be alone and . . ."

"Carla can take care of herself. She'll be able to visit you in Washington, and, heavens, you can go to Westport as often as you wish. But you must have a base in Washington, that's all."

"I hadn't realized that."

"What's there to realize? It's time you had your own place. Don't you agree, Carla?"

Mother had been looking at me, her eyes wide. Now she looked at him. She said nothing.

* * *

I do not know how much time elapsed before David moved into his Washington apartment. Several weeks surely. Nor do the tapes reveal where the apartment is. It is just "an" or "the" Washington apartment. No address is given, not even a section of town.

David never describes the apartment. Why should he? He was after all not writing a book but simply talking into a microphone for his own amazement. I can only surmise that since David was accustomed to living in considerable luxury, his apartment must have been comfortable and reasonably well-appointed. His mother visited him there. It is hard to imagine her sleeping in a hovel. The tapes indicate the apartment consisted of a living and dining room, probably connected, a kitchen, and bath. There was one bedroom. Reference is made to a second bedroom.

I also do not know how much time elapsed between David's moving into the apartment and his installation of his tape-recording system. The voices on the tapes indicate that he had at least two microphones in the apartment, in the living room and in his bedroom. Since neither Morrison nor David's mother give the slightest indication of knowing they were being recorded while in his apartment, it must be assumed the microphones were cleverly concealed. I don't know whether David did the installation himself or had it done. I have no indication he had the ability to make such an installation. On the other hand, it seems unlikely that he would have risked having anyone else know about his equipment.

The quality of the recordings is good. The voices are quite audible even when the person is some distance from the microphone. The only problem is that the microphone also picked up extraneous noises. When a coffee cup is set in a saucer, for instance, the sound is—oh, I'm no writer—it's loud, believe me, crashing. I can report that the system was not voice-activated. David turned it on when there was something he wanted to record.

That which follows is obviously the first tape, the true beginning of David's narrative. He must have set aside an evening to begin, or perhaps he found himself alone and decided to begin on impulse. He mixed a drink; the sound of ice in a glass is clearly audible. He said, "I've got this new toy. What am I going to do with it?" He played those words back to himself, I imagine, assuring himself the device was working, then pressed the record button again. He commented that his voice sounded strange. That was reasonable. People are always surprised by the recorded sound of their own voice. And his voice was strange in another way. "It's funny to hear your voice in an empty room." And I can understand that. I've lived alone for many years and talk to myself incessantly. But never aloud. I would think myself peculiar if I did so. He tried again. "Lord, but it's quiet in here." The room really wasn't quiet. The microphone heard better than he. There is a hum in the background, perhaps an air-conditioner, maybe a refrigerator. A clock ticks faintly in the distance. There is a little noise from the street. A car horn can be heard. He makes a couple of false starts. "I really don't know what to say." A pause, then, "How do you say where your life begins, the cradle, the womb?" Another pause, then he truly begins.

* * *

The number fifteen has been important in my life. I was born on the fifteenth of May. My father was fifteen years older than my mother. My mother is fifteen years older than me. It sounds like a tennis game. Fifteen love. Thirty love. Thirty-fifteen. Deuce. Advantage Mr. Callahan.

Having a son only fifteen years younger than herself has posed some social difficulties for my mother. When I was five, she was twenty. When I was ten, she was twenty-five. That was all right. No one thought much about a young woman trailing a little boy along. But I had a tremendous growth spurt when I was twelve or so. I had my full height by the time I was thirteen. It was something else for a gorgeous woman of twenty-eight to introduce a gangling, six-one kid as her son.

On more than a few occasions I heard her lie about her age—or try to. She'd pick a number—thirty, thirty-one, even thirty-three or thirty-five. This was ridiculous, of course. My mother had enough trouble passing for twenty-eight. She's almost forty now but doesn't look thirty. If she said twenty-five, no one would question it. She'll always look young, I think, even if she ever permits a wrinkle to appear on her face. It's her bones, I guess, fragile, delicate. Or maybe it's the shape of her face. She has one of those almond-shaped faces with high cheekbones that photographers love. Most likely it's her eyes. That's what everyone notices most about her. If she'd had brown eyes or washed-out green ones, few would consider her a great beauty. But the irises of her eyes are of the deepest, richest blue and so large they seem at times to fill her whole face. When she looks at you unblinkingly, you feel they are two blue pools enveloping you. Many times I've had the sensation of falling into them. Indeed, I sometimes dream at night of standing beside a pool of still water and wanting to dive into it. I always wake up before I do, however.

When I was in prep school, and particularly college, strangers routinely assumed Mother was my sister or even my lover. It became embarrassing to explain that she was my mother. The comments were predictable and tactless. "You can't be his mother!"—which of course she was and is. Or "Heaven's, how old are you?"—which was even worse. Or, totally insulting, "You must have been a child bride." I don't believe Mother and I ever encountered anyone who could handle this matter of ages and appearance with tact. So we learned to avoid it. We introduced each other without giving relationships. Or, if someone assumed a relationship, we'd let them.

In recent years, Mother has taken to lying about *my* age. I've seen her lop five years off my life. She does this in situations where I have to be introduced as her son and where she wishes to impress some dignitary. I don't like being tolled back to my teenage years. I think it is silly of her. But I do understand her reasons. She's a beautiful and rich widow. To have a twenty-four-year-old son. Well! Heads do turn and people do talk. And just now I'm not supposed to be visible on the social scene in Washington. Hopefully, all this super-secret-government-agent-master-spy crap will end shortly, and I'll be able to go back to a normal life—if I've ever had such a thing.

[There are sounds on the tape, a sharp noise, a rustle of fabrics, soft footsteps, the clink of ice in a glass, and a variety of other sounds indicating that David had gotten up and made himself a drink. He then returned to his narration.]

I have tried many times to imagine the meeting between my mother and my father that resulted in my birth. It is not very easy. I know better, but other people see my mother as cool, icy cool. I once heard a fellow at a party call her a "beautiful ice statue" and heard the other guy reply, "Yeah, and I'd sure like to melt her." This is a gross misreading of my mother, but I can't blame them. With other people, my mother is always aloof, diffident, largely silent. She appears to be listening, although I'm not always certain she is. She seems to be interested in what others are saying, but she rarely speaks. I've watched her time and again. A situation will arise in a conversation—if a monologue can be called a conversation—when it seems inevitable that she must speak, if only "yes" or "no" or "how interesting" or some banality like that. But most often she doesn't. She says nothing. Maybe she just looks at the person expectantly, waiting for them to continue. They do. It isn't awkward. There is no embarrassment. I suspect people don't even realize Mother hasn't said a word. It is uncanny how she does it. I've tried it, and it's a dud. I've never seen anyone do it the way she does. Her passion for silence gives her this aura of coolness. With others, she seems always calm, placid, always controlled. There is nothing spontaneous about my mother. In fact, she tries to avoid any situation which is not planned. She wants everything to be familiar, practiced, even rehearsed, at least in her mind. So it is impossible to imagine my mother, cool, calm, controlled, always sophisticated and elegant, involved in a tumble in the hay somewhere or in the back seat of a car, sweating and panting while I was conceived.

Imagining my conception is also difficult because she never talks about it. She gives the impression of being born when I was born, of having sprung into life at age fifteen. She never speaks of her childhood. There is no mother, no father, no origins of any kind. There are no photos of her as a child, no mementos or souvenirs. She just hatched whole.

My father talked about their courtship a little—if courtship is the word. Their meeting. I think he would have spoken more about it, but he felt constrained. She didn't talk about it. She didn't want him to talk about it. I pressed him for details. He knew I had a right to know something. He told me a little. It was not enough to satisfy me.

So I must imagine my father driving along a highway in Massachusetts toward Boston. He would have been driving a sports car, an MG probably, white or yellow with a black interior, the top down, his red hair tousled by the wind. The radio would have been playing, loud music most likely, or a political discussion of some kind. What was he going to Boston for? He would have been twenty-nine, rich, handsome. He could have been on his way to some kind of business meeting, but that seems unlikely. Maybe a meeting with friends, perhaps a political discussion of some kind. Why were you going to Boston, Dad? Well, I really don't remember why, son. I was just going. I never thought to ask my father that.

My mother was hitchhiking. That in itself seems an imponderable impossibility. The elegant, always impeccable Carla Callahan—I don't know what her maiden name was—standing beside some lonely road in Massachusetts, her thumb upraised to halt a car, any car, my father's car. What was she wearing? Dirty blue jeans? A tacky sweat shirt? Her hair dull and limp and dirty, blown in the wind from passing cars? Impossible to believe. It cannot be believed. Yet she *was* hitchhiking and my father *was* driving down that road and he did stop and pick her up. Did he see her far ahead and slow

to a stop when he saw she was a girl, any girl?
Was he horny and couldn't pass even an in-
discriminate opportunity? Or did he pass her,
see how beautiful she was, then stop with a
great screeching of brakes and a cloud of road-
side dust? Did he turn around and come back
for her? Or did she run after the car, a long
way maybe, arriving breathless, panting, her
chest heaving, to hop in for a ride? My mother
runs beautifully. I think she ran after the car.

It was late afternoon. Dad said so. Did they
stop somewhere for a drink? Hi, I'm Brendan.
Brendan Callahan. Who are you? Carla. Carla
what? Or did she just say Carla and not give a
last name? Or was her name really Carla at all?
Maybe it was something mundane like Myrtle
or Blanche. I've always had the feeling she invented the name Carla to go with Callahan.
There is no way of knowing. She has no birth
certificate. When she got her passport, she had
a new certificate drawn and legalized. This
place'll do. The car stops, too quickly probably;
she lurches forward. He hops out. Does he come
around and open the door for her? Today,
surely. She'd wait in quiet insistence. But then?
They go inside. What'd you like to have? Did
she say martini? That's her drink today. Did
she like them then? You look awfully young to
drink. How old are you? Did she lie her age?
She was fourteen. She must have looked ten.
Maybe she asked for a coke. No, my mother detests coke. Orange juice? Yes, my mother would

have had an orange juice. Dad had a beer. Imported beer. On tap, preferably.

My mother was running away from home. I know that. She told me. She was adopted. Her parents divorced. She saw no sense in remaining any longer. Had she just left? Was this her first ride? Or had she traveled many days? Had there been many rides, many drinks, many motel rooms? I wonder about that, sometimes quite a lot. My father and she talked over their drinks. What did they talk about? Today—or I should say until he died—he talked a lot, and she mostly listened. Did he ask her questions about herself? Did she give noncommittal answers? Did she put him off by asking about him? Did she get him talking about himself? She does that so marvelously today. Did he prattle on about himself and his activities, his dreams, his opinions, while she nodded and tilted her head to the left and smiled faintly, saying almost nothing? Did it grow late until he suggested dinner? Did dinner take a long time until he suggested the motel?

How did my father get my mother into bed to conceive me? He was twenty-nine, the scion of a wealthy Connecticut family. She was a fourteen-year-old runaway he picked up hitch-hiking. Impossible. Yet it happened.

"How did you and Mother meet, Dad?"

He turned his head a little to look directly at me. His eyes squinted a trifle, then he smiled his broad, Irish smile. "Oh, your mother was hitchhiking up in Massachusetts. I gave her a lift." He tried to make it light, a small joke, but he knew I wasn't satisfied. He was expected to say more. His smile faded, and he looked away from me. When he spoke, his voice was low, soft. "Your mother was the most beautiful girl I'd ever seen. I loved her from the first moment I saw her. I've always loved her."

Was he a love-struck young man, hopelessly infatuated with a beautiful young girl he had just met, driven by passion to bed my mother? It could not have been that way. My father, if he was nothing else, was a compassionate man. I guess more than any person I've ever known, he genuinely loved people. I cannot believe that he used a ride in a car, a drink and a free meal, to bribe a fourteen-year-old runaway into being balled by him. No. Never. However much he may have desired her, he would have taken her home or found her a place to stay. He would have looked after her, given her money, protected her, helped her. He would have slept with her, to be sure. My father was no saint. But not in lust. He would have had to feel he was helping her. He would have had to have it all worked out so that sex was an act of virtue. He was doing good. My father was a do-gooder.

But there couldn't have been time for all that. My mother was fifteen years and five months old when I was born. I believe that to be true.

If she was going to lie about it, she'd have lied her age the other way. Subtract nine months from fifteen years and five months. There wasn't much time for romance and courtship. They must have copulated when they first met or shortly thereafter.

There is another possibility.

"Mother, when you first met Dad, did you know he was rich?"

I don't remember when I asked that. I was quite young, I suppose. She looked at me. Her blue eyes were very dark, questioning. "Why do you ask that?" My mother is nothing if not guarded in her speech. I have never seen her caught off that guard in some unwitting, unwanted self-revelation.

"No reason. I just wondered, that's all."

She looked at me a moment longer, then decided the question was innocent and required an answer. "Did I know your father was rich?" A repetition. More time to think. Her mouth started to frame the word no; then she changed her mind. "Yes, I suppose I did. Not at first, but soon. It's hard to say." I submit that is an answer that is no answer. My mother should have been a politician.

Did my mother have a plan at age fourteen? Or was it all just an inspired impulse? Did she see his car and his clothes? Did she listen to his guileless candor about himself, his family, his activities? My father never felt the slightest need not to reveal anything to just about anyone. He never had anything to hide. Did she discover he was rich and unmarried and then have an instant insight to the possible future for a penniless runaway girl, particularly one he obviously desired? Did she keep him talking, dawdling over dinner until it was too late to go on to Boston? Did she encourage him to drink too much until he was high, or maybe a little drunk? Was he so enchanted with her that he forgot the time and where he was and where he was going? Did he shake his head, smile boyishly, and apologize for drinking too much? We'd better stop somewhere for the night. Don't worry. I won't touch you. How did he sign the register? Mr. and Mrs. Callahan? Not him. Maybe Brendan Callahan and daughter. More likely Brendan Callahan and whatever name she'd given him. My father detested dishonesty. You take the bedroom. I'll sleep here on the couch. It'll be comfortable enough. There's a shower there if you want. She emerged from the shower—wearing what? If she was hitchhiking, she must have had some clothes with her. A nightgown? A robe? Perhaps she wrapped herself in a towel. No. His shirt. She took his shirt as a robe. She came into his room—just to thank him and say goodnight. She went close to him. He smelled the sweetness and cleanness of her. She extended her hand. He felt its softness and smoothness and strength. He looked into those blue eyes and felt himself being enveloped by them. She smiled and reached up to give him a coquettish peck of a kiss. He felt her softness and nearness. Her shirt fell open. His hands could not resist. Silken curves. A saturation of softness. And he could not resist. I think my mother seduced my father that night and I was conceived. Yes. It could only have been that way.

Yet, who knows? My mother certainly will not talk of it, and my father is dead and gone and can't. Besides, neither one would have told the truth. My father would have protected my mother, and she would either not remember or not recognize or utter the truth. I can guess some sort of seduction must have occurred; yet seeing them later it is hard to believe. I guess it must always be that way. A child sees his parents, grown, mature, careful, safe, and old— although my mother is anything but old—and finds it hard to imagine them as young, careless, and in love. I just can't imagine any grubby grappling in a motel room. Was she a virgin? Was she tight and frightened? Did it hurt? Did she cry out in pain as he forced his way inside her to eject the seed that made me?

* * *

This curiosity about how his parents met and his conception was not just idle rumination to David. He pursued the matter on two other occasions, with his mother and with Morrison. I have extracted both conversations to complete this episode.

On the one tape, David is having dinner with his mother. They are having a rather animated conversation. He seemed to have her relaxed—relaxing Carla Callahan was always a large production—and enjoying herself. He had her reminiscing. I think all of that was a lead-in to this question:

"Mother, how did you and Dad meet?"

She said nothing. It was a long silence.

"Oh, come on, Mother. It's fair question. I have a right to know."

Nothing. There is no sound on the tape.

"Look. It's no big deal. I'm not invading your privacy. It's not important. It's just a curiosity. A person wonders about his parents, that's all."

Still nothing. And nothing. And nothing.

It went on forever. I would have thought the machine broken except the tape was moving and I could hear the familiar background noise of his apartment. It was the most devastating silence I've ever heard. I timed it. It went on for one minute and twenty-three seconds. I had the impression she might never speak again, except that she loved him and took mercy on him. She opened her mouth and finally spoke:

"How is your work going, David?"

He had more luck with Morrison.

* * *

"Uncle Richard, do you know how my parents met?"

"I didn't know there was much to know. She was hitchhiking. He gave her a ride. The rest is you and a most interesting history."

"I know all that. I just don't believe it."

"Why on earth not?"

[He sighed. There is a silence, then the monstrous sound of a cup being placed on a saucer.]

"Look, I'm not much younger than my father was when he met my mother. Like him, I'm the scion of a wealthy family. I've been to college. I'm informed. I know which way is up. I've things to do. My mind is occupied. I, too, am unmarried. I simply cannot imagine the cirmumstances in which I might be driving down a road in Massachusetts, spot a fourteen-year-old girl hitchhiking, take her to bed, father a child, and then marry her, living happily ever after. It just won't play in Peoria."

[Long pause.] "Did you ever ask your father?"

"Yes."

"And what did he say?"

"He said he fell in love with her the first time he saw her."

"And you can't believe that."

"Sure—if my mother were standing out there hitchhiking today." [He laughed.] "That, I submit, is a little hard to imagine." [Both laughed.] "My mother's gorgeous. Lots of men have fallen for her. She could have anybody she wants, I suppose. But at fourteen? I look at fourteen-year-old girls. And fifteen, even eighteen. I make a point of it. They're children. Don't you see my point?"

"I do. Of course, I do." [There was another pause.] "I was called out from New York. Your grandmother phoned expressly to have me come out to Westport and talk to your father. I had not met your mother when I confronted him. I said something like, 'Brendan, what sort of nonsense is this? A fourteen-year-old girl? Pregnant? We are all of the flesh. I can understand a dalliance. We all make mistakes. But why perpetuate it with marriage?' "

"And what did he say?"

[Morrison sighed.] "It's hard to remember. He may not have said anything. He was angry. I remember that. He didn't want any of us to interfere with his life. He was very protective of your mother. She was his wife and we were to accept her. He may have just glared at me and walked away. He may have told me to mind my own business. Something like that."

"But, Uncle Richard—"

"David, you and your father are alike in another way. If you think of that, it'll help you understand your parents. I've watched you grow up. I've never seen you with a girl. Oh, I'm willing to believe you've sowed your oats, but you can't really have had much experience with women." [David said nothing.] "Your father was like that. There was never any question of his masculinity or virility, but he just wasn't interested in girls. It seems to be a family trait. All the Callahan men seem to marry late. I think he saw your mother, knew she was the one, and married her. It's as simple as that. Nothing complicated about it."

"But a girl of fourteen? A runaway? Hitchhiking?"

"Why not? Your father was always a Democrat, egalitarian, humanitarian, a kneejerk liberal. He wouldn't have been attracted to a phony finishing-school product. The whole idea of a debutante appalled him. A runaway, an orphan, a hitchhiker. Now *that* would have appealed to him. At least it wouldn't have mattered."

"But fourteen?"

[Morrison sighed and cleared his throat.] "That's always been the problem. It certainly was at the time. She was so damnably young and looked even younger."

"So how do you explain it?"

"You don't—at least I don't. I don't see any need to. It just happened, that's all." [He laughed.] "But that's not enough for you. You want to *know*, don't you? All I can tell you is to look at your mother, really look at her, and know her. If there is a more extraordinary woman in the world, I don't know the lady. Your mother is extraordinarily beautiful. Everyone sees that. But she is also very intelligent

50

and extremely well-disciplined. Your mother has a will of iron. She gets what she wants. And she is capable of anything, I think. When I first saw your mother, she was a waif. But she had those big, big eyes. I thought her all eyes at the time. And even then she was silent. Kings, presidents, diplomats, most of the politicians of the world, should take lessons from her on the ways and uses of silence. There was just something about her. If still waters run deep, then at age fourteen she was a bottomless pit. What's that place out in Ohio? The Blue Hole? Supposed to be bottomless. That's your mother —then and now."

[Pause.]

"All I can tell you is that your father was like an explorer. Say he was in South Africa or someplace. He finds a rock. Millions had walked by the rock and not noticed it. But he picked it up and very quickly recognized it for what it was—a precious diamond. I think your father recognized that your mother was a gem of great value. A little polishing, a little shaping and— need I say more? Isn't that what she's become? I think your father's prescience in women is to be admired. Does that satisfy you? It may not be right. It may be entirely wrong. But it's the best I can do for you."

[David said nothing. But apparently he was satisfied, for the matter is never brought up again.]

"Go on, Uncle Richard. What happened after that?"

"After what?"

"After Mother married Dad. I've never known what happened. Neither one will talk about it."

"Yes, you would have trouble getting your mother to talk about it. And thereby your father wouldn't have said much either."

"It must have been a difficult time. Things happened that have affected my whole life. We're not close to the rest of the family. Aunt Maureen obviously detests my mother. I think I have a right to know why."

"Yes, I think you do. The problem is that I'm not sure I have a right to tell you."

"Mother won't. Who else is there? You have to."

[He sighed deeply and paused.] "All right. I first met your mother in the house in Westport, in the living room. It was your grandmother's home then, and the house was different. The living room was smaller, rather dark and depressing, full of antiques and bric-a-brac. Your mother did a smart thing when she opened up the house and made fewer rooms. At the time I was appalled at her enlarging the windows. But she was right. She didn't give a damn about Georgian architecture. She cared about living. She wanted large rooms and airy rooms with lots of light. A house is for people. A house should be lived in, she said, and she was right.

"I had been summoned by your grandmother. A family crisis. Brendan had committed another folly, only this time it was a disaster. Brendan had met a girl, got her pregnant, and married her. And she was only fourteen. Your grandmother sat in a chair close to the fireplace. I remember it was a straight chair. I suggested a more comfortable one for her, but she wanted to sit upright, ready for battle. Brendan wouldn't listen to reason, so she, as head of the family, would have to do what was necessary. Your grandmother could be a forbidding old battle-ax.

"Your grandmother got your father out of the house on some pretext, then summoned your mother downstairs. I thought it cruel of her. I said she ought to give the two of them a chance to speak. She wouldn't hear of it. She was going to end this folly once and for all.

"I'll never forget the sight of your mother. She was a child, and one of the most forlorn and pitiful I'd ever seen. Fourteen years old? If they'd said twelve, it would have been more like it. You could see that she was pretty, or could be, but she looked ghastly. She wore her hair long then. It was blonde all right, but limp and stringy. She wore a dreadful dress, a blue polka dot, I think, ill-fitting and most unflattering. She came over and was not invited to sit. I was introduced. I smiled at her. It seemed the poor child needed a friend somewhere. But she just looked at me with those big blue eyes of hers and didn't move a muscle.

"Your grandmother launched into her prepared speech. Brendan's conduct was inexcusable, almost criminal. He had taken terrible advantage of a young child, and marrying her was no way to make it right. While she didn't approve of divorce, it was the only thing to do in this circumstance. The 'other problem,' as she called it, could be taken care of too. Fortunately, medical science had progressed. She would see that your mother got the best possible care and was provided for. She had her schooling to finish, a career perhaps, a real marriage, and family. Your grandmother was doing it all for her own good.

"Your mother didn't twitch. She just looked at your grandmother unblinking, not uttering a sound. It was most effective. Your grandmother was left to run on at the mouth. She began to repeat herself and then finally ran down, realizing she was being anything but affirmative and imperious. There was a long silence. A real long one. Finally your mother said, 'I want my baby and I'm going to have it.' Your grandmother sucked in her breath. It made a quite audible gasp. I've heard many older Irish women do it. She said that your mother's attitude was most commendable. She was happy to see she had some moral values. The church, of course, did not approve of—she couldn't say the word abortion. I think she used an expression like 'those operations.' There were suitable homes for young ladies in difficulties. She would see that your mother received the best possible care and suitable adoption was arranged.

"Your mother gave her first reaction at the word adoption. She looked like she had been slapped. Very quietly, but with steel in her voice, she said, 'My baby will never be adopted.' Your grandmother was aghast. She tried to remonstrate with her, explaining the impossibilities of an unmarried girl with a child. Your mother interrupted her. 'My baby is going to have a real mother and a real father and a real home. This home. You might as well get used to me.' She turned on her heel and walked out.

"Your mother was offered a lot of money to leave and divorce your father. I believe it started at five thousand dollars and went up in increments. I made the final offer of fifty thousand in cash and a thousand a month until she remarried. It was all drawn up in a legal contract and put before her to sign. I was supposed to make dark, legal threats to scare her into signing. But that was silly. She had every legal right and knew it. Besides, I liked her and felt sorry for her and couldn't threaten her. Instead, I made a little speech. I said, 'My dear, I think I understand how you feel. You were adopted. You cannot bear the thought of your child having a similar fate. I respect you for that. I really do. And under any other circumstances I would encourage you. But this is impossible. Oh, I think in time you'll make a good wife for Brendan, but that's the least of it. You are a poor, homeless girl. You may think of yourself as older, but you are only fourteen. You cannot forsee the future as I can. Your husband is twice your age. He is the scion of a wealthy and prominent New England family. He may love you now, but in time his ardor will cool. He'll find someone closer to his age and from a similar background. There will be a divorce, and you will still not have what you desire for your child. Even if that doesn't happen and Brendan continues to love you, your situation is still impossible. Your mother-in-law is head of this family. She largely controls the purse strings and will until her death. She is, shall we say, a most strong-minded woman. This is her house. She will do everything to break your marriage and, indeed, to break you. And, I assure you, what diabolical depredations she fails to think of, Maureen will. She is already jealous of you. For some reason, she had it in her mind that Brendan would never marry. She expected to inherit and become mistress of this house. You are an intruder. Do you begin to understand? You have been most uncomfortable in this house already. It's only started. This is a big family. There are aunts and uncles and cousins. You will be snubbed and put down and ostracized. Your origins will be fully remembered and grossly exaggerated. You will be called a tramp, a money-grabbing snippet who ensnared poor Brendan. Even he will come to believe it. You are a fourteen-year-old girl who has entered a world you know nothing about. You have not the education, the background, the breeding. You might as well be on another planet.'

"That was more or less what I said. I might as well have saved my breath. She just looked at me with those big eyes. I felt like I was foundering in a great blue sea. She smiled a little, you know, that wan sort of edge of a smile she has. 'Would you like to be my child's godfather?' she said. Oh, she was something else. But I got to her. I said, 'All right, if you don't care about yourself, do you care about the child? Has it ever occurred to you what life is going to be like for your child here?' She hesitated. Her eyes got a little larger and her mouth firmer. 'I've thought about it,' she said. 'I've thought a lot about it. It's gonna be grand. It's gonna be the grandest life ever.' David, my boy, I guess you're the one to say how well she succeeded. I gather it hasn't been too bad for you."

"What was my father doing all this time? Didn't he try to protect my mother?"

"Of course he did. If he'd known of the bribes and threats, he'd have raised hell. But he didn't know. It was your grandmother's whole idea that he not know. Your mother could have told him, but she didn't. She was spunky. She didn't want him to think she had any problems she couldn't handle. Of course, Brendan saw how nasty his mother and sister were being to your mother. He threatened to move out into his own home. Maureen would have adored that. It was just what she had in mind. Your mother wouldn't hear of it. She'd found her nest, and she was going to stay in it, no matter how many predators were flying around."

"But how?"

"How what? How did she win? You'll have to ask her that, but then I guess she wouldn't tell you. She may not know herself, but then it seems to me that she must have had some sort of plan. She's too intelligent, and the obstacles were too great for her not to have developed a strategy. What I'm trying to say is—I don't know what she thought or did, for the most part. I only know, or can see, the result. I doubt very much if she thought in these terms. She may have thought she was doing something entirely different. But the result, the bottom line of what she did, was so simple, so easy. I thoroughly enjoyed watching it happen."

"What?"

"All right. It's a good question. You should know the answer. Everybody should know the answer. It should be taught in every schoolroom as the most important thing to be learned in life. It's how anybody succeeds at anything. How can I explain it to you? Oh, yes, you play sports. Did you ever talk to a successful athlete,

I mean a really topflight one, who thinks about what he is doing?"

"No."

"I have. Several of them. What every one of them does is play to his strengths, his assets. He finds out what he does best and does it—and does it and does it. In baseball, a pitcher finds out what his best pitch is on a given day, and he gives the batter nothing to hit but that. At the same time, the batter stands there and waits and waits until he can get the pitch he likes to hit. It's a stalemate. That's what makes the game so slow-moving. The shortstop likes to move to his right but not his left. He shades second base, protecting his weakness and inviting a ball to his strength. It happens in every sport. The basketball player likes to take a certain shot from a certain spot on the floor. He'll do it everytime, if the opponent is dumb enough to let him. The quarterback likes to throw a certain kind of pass. The defensive end adores a particular pass rush. They'll continue to do it unless they are prevented from it and forced to do something they don't like to do or don't do as well. That's what sports are about. And it's not just in sports. Bankers like to make certain kinds of investments they know the most about and understand the best. Lawyers are at their best in certain types of cases. Artists use certain colors best and paint certain types of canvasses best. Writers have certain kinds of stories they write best. That's the secret of success, David.

Find out what the hell you do best; then work like hell doing it. The flops and failures spend their time doing something they aren't very good at."

[Morrison paused. There was more sound of cup and saucer.] "I guess I already know your next question. What was your mother's strength?"

"Yes."

"What do you think it was?"

[Silence.]

"What's the most obvious thing about your mother?"

"Obvious?"

"Yes, obvious. What's the first thing people notice about her?"

"Her eyes?"

"That's true. What else?"

"Well, she has a nice figure."

"That's also true. Most people do notice her shape. You keep listing trees for me. I want the whole woods. Your mother is beautiful, isn't she?"

"Very."

"I don't know whether she ever thought in these terms—probably not, but the bottom line was that she took the one asset she had at age fourteen, developed it, and used it, just like Lefty Grove or Bob Feller used their fast balls. Even the first time I saw her as a bedraggled waif, she was beautiful. She quickly learned how to fix her hair and make herself up and how to dress so that she became more beautiful. And as she grew a little older and her features matured, she became a true beauty. That's all there was to it. Her one asset was beauty, and she used it in every possible way. Looking back on it, it seemed so easy, although I'm sure it wasn't. She has spent her whole life being beautiful, every day and in every way. All those exercises she does, her diet, everything, all is preserving and developing her asset. And, as she ages, she simply becomes more remarkably beautiful. And it wasn't just her appearance. She wanted to become beautiful in all ways. She wanted to be surrounded by beauty. She wanted to live in beauty. She had very little schooling and no background, so she learned what she had to learn to be beautiful. She learned beautiful manners. She learned to set a beautiful table. She bought beautiful clothes. She wanted a beautiful home, so she called in an interior decorator. When she opened her mouth, she didn't want ugliness to come out of it, so she took elocution lessons—I may be one of the few who knows that—and read and read and read so she'd have something beautiful to say. Yes, she read and studied and took lessons and watched others and learned from everything she saw or did. She was a blank canvas when she married your father, one awaiting beauty to be spread upon it. Do you understand, David? Beauty was her asset. She developed her asset to the fullest extent possible in every way possible. She knew she'd never be an intellectual giant, a great earth mother, a career woman, a dozen other things. But she knew she was beautiful. Yes, she was that. I enjoyed watching her develop and use her beauty."

[Morrison paused.]

"She had one other asset, a truly rare one that I'm not sure she fully appreciates today. Want to guess it?"

"I'm sure I couldn't."

"I don't think you could. Silence. Your mother has the most gorgeous silences in the world. She can destroy people without saying a word. She knew how to do that at age fourteen. It was a natural gift. She just says nothing, and everyone is sure she has a lot to say. I suspect her silence may be a product of her own insecurity about her intellectual attainments. She is perhaps afraid of saying the wrong thing. It may be simply that your father talked so much she didn't get a chance. The reason doesn't matter. The point is that, for her, silence is not just golden; it's priceless."

"So what happened?"

"With your grandmother, you mean? Not a whole lot, I guess—although I could spend all afternoon telling you what didn't happen. But I'll tell you the essence of what happened. Your mother gave them beauty, and she gave them silence. And ugliness and noise just naturally disappeared. Your Aunt Maureen was the first to go. She wasn't much older than your mother.

There was no way a person as physically unfavored as her—your Aunt Maureen is a marvelous person with her own assets, mind you—was going to hang around your mother if she could help it. Your grandmother lasted awhile longer, but in time she came to look so angry and bitter and ugly and conniving—I guess you might say she was hung on her own tongue so often that she decided the climate was better in Florida and she ought to retire there. She died a few years ago, as you know. Oh, I'm sure it was much more difficult for your mother than I'm making it sound, but from where I sat it looked so easy. Your mother didn't let anything bother her. She didn't fight your grandmother. She accepted her with apparent equanimity, didn't impose herself, didn't ask or demand. She was always sweet and polite. She seemed to ignore almost everything. In a situation that was nasty and ugly, she found her own virtue and covered herself with it. As a result, she simply became more beautiful. She occupied herself with beauty and being beautiful. It was a lesson, I'll tell you."

* * *

This ends the extract from a later tape. We now return to what I believe to be the first tape in which David is reminiscing about his childhood.

Mine was a happy childhood. It may have been the happiest of all possible childhoods. I felt enveloped in the love of my parents. I lived in total security, security of home and surroundings, security of familiarity, security of the love of my mother and father. I have never been so happy since. When I became thirteen and went away to school—at my father's insistence—my life began a long slide downhill. I have spent most of the remaining years away from home. All I want to do is return home. I guess there must be something wrong with me. I'm unhappy here alone in this apartment. There has to be something wrong when all a grown man wants to do is go home. Or should I say return to my childhood?

I loved our house in Westport. I remember every brick, every board, every blade of grass. It was a house to be lived in and to be loved, and Mother did it. She believed the names of the rooms conveyed their purpose. A *living* room was to be lived in, a *dining* room to *dine* in, as elegantly as possible, a *bedroom* to sleep in. And if she could, she would have forbidden the sun not to shine on the *sun-room*.

It was a strange house, I suppose. It looked like a very large brick mansion of Georgian design, but by the time Mother finished with it, there weren't that many rooms in it. It was hidden from the road by trees and a high brick wall. When you entered the gate, you drove into a circular drive in front of the house. The garage was to the left, making the house look larger than it was. You entered a large foyer. It was rather pretentious, but I gather my grandfather who built the house was a pretentious guy. The foyer was tiled in black and white—what else? There was a rather grand staircase leading to the bedrooms upstairs. The living room was to the left as you entered. I always thought it monstrously large, but it had its uses. It could host quite a large party, for example. For just the family or a few guests, there was a cluster of chairs around the fireplace. It made a conversation center at the end of the room. This was where we relaxed, read, talked, or had cocktails before dinner. If my father had friends in for a political discussion, the conversation area could easily be enlarged with a few more chairs. Everyone was close enough to be heard easily, yet far enough away to keep from coming to blows. Some of my father's political discussions were apt to border on bloodlettings. My father's library and study was off the living room toward the back. It was crowded and leathery and musty from books and papers. Mother and I often sat with him there in the evening, watching television or talking.

The dining room, also large, was to the right of the foyer. The kitchen was in back of it. Beyond the dining room was the sunroom with my mother's flowers. It was a comfortable, warm room, particularly in winter. You went through double doors to reach the patio, terrace, and pool.

The upstairs had probably contained more bedrooms at one time, but my mother had had it remodeled for more utilitarian purposes. Her suite was at the extreme left. Yes, suite. She had her bedroom and a large bath, a dressing room with a large walk-in closet, and, beyond it, her exercise room with its apparatus. It was at the extreme end of the hall with a separate door. My father's bedroom and bath were to the center. My room and bath were to the right along with the only extra room and bath. Uncle Richard was about the only person who ever used it, and that wasn't very often. Thus, all this space converted to a four-bedroom house. But it was hardly the neighborhood split level. The rooms were very large. A couple of the bathrooms could have housed a significant cocktail party.

I loved that house. It was formal and elegant, yet lived in, a combination I've seen in few other homes. It had places for the things we liked to do. There was privacy, yet places to be together and bring people together. It was open and airy and spacious. There was an absence of knickknacks and ruffles and frills and fancy furniture and ornate silver and crystal, such as you see in many homes. I suspect the house was easy to maintain and keep clean. It was a cinch my mother was going to do very little of it. Mother maintained the house with the effortlessness with which she did everything. There were no live-in servants. Mother wouldn't have had them, even if she could have found them. Rather, she had day help and took great pains to keep them. The key to it was Mrs. Riordan. She was an ample woman, actually not much older than my mother, as Irish looking as her name. She seemed to have genuine affection for my mother. That was remarkable, for not very many women like my mother. Many thoroughly dislike her. I also believe my mother was genuinely fond of Mrs. Riordan, and she may have been a unique individual in my mother's life. She just did not have girlfriends. I cannot believe they were confidantes. They always addressed each other formally, Mrs. Riordan and Mrs. Callahan. But there was an aura of mutual understanding, appreciation, and trust.

In any event, they had a good arrangement worked out. Mrs. Riordan had her own home and family in Saugatuck. She came in the early afternoon, about one, having stopped to order groceries or buy necessary articles. She cooked lunch and dinner, leaving about nine, after dinner was served. She would usually serve it, or one of her daughters would come in one or two evenings a week to help out and serve. Mrs. Riordan thought it good training for them. Her husband or one of her sons looked after the lawn and garden. Thus, care of the Callahan house was a sort of Riordan affair. I don't know, but I suspect they were generously paid. My father disliked the whole idea of privilege and a servant class. I'm sure he would only have accepted it on the basis of offering employment and paying well for it. The laundry was sent out. A commercial firm came out from Bridgeport once a week for the major cleaning.

So my mother had a rather effortless life—in so far as housekeeping went. We all sort of made our own breakfast. Lunch and dinner were provided. Mother would meet with Mrs. Riordan in the afternoon to work out menus and resolve any household problems and expenses. That seemed to take about ten minutes, and magically the house was managed to perfection. My mother never did a dish. She has beautiful nails. She can't cook a lick. Oh, she'll try some scrambled eggs once in a while, but with no notable success. It is not that she is lazy. Far from it. You never see her idle. It is just that she has no interest in domestic activities and has arranged affairs so as to make them disappear from her life or nearly so. I think she's amazing to be able to do it.

My mother arises at six o'clock every morning—*every morning*: Sundays, holidays, 365 days a year, 366 in leap year. It doesn't matter what she did the night before or how late she was up. I know she has been up all night and still done her six A.M. exercises. I don't know how she gets up. She just does. No alarm. She wakes up, gets up, puts on her leotards, and begins an exercise regimen calculated to exhaust a fullback. She starts with stretching or limbering-up exercises, a great array of them. She commences with her fingers, then her arms, her neck, torso, legs, and toes until every muscle in her body must have been brought into use. She runs through these very slowly at first, then repeats them again and again at an accelerating tempo until it is impossible to count how many leg lifts or sit ups or scissor kicks or what have you she has performed. She does it to music. I'm convinced my mother is tone deaf, or nearly so. She would never admit it. It is one of her deepest secrets. She pretends to love music. She has it on in the house most of the time. But I think that is just an exercise in doing what she ought to do. Music is supposed to be beautiful. People are supposed to enjoy it. So she has music around her and acts like she enjoys it. But I know my mother well. I think she is faking. I have an idea the music is little more than noise to her. Except for the rhythm. She can feel that. She can dance, for example, rather well. She had a tape made to accompany her exercises. It is an incredible assortment of classical, popular, jazz, martial, and rock music. That's how I discovered she was tone deaf. She'd be doing some ballet steps to the *Washington Post March* or something similar. But the rhythm was right for what she was doing. She uses the tape for rhythm, I believe, and to time her exercises. The music signals the tempo of the exercises to her and what to do next in her program.

After her limbering-up exercises, she begins what might be called a dance section. She has a practice bar, the type used by ballet dancers, on one wall and a large mirror. She practices at the bar and performs a series of ballet positions and steps. I suppose they are all rather simple, but she does them with considerable grace. It is a pleasure to watch her. The ballet gives way to a variety of other steps and leaps and high kicks. All are done with great precision and energy. At the climax she does a whole series of high kicks. For once the music, the *cancan*, is appropriate. From dancer she becomes gymnast, doing a whole series of exercises on the balance beam. She follows that with some really startling acrobatics on the floor mat and tops all with a short program on the uneven parallel bars. You wouldn't believe the ceiling in her room was high enough. The first time I saw it, I was sure she would crash into it, but she had it measured with an inch or so to spare.

I asked her once where she learned all of the exercises.

"Oh, I just picked them up through the years. I'd see somebody doing something on television or somewhere. I'd try it. I used to go to a gym and take lessons. He was an outrageous queer. He showed me what to do, how to develop certain muscles, that sort of thing. I used to take you along. You were a marvelous protection. No one bothers a young woman when she has a baby tagging along. But I guess you were too young to remember. When I had this room put in the house, I dispensed with the instructor and went on my own."

Another time I asked her why she worked at it so hard.

"It's good for the figure," she said. "Did you ever see a fat, ugly ballet dancer or gymnast?"

"Some of those Russian gymnasts are pretty husky."

"That's their basic bone structure. And they've overdone it. They've concentrated on perfecting certain events. They overdeveloped certain muscles. I do a great variety of exercises."

"So all this work and sweat is an exercise in vanity."

She looked at me. I'd almost said the wrong thing, gone too far. I may have been the only person who could get away with such a remark. Even then I had to smile broadly to show I wasn't serious. I was relieved when she accepted it as an innocent remark and replied.

"Not entirely. I enjoy this. I really do. I enjoy the effort and the accomplishment. I always feel better afterwards. And I think I'm good at it, don't you?"

I said I did. And I meant it. Some of her work, particularly on the balance beam and the floor exercises, compared favorably with what you see on television, the Olympics and that. I don't know the terminology, but she can do a beautiful handstand, hold it, then gradually fall into a walkover leading into a full split, then slowly reverse the process back into the handstand. That sort of thing.

"I can't explain it. This is my time, my thing. I enjoy it. It's the only thing I'm really good at. I see other women, flabby, soft, their flesh and bones giving away even as they walk. I know I'm better. I'm superior at something. And I feel good. It's wonderful to feel good and healthy and strong. Knowing you've conquered your body—knowing you can make it do anything you want—"

She never finished either sentence. That was about as much self-revelation as you are likely to get from my mother.

After the gymnastics, she works out on some equipment, stationary bicycle, weights and pulleys, that sort of thing. If it is raining or really cold and unpleasant, she'll run in place. Most days she gets into a sweat suit and runs on the beach. She'll do it for a long time, several miles at least, and I don't mean jog. She runs, hard, in a series of wind sprints. She finishes up with a sauna—so hot it is like an oven—then jumps into the pool, summer or winter, for a ridiculous number of flat-out, hard-as-she-can-go, laps.

About nine or nine-thirty, having showered, she appears in the kitchen for orange juice, toast and coffee, wearing an immense white terry-cloth robe, a towel wrapped around her head. It always seems to me she should be exhausted, but she is never more alive, more shining and vigorous, than at that moment. And that isn't the end of it. After breakfast, she'll go horseback riding a couple of days a week, or bicycling. Other days she'll go shopping, sometimes at Alexanders or in White Plains. Sometimes she'll take the train to New York. On occasion she'll drive. She returns in the late afternoon. There's another dip in the pool. Then she'll soak in a leisurely bath and appear once again beautiful and elegant for cocktails and dinner. She tends to retire early. With her regimen it is no wonder. She is highly regular about all of this. When Dad was alive, she could vary her schedule and did when it was required. But she didn't enjoy making changes in her routine. And nothing, absolutely nothing, would keep her from her morning exercises. I suspect that is why she did them so early when there could be no interruptions. And *every* morning. If she'd been up late or felt out of sorts, she worked harder at them. I remember a few occasions when she was downright ill with a cold or something. She dragged herself through her exercises, then fell into bed exhausted. I worried about her. Dad called the doctor, who told her she was a damned fool.

The result of all this "foolishness" is a figure that I can only describe as devastating. I may be prejudiced. But I think not. I've seen how other men look at her. She is tiny, about five-foot-three, not more than ninety-five pounds or so. She wears a bikini like no one else. It must have been invented for her. She is all muscle, not a speck of fat anywhere, long, taut, yet rounded muscles on which the skin is stretched tight as a drum. Her waist is incredibly tiny—twenty-one inches she told me once—and her arms and shoulders so slender you'd expect them to break. Yet she is not bony or skinny or hard. She is rounded and firm. There are men who look at breasts and bottoms. My mother has those. Not large or excessive or obvious. To me, the sexiest thing about my mother's figure is a hollow that runs up her thighs and deepens and disappears at her pelvis. You seldom see it in women. Fat collects there. A woman has to be very thin and her muscles honed to a fine edge for it to be seen. I used to watch that hollow appear and disappear as my mother exercised or walked beside the pool. I used to lie in bed at night and think about that hollow and remember it and visualize it. It was terribly exciting to me.

Three A.M. Got to go to bed. Really am beat. [He yawned loudly.] Big day tomorrow. Mother is coming—and Uncle Richard. Mother, do you have any idea how much I miss you? Can't stop thinking about you. You know that, don't you? Yeah, you know. You always know everything about me. But I'll see you tomorrow. At last. I just wish Uncle Richard wasn't coming. Can't I ever have any time for myself, do what I want to do? All this stupid intrigue. Well, he's coming. I've got to get something settled with him—whether he likes it or not.

* * *

David shut off the machine. I don't know what time he turned it back on. In the afternoon, I presume. Morrison was already there.

They have apparently been involved in some kind of light conversation. Carla Callahan is late, and they are awaiting her arrival before beginning a serious discussion. David uses the time to ask his "Uncle Richard" about his parents' marriage and his early childhood. He turns on the machine to record Morrison's revelations. As the reader now knows, I lifted their discussion and used it already to aid the narrative flow. This conversation was terminated by the arrival of Carla Callahan. I am not very good at describing voices. Hers is rather low pitched, throaty, somewhat breathy, as though she expends too much air for the sound she makes. I suspect she trained herself to talk this way. When she is angry, she reverts to a voice that is higher pitched, even shrill. She apologized for being late, blaming the traffic and the Eastern Air Lines shuttle from La Guardia Airport in New York. There is a bit of small talk about how everyone is and how they are doing. Coffee is made. Cups clang.

Voices fade a bit as the three people move around the room. Eventually they settle down. David left his infernal machine running, I suspect not by accident. Morrison spoke first.

* * *

"You asked for this meeting, David. What's the problem?"

[David hesitated, made a false start, cleared his throat. His voice sounded strange, a little higher pitched and tight. All indicated he was nervous or had a rehearsed speech in his mind.]

"Uncle Richard, you asked me to do this—"

"And the President. Remember that."

"Okay. You and the President asked me to do this, to maintain contact with Ephraim Squires and his so-called revolutionaries. I'm trying. I do the best I can. I visit them, or try to, two or three times a week. I give them your money. I try to be one of them, to pretend I'm friendly and in agreement with them."

"I think you've been doing fine."

"That's just it. I'm not. I'm not getting anywhere. It's all a huge waste of time."

"I assure you it isn't."

"Look, Uncle Richard, I'm not my father. He was fifty-three years old when he died. He had devoted thirty years or more to liberal causes. He was knee jerk to the core—and out of conviction. He wasn't pretending as I am. He believed what he said and did, and everyone knew it. He gave a fortune to liberal causes—"

"How well I know. He'd have given all his money away if I'd let him."

"That's just it. He bankrolled the causes he believed in—sometimes programs he merely thought a good idea or interesting. He was known and respected by every left-wing do-gooder and liberal politician in the country. He had contacts all over the nation—hell, the world. When he had something to say, people listened. They sought out his opinion. Don't you see? I'm not him. No way I can be."

"Yes, I do see that. You're what? Twenty-three, twenty-four? You're young, not known, not trusted."

"Exactly. I'm wasting my time and your money."

"Tell me how they treat you. What's their attitude toward you?"

[He sighed.] "Okay. When I first went to see Squires—and he is a hard man to see, believe me—he was nice to me. He expressed sympathy on my father's death. He spoke of his regard for Dad, what a loss his death was, that sort of thing. He was positively decent. We had a nice enough chat. I told him a lie. I said that before he died, Dad had asked me to carry on for him. I don't think Squires believed me. He said, 'The papers said he died in his sleep.' I said he had, but we had talked about it before he went to bed. Looking back on it, I said, I figured he must have had a premonition that he was going to die. It was a lousy lie but the best I could think of at the moment. Squires wouldn't let it go. If you'll remember, Squires, Sam Dan Cooper, and their entourage had been to our house the night before Dad's death. I had driven Cooper and his wife to Squires's motel room. That's where I saw their perverted sex going on. Squires remembered all that. He said, 'You mean you and your dad went home and rapped before going to bed?' I said that was right. We often did it."

"Did he accept that?"

"I don't know. Maybe. But whether or not he did, I wasn't helped. I told him I wanted to carry on as my father had, help in anyway I could. He scoffed at me. 'No way,' he said. 'You're not your old man.' I admitted I wasn't, but I wanted to try to be."

"Sounds fine to me. Didn't he accept that?"

[Another deep sigh from David.] "That's it. I just don't know. I'm accepted in the sense I'm allowed to come around, give money, make a comment or two, ask a question. But at the same time, I'm an outsider. I'm anything but trusted. Everyone watches what they say to me. I'm never alone in a room. I'm a fringe person, a pariah, a camp follower of the liberty army whose purse is his only usefulness."

"That's about all I expected."

"Let me finish. Lately, it's gotten worse. I'm mostly ignored. No one talks to me. If I ask a question, no one answers or maybe I get a noncommittal monosyllable. I feel like a kid, a little leaguer hanging around the big league dugout getting in the way. It's no fun I tell you. If I want to 'make a contribution,' I'm handed over to a flunky with his hand out. If I insist on giving it to Squires and wait long enough, he shows up to take the money. Lately, he's begun to openly ridicule me. He calls me 'kid.' Once he said, 'Good thing you got bread, kid, 'cause it's a cinch you ain't got nothin' else.' I protested and asked what he meant. He laughed and walked away. He's openly contemptuous of me, sneeringly so. His girlfriend, Edna, is worse, always has been. Her mouth is a cesspool of ridicule. Don't you see? I'm not wanted. If I had a shred of self-respect, I'd walk away and never come back. But that's not what you want me to do. You want me to stay in there."

"Yes, I do, very much so. I know it's hard for you, but I know you can take it."

"It's not a question of taking it. I could do that if I were accomplishing anything. But I'm not. I'm wasting my time and your money."

"I should decide that, I think."

[An even deeper sigh.] "Look, Uncle Richard, I despise Squires and all he is and stands for. Hanging around him and being ridiculed is a first-class hell. What's it all for?"

"I assure you—and the President would want me to assure you—that it's for a good purpose."

"Uncle Richard, I'm not a complainer. You know that. But I'm not very happy rattling around this apartment by myself. I worry about you, Mother. I don't like having you alone up there in Westport, me down here."

"You needn't worry about me, David. I'm perfectly safe."

"But you have to be lonely."

"Of course I'm lonely. But I keep busy and—"

"David, your mother can take care of herself."

"Lord, I know that. But is it so bad for me to love my mother, to want to be with her?"

"Oh, darling, I miss you too. But Richard has said this won't go on for very long. Isn't that right?"

"Yes."

"Okay, so how long is not very long?"

"I can't give you a terminal date."

"A year?"

"No more than that I should think."

[They lapse into silence for a moment; then Carla Callahan speaks, her voice low and controlled.]

"I know a year is a long time at your age, darling, but it isn't really . . ." [Her voice trailed off, another unfinished sentence leading to a prolonged silence. I have the clear impression that David was upset. The conversation wasn't going the way he wanted it to. He felt badgered into a corner. In his frustration, he tried a new tack.]

"All right. I'll continue to put my head in that meat grinder across town. But it seems to me that if I'm going to be this unhappy, if I'm giving up what to me is a big chunk of my life, then I've a right to know what for."

"Because the President wants you to."

"I'll be frank, Uncle Richard. That may be enough for you, but it sure isn't for me. I think I've a right to know what's going on. If I'm to play a big deal mastermind spy, then I should know what I'm looking for. I've a right to know what I'm getting into. It's only fair—and it's my neck I'm sticking out."

[Morrison paused.] "I know how you feel, David, but I can't. I just can't."

[More silence; then Carla Callahan sided with her son.]

"David's right. Both of us have been made a party to something we know nothing about. We are being asked to make sacrifices of our personal lives. We ought to know what for."

[Silence, studded this time by deep sighs from Morrison.]

"I realize what you're saying, both of you. Believe me, I sympathize with your position. But I feel—all of us feel—it is better for you not to know too much at this point. I'm sorry, but—"

"Not know too much about what?"

"Just a minute, David. Let me speak."

"Wait, Carla—David, too. What I'm saying is that I hope, I believe, your respect for the President, as a person and as an office, will be enough for you. Just now at least."

"Yes, Richard, but—"

"I'm asking you to trust me and to trust Merrill Lampton."

[Silence lasting twenty-seven seconds. It was Carla Callahan at her best, commanding attention with silence.]

"Are you finished, Richard?"

"Yes."

"I've something I'd like to say then. Of course, David and I respect the President. And we trust you. But that is a two-way street. We are entitled to some respect and trust too. You are asking David to mingle with these revolutionaries. That's what they are—*revolutionaries*. I've met Squires and some of his people. They're goons. They carry guns into people's homes—into my home. I've never forgotten it or forgiven them. Clearly, Richard, whatever your motive, you are putting my son into a situation of danger."

"I hardly think that."

"You may not think so. I'm sure you don't mean to. But the fact is these people are armed and dangerous. They ought to be locked up. You are our oldest and dearest friend. You have been like a father to me all these years. You are David's godfather. I cannot believe you would impose the slightest risk upon him without good reason. But I'm telling you now, Richard, that I will not allow him to go on with this unless and until you confide in us just what is going on."

[It is not hard to figure Morrison's consternation. He was trapped. He needed David in the cabal. The beauteous Carla was making it impossible unless he opened up. He hemmed and hawed and cleared his throat and sighed. Ultimately, he got to it.]

"All right. Let me say first there is no plan as such. There really isn't much to tell you, simply because we don't know ourselves. We have only the vaguest sort of idea, almost a principle."

"About what?"

"Be patient, David. Give me a little time. You've got to realize what is going on in this country, politically. The election is little more than a year away. You don't have to be very smart to figure the Democrats are going to unite behind Houston Walker. He'll be a tough candidate, young, appealing, full of liberal hogwash that appeals to all the do-gooders—and, I might add, has gone a long way toward the ruination of this country. Walker looks unbeatable. Who's the G.O.P. have? Nobody. Lampton's biggest mistake was in not grooming a successor. He took that doddering old fool as his running mate. He didn't think ahead. Eight years seemed forever until it was too late. Now there's nobody with the stature to stand up to Walker. Or is there?"

[Morrison seemed to pause for effect.]

"Merrill Lampton is the best President this country has ever had. I'm hardly the only one who thinks so. He is strong, dynamic, knows what he wants, and has the guts to do it. All his wrangles with Congress. Greatest thing that ever happened. He vetoed every damn one of their spending measures. When Congress overrode his veto, he impounded the funds. When Congress voted that he couldn't do that, he did it anyhow. Their only choice was to impeach him, and they haven't the guts to try. Lampton argued that he was upholding the law—as he is sworn to do by the Constitution. He wasn't going to see the country ruined with inflation while he sat in the White House. And he made it stick. You remember that, don't you? Fiscal integrity. That's what we need in this country and have under Merrill Lampton. Walker will be a disaster. He has no economic sense. He's just a cheap politician buying the votes of those too lazy to work for a living. And if you think taxes are high now, just wait till Walker gets in office. He'll raise them out of sight. He's already advocating higher taxes for the rich. Pay their full share, he says. Close the loopholes. The bastard. If he's elected, there will be the greatest flight of capital out of this country you've ever seen. It'll either be that or give it all to the government to waste. I tell you Walker must be stopped."

[David.] "Then this is just a political—"

84

"Another thing. Remember all the furor over the amendments to the Freedom of Information Act? Censorship they called it. We simply argued that fair is fair. The networks with their pinko commentators can say anything they want, but give the rest a chance. Oh, did they scream. Freedom of the press, the First Amendment, all that hogwash. We simply argued that no damn newspaper or television reporter had a right to steal government secrets and threaten the security of this country. And we were right. What a fight it was. We rammed it right down their throats. And when the pinkos took it to court as unconstitutional, the high and mighty judges backed away from it. No real constitutional issue. Refused to hear the case. That shows you what good court appointments can do. I'm telling you Merrill Lampton is the best thing that ever happened to this country. We need him—bad."

[Silence. Morrison seemed to have the Callahans spellbound with his speech, however ridiculous its content.]

"So we can't run him again, can we? That damn two-term amendment. Worst mistake this country ever made. Oh, I know it was my party that did it after FDR. But it was done too hastily. It was wrong then. It's a tragedy now."

"Revoke the amendment. It shouldn't be too difficult. There was a movement underway when Nixon was in the White House. Just at the start of his second term."

"There isn't time. Even if we tried, it wouldn't work. All those state houses. The legislatures only meet on off years, and the Democratic governors would never call a special session to reelect Lampton." (Morrison paused, then stated with great emphasis.) "*We've got to keep Merrill Lampton in the White House.*"

[David laughed.] "How? A military coup?"

"It would never work."

"You're right. But there is a way, isn't there? Watergate II. That's what you're doing, isn't it? The similarities between Lampton and Nixon are too many to be casual: strong men, fiscal integrity, law and order, government by veto, impoundment of funds. Only it didn't work then, and it won't work now."

"What do you mean, it didn't work? Watergate was just a warm-up, a mock-up to show how it really could be done. And it was a howling success. It wrecked the election process. The country accepted an appointed President, didn't it? Prior to Watergate, could you have imagined the circumstances in which we'd have an appointed President? Watergate was no failure. It broke the mold built during two hundred years of the Presidency. It's made all things possible in this country. And it would have done a lot more if it hadn't been for those bumbling CIA agents, creepy Cubans, and dumb clucks in the White House. That was the only real mistake, putting dummies in charge of it and running it from the White House."

"So it is to be Watergate II."

"I don't know what it's to be. All I know is we have to keep Lampton as President."

[Long pause.]

"It'll never work, Uncle Richard."

"Why not?"

"The Constitution."

[Morrison snorted in ridicule.] "Nonsense."

"No it's not. Madison said it best. What was it? Something about ambition counteracting ambition. I've got the exact quote here someplace."

[There are sounds hard to describe. Obviously David went to a bookshelf.]

"Here it is. James Madison writing in *The Federalist* No. 51. I'll read it. 'Ambition must be made to counteract ambition. The interests of the man must be connected with the constitutional rights of the place.'"

[Carla Callahan.] "What does that mean?"

"In plain language it means the founders built personal motives into the Constitution. The power is spread around. The President has come to have most, but there is still plenty of power spread around in little pieces. A guy has a job—a place—and that gives him power. Every time somebody makes a grab for more power, there are lots of people trying to shoot him down—one hundred senators, 435 representatives, hundreds of department and agency heads, millions of bureaucrats, judges, and DA's, battalions of military officers. All are ready to defend their bailiwick. The power grab always fails. It failed in Nixon's day. It'll fail now. It was the genius of the founders."

[Morrison snorted again]. "The hell you say. It's worked many times. The only times it doesn't work is when some jerk is obvious about it. Look at Teddy Roosevelt. He sent the fleet to the Pacific against express orders and won the Philippines. He had vision and guts. Look at FDR and how he got us into World War II. Look at Johnson in Vietnam. It's worked dozens of times."

"Sure it has, in a war, in a particular policy. But that's hardly seizing the White House."

"That's happened too. You just don't know your history. How did Rutherford B. Hayes become President? He lost the election. Tilden had him defeated—by a wide margin in the popular vote and by plenty in the electoral vote. So how did Hayes become President? I'll tell you. A single individual did it. And he wasn't even in government. I forget his name, but he was an editor for the *New York Times*. Reid, I think. He hated Tilden. He wanted Hayes. Couldn't bear the thought of his losing. And he had the vision. He saw how it could be done, and he had the guts to do it. In the wee hours of the morning, he sent telegrams to the Republican electors in three states that had not yet reported: Louisiana, Florida and South Carolina. He had them challenge the election results. The whole thing went to a special electoral commission. It was rigged, and Hayes was voted the winner. And Tilden accepted it, 'cause he didn't want to fight."

"That's hardly likely to happen now. NBC tells you who has won in seconds."

"Nonsense. Nixon could have pulled it off with Kennedy in 1960—only he didn't have the guts. Look, I'm not saying this will work again. I'm just saying that American history is studded with times when people of guts have seen the moment and seized it. I'm just saying it's important that Merrill Lampton stay on as President. If the moment appears, I want to be ready for it."

* * *

I should not interrupt this, I know. But I am a college professor of political science, or used to be, and I cannot allow this Morrison drivel to go unchallenged. David Callahan was a political science major in college, but he clearly is no match for either the maturity or cynicism of Morrison. Few people are. And that is the fatal weakness of democracy. The whole process of democracy in the end depends upon the good will of the leaders, upon their dedication to the process of democracy, their surrender of their native desire for power to it. Few democracies

exist in the world. The United States was the
world's oldest among the major nations until it,
too, finally, ultimately, I guess inevitably, suc-
cumbed. I don't know how to combat it. In
my heart of hearts, I think that maybe if the
men of intelligence, reason, knowledge, and
goodwill speak out, the people will listen to
them and adjure false leadership. But I am not
conviced of it. Nonetheless, succored in my
contented Cotswolds hills, I will have my say,
whether anyone ever hears me or not.

Richard Morrison is talking nonsense. He
parrots all the conservative gibberish. Hard
work is what made our country great. The lazy
and the shiftless, along with the "do-gooder" no-
tions of helping people who can't help themselves, are ruining America. It is rhetoric of the
purest sort. With precious few exceptions, to
tell an unemployed person to go to work is to tell
him to flap his arms and deliver the airmail.
There simply are no jobs for tens of millions of
the young, aged, widowed, divorced, unedu-
cated, and unskilled. Most jobs in the United
States pay the minimum wage or slightly above,
in any event hardly enough to support a single
individual, let alone a family. To simply work
in the United States sometimes hardly means
survival, let alone the accumulation of pos-
sessions, gadgets, doodads, and luxuries dis-
guised through advertising as necessities. It
takes a great deal of money to belong to the
middle class in America, so much so that only

the highly educated, technologically proficient, most persevering, and downright lucky can enter it. Tens of millions of Americans do not have a prayer of such accomplishment and have been in that condition for generations. For Morrison to label these people as shiftless and to uphold himself as saving the nation is both totalitarian and obscene.

His gloating over the "triumph" of the Freedom of Information Act is more than I can bear. It was a vital cog in Lampton's wheel of dictatorship, perhaps the whole key to it. That malicious, infamous act, bludgeoned through Congress and the court, enabled Lampton and Morrison to muzzle the press. Did we never realize the importance of the First Amendment guarantee of freedom of the press? When (oh, when!) did it stop occurring to us that the first act of any dictator of whatever persuasion is to seize the broadcasting stations and close down the newspapers? America remained a democracy for two hundred years, not because of political parties, not because of free elections (for how many times were they not truly free but sold to the candidate with the most money?), but because of the First Amendment rights of the freedom of religion, press, speech, assembly, and petition. We were a free people because we had a press free of the threat of prosecution regardless of what outrageous thing it printed or said. The American democracy depended upon the free publication of information and opinion, no matter how outrageous its form or substance. When the federal government, in the name of national security, was given the power not only to muzzle the press with secrecy (which had been going on for years previously) but to prosecute editors and publishers because they managed to puncture the veil of secrecy, American democracy was doomed at that point. How stupid we were. How misguided. We gave away our birthright in the name of national security. I am shocked beyond reason, saddened and disillusioned. I had believed in the people more.

If I didn't have the benefit of hindsight, I would have said David won the argument with Morrison. His understanding of the Constitution and how it works—or, as I should say, *worked*—was both classic and precise. It might have been better if he had quoted *The Federalist* No. 10 in which Madison wrote: "The great security against a gradual concentration of the several powers in the same department, consists in giving to those who administer each department the necessary constitutional means and personal motives to resist encroachments of the others." *Personal motives*. Each person in government had his own nest to feather. It was a beautiful system.

Yet, David's quotation from the fifty-first *Federalist* is good. "Ambition must be made to counteract ambition." Yes, that says it.

It pleases me that David was such a good

student and understood this. I would have sworn that Morrison was wrong in his venal analysis. Yet, with hindsight, he was right, David wrong. I wonder why. Why did the brilliant system of the founders ultimately fail?

I feel a chill everytime I hear Morrison's scornful voice saying Watergate was a howling success. Of course, he means the *attempted* subversion of the Constitution, not the thwarting of the attempt. He was right, of course. Americans went on a binge of self-congratulations right after Nixon resigned. The very instant Gerald Ford was sworn in, Chief Justice Warren Burger said, "Thank God it worked." Oh, yes, it was constitutional. Gerald Ford was a well-meaning man, hardly the stuff of tyrants. He performed his role as caretaker president, if not well, at least acceptably. But his very existence in the White House was an affront to the system. He was living proof that the political system was flawed—an *appointed* President. If there had been real reform, if Presidential power had been reduced, if Congress had truly reformed itself so as to become an effective organ of government, then the lessons of Watergate would have meant something. That trauma of the 1970s would not have been Morrison's "howling success." I wonder. Was there a conspiracy even then? Were some people aiming even then at just the sort of coup that Lampton has performed? Was Watergate just a trial run for Merrill Lampton?

The problem back in the seventies—and I am guilty too—was that we Americans thought of dictators in terms of a military coup, the proverbial man on the white horse, or of a strutting peacock like Mussolini, Franco, or Hitler, brown shirts, black shirts, salutes, martial music, and all that. We didn't realize until it was too late that a dictator can wear blue serge or pin stripes and wrap himself in the status quo, declaring allegiance to God, flag, country, and motherhood. We may even—probably will—have serial dictators. Lampton won't live forever. He'll be succeeded by someone just as undemocratic, just as addicted to regimentation and military force in the name of "law and order." We may even elect him, as we did Lampton.

I think about the discussion between David Callahan and Morrison, David spouting the practical idealism of Madison, Morrison voicing native cynicism. In a way, theirs was a case of youth versus age. Madison had been young when we wrote those words, only thirty-six, not much older than David. Morrison is in his late sixties, wise in human nature, and very cynical. He saw the flaw in the system and exploited it. And I now see it too. Actually, it has always been intrinsic to the American political system, its fatal weakness. That it was not used for two hundred years led Americans to forget that it existed. We were warned, all of us, by the very men who wrote the Constitution in that sultry summer of 1789. No matter in their debates concerned them so much as the powers of the President. They were obsessed by the problem. I've always liked the descriptive passage in Catherine Drinker Bowen's book *Miracle at Philadelphia*. "No fewer than sixty ballots were needed before the method of selecting the President was decided; repeatedly, delegates fell upon it as if never before debated. Five times, the Convention voted in favor of having the President appointed by Congress. Once they voted against that, once for electors chosen by the state legislators, twice against that, and then voted again and again to reconsider the whole business."

A President appointed by Congress. Five times voted by the founders, then ultimately rejected. The United States in its two hundredth year of independence came to that and has now passed beyond.

In the middle of the convention, Hugh Williamson of North Carolina, who disliked the whole idea of a chief executive, spoke the truth, saying it is "pretty certain that we should at some time or other have a king." He said it might be an elective king, but he would "feel the spirit of one. He will spare no pains to keep himself in office for life and will then lay a train for the succession of his children." Williamson saw this—oh, now prophetically—as inevitable and suggested that all be done "that might postpone this event as long as possible."

But that was not the only warning or even the most succinct. The delegates wrangled over the powers of the President all summer. Finally, weary of it, they compromised and in effect designed the office to fit the personality of the man whom they all knew would be the first President, George Washington. He sat before them as the elected president of the convention. When it was finally over, wise, crafty, Ben Franklin, at eighty-one the oldest man at the convention, struck to the heart of the problem and illuminated the ultimate flaw in the system, which Morrison saw—and seized. Said Franklin, "The first man at the helm will be a good one. Nobody knows what sort may come afterwards."

It took two hundred years, but we now have that "sort"—Merrill Lampton.

Morrison and David Callahan continued their discussion. Rather typically, Carla Callahan had little to say. Politics was not her metier.

* * *

"So you want to keep Merrill Lampton in the White House. What has that got to do with me? More than that, what has Ephraim Squires got to do with it?"

"I told you we have no definite plan. Our thinking is ad hoc. We have only a—a principle. I don't know what else to call it."

"All right. What is your principle?"

[A deep sigh. Morrison was clearly reluctant.] "You two do make it difficult. I don't think you need to know everything. Indeed, I

don't think you ought to. But what can I do?"
[Pause.] "Let me put it this way. I've already
mentioned the Hayes-Tilden election of 1876.
I'm a bit of a student of it. I've read every
word about it I can get my hands on. It was the
greatest constitutional crisis in our history. Our
whole form of government almost came tum-
bling down. And it could happen again. The
flaw in the election process was never corrected.
Are you familiar with that election?"

"Yes. You are suggesting some sort of disputed election, some kind of constitutional
crisis, that will require Lampton to stay on as
President past his elected term."

[Silence.]

"It's a wild idea, Uncle Richard. Real wild."

"I never said it wasn't."

"How do you propose to do it?"

"I said we have only a principle, not a fixed
plan."

"Forgive me, but I think you do have a plan.
Oh, maybe not a neat and tidy plan with everything all worked out. But you've got a good
idea, don't you?"

[Deep sigh from Morrison.] "We have a
thought. I'm not sure I'd dignify it by calling
it an idea."

"Okay, what thought?"

[Another long pause. I can almost feel Morrison squirming. He turned to Carla Callahan
for help.]

"Will you tell your infernal son to let it go? I've said too much already."

"Don't make so much of it, Richard. We are practically family. I certainly don't understand what this has to do with David and me. I'd like to know."

[Another sigh, this time of resignation.] "All right. All right. We don't know, but we think that maybe, perhaps, with luck and all that, Squires is the key to this thing. He wants a revolution. The system is all bad. Destroy it. Blow everything up—"

"I don't think he wants to blow up anything."

"Maybe not, but he wants to tear down our system of government, break up the corporations, embrace communism or Maoism—whatever that is."

"He talks about liberty and returning to the principles of the founders."

"I know what he says. But that's bullcrap—forgive my language, Carla. He's an anarchist. He wants to destroy, you, me, all we stand for, this nation, our way of life. I don't care how you define it. I don't care what language he uses or you use."

"Look, I'm not with him. You know that."

"I'm sorry. You're pressuring me, and I'm a little annoyed."

"I'm sorry, too. Why not say it and have it over with?"

"I suppose you're right. Our thought is that

if we can get Mr. Squires to stage his little revolution on schedule, he might cause enough disruption to interfere with the election. A claim could be made that it is not a fair election."

"And President Lampton stays in the White House till there is a fair election?"

[Long pause. David finally breaks it.] "It would take a lot of disruption."

"I never said it would work. It's a long shot. Like you say, we are probably wasting our time. But to me, Houston Walker will be such a disaster that no effort to keep him from power is entirely a waste."

"Uncle Richard, I'm sorry you found it so difficult to tell me all this. I'm neither shocked nor against you. I'll do anything I can to help. But I still don't understand what you want me to do."

"For the moment, just what you've been doing. Stick with Squires and his goons, as Carla calls them. Find out what they're up to, what they're thinking, what makes them tick. When the time comes, maybe we can plant a little seed of trouble in their midst."

"Like what?"

"I really don't know. So there's no point in asking. The point is this: Are you with me? Will you go on as you've been doing, as hard as it is for you, as vague as it is, as unlikely as there is of any good coming from it?"

[Carla Callahan interrupts at this point.] "I have a question. A simple one. Why David?

Why not the FBI or somebody? They're paid to do this sort of thing. They're trained for it."

"It's a good question. And the answer is simple. The FBI, the CIA, the White House, every government agency has proved itself to be a bundle of leaks. There are no secrets in official Washington. David is right when he talks about the division of power all over the government. Everybody is feathering his own nest. They see somebody getting a leg up on them, and they call the press. The story is leaked, and a good thing is ruined.

"Everybody talks about the lessons of Watergate. Okay, we learned a lesson too. The big mistake in Nixon's day was that the effort was made from the White House. Oh, Nixon tried to hold it close, but there was no way to keep it secret. The President lives in a goldfish bowl. And Nixon had that goddamned tape recorder running. The sheerest stupidity. Hand the proof over to your enemies. This time we are determined that no one, absolutely no single individual even remotely connected with the government, shall have any role, not even a speck of a role, in what is going on, not the White House, not the Defense Department, not the FBI, nowhere. That's why we need you, David. That's why you are being kept as far from the White House as possible. As far as anyone but us three—and the President—knows, Merrill Lampton never heard of you."

"But the President knows you. The press

knows you as his good friend, confidant, and advisor."

"Oh, sure, but I'm harmless. I'm just a doddering old fool, a Bernie Baruch type of character. I've no official position. I just talk, and always about politics at that. I never open my mouth—at least publicly—about anything else. I'm too well-known, you might say. I'm the favorite whipping boy of the liberal press, the archetypical political boss, soon to be defunct. Okay. Fine. Splendid. I like it that way."

[David.] "In other words, you are so busy being blamed for what you don't do, that nobody notices what you do do."

[Morrison laughed.] "Sometimes, Carla, I think you have too smart a boy there." [His laugh trails off.] "I must pressure *you* now, David. I ask again. Are you with me? Will you help?"

"Help keep Merrill Lampton in the White House?"

"Yes."

"I will, yes. I'll do anything I can."

"And do you approve, Carla?"

"Don't be so melodramatic, Richard. If someone will make me a martini, I'll toast our President—present and future. But you won't let David get into danger, will you?"

"Mother, I can tell you Squires is all talk. He's harmless. I suspect that is why Uncle Richard's plan is doomed to failure."

If this were all I heard of these tapes or knew of events, if, indeed, this isolated conversation is all that had occurred, Morrison's ramblings could be dismissed as evidence of senility. I suspect there have been many times, perhaps as often as every four years, in which men obsessed with politics have concocted schemes to capture the White House by any means, fair or foul. The very idea that your man is the savior of the nation and the other fellow a threat to civilization is the nature of politics itself, at least in the United States.

The Hayes-Tilden election of 1876 was the greatest electoral crisis in American history. As a constitutional crisis, it is probably exceeded only by the Civil War and Watergate. Yet to have Morrison offer a half-baked scheme for recreating the election of 1876 and keep Lampton in the White House because no successor had been chosen would seem to be the ruminations of a fool. It is like standing in Times Square at high noon on a sunny day and waiting for lightning to strike you dead.

Morrison is no fool, however. Pressured by David Callahan and particularly by his mother, Morrison came up with a plausible scheme so as to seem to confide in them. He was clever. He told them enough to satisfy them, yet kept concealed the true machinations. Less trusting, more astute questioners would have gotten it out of Morrison at that moment. The Callahans did not. Since they did not at that time, it is perhaps best that the reader be forced to wait to find out the Lampton-Morrison plot, as David Callahan had to.

Carla Callahan stayed some time with her son during that visit. I cannot tell how long it was. Some conversations between them were recorded, but these appropriately belong to sections of David's reminiscences. I am reserving them to that point.

Nothing in these tapes is more futile than David Callahan's efforts to understand his father. Again and again he reaches out to him, but the portrayal which results is of an ill-defined figure who, however important in his life, remains shadowy. There is a reason for this, but David is understandably reluctant to talk about it, so he tries again and again to come to grips with the problem of his father.

* * *

I never knew my father. I feel I ought to regret it, but somehow I don't. It is strange to realize that I don't know him. I spent a lot of time with him, perhaps more than most sons do with their fathers. He talked to me a lot. He loved me. He was open and guileless. He kept no secrets from me that I know of. He wanted only the best for me and tried in every way he could for me to have it.

103

If I am to speak the truth, I guess it is not my father's fault that I never knew him. He tried. But I couldn't accept him. I hated most of the time I was with him. I did it because it was necessary, because he wanted it, and because my mother wanted it.

I look like my mother, not my father. Perhaps that is part of the problem. I am blond like her and slender and small-boned. My blue eyes could have come from either of them. About the only physical characteristics of mine that I can assign to my father are the reddish tint to my hair and my squarish jaw. The Callahans do not have weak chins. No, I don't look like my father. He was a big man, bigger than I, six-foot-three, with heavy shoulders and chest and muscular arms. He must have weighed two hundred and fifty pounds when he died. He had been quite an athlete when he was young, football at Harvard and all that. He loved competitive sports. He once said his only regret in life was that he had not tried to play professional football, although I think he later altered his views on that.

The most obvious physical characteristic of my father was his brilliant red hair. There must have been every shade of red in it from bright orange to ruby oxblood. He wore it fairly long, so that it had some curl in it. It really was beautiful, and he was very proud of it. There never was any problem in picking my father out in a crowd. He came equipped with his own beacon. That red hair was only part of the Irish in him.

He had very fair skin, and when he went out in the cold, his cheeks would glow apple red. He had the sort of earthiness and jolliness and vigor and love of life that we associate, at least, with Irishmen. And he was Irish too, in his absolute absorption in politics. He loved politics, politicians, talking politics, arguing politics, and finding a political motive behind every human action. Yet, Dad couldn't really have been Irish. His ancestors were, certainly. He got all those Irish characteristics and an Irish name from them. But he was four or five generations, depending on how you count them, removed from Ireland. We visited there once when I was about ten. He thought it pretty and peaceful, but he was bored and couldn't wait to get home. About all I remember was looking up O'Callahan in the phone book. My father said that had been the original name. If you counted the spelling that has a "g" in it, there were pages of O'Callahans and O'Callaghans.

I asked both my father and Uncle Richard how much money we had. I never did get a satisfactory answer. Dad professed not to care. Uncle Richard said something like, "I doubt if anyone really knows. You have enough, so forget it." That was good advice. Certainly neither Father, Mother, nor I give much thought to money or where it comes from. I have learned that my Callahan ancestors both made and married money. They were shrewd Irishmen. Some of the money was made in textiles. I believe

105

some branches of the family are still in textiles down South. A lot of the money was put into land, and that became the basis for the fortune. I've heard a whole milltown in Connecticut mentioned. I know a large piece of Fairfield County was owned by the Callahans at one time, and that couldn't have been too bad.

I believe we have what is called old money. My grandfather was the last Callahan to actually go out and earn any. My father, my mother, and now I—Aunt Maureen and Uncle Edgar, too— simply live off the income. It is all in trusts, securely invested in God knows what. Uncle Richard takes care of all that.

Uncle Richard and my father disagreed on almost everything; yet they were close friends. My father trusted Uncle Richard to look after the family money. It was a cinch Uncle Richard did not trust father to do so. I heard him say to Dad once, "Why do you resent your money so much? It really isn't so awful. You don't have to work so hard at giving it all away." Dad replied, "You don't mind my giving it away, Dick. You just mind who I give it away to." What that meant was that Uncle Richard was—is—a dyed-in-the-wool Republican conservative straight out of Wall Street and Dad was a liberal Democrat of the most knee-jerk variety. Dad supported every liberal cause there was—

No, that's not fair. My father had genuine compassion for people, all people, even conservative Republican bankers, as I heard him tell Uncle Richard once. He couldn't accept that people were hungry in this country while food was being thrown away and ground lay idle. He couldn't understand why people walked around sick when we had the finest medical facilities in the world. He couldn't accept his living in a mansion while others had hovels. He simply could not understand what pleasures people got out of having money or making money or spending money. My father was a liberal knee jerk in the sense that he was for whatever the latest liberal cause was at the moment. Yet, there were certain touchstones to his beliefs. He detested violence, whether it was war, terrorism, or simply slapping someone's face. He also detested a closed mind—

Oh, shit, that's awful. Ridiculous drivel. I've more insight into the corner butcher. He cuts his lamb chops with loving care. It is a point of honor to him to trim the fat. Shit and shit again. My mother would die if she heard me using that word. Why can't I reach out to my father? Christ, that's shit, too. He's dead, you sap. And while he was alive, all twenty-three years you knew him, you kept him at arm's length. You wouldn't let him know you, so how the hell can you expect to know him?

Oh, shit, again. That's not true. I loved him when I was little. I thought he was the most wonderful father. We played ball in the yard and ran on the beach. He was wonderful to play with. He'd get me on his shoulders and dash madly into the surf, while I screamed with delight. I'd stand up and he wouldn't be there. Then suddenly he'd appear out of the water, pretending to be a whale, spitting a stream of water out of his mouth and making noises like a giant fish. Or we'd play football. He'd be the fullback, charging across the yard or beach while I chased him, giggling until I could hardly run. He'd let me catch him, and he'd fall, pretending to be tackled hard, groaning and grimacing in pain until I almost believed him. "Daddy, you all right?" He'd groan harder, then suddenly grab me and laugh. And I'd laugh, in relief. He was wonderful when I was little and I loved him. Then a wall came between us. No, not a wall. He would have smashed that. A curtain, a silken curtain. He flailed at it, but it just billowed and enveloped his fist and returned, always between us. He knew something had happened between us, and he resented it. "What's the matter, son? You don't seem to be enjoying yourself." Or, "If you don't want to do this, Davie, you don't have to." I'd always deny it and insist I wanted to and nothing was the matter. But there was. I knew it. He knew it. I came to see the frustration in his eyes. If I speak the truth, I guess I have to say I enjoyed seeing that. And if I speak the truth again, I guess I have to admit I was particularly cruel. I think it would have been easier for my father if I'd been rebellious or defiant or nasty. But I wasn't. I went along with whatever he wanted me to do. Obedient, I surely was, but I only gave him the letter, not the spirit. That hurt him more than defiance would have.

* * *

David Callahan was not without self-perception. He had started this secret verbal exercise in search of some understanding of himself. Presumably he was unhappy and dissatisfied. There were great emotional forces at war within him, it is to be imagined. He hoped he could in some way talk this conflict out of existence. His father was the key to his problem, he believed. He tried, unsuccessfully as we have seen, to "explain" his father. He had the perception to realize he was not doing very well.

David Callahan knew what the problem was. But it was difficult for him to speak of it—even to himself in the privacy of his apartment. I might add that that was only understandable. If I were he, I couldn't have spoken of it either. When he resumed his recording, he obviously had faced the fact that he must speak of the central problem of his life. The reader should be warned that he approaches this in the most oblique, roundabout way.

* * *

My mother has talked a little about her background. I don't think she wanted to speak of it at all, but she felt she had to tell me something. Doubtlessly, she had thought carefully of what to say. When she did so, the words came out quite vehemently.

"I never knew my real mother and father. I was put out for adoption as an infant. It was all a huge mistake. The adoption agency goofed. My adopted parents didn't love each other, and they didn't love me. They didn't know what it meant to be parents, and I was a huge nuisance. When they finally, mercifully, divorced, I left home and met your father."

I remember her reaching out and taking my face in her hands and saying with great intensity. "When I had you, all I wanted in the world was for you to have a real mother and a real father and a proper home. I just wanted to love you and love you and love you. I didn't ever want to leave you, and I didn't want you to ever leave me." There were tears in her eyes as she said, "Do you understand?" I said I did, and we both cried and embraced. I remember exactly when that happened. I was thirteen and going away to school for the first time. I didn't want to go, and she didn't want me to go. My father insisted.

My mother was the most wonderful mother. My earliest memories are of being with her. She took me everywhere. I am to this day the only person allowed to watch her do her exercises.

When I was little, she'd take me in the room. I'd play while she exercised. I remember trying to emulate her and falling down or getting my legs and arms twisted into hopeless knots. She'd stop what she was doing and laugh and pick me up and hug and kiss me. She'd show me what to do and help me through a forward roll or back roll. I can remember lying on my back, my legs in the air, trying to keep up with her on a scissor kick. I remember running on the beach with her, or trying to. She'd race ahead of me, then come back and scoop me up on the run and run with me while I squealed with delight.

Others, I know, think of my mother as icy cool, aloof, even diffident, a beautiful but untouchable china doll. I do not think of her that way. To me she is all warmth and softness and hugs and kisses and laughter. We laughed a great deal together. We always had something to talk about. My mother was positively garrulous at times with me. We played games together, and the usual end of them was a fit of laughter. I was always ticklish, still am, and she would poke me and start to tickle me, and we would both end up laughing until tears ran down our cheeks. We went horseback riding and bicycling and swimming and running. She took me everywhere. I did what she did. I never wanted to do anything except be with her. I begrudged the time I was in school. I was hesitant about being with my father. But she said it was important that I spend time with my father. I often begged her to come with us, and sometimes she would.

I was never a behavior problem with her. I have not a single recollection of her being angry with me. She'd simply look at me and say what I had done wrong and what I ought to do. There was no rancor to it. It was never an accusation. I truly grew up without much sense of guilt about any of my actions or inactions.

[On another occasion David discussed his childhood with his mother.]

"I think I loved you too much, David. I could feel you growing within me, and I loved you even then. I wouldn't let the doctor give me any anesthetic. I had you by natural childbirth. I wanted to feel everything and know everything about you. And I had a hard delivery. There were hours and hours of pain, but strangely I enjoyed it. I knew you were coming and you'd be strong and healthy and wonderful. I just knew the hurt would make me love you more and it did.

"You were the most beautiful baby ever born and the happiest and healthiest and most wonderful. I was consumed with love for you. I wanted you with me always. I hated it when you had to sleep, and I used to come in and watch you sleep, just to be near you. I didn't think I could stand it when you went off to the first grade. I couldn't wait for the school bus to return you to me. I often drove to school and picked you up. I was even jealous of the teachers who had you so many hours a day. I refused to have another child. I didn't want to have to share myself with anyone else.

"I know other mothers don't feel this way. I suppose there was something unnatural in my love for you. But when I was a child, I felt such a sense of loss that I didn't know my real parents. I felt it was the cruelest thing in the world not to have a real mother and a real father. I used to look at people to see if they would give some sign, some recognition that I was their child. I felt they ought somehow to know me. Even animals know their own offspring. I used to make up incredible fantasies about my parents finding me and knowing me and coming at last to love me. I couldn't wait to have a child of my own to love, and I had you and I loved you as no child was ever loved."

There was boundless affection between my mother and me. We were always hugging and kissing and touching in some way. When I'd come in the house, from school or even from a short play outside, she'd embrace me and kiss me and stroke my hair back and ask me about what I'd been doing. I guess other kids throw their hats in the house after school, say hi, and go out to play. I went straight to my mother to hug her and be hugged and to express our sheer delight in each other's company.

113

My going to bed was a ritual. She bathed me every night far beyond the age, I think, when that sort of thing usually stops. I guess I was nine or ten before I began to bathe myself. Even then she was sort of in and out of the bathroom, bringing a towel, turning down the bed, fussing with my clothes, and telling me to hurry up. Even when I was as old as twelve, she'd frequently wash my back and scrub my ears and dry me with a soft towel and button up my pajamas. Although she was never nude, I never had any sense of embarrassment at my own nudity in front of her. Even when my scrotum hardened and the pubic hairs started to grow and my voice deepened, I was not embarrassed. She said what a fine man I was becoming. And when I had a hard on, that, too, was not unnatural.

When I was dressed in my pajamas, she'd comb my hair and tuck me into bed. She'd sit on the edge of the bed, and we'd talk, usually about what we'd done that day and what we were going to do tomorrow. It was a precious time for me, just we two alone, talking in the most intimate way. Then she'd get up and smooth the covers and bend over and kiss me good night. My mother's kisses were not like other kisses. Even if she just brushed me with her lips, I felt a tingle all through me. I know she did too. Sometimes she'd say, "Wow!" and laugh and say, "Oh, I pity the girls when you grow up."

114

"You had the most beautiful body, David. When you were little, you were all warm and soft. And as you grew, you were straight and tall and lean and hard. I always liked touching you. You were my son. It was to me only natural to touch. I loved you. I didn't want any secrets between us, any hiding and shame. I didn't want anything to spoil what was between us."

The first time she masturbated me it was the most natural thing in the world. I was twelve. She had gotten up from the bed, smoothed the covers, and kissed me. My hard on was a bulge in the covers. She patted it, smiled, kissed me lightly, and said, "We'll have to do something about that." She reached under the covers and took hold of me. Her hand was like silk, and she sent shivers through my whole body. She took her hand away, went into the bathroom, and came back with a towel. She turned back the covers, told me to lie still, as if I could move, knelt beside the bed, and began to stroke me. I didn't know what she was doing or what was going to happen, but the sensations she caused enveloped and immersed me. When I finally came, it seemed to go on forever while my body writhed with the most extreme pleasure. I swear I could feel every nerve in my body, and a most pleasurable warmth spread down my legs and knees and ankles to my toes. She said, "Good heavens," lightly, almost with wonder in her voice.

She covered me back up and sat on the bed once again.

"Was that nice?"

I said it was, although I could barely speak.

She kissed me lightly. "I'm glad," she said. "Was that the first time?"

I said it was. That I hadn't known.

Then she kissed me harder, even passionately. "I'm so glad. I don't want you ever to do that to yourself. I couldn't bear the thought of you sitting in the toilet or some place doing that to yourself. It's degrading and dirty. Promise me you'll never do it."

I promised.

"If you have a problem, simply tell me. I'll help you. All right?"

I said that was all right.

"And David. This has to be our secret. You must never, never, tell your father, your friends, anyone. It is our secret. Promise?"

I promised again.

"I had read books. I knew what happened with boys your age. I simply could not bear the thought of my beautiful son hunkered down somewhere masturbating himself. Nor could I stand the thought of your being uncomfortable. It seemed only natural that I should do it for you. I fed and clothed you. I looked after you when you were sick. I talked out your problems with you. Why shouldn't I tend to your sexual needs? And so I did. It brought you pleasure and relieved your needs. I couldn't see any harm in it."

My mother's action awakened my sexuality. Awakened? Aroused? It became a storm within me. I laid awake a long time that night and for many nights thereafter. I desired my mother as I have never desired anything in my life. My nights, days too, were filled with bizarre sexual fantasies, all involving her. I wanted her. I wanted her. My penis was like a hot iron and my groin ached, but because of my promise to her there was nothing I could do or say. She tried to help. Masturbating me became an almost nightly ritual, a great intimate moment between us, but I think it only made my problem worse. I ached at the slightest, most casual, touch of her hand. Our hugs and kisses were a torment, both in the doing and in the not doing. I hated school and every moment I was not with her; yet when I was with her, the mere sight of her made me ache with passion. My penis oozed constantly. My shorts were forever wet. More than once I came in my pants just watching her. One time I came just as she kissed me, when I arrived home from school. She felt it, hugged me close till I finished. "You better go change," was all she said.

I suffered. That's the only word for it. I had

a chronic condition for which there was no known cure.

One afternoon when we were alone—we were in a restaurant some place—she said, "David, you've got to stop looking at me that way."

I asked what way.

"Like you are right now. Your eyes are blue flames burning me. People will notice. Can't you forget it?"

I said I couldn't.

"You must, David. I'm sorry for you. But I don't know what else I can do. You've got to promise me to try to forget."

I promised.

If we had company or she and Dad had gone out and she couldn't come to me at bedtime, I'd lie there sobbing with the pain of the wanting. On one occasion she missed three nights in a row. I thought I would die of frustration. When she finally came the fourth night, she fussed over me and told me she was sorry but it couldn't be helped. When she finally did it for me, I lay there on the pillow crying.

"Oh, baby, baby, what's the matter?"

I couldn't speak.

"David, please talk to me."

I said I wanted to see her. Her body. I put my hand on her breast. I felt its softness through her dress.

She took my hand away and pulled me to a sitting position and hugged me close. "Oh, David

. . . David . . ." She said it over and over.

I said I wanted her. I said I had to have her.

"Oh, David . . . David . . ."

"I had a terrible problem, and I didn't know what to do. I had no idea—I'd never dreamed that you would have such a towering sex drive and suffer so much with it. And your pain was my pain. I felt dreadful for you. But I didn't know what to do. I released you from your promise not to masturbate. I thought maybe that would relieve you. But you refused."

"I have never masturbated to this day."

"I didn't know what to do. It was a terrible dilemma." [She paused a long time.] "My mind was made up when your father decided to send you away for school the next term. I opposed it. We had a terrible row, but there was nothing I could do except accuse him of inconsistence. He wanted his son to have the common touch. Growing up with money was bad enough. He didn't want you to feel privileged. Now, he'd changed his mind. The junior high in Westport was a mess. He wanted you to go to a school with more discipline, a better academic and sports program. It would help you through the difficult years. I couldn't argue with him. All I could do was get him to allow me to tell you when the time was right, after the school year ended or sometime over the summer."

119

It was my thirteenth birthday. I remember it precisely. Dad had to go away. Some meeting on the West Coast. He was sorry, but he couldn't help it. He gave me my present early. I don't remember what it was.

Mother kept me out of school so we could spend the whole day together. She got me up when she awoke, and we did exercises together. Rather, she did her exercises while I watched her hot-eyed. We changed into our swim suits, put on the sweat togs, and ran along the beach, hard, for a very long time, came back, took a sauna, and swam—her daily ritual. After a shower and breakfast, we went horseback riding. We returned, showered and changed again, and went out to lunch. Afterwards, we shopped for my birthday present, a blue cashmere sweater I've kept all these years. We returned home about four and took a long swim.

Mother was particularly animated all day, very happy and affectionate. We put our arms around each other as we walked through the house and to and from the pool. We held hands walking down the street. She held my hand during lunch and touched my knee with hers. She kissed me lightly several times and once made a joke. "You're getting so tall I can't reach you. I've either got to get a stool or start kissing you on the navel." We both thought it very funny. None of this sort of affection was extraordinary between us; yet there was a difference. Or was I imagining?

About five she suggested we dress for dinner. She wanted to see me in my new tux, and she had a new gown for the occasion. I went to my room and showered again, dressed and came downstairs. I had to wait a long time for her to appear. Nothing, but nothing was going to rush my mother's bath. When she finally appeared after six-thirty, she was a vision. I'm sure I blushed and gasped when I saw her. She had never worn a gown like that before. She usually wore severe, rather concealing clothes. This dress was electric blue satin, backless, cut low in front and very formfitting. There was a slit up one leg so she could walk. She laughed and did a slow turn for me to see it. "You like?"

I assured her I did.

She laughed again. "Oh, it's silly and obvious. All this skin. But I thought I ought to own one sexy outfit."

Taking her cue, I said it sure was sexy.

Quite unexpectedly, she reached up and kissed me lightly, just brushing my lips. She might have been wired for electricity, the sensation she caused. "Now, my boy," she said, "it's time you learned to make the perfect martini." She instructed me in what to do and declared it perfection. I tasted it but said I didn't like it. She suggested a sherry. I didn't like it much better, but dutifully drank it.

"I had Mrs. Riordan lay out a buffet for our dinner. I hope that'll be all right for your birthday."

I said I wasn't very hungry. She said she wasn't either.

"I told Mrs. Riordan she could leave early. We've the whole place to ourselves."

Mother became quite gay and animated on her drink. We walked out by the pool and enjoyed the warm spring evening. We sat on the patio for awhile, then about eight came in for dinner. There was some soup and salad, beef stroganoff and rice on a warmer, and a napoleon for dessert. Mother had me pour some wine. We each had two glasses. I began to feel a bit giddy. Mother ate very little and I still wasn't hungry. There seemed to be a lump in my throat that made swallowing difficult. Mother asked me if I minded not having a birthday cake. I told her I hadn't even thought of it. I hadn't.

After dinner, she put some music on and suggested we dance. I protested that I wasn't very good. She said it was time I improved. I don't remember the music. It sounded very old-fashioned, sort of dreamy. Or maybe I was just dreamy. As I took her in my arms to dance, I felt enveloped in the nearness of her and in her perfume. Her hand in mine, the flesh of her back against my other hand, felt like cold fire.

"You're trembling, David."

I said I couldn't seem to help it. We began to dance. I felt my hard on pushing into her. Embarrassed, I tried to move away. She moved back against me, not seeming to mind. The roundness and softness of her curves against me made such an ache in my loins that I could barely move. Her perfume, the exquisite sweetness of her, enveloped me. We danced awhile and sipped some wine and danced some more. We didn't talk much. I lost all track of time. I still don't know what time it was when she suggested it was time for my bath. I protested. I didn't want to be sent off to bed. She laughed a little, patted my cheek, and kissed me lightly. "Mother knows best," she whispered. Then, aloud, she said, "You go ahead. I'll lock up and be along in a minute."

I had finished my bath and gotten dressed in my pajamas when she opened the door to my room. She had changed into a negligee. For the life of me, I can't remember the color of it, but it was soft and very thin. I could see the contours of her body, the soft mounds of her breasts, the nipples straining against the fabric. She came to me, stroked my hair back as she so often did, then kissed me, lightly like she always did.

"Did you enjoy this evening?"

I said I enjoyed the whole day. It was the best day, the best evening, of my whole life.

"I'm glad, I so wanted it to be right for you. I wanted everything to be perfect."

She unbuttoned my pajama top and began to rub her hand over my chest.

"I want your first experience to be the most beautiful and wonderful possible."

She removed my top and then undid the tie and helped me step before her naked. She ran her hands over my chest and sides and abdomen and lingered a moment over my loins and buttocks and the thighs between my legs. She caressed my distended penis lovingly. "You have such a beautiful body," she said. "And you're so wonderfully big." Her hands were like cool water on my aching organ. "You can do anything to me you want, David."

I began to tremble. I felt so foolish, but I just couldn't help it. My whole body seemed racked with violent spasms, so much so I could hardly undo her gown. When it slid whispering to the floor, I moaned. I couldn't help it. I touched her with one trembling hand, on the breast, and felt the hard nipple beneath my quivering fingers. I moaned again and felt her other breast and then held both, filling my two hands. I moaned again and again as I ran my hands over her. She was like silk. Her skin was soft and smooth, but I could feel every muscle beneath. I knelt before her and put my arms around her and felt the delicious curve of her buttocks and laid my face against the hard flatness of her stomach and felt the down of her pubic hairs against my chin. Remembering, I touched the hollows in her thighs and followed them to the secret place they led to. Again and again I did that. Oh, how I'd longed to do that. And she began to tremble too. I buried my face against her breast and felt her nipples go soft against my tongue.

"Now, David, now."

We laid on the bed. I caressed her thighs, and she moaned and opened them wide for me. I seemed to know instinctively what to do. Or was she helping me? I got to all fours above her. She caressed my penis, that aching sword, one more time, then guided me into her. It was a scalding cauldron. I cried aloud at the heat of it. She put her arms and her legs around me and squeezed so hard I couldn't even move. "Oh. My God! *My God!*" she said. There was both shock and dismay in her voice. And before I had even made a movement, indeed I could not move the way she held me, she began to shudder and writhe beneath me and moan and gasp and say over and over, "*My God! My God!*" Her orgasm seemed to continue for the longest time. She tossed her head from side to side. Her whole body seemed to dissolve in a paroxysm of shuddering. Her legs gripped me so tight I felt pain. As her orgasm subsided and her hold on me relaxed, I began to move inside her. It was strange. So many times I'd dreamed of this. So many times I'd ached for this. I'd come in my pants just looking at her. Now, inside that burning tube, I figured to go instantly. But I didn't. I felt strangely satiated by the smell and softness of her and the wonderful doing of it. I wanted it to last forever, never to end. As I thrust into her again and again, she began to moan. And writhe. "Oh, my *God!*" she said again, almost screaming, and began to shudder again, worse than before, and I squirted into that shuddering, writhing flesh of hers. As I did so, I began to cry. I sobbed. Tears ran down my cheeks, and I suddenly realized she was crying, too. And crying in each other's arms, we came again. I couldn't seem to stop, nor she.

Finally, mercifully, spent, I rolled off of her and we lay in each other's arms, still sobbing. I asked her why she was crying. Had I hurt her?

"Oh, no, you didn't hurt me. It was— Oh, God, David, what have we done? I thought— Oh, God, I never thought it would be like this. I've never gone like that . . . even once like that . . . and then, again and again, each more than the last. I didn't know it was possible."

She got up and went into the bathroom. I heard the sound of running water and the toilet flushing. She returned, still naked, and sat on the edge of the bed.

"It just can't be," she said. "It just can't be." The words seemed a mesmerizing chant to her.

"What?"

"It just can't be. It can't be."

"What?"

"You. You're thirteen years old. A seventh-grade boy. It can't be this way. It just can't."

"You didn't like it?"

Suddenly she must have realized that I would have no way of knowing what she meant. "Oh, David, you silly. Mothers and sons aren't supposed to do this, have intercourse. You've got to know that. It is supposed to be the most forbidden thing people can do. But the more I thought

126

about it, the less I could see why. If there was
to be a child, between you and me, I mean, that
would be the sin. But I take the pill. I wouldn't
have a child by you. I figured you'd be doing it
soon anyway. I didn't want it to be some ugly,
sweaty, rutty thing. I wanted it to be beautiful
and wonderful for you. I wanted you to learn
what to do and be good at it and enjoy it. I simply couldn't see why I had to leave all this to
someone who might hurt you. I saw no reason
why I shouldn't teach you the most important
thing in life. I tried to make it beautiful. I
planned this whole evening for a long time. I
even bought a special dress. I thought you'd
find it pleasurable. When you'd finally done it,
your curiosity would be gone. I thought everything would be easier for you. I simply never
expected *this*. I never dreamed of it."

I still didn't understand. I asked her what
she didn't dream of.

"I never expected to come myself. I thought
it would be just your thing. I never expected to
be turned on myself. But when I touched your
slender young body and you touched me with
your trembling hands, it was—I was just gone,
that's all. I guess you can't know or understand,
can you? I don't very often have any orgasm. I
fake it lots of times. And to come, like that,
with you, so quickly, so shatteringly, like my
body is breaking apart, and to do it again and
again, being unable to stop doing it— David,

127

don't you understand? You're fantastic. You're ten feet tall."

I remember lying there on the bed, grinning with pride and pleasure. I asked if we could do it again.

"You're kidding." She looked down at me. "I guess you aren't kidding."

I don't know how often we did it that night. I believe at least twice more. She came in bunches, shuddering under me, or over me, again and again. I couldn't possibly keep up. I don't remember falling asleep, but I awoke in the morning to find her gone. I felt an impenetrable loss.

I found her doing her exercises. She wasn't using her music or doing her regular routine. She was peddling ferociously on the bicycle, the sweat dripping off her. She did her other exercises with a particular savagery and violence. I went with her when she ran. I've never seen her run longer or harder. She seemed to be punishing herself. She ran and ran until even she was stumbling with fatigue. We went into the sauna, and she turned the heat up high. There, on the floor, in the blistering heat, sweat pouring off our bodies, slipping and sliding, salt bitter in our mouths, we made love again, repeatedly, shatteringly. She stood up, her beautiful body glistening, my sperm a rivulet down that hollow in her thigh. Suddenly, quite naked, she opened the door and jumped headlong into the pool. I don't think she gave a thought to

whether Mr. Riordan was gardening. He wasn't.
I jumped in the pool after her. We had not yet
spoken a word to each other that day.

* * *

I wish as I have wished for few things in
my life that I did not have to describe this
incestuous relationship between David Callahan
and Carla Callahan Lampton. It disgusts me. I
feel like a voyeur. More, it fills me with loathing for that woman, seducing her son at his most
impressionable age, ruining his life before he
ever had a chance to live it. I wish I didn't
have to print this information. I wish it would
just go away. But it won't. There is no understanding David Callahan and what he did to his
country except in terms of his incestuous relationship with his mother. I even wish there
were laws of libel to keep me from printing this.
But the proof of the incest—a nasty word both
mother and son find so difficult to speak—is unmistakable. There is a tape, a horrid tape, in
which she comes to dinner at his apartment.
They have drinks. He tells her she looks tense.
She says she is. He asks if she has a headache. She
says a little one. He says he has a cure. There is a
pause. I can't imagine what is happening. She
says, "Now?" He replies, "I can't think of a
good reason why not."

He leaves the tape machine running while
they do it. Yes, my God, he recorded himself

having sex with his mother. As near as I can figure, he was twenty-three or twenty-four and she was thirty-nine. It's all there on the tape, the moans and groans, the monotonous repetition of the word "hold," the calling of his name over and over, all as he describes it so often. It went on for a time that can only be described as indecent. The pair of them were nothing if they weren't insatiable.

Afterwards, they come back in the living room and have some dinner. He asks her not to dress. He wants to look at her. She laughs a little, calls him silly, but agrees. He tells her repeatedly how beautiful she is and comments on her anatomy.

It is on this occasion that he gets her talking about their relationship and how it began. It is not very easy. She is most reluctant, but he begins to reminisce and asks her if she remembers various times and happenings. At first she says, "We've talked about this before, David. Why go into this again?" She, of course, does not know it is for the benefit of the tape recorder. He gradually gets her talking. Most of her remarks and explanations of the incest that I have already used and will use in other places come from this tape. They talked for a long time, then went into the bedroom and did it again, and David recorded that session, too. All in all, he used almost an entire reel on that night's incest.

David Callahan has on tape the erotic sounds of several lovemaking sessions (if that's what it was—it was their term for it). This is in addition to his own seemingly endless descriptions of his affair with her. There can be no doubt that Carla Callahan Lampton, wife of our esteemed presidential dictator, carried on an incestuous relationship with her son for twelve years.

To me, her "explanations" are really self-serving excuses unworthy of consideration. The simple facts are that under the guise of smothering mother love, she attracted and seduced her son into incest. That she didn't know, that she didn't believe any harm would come of it until it was too late, is patently baloney. The incest taboo is the oldest and strongest among mankind. It is both vile and psychologically sick that she found her son so attractive. Unhappy and frustrated in her marriage to Brendan Callahan—who was the only decent person in this whole miserable affair—she trained her son to be her perfect lover. I have heard that many mothers do this with their sons, although it is impossible for me to believe it in the case of my own mother. But the taboo operates to keep mothers from actually copulating with their sons. Or at least I do strongly believe. The mother can't break the taboo. The son fears the father until he reaches an age where he no longer finds the mother physically attractive. I believe that incest does occur, but it is usually between father and teenage daughter in what amounts to rape. But incest between mother and son is rare, I truly believe. I

would not believe it in this circumstance were
not the proof inescapable.

There are ameliorating circumstances, such as
Carla Callahan's unhappy childhood, her inordi-
nate love for her son, the very unusual disparity
in their ages. Yet, the fact remains that she did
seduce him and quite consciously and deliberately. More, she then maintained the relationship for her own morbid and erotic pleasure.
She broke a fundamental law of nature and tried
to get away with it. The piper was playing for
them both, but for a while the music was very
sweet.

*　*　*

"That first night, David, while you slept, I
lay there beside you, wide awake, rigid with
what I can only describe as terror. I had done a
terrible thing. I had been so dumb. I hadn't
thought. I hadn't realized what would happen
or what could happen. I knew for a mother to
make love to her son was wrong. But if there
could be no child, I couldn't see how it could be
very wrong. Oh, I knew about Freud. But that
was supposed to be with young children. You
were over six feet tall, a beautiful young man. I
did the other thing for you—the masturbation.
You never revealed it. I knew you could keep a
secret. I also knew how you were suffering. I
thought that if we made love—had real intercourse—it would be good for you. You wouldn't

wonder any more. You'd know. And if I made it beautiful and if I made you feel beautiful and strong and manly, it would give you confidence. I truly didn't think it would be much, just some nakedness and warmth. I thought it would be soft and cuddly, like holding you as a baby in my arms. I thought it would be just romantic, hardly sexual at all.

"I laid there that night knowing how wrong I'd been and what a terrible mistake I'd made. I was petrified for you. I felt there was no way you'd ever keep this a secret from your father. You'd blurt it out in some moment of anger or petulance at him or me. And even if you kept it a secret, it would show in your face, your eyes, the way you looked at him or me, a smirk on your lips that you thought no one saw. You'd say something when you thought we were alone and be overheard. You'd touch me, on the stairs, passing in the hall, sitting beside the pool and be seen. Questions would be raised. He, Mrs. Riordan, Richard, people just visiting the house would begin to wonder. There would be doubts. Talk. Accusations. My life—and yours—would be in ruins. It was inevitable. There seemed to me to be no way to prevent it.

"And I was scared for myself. I was numb with fear. You had done something to me that I didn't know was possible. You had awakened some—some beast in me. You had transformed me into someone I didn't know I liked or wanted to be. I had never really enjoyed sex very much. It had always been sort of messy and grunty, more sufferance than pleasure, more fraud than passion. That night, when you touched me, something in me came alive. It devoured me. When you entered me, I came instantly and in the most violent way. I couldn't tell whether it was pleasure or pain. It hurt. I swear it did. It must have been pain. And it wouldn't go away. It kept crashing over me in waves. It would subside and then bear down on me again. I felt helpless in some terrible pounding surf that kept throwing me again and again against the shore. Everytime I tried to rise, to escape, a new wave bore down on me and immersed me.

"And that was the least of it. I laid there beside you that night. I was bone weary from all we'd done. My insides ached. I had been unable to move. Your semen had run out of me and soaked into the bedsheet. I could feel its dampness. Despite it all, despite my weariness and my fear, I laid there wanting you, wanting you, wanting you. It was all I could do to keep from waking you."

"I wish you had."

"No, let me finish. I'll never be able to say this again. I knew I'd changed forever. There was now some terrible urge inside me. I felt it would never go away. I would have to live with it forever. I got up, determined to drive it out of my body. I showered. I tried to wash it away. I did my exercises. I would drive it out by sheer weariness. If I were exhausted, this feeling, yes, this damnable lust, would leave me. I tried. I tried as hard as I could. I ran until I could barely move. Then when we did it in the sauna, slimy with sweat, slipping and sliding, all salt and lather and foam, I knew I was lost. I was terrified, David, simply terrified."

My mother climbed out of the pool and ran into the house and upstairs to her room. I'll always have a vision of her running into the house, her beautiful naked body flinging water as she ran. I followed her in a bit, but more deliberately. I dried myself at poolside, wrapped my nakedness in a towel and went to my room. I showered quickly and dressed, then came downstairs for breakfast. I was ravenous, I remember. I think I ate breakfast cereal. I usually do.

I knew I had changed. I didn't know how or, I guess, understand why. But I knew I was different. Looking back on it, I suppose I did a lot of growing up that night and morning. I felt very relaxed. I remember that. And I guess I felt very strong and confident and masterful. Looking back on it, it seems to me I should have felt very dreamy and full of the wonder of all that had happened. But I don't remember feeling that way. I suppose I was still too close to it. That came later.

My mother didn't come down for a long time. She usually showered very quickly and came down in her robe, starved after her exercise. This time she came down dressed in white pants and a blue sweater. She had dried and fixed her hair. That never seemed to take much effort. But she had put no makeup on. I saw her hand trembling. I suppose that is why she hadn't been able to fix her eyes and do her lipstick. She looked very wan and tired and tiny and so beautiful. I felt very protective of her.

I poured her a glass of orange juice and made her toast and laid out the marmalade for her. She liked orange marmalade on her toast. It gave her quick energy after her exercise. She didn't eat that morning. The silence was a shroud between us. Finally, I said, "Mother, we've got to speak to each other some time." She looked at me, but she did not speak.

I didn't know what to say. I felt a sense of helplessness. Yet, I knew I had to do something. I went over to where she sat at the table and stood close to her and put my arm around her shoulder and pulled her to me so her head lay against my stomach. She was trembling. I said, "Mother, I love you." She finally spoke my name, "David, David—" very sadly, forlornly, as if the words were a great weight.

I asked if she were ill.

She sighed. "No, I'm not ill. I'm just very tired. I didn't sleep all night." She lifted her head and looked at me and smiled her little, almost imperceptible smile. "Somebody kept me awake almost all of it." She clutched my waist harder. "Oh, David, David. What are we going to do? I'm so afraid."

I repeated the word as a question. "Afraid?"

Then she poured out her fears. We had done a terrible thing, an evil thing. We would be caught. People would know. There was no way to hide such a thing. She hadn't intended it. But she hadn't known. She talked a long time. The words cascaded out of her. At times she trembled so much her voice quivered and she became almost incoherent.

Mrs. Riordan came in, damnably early, damnably cheerful, and insufferably talkative. She gabbed about this and that. Had I liked my birthday? I was almost a man now. Mother roused herself, quite marvelously really. She talked with Mrs. Riordan, inquired about her family, talked of household things. I doubt if Mrs. Riordan knew there was anything wrong.

Mother and I went out. We were too tired to do anything but drive around. I remember we ended up at Compo Beach. We parked, sat in the car overlooking the sea, and talked. The weather had changed. It was now a gray and windy day, on the edge of rain, and a bit chilly. We were almost alone on the beach. It was very quiet inside the car. I could hear the surf, although it sounded a long way away through the closed windows. I could hear the seabreeze whistling through a crack around the windows. The automatic clock in the dash clicked the passage of time.

I told her not to be afraid, that everything would be all right, that I would never, never tell. She said I didn't understand, that I couldn't possibly understand. We had both changed. We would never be the same again. She could see it in me even then. We wouldn't be able to look at each other in the same way or touch each other. We'd be stilted and strange and afraid. Everyone would notice. I said that wasn't so. I would be exactly the same. So would she. No one would see any difference. Mrs. Riordan hadn't thought us any different, had she? Mother said, "I wish I could be sure of that." I talked a long time, trying to reassure her. I described our days. I said she'd do her exercises and run and swim and come down to breakfast and horseback ride and shop. How I'd go to school and come home and hug her and kiss her and sit and talk with her as we always did.

She didn't believe me. "There's another thing, David. I've seen you the last few months, ever since I started doing the other thing—masturbating you. You've been tense and nervous, hot-eyed and jealous. One reason I did that last night was in hope you'd get over it before your father started to wonder what was wrong with you. I know now I've made a terrible mistake. Oh, you're fine now. But in a day or two your sexuality will return. You'll be tormented. You'll want me again. I know that. You'll be hot-eyed and jealous and irritable. It'll all come out when you least expect it. You won't want it to. I know that. But it will, it will. And even if it doesn't, you'll suffer. You'll do poorly in school. You'll—"

"I won't, Mother, I won't. I promise you."

We were silent then a long time. Looking back, I think that was the smartest thing I could have done. There was no way I could convince her. But she could understand silence. When I finally spoke, I remember very clearly what I said. When I think that I was only thirteen, I find it very hard to believe I said it. Yet I remember the words exactly. They just seemed to come out. I don't remember thinking of them in advance. Very quietly and matter of factly, I said:

"Mother, there is nothing to be done about it now. We did it. We are not going to be able to stop doing it. We will simply do what is required to keep Father and anyone else from knowing."

I had spoken the simple truth, and she knew it. She looked at me quite surprised, even startled.

"Your father is sending you away, David, to school, St. Albans in Massachusetts. It has nothing to do with last night. Don't ever think that. He decided you needed a better school than the junior high in Westport. I tried to talk him out of it. I couldn't. I'm sorry. It'll be very hard for you—and me."

I felt I'd been struck in the face, a hard

139

blow. I seemed to have trouble breathing. I could only ask when.

"In September. For the new term."

I didn't speak for a time. When I did, I was quite calm. "We have all summer then. I don't want to waste a moment with you. I want to learn. I want you to teach me everything."

She shuddered. "You already know too much, David."

"Let's go home. Get rid of Mrs. Riordan again. I want to do what we did last night again. Everything the same. Your dress. Dancing. Everything—and more."

"David, I'm—" She smiled, quite beautifully. "I started to say I'm already sore from last night and this morning. But no. You're right. Let's do go home." She started the car, then turned to me. "David, you're right. I'm amazed at your wisdom. We can't really help ourselves. But we'll have to be careful always. We must never be impetuous and foolish and stupid and take chances. We'll have to be patient and wait. It'll be hard, at times too hard."

"I know."

"It will have to be that I always come to you. Only I can know when we can be alone and safe. And don't make it harder for me. Don't ask me. Don't beg me. Don't urge me into unnecessary risks."

"I understand. I won't. I promise. But when we are together, I want it always to be good between us. I don't want us to be worried and afraid and—and guilty. I want it to be always—"

"Like last night."

"Better."

She looked at me a moment, smiled her imperceptible smile, then backed the car off the beach.

"When you talked to me later that day, you were the most amazing child. I say child because—well, it was the day after your thirteenth birthday. But you were no longer a child. You seemed to have grown up overnight. You were calm and controlled and—reassuring. I began to feel almost that our roles were reversed. I was the child and you the parent. I still think it amazing, almost unbelievable, what happened to you, to us that day."

I heard my mother say, "Why don't you leave early again today? With Mr. Callahan away, David and I will just eat something light, a sandwich or something." Mrs. Riordan was grateful. She said there was roast beef and ham in the refrigerator. She'd make a platter with cheese and whip up some potato salad before she left. Mother said that would be fine.

Mother and I forced ourselves to take a swim, forced because we were both tired, forced because we both wanted to do something else but couldn't, forced because it had turned cold and windy. We came out of the water shivering, toweled off, and wrapped ourselves in terry cloth robes and sat in the sunroom. We talked. We both tried to look at each other and talk as we always had. We were practicing, seeing if we could do it. I thought it went rather well.

When Mrs. Riordan left, we both went upstairs and dressed. We each went silently to our separate rooms. They seemed an eternity apart. I dressed in my tux and came downstairs. She came down more quickly than she had the night before. She looked wan and tired, but somehow it made her even more fragile and beautiful in her sexy dress. She had put on long matching gloves, which she had not worn before. I liked the gloves. I had not realized how sexy her upper arms were. I wanted to touch that soft, milky skin. Then I realized I could. I touched her and bent over to kiss her. She turned away. "Don't kiss me, or we'll be doing it here on the floor in front of God and everybody."

I made her a martini. I had part of one myself, determined to try to like it. She had a second. "Do you realize I haven't had a bite of food all day?" We tried to eat, but managed only a few bites with a lot of poking at the potato salad. We weren't hungry. Much earlier than before—it was hardly dark—I put on the same music. We danced or tried to. This time, it was she who was trembling in my arms. She tried to dance close to me and feel my erection against her. She shook her head and gave an expression that surely meant she couldn't stand it and moved away from me.

It wasn't the same upstairs, either. She went

directly to my room and stood there trembling while I undressed her, her gloves first. I unzipped her gown and removed it from her shoulders and held her hand while she stepped out of it. Her panties came the same. She stood there, naked and silent, trembling constantly, while I, too, undressed.

It was strange, wonderfully strange, our love-making. So different from the night before, yet so much the same. She never said a word. She never lifted a finger to touch me once. She just stood there, rigid, trembling uncontrollably, while I fondled and caressed her. And when I took her to the bed, she just lay there on her back still trembling. And when I touched her and opened her wondrous thighs, she did not resist. And when I entered her, she did not come immediately as she had before. But when I began to move, thrusting into her, very slowly at first, she moaned. There was a louder moan. And a third. Then her orgasm came crashing into her. She cried out and shuddered and writhed and gripped me savagely and ferociously. Again and again it happened. I was again unable to move in her grip. And, as before, when she relaxed and I began to thrust into her again for myself, she shuddered and writhed and gasped under me each time I came.

We both fell asleep exhausted. Some time in the middle of the night I awoke. It seemed strange. With delight I realized her body was there, warm and soft against me. I cupped her soft breasts and ran my hand over her abdomen and touched the moist hair between her thighs, and they opened again, and we were in repetition. More than before, if that was possible. I fell asleep. Toward morning—I could just see a faint light through the curtains, the first graying of day—I was awakened by her hand on me. She touched my groin and my testicles, and I had an erection. There was a rustle of covers, and she was on me and I was in her. We tossed and turned and rolled and struggled on the bed. That was when she dug her nails into my back and scratched me. I fell asleep, truly exhausted.

"I used to worry about our doing it so much. It might not be good for you. But I couldn't seem to do much about it anyway. I read somewhere—a woman of thirty and a teenage boy are at the height of their sexual powers. Does that account for the insatiable way we were? And I'd never had much sexuality to speak of before you. Maybe I was making up for lost time."

"Oh, I think there was a better reason."

"You mean that it was forbidden—what we were doing?"

"Hmm. That, too, I suppose."

"And we had to steal all our time together. And it was precious. We felt we couldn't waste a moment."

"Yes. But something else."

"What?"

"It's simple. You were the most beautiful, desirable, and sexiest woman in the world. You still are."

[That was when they went back into the bedroom.]

My father had left early Thursday morning. That had been my birthday. The next day had been Friday. My father was coming home on Sunday evening, and most of Saturday was a waste. It began with my sleeping late. When I awoke, the house was full of Riordans—mother, father, daughter, cooking and cleaning and gardening. Mother had done her exercises, had breakfast, and even dressed by the time I came down. I felt a surge of anger that I'd wasted so much time in sleep.

She was in the kitchen with Mrs. Riordan. "Good morning, sleepyhead," she said.

Accusingly, I said, "You didn't wake me."

She looked at me, that almost imperceptible smile on her lips. There is nothing I associate with my mother as much as that almost unnoticeable smile. Indeed, she is smiling mostly with her eyes. For me, what La Gioconda is smiling about in the Mona Lisa is no mystery. "I thought you needed your rest," she said.

My cornflakes were set up on the table in the terrace. She sat with me and had coffee while I ate. Mr. Riordan was trimming a hedge some distance away. There was a little privacy, but not much. I tried to speak. "I wanted—"

"I know what you wanted. It wasn't possible." She made a slight motion with her head toward Mr. Riordan.

I munched my cereal for awhile, my petulance gradually fading. Finally I said, "How did your exercises go?"

She took a sip of coffee. She seemed to be studying Mr. Riordan's gardening intently. "For some strange reason—I can't imagine why—I didn't seem to have my usual energy."

We left the house. There seemed no point in being there. We drove around, killing time, and pretended to shop, killing time, and pretended to have lunch, killing time. "How about a movie?" she asked. I didn't want to go to a movie. We wandered around some more stores.

At lunch she said, "I told you it wouldn't work."

"What?"

"This. You. You're upset, angry, sullen, impatient. You can't wait."

"It's just—"

"There'll always be justs."

"—that he's away. He's coming back tomorrow. And they're there. Cleaning. Doing God knows what. We could be—"

"We can't. We have to wait."

"What time do they leave?"

"Five or six."

I sighed. "I can wait. I'm sorry."

"There'll be lots of waiting, David."

"They're off tomorrow. The Riordans."

146

"Your father's coming home. We have to be ready."

I said nothing. We both said nothing. We poked at our food. We tried to eat.

"Mother."

She looked at me. It was her way of signaling her attention. She did that often.

"Is it hard for you, the waiting I mean? It would be easier if you, too . . ."

She looked down at her plate and moved her fork, as though drawing a design in the food. "Extremely," she said.

We tried to have fun after that, sort of sharing our misery. But we weren't very successful. We were both too tense.

When we arrived back home, the phone was ringing. I got to it first. It was Father from California. He was sorry. He had to stay over another day. He wouldn't get home until Monday evening. I had to choke back a yelp of glee. He wanted to know how things were. I said fine. Did I have a good birthday? I said it was very nice. He was sorry he missed it. I said I was too, but it couldn't be helped. He asked for Mother.

I pretended not to hear. "Did you want to talk to Mother?"

She was standing right there. She shook her head, quite violently.

"She's not here. She went out for a moment."

"That's okay. It wasn't important."

"She'll be sorry she missed you."

"It was nothing. Just tell her I love her. I love you both. I'll see you Monday evening."

"All right."

"Goodbye, son."

"Goodbye."

We went upstairs as soon as the Riordans left. We made love with a passion that was almost painful. It was almost dark when we finished.

"I'm starved," she said. "Are you?"

I reached for her.

"I mean food, silly. C'mon."

She jumped out of bed. It was then she saw the scratches on my back.

"Good Lord! Did I do that?"

I said I guessed she had.

"That's terrible. Does it hurt?"

I said it didn't.

She got some alcohol from the bathroom and dabbed at them. "That's awful. Just awful. How could I? I've got to be more careful."

"Forget it. I liked it."

"You don't understand. This is terrible. If your father sees this . . ."

"I'll tell him a branch scraped me."

"Oh no you won't. He'll never believe you."

"Why? Have you done it to him?"

"Please, David. Don't. Don't ever ask me about anything I do with your father."

I said I was sorry.

"He'll know what they are. That's all. Anybody can see what they are." She turned me around. I could see the fear and desperation in her eyes. "You can't swim until they heal. You can't have your shirt off. No one must ever see these."

"Okay. Okay. I won't swim. I promise."

"I just hope they don't scar." She kissed me lightly. "We've just got to be so careful, David."

I said I knew that.

"Okay. Let me use your shower."

When she came out, using a dryer on her hair, she was still naked. I sat on the bed watching her until she finished. It only took a minute.

When the motor was turned off, she said, "Food. Remember? I said food."

"Let's go down this way."

"No clothes? Don't be silly."

"We can pull the drapes. No one will know."

She smiled. "Heavens, what a greedy child." She handed me my robe. "I'm sorry. We have to wear something." She went to her room and came back wearing the negligee of two nights before. "How's this for a compromise?"

I said it was lousy.

I made her a drink. We ate ravenously. Afterwards I asked her if we could go back upstairs.

She laughed. "Now? After all this food? I'm going to stop feeding you. It gives you too much strength."

I was hurt, stung. "Mother, I love you. I don't want to ever force you."

Her smile faded, and she got up and came around the table to where I sat. "David. You blessed boy. I'm so sorry. I don't ever want to refuse you—when we can." She undid her negligee and let it fall to the floor.

We came down again later and raided the refrigerator and had sandwiches and milk. She said she was probably going to get fat, and it would all be my fault. We spent another night together, sleeping only spasmodically. I arose with her, and we ran together but not very far or long or hard. When we went into the sauna, she brought a mat with her, grabbing it from a poolside lounge chair. It lay on the floor between us. We both looked at it and each other and laughed. And we used it. And when she stood up, her body glistening as she wiped away my semen and got back into her bathing suit, she said, "David Callahan, I don't know what you do or how you do it, but you are something else." I reached for her. She darted from me, saying, "Oh, no!"—opened the door and dived into the pool. She was laughing as she did so.

She left the pool before me, reminding me it had to be my last swim for a few days. I swam awhile, got out, toweled, put on a robe, and went upstairs. I went to her room. She was just getting out of the shower. We did it in her bed. It was the only time ever. Afterwards, she said, "It's too risky."

"Why?"

"I don't know. I can't explain. It's a bad precedent. Never again—not here."

"I just wanted to be in your bed, with you."

"It's all right. But not again."

We made love in the afternoon and again at dusk. Afterwards, she made me bathe and dress. She did, too. She wore a white pants suit, I remember. It made her look very slender and tiny. We ate; then we went into Father's study and sat together on the couch. She turned on the television. It was a crime show. I wasn't interested.

"David, I'm exhausted. I've hardly slept in three nights. I've never been so weary in my life. Every bone in my body aches. You've made me so sore it hurts to urinate. We've got to stop. We've got to get ourselves together. You've got to go to school tomorrow."

"Why?"

"Because you do. Everything has to be normal by tomorrow night."

"I know. But I thought—"

"Don't think, darling. I know I'm right. It will be hard enough to explain the two days you missed."

"We don't have to tell."

"Oh, but we do." Her voice took on great urgency. "We mustn't lie, David. It's bad enough as it is. We can't make it worse with lies. We'll get caught in them. We'll—"

"I told you not to worry. Everything'll be okay. You'll see."

We watched or pretended to watch the dumb TV program. I didn't even know what it was about. I asked if I could kiss her.

"Of course, silly." She gave me a light peck.

"No, I mean really kiss. I feel like I've done everything but kiss you. I'm not a very good kisser."

She laughed. "You teenage boys are all alike. All you want to do is neck."

I bent over and kissed her, hard. I remember opening my eyes and seeing her eyes. From that close they were infathomably deep pools. "I didn't know what soft lips you have. I'd only ever seen your eyes." I kissed her again.

"Open your mouth a little," she said.

I did.

"More."

Suddenly there was a whole new world of sweetness and softness, moist and warm, speckled with sensation. Her tongue came into my mouth, tiny and smooth and sweet, stunning me with sensation. It explored my tongue, gently, over and under and along the sides, and ran along my teeth and inside my lips and back inside as far as it would go, finding and caressing with a sweetness that exceeded all taste. I trembled under the onslaught of sensation. She withdrew her tongue, inviting mine, and I shuddered as it entered that delectable cavern. I did as she had done, exploring, seeking out every smoothness, every softness, every fold of her flesh. Slowly, she pulled it inside, sucking on it, pulsatingly, gently, then harder until my mouth was wide open and my tongue filled her whole mouth and I could feel pain at the base of it. In wonder, I opened my eyes. In a moment her eyelids fluttered and I could see the desire like a mist in the half-revealed pools. I was suddenly aware of her body, rigid, arching against me, her hips and thighs moving, pulsing, her breath coming rapidly, its sweetness warming my face.

In a moment she released my tongue. I stood up and pulled her to her feet.

"Here?"

It was somehow both a question and a negative.

"Yes."

She looked around the room. I could see hesitation, even a little fright in her eyes. She went behind Father's desk and checked the drapes. She turned off the light and then closed and locked the door. I started to turn off the television, then realized I didn't want it to be dark. I turned off the sound, and in the flickering light from the boob tube, we undressed.

There was a full-length mirror attached to the inside of the door to my father's study. It was incongruous in the book-lined, masculine room, but it was the only such mirror downstairs. My mother used it frequently to primp herself and check her appearance before she went out. We all used it for that. Now, we stood before that mirror and looked at ourselves looking at each other. I saw myself looking at her beautiful body. I saw my hands upon her. As I felt the softness of her breasts and the hard nipples between my fingers, I both felt and saw in the

153

mirror. As I ran my hand over her tiny waist and slender hips and felt the soft curves and silken smoothness atop the firm muscle, I saw what my hands felt. I eyed the hollow in her thighs and saw it form and disappear as she moved under my touch. And when we embraced, I turned to be able to see as well as feel my hands cupping the pillows of her bottom, our flesh pressed together, her breasts bulging against my chest. Her face turned against mine, her mouth open, her cheeks and throat moving as she sucked my tongue.

She laid on the couch, her thighs spread inviting me. Instead, I knelt beside her. I explored every facet of her body. I said over and over how beautiful she was and how beautiful each part of her was, and I told her how it felt to me and asked her how it felt to her, and she told me, if only with a moan or a sighed word like "Wonderful." She kept trying to pull me up to her, but I wouldn't let her. I wanted to see and know. I moved her thighs and saw how that wonderous hollow was formed. I parted her moist down and looked and explored with my fingers. Moaning, she explained about the clitoris and vagina.

"Is that where the pee comes out?" I asked.

She was still my mother. "Urine."

I rolled her over and explored her back and bottom. Again and again I explored her body, marveling in it. I wanted to know it all. I began to kiss her all over and then to lick her, every inch of her, every curve, every crevice, every fold of skin. When my mouth became dry, I sucked her toes and fingers, her tiny ears, her nose, her nipples. I probed every orifice with my tongue. Again and again I did it, insatiable. Her smooth armpits were a treasure, behind the knee, the small of her back. She moaned and writhed and shuddered under my touch. It went on for the longest time. When I finally entered her, our paroxysms were particularly violent, even savage.

As we lay beside each other on that couch, the light flickering over our bodies, I asked her how it felt.

"What?"

"When you come?"

She shivered. "I don't know. I can't explain. Hemingway once said the earth moved. I don't know. With me, it's more like an earthquake. I've never been in one. I don't know. But to me it is like the whole earth is shaking. I can't stand. I can't move. I'm helpless, paralyzed. Everything stops. It is like there is great thundering noise. Only I don't hear it. And it seems to happen again and again. Each time harder. It pulses. It comes in great shocking waves, over and over. I don't know. I can't explain. Could it be like death? Is that how a person feels in death, shocking violence, paralyzed, helpless? Then you are alive. So wonderfully alive." She kissed my chest. "But so terribly tired."

We lay there awhile. "How is it with you?" she asked.

I thought. It was hard to answer. "Maybe an earthquake," I said. "I don't know, either. It's a great feeling of release. All the strength goes from my body. Sometimes I feel a great warmth all over me. It seems to rush down to my legs and feet. I can't move. But not always. It's different every time. Sometimes when I come, it is like some dreadful eruption. From deep inside me. And it hurts here." I touched my testicles.

She raised her head from my shoulder and cooed. "Oh, baby. We're doing it too much."

"What makes you come?"

"You do, silly."

"No. I mean, what do I do that makes you go?"

She laughed and snuggled deeper inside my arm. "It looks like all you have to do is exist on the face of the earth."

"I mean it. I'm serious. You said your thing, the clitoris, was like a little penis. Does that make you come?"

"Yes. But sometimes it's just having you inside me. You're so big. I can feel you inside, poking at something. I feel you all the way in. That makes me come sometimes. You don't even have to move. Just exist, I guess."

We laid there a long time. Then she stirred and scrambled up and stepped over me and knelt on the floor. "Now you," she said.

I tried to protest, although I don't know why.

"Turn about," she said. "Only fair." And her exquisite torture of hand and mouth and tongue began. At one point she almost squealed. "Why, they're moving. Look at them. Is that you making more?"

Later, she was truly exhausted. I picked her up off the couch and carried her upstairs and put her in my bed. I came back downstairs for our clothes and to turn out the lights. When I came up, she was asleep. I got in bed beside her, and we slept in each other's arms all night, our first, undisturbed, together.

In the morning I got up and went to school. She made only one reference to all that had happened. "You forgot to wipe off the couch." She smiled almost imperceptibly. "I hope the odor comes out." She kissed me lightly and shoved me out the door.

* * *

I am a political scientist. I qualify as somewhat of an expert in various forms of government. I am not an expert in child psychology or sexual conduct, if indeed anyone is expert in these matters. I suspect these professional disciplines have so much difficulty establishing themselves simply because there is nothing to be expert about or the expertise is so widely held that everyone qualifies as one.

I have never married, but I am not virginal. I have had experience with several women. I have loved two women, one of them enough to ask her to marry me. She had the good sense to refuse me. I find the sexual excesses of David and Carla Callahan—some of the worst is yet to come in this narrative, I'm sorry to report—both ridiculous and disgusting. There is a great deal that is pathologically wrong in their feverish clutching and copulating. Yet I was touched by David Callahan's description of what transpired in the father's study. If that is all there had been, if it had all ended there, I might be able to forgive Carla Callahan. They were as children, touching, exploring, delighting in each other's bodies. There was a naiveté, an innocence that warms even an old stone such as I. And they were children. Both of them. At thirteen, David was very much a child. And Carla Callahan, even at age twenty-eight, was still a child, a child woman. She had been a child bride and a child wife and a child mother. She had adopted a veneer of sophistication. She seemed poised, capable, cool. Icy beautiful was the description David gave of her. But at heart she was sexually a child. I can believe, truly, that in her incest with her son she was sexually awakened. I can believe, as that scene in the study shows, that with her son she experienced a childlike rapture of touching and exploring and sensation she had never known. She was reborn with her son in the sense of discovering and experiencing what was so regrettably missing from her own nonexistent maidenhood. I am touched by their innocence, their sense of delight, the frankness and simplicity of their conversation, as David reports it. I wonder if we do not do something terribly wrong in our still-inhibited society in not allowing the young to discover and delight in each other's bodies.

As I said, I can *almost* forgive Carla Callahan. But the fact remains that she was a twenty-eight-year-old married woman who seduced a thirteen-year-old boy. Leaving aside the fact he was her son, it was still a heartless act. Twelve and thirteen, the onslaught of puberty with its drastic hormonal changes, is a crucial time in a boy's life. The influences of those years will often decide the course of a lifetime. Freud was wrong in his emphasis on the first five years. It is twelve and thirteen that matter; at least they are equally important.

Carla Callahan and her intentions be damned. What she actually did was play havoc with her son's natural sexual development. At a time in his life when he should have been holding hands with a girl in the movies, he was using every bit of his energy trying to satisfy his insatiable mother. Yes, it was touching, his receiving his first kiss at age thirteen. I could have moved to tears of nostalgia for my lost youth were it not for the fact he had already had intercourse, several times, and in the most bizarre and licentious fashion. To me—and it does make me want to cry to realize it—what David Callahan was really doing when he kissed his mother there in that study—"I'm not a very good kisser," he said—was to reach out one final, desperate time for his own childhood that was slipping away from him. In the end, the incest aside, the terrible, unforgivable thing Carla Callahan did in that incredible, orgiastic four days in May, was to kill her son's childhood, much as her own had been. She had never been a child. David Callahan was never to be a child either. We humans are cruel.

* * *

I got home from school a little after three-thirty. I don't remember much about that day at school. Most days at school are pretty much like every other day anyhow. When you've been to one, you've been to them all. I'm sure it was endlessly long, however.

Mother was in the sunroom when I came into the house. I went to her, as always. I stopped in the doorway, I remember. The strain in her eyes and her face was a scar. She was a hunted animal. I went to her and kissed her, again as always. She was rigid with tension. She seemed almost brittle, as though she would break at a touch. I whispered close to her ear. "Don't worry. It'll be all right."

"How was school?" She tried to say it brightly. She tried to smile.

I said something about school.

"Did you remember your excuse?"

I had remembered my excuse.

She put her arm around my waist. It felt like a stick of wood. Her body against me might have been marble, cold, hard, lifeless. "Do you want some cookies and milk?" All of this was playacting, an excruciating effort at normality for the benefit of Mrs. Riordan, in case she was paying any attention to us.

I said I wasn't hungry.

The minutes dragged by, an exercise in the repetition of eternity. We went into the living room. She stood by a window looking out at the road and driveway. I think I paced the floor. I don't remember. A long time passed, or it seemed long. I kept looking at her. The skin seemed stretched on her face, so tight it seemed likely to split. I could see a twitch in her temple. An artery throbbed in her throat.

I suggested she take a swim. It would relax her.

She shook her head but said nothing.

I heard the clock over the mantle. Mrs. Riordan ran the mixer in the kitchen. The phone rang. We both jumped. Mrs. Riordan answered in the kitchen. We heard her voice. It must have been for her. She never called us.

"I'm going to bathe," Mother said and went upstairs.

She came down fairly quickly. She wore a long, slender, black velvet skirt and a white frilly blouse with ruffles at the throat and cuffs. She looked very prim, very beautiful. I said so. She glanced at me. It meant nothing. She said nothing. She went back to her vigil at the window.

He came. The tires of his MG crunched the gravel as he wheeled by the windows to the garage. I looked at my watch. Seven-thirty-five. I ran out the front to the garage, arriving just as he stepped out of the small car. He seemed ridiculously big beside it. I hugged him and said I was glad to see him. He said it was good to be home. I picked up his bag while he carried his raincoat and briefcase. I shut and locked the garage door, then put my arm on his shoulder as we walked toward the front door.

"You're late," I said.

He sighed. "Yes. Hate Kennedy at this hour. Plane circled for an hour, then taxied another half hour. Baggage was slow and traffic a disaster. I thought I'd never get home."

Mother met us at the door. She said she missed him. He said he missed her. They kissed. I didn't look. I hustled inside with his bag.

When I straightened up, they were inside, the door closed. He had his arm around her waist. He was looking at her intently. "Are you all right?" he said. "You look tired."

She smiled. "I'm fine, dear. Just a little headache. It'll go away in a minute." She reached up and kissed him lightly as some sort of proof. "It *is* good to have you home."

"Yes," I said. "I mistreated her terribly."

I saw the whites enlarge in Mother's eyes. Her mouth came open in a silent gasp.

"So he was bad, was he?"

I smiled.

Mother caught herself. "Terrible child, really." She smiled now, almost in relief, understanding the banter. She reached out her hand to me, and the three of us went into the living room.

"Mother taught me how to make martinis," I said.

"Really? At his age? Hope you didn't drink any, son."

"I tasted it. Not bad."

"My son, **a** teenage alcoholic."

"Don't worry. They'll never replace Gatorade."

I went to the cabinet that served as a bar and started to make the martinis.

"I don't know if I'm ready for this development, son. I'd better—"

"He's pretty good, actually. I taught him the secret formula."

"No ice," I said. I hurried into the kitchen with the bucket. When I returned, they were embracing. I felt pain in my stomach and looked away. I busied myself with the bottles and pitcher and ice. I poured into stemmed glasses.

"Straight up," I said.

Dad took the glass. "Hmm. Chilled. Twist of lemon." He sniffed the glass. "Fragrance of gin and vermouth." He sipped. "Not bad. Not bad at all. A trifle too much vermouth, maybe."

Mother smiled. "David, I told you not to wave that vermouth bottle over the gin too long."

We all laughed. It was working. I had known it would.

If only he'd take his arm from around my mother.

She moved away, as if leading us further into the living room. We followed. We all sat near the fireplace.

"Did you have a nice birthday, son?"

I said it had been marvelous.

"What did you finally get him, Carla?"

I showed him the sweater I had on.

"Very nice," he said.

"Cashmere," she said.

"Did you have a cake?"

"I didn't want one," I said. "Mrs. Riordan had napoleons."

"No cake? At your age? How strange."

There was a silence. It seemed strange, strained.

"You seem different, son."

I could feel my mother's panic, her eyes boring into me. I forced myself not to look at her. I kept my eyes on him.

"How am I different?"

"I don't know. You've been so nervous and withdrawn lately. You seem more—I don't know, more relaxed, different somehow."

"More grown up?"

"Yes, that's it."

I smiled. "There you have it."

"Have what?"

"The change. I'm a teenager now."

He liked that. "My God, that's right. Carla, we've got a teenager in the house. Isn't that wonderful!"

She smiled broadly in approval—and relief.

"Don't tell anyone," she said. "Let's keep it a secret. I'm too young to have a teenage son."

"You want me to wear short pants and knee socks?"

"It might work."

"How about going back to the second grade?"

"You're a little big."

"And how is school?"

"I missed a couple of days."

"Missed!"

"It was his birthday. He wanted to stay home. I let him. Friday was a half day anyway."

"But Carla—"

"Don't worry, Brendan. The year's almost over. They aren't doing anything anyway."

He seemed unconvinced. "You'd better catch up on your homework then."

"I already have," I lied.

Mrs. Riordan said dinner was ready.

On the way to the table, I asked about his

trip. He said it had been okay. I asked a couple of questions. It got him talking about it. He told a rather involved story about the California governor. Mother made a comment or two. Most of the dinner hour was consumed with that.

When the conversation dragged into silence, I said, "Mother tells me I'm going away to school in the fall."

He seemed startled. He looked at Mother. "I thought you weren't going to tell him right away."

She glanced at me. "It just came up. I don't remember how. It seemed the time."

"I'm looking forward to going." I tried to say it with conviction.

"Really, son? I was afraid—"

"No. It'll be good to get away."

"I'm so glad to hear that. I've been afraid—"

"No, I want to go."

He looked at Mother. "What a relief that is."

"Mother says it has a good sports program."

"Oh, it does. St. Albans is a fine school. Tough. Disciplined. High standards. You'll have to work hard, son."

"I know. I want to."

He looked at me, then at Mother, back to me. He seemed very relieved, very happy. "We'll miss you. It'll be godawful lonely around here, won't it, Carla? Just us old folks."

It seemed incongruous to call her old.

"Yes," she said. "I don't know what I'll do." She deliberately did not look at me.

"Oh, you won't even notice I'm gone."

"Yes we will, son. You can believe that."

"I'll miss you both." I looked at him. "You especially." I hoped I wasn't pouring it on too thick.

"Me? Why me especially?"

I was stuck.

Mother rescued me. "Good heavens, you two. He's not going till September." She laughed. "Anybody'd think we were trying to get rid of him."

I don't remember much of the rest of the evening. From my brief glances at Mother, I could see that she was still tense, on guard, expectant.

It was past ten-thirty. I knew I had to leave before it became an issue.

"Is your headache better, Mother?"

"Yes, David, thank you."

I knew she was lying. I looked away from her. As casually as I could I said, "Everything is all right then?"

Her hesitation was almost imperceptible. "Yes."

I stood up. "School tomorrow. I better take a bath and hit the sack."

Mother said, "Yes."

I went over and kissed my father. "Good night, Dad."

"Good night, son."

"I'm glad you're back."

"Better believe it."

"I'll be up and tuck you in in a minute."

167

I was in bed when she came to my room. She sat on the edge of my bed. She whispered, although she didn't have to in the closed room. "You were magnificent. I couldn't have made it without you."

"I know."

She kissed me passionately, then reached under the covers. I took her hand away. "No," I said. "Never again that."

"Oh, David . . ."

"Are you and he?"

"Oh, David. Don't ask. Don't ever ask. Don't torture yourself. Don't torture me."

"I'm sorry."

She kissed me again. "I'd better go."

"Yes."

When she was at the door, I said, "Good luck." I heard her go to her room. A few moments later she went back downstairs.

I laid awake a long time, numb, hardly breathing, my every sense alive, straining to hear anything. After awhile I heard the sounds of locking up and their steps and voices on the stairs.

"Did you do it that night with Father?"

"I thought we were never going to talk about your father and me, David. It's pointless. It's just cruel all around."

"I know. I agree. But it was so long ago."

[The tape was silent. She did not reply.]

"Just this once, I thought—".

[She sighed.] "All right, all right. Yes, we did it that night." [A pause. A hesitation. She must have been searching for words.] "I had to. He was very affectionate, sexy. I knew this was a crisis I had to face. It had to happen sooner or later. I might as well get it over with."

[There was another pause. I could feel her distaste for what she was saying. I almost wished David would reprieve her. Yet, I had my own morbid curiosity.]

"We went to our rooms. He wanted to come to mine. I said no, I'd come to his. We made love—"

"Love?"

"We had sex. He was very passionate. I tried to respond while trying to make everything just as it had always been, exactly the same." [Pause.] "It was very difficult."

"Did it work?"

"Yes. I think so. He never said anything."

"Did you come? With him?"

"I don't think so. I don't remember."

"You don't remember?"

"No. I don't remember."

"It happened so often. It must be hard to remember."

[She said nothing.]

"Did you come more than once?"

[The silence lasted one minute and eleven seconds.]

* * *

Morrison came to talk to David. I wouldn't have known that their conversation occurred at this point in David's narrative except that, mercifully, Morrison's visit came in the middle of the tape. I suspect David was surprised by the visit. At least, he did not have the recording machine turned on. Apparently, when he realized something important was to be discussed, he switched it on, then had the presence of mind to have the subject matter titled. "I'm sorry," he said. "I didn't hear what you said. Would you repeat that?" Morrison raised his voice. "I said I want to know everything about Ephraim Squires." David protested that he had already told him most of it. Morrison insisted he wanted to know *everything*, even if he had heard it before. He wanted no detail omitted, no matter how small or seemingly unimportant.

David then recounted the following episode, largely uninterrupted by Morrison. To avoid the inside quotation marks and thus make it easier to read, I am presenting this in the same form as David's other narration.

* * *

As you know, I came home from college sort of at loose ends. I really didn't know what I wanted to do with myself or my life. Dad suggested I attend some of his political meetings. He'd introduce me to some people. Maybe I'd get as interested as he was. If not, at least it would give me something to do for awhile. I agreed. I made a few trips with him, Boston once, New York several times, Washington a lot, once to Chicago and the West Coast. My job seemed to involve being introduced to a lot of people and reacting in an appropriate manner. I met a number of congressmen and senators and sat while Dad talked earnestly to them about the country and the perils of Merrill Lampton. You know what Dad thought of the President. It became a joke between us. The "perils of Merrill" I called it, and Dad thought it funny and picked it up.

Mostly Dad was spending his time maintaining contact with various revolutionary groups. He really was very big on them. He felt they were important and, I guess, potentially dangerous. He felt it important that he maintain contact with them to try to keep lines of communication open. I met a great many of these supposed revolutionaries: blacks, women, queers, and white liberals. All seemed to exist in rather drab surroundings. All were quite conspiratorial and terribly earnest. I sat through a great many bull sessions. It reminded me of college.

To a person—the word "man" having taken on the connotation of a vulgarity to be expunged from the language—these people believed in the inevitability of revolution. It was not an "if," only a "when." It was all terribly vague. The economic and political system would be toppled and the social structure with it. The Constitution would be thrown out as an archaic nineteenth-century document and a new one written. The corporations would be broken up, along with the churches, universities, and most of the known institutions. Power would be returned to the people, all of whom would enjoy untrammeled liberty to do as they wished. At times it sounded like anarchy. At other times, it had distinct Maoist overtones—retraining the people, eliminating the competitive spirit, evacuating the cities, constructive work, cooperating and sharing. Much of this talk struck me as juvenile and naive. I longed to argue with them and point out the holes in their doctrines. But I remained silent. I was determined to keep my mouth shut.

I couldn't tell what they thought of me. I was mostly ignored, yet accepted as my father's son. They seemed to automatically accept that I agreed with everything my father said. I did nothing to dissuade them. Dad seemed to be accepted by the various groups. Even when he was meeting the people for the first time, he was known by his reputation, and that reputation gave him instant approval. His constant theme was nonviolence. The revolution didn't have to be violent to succeed. Violence would only hurt it. Everytime some unwitting person made a reference to "burn, baby, burn," Dad would relieve himself of a fairly pat lecture on Mahatma Ghandi, Martin Luther King, Jr., and the war protests of the 1970s. He'd cite a stock list of successful nonviolent revolutions and an equally long list of violent revolutions that had gone sour. His speech was quite good. It was successful in that talk of violence ended in his presence. I was far from certain he had convinced his listeners, only silenced them.

Dad and I would talk about the meeting or the people I'd met. We'd be riding home in the car or plane or sitting in the hotel room. Invariably he'd want to know what I thought. I would have preferred to give a noncommittal answer, but I knew that wouldn't do with him. I had to be a part of what he was doing. He wanted me involved. I was expected to argue with him. With some conviction I would say that it struck me as a strange revolution. Nobody seemed to have a very clear idea what they were revolting to. His usual answer was:

"That's the way with most revolutions. It's easy to hold a revolution, but hard to govern afterwards. Most revolutionaries turn out to be lousy governors. It takes different people. One destroys; the other builds. It's also why most revolutions, particularly violent ones, have turned despotic. The revolution stirs up everybody's passions, their hopes. When it's over, somebody has to restore order, usually by force, tyranny. The aims of the revolution are lost. The stage is set immediately for the next revolution."

He could relieve himself of a long discourse on the French and Bolshevik revolutions to prove that statement.

Sometimes I'd argue that these groups seemed more a political movement than a revolution. It looked to me, I'd say, that this "revolution" would go the way of so many others in American history—the populists, the labor movement, the blacks. It would simply be absorbed into the political system. One political party or the other would simply take over its program, or enough of it, so the revolution would peter out. The Republican party had been born out of the abolitionist movement. It later became the vehicle for the industrialists, businessmen, and the middle class. The Democrats had absorbed the populists, the unions, the blacks. It had all been so simple, I said. The Democrats nominated William Jennings Bryan. The Labor leaders were made Democratic power brokers by FDR. Lyndon Johnson had ended the civil rights movement in a single speech to Congress. "We shall overcome," he said, and the movement ended right there. In the 1970s, the Democrats nominated McGovern, and the antiwar movement went the way of all American revolutions.

I would make this sort of argument over and over. Dad would be impressed with my knowledge of American history. He acted like I was a dividend on the money he'd spent for my education. But he always had a reply. He hoped I was right. He hoped fervently. It was what he—and I—were working for, to make this a political revolution. But there was a problem.

Ephraim Squires. "He's a true revolutionary," he said. "He's Sam Adams."

I did not meet Ephraim Squires for over a year. I always seemed to miss him. He'd just been there, or he was due in the next week. I became curious about him, for I heard his name mentioned a lot. A letter from him would be read at a meeting, or there would be a phone call reported to the group. Some article he'd written or brochure would be cited or quoted. He was clearly the leader of this would-be revolution. People often referred to him as Sam Adams. I was eager to meet him. Dad said I would—and be surprised.

I started making excuses to avoid traveling with Dad. The simple fact is that I was bored with being a revolutionary. I hardly went with him at all over the next spring and summer. It got to be embarrassing to explain. More often than not I simply didn't bother to explain. I simply asked him to let me skip that one—and the next and next. It was early September when he asked if I wanted to attend a meeting in New York that night. Before I could think of a reason not to go, he said, "Ephraim Squires will be there."

On the way into New York in the car, Dad explained that Ephraim Squires had been in the city for several days—exactly where he was in from was never explained—holding meetings with leaders of various groups in the New York area. These sessions had concluded. Tonight was a social evening at which all of these people were to come together, mingle, and get acquainted.

The meeting was held in a large, second-floor hall in lower Manhattan. Dad was driving, so I didn't pay much attention to where it was. And if I ever knew the name of it, I've forgotten it. Doesn't matter anyhow. It was a rather shabby place, entered through double doors on one end. The floor boards were worn and creaked. The windows hadn't been cleaned in the memory of man. The walls were painted an insipid green, and the paint was peeling. I guessed the place had once been a warehouse. Some attempts at decoration had been made. One wall was graced with a large replica of the revolutionary flag, stripes of various shades of black, brown, tan, white, yellow, and copperish red, each to represent the races of the earth. Apparently a lot of argument had gone into the exact shades, order in which the colors were displayed, and so forth. A white dove of peace marked the center of the emblem. I decided it really wasn't a bad-looking flag. The other wall was decorated with a long sign bearing crudely made letters that read: UNITY AMID DIVERSITY. This was apparently the revolutionary slogan.

I had no way to judge the unity, but as I looked over the crowd and wandered around the room, the diversity was obvious. Every minority, every screwball outfit in the city, seemed to be there. Some were obvious; others had to be identified by their name tags or organizational buttons. There were lots of blacks, of course, and Puerto Ricans. But I hadn't realized that New York had such a large resident Indian population. It may have been my imagination, but a disproportion of the whites seemed to be women, for the various women's lib groups were out in force. There seemed to be an unusual number of attractive young white women, suitably braless and enjoying themselves. The gay liberation movement was extremely well represented, with homosexuals and lesbians parading about in their various costumes and making no effort to disguise their great affection for each other. To my surprise, there were several religious groups present. There were representatives of some Jewish radical bodies in majulkas. There were no Arabs there that I could detect. Some Hare Khrishna kids were there, with their yellow robes and cymbals. Dr. Moon had several people there. I even spotted a couple of Jehovah's Witnesses, which positively shocked me. To this mix were added several old-line Socialists, looking quite erudite. Faculty members, I presumed. There were a number of welfare mothers, large, buxom, and very militant black women. Most surprising was the delegation from gray power. They sat in one corner and seemed stunned. I had great sympathy for them and felt like joining them. I have not given you a complete list of the organizations represented there. All I can do is try to convey that it was an extremely motley collection of down-and-outers. If anyone had doubted the existence of a lunatic fringe, they should have seen that hall.

When I entered, and most of the time thereafter, the crowd seemed engaged in random movement and noise. There were several hundred people in the hall, with people coming and going constantly. It struck me as a very large, very bizarre, cocktail party, although that was hardly encouraged by the beverage, something called "liberty punch." It seemed to be a concoction of lemonade and grape juice. People—the queers loved to do it—circulated with pitchers, pouring the vile stuff into paper cups. Everyone seemed to be carrying a flask to spike the punch, so characterizing it as a cocktail party was perhaps not too wrong.

I wandered about, reading nametags, and acting very official so as to escape a particularly loud voice or raucous laugh in my ear or an insufferable permeation of cheap perfume from a queer, or the suffocating "official" welcome from a battleax libber who wanted to know *all* about me, the organization I represented, and wasn't this a grand gathering.

I was mercifully saved from this lady by the sharp ringing of a bell from the center of the room. It was such an incongruous sound that there was almost immediate quiet. Suddenly a figure arose, head and shoulders above the crowd. There was applause and cries of "Let's hear it, Sam." This, I assumed, was Ephraim Squires, the Sam Adams of the revolution. He certainly looked the part. He was a tall, slender, extremely handsome black man with beautiful coffee-colored skin and even, Caucasian features. He wore a well-tailored black suit, white shirt, and striped tie. He raised the bell and peeled it again, several times. When he spoke, his voice was one of the richest, most mellifluous, I'd ever heard.

"My friends, and I do mean friends, each and every one of you, I thank you for coming . . ." He clanged the bell twice. "I ring this bell to remind us all of why we are here. Liberty." There were cheers and a smattering of applause. "Liberty is what brings us here. What unites us all. We have come here, all races, all sexes, all religions, seeking but one thing, liberty for ourselves and our brothers and sisters. All of us want in one way or another to throw off the yoke of oppression fastened to us by our corporate masters and their lackeys in government."

Each phrase in his speech was now being cheered. There were cries of "Give 'em hell, Sam" and "Tell it like it is."

"There is much that divides us. Our skin, the color of our eyes, the clothes we wear, the shapes of our bodies, our life-styles, our education, the way we worship. Yes, each of us is different, a unique human being. For too long, for far too long, the oppressors have enslaved us by preying on our differences, turning brother against brother, sister against sister, brother against sis-

179

ter and, yes, sister against brother. It must now all end. It is NOW all ending. In this very room, as I speak, in rooms all across the nation, indeed around the world, oppressed people are forgetting that which divides them and uniting in a common cause—*liberty*."

He rang the bell again amid loud cheering.

"*Liberty*. Precious liberty. It is what we all want. It unites us as one indivisible force that will rise up and smite the corporate-governmental-military oppressors—once and for all. We will not be divided again. Our quarrel is not with our sisters and brothers. Our quarrel is with the oppressors. They are the enemy. United, victory is ours. United, liberty is ours."

There were deafening cheers. He raised his paper cup.

"And so, my friends, my brothers and sisters, let us drink our liberty punch. Let it wash away the taste of oppression from our mouths and bring unity, sisterhood, brotherhood, to our hearts. *Down with the Oppressors*."

With an exaggerated movement he chuggalugged his paper cup of liberty punch and clanged the bell with great vigor. But even its noise was drowned in the cascade of cheers.

I was impressed. What he said might have been nonsense, but there was no doubt that Ephraim Squires was a spellbinding orator. A good old-fashioned stem-winder he was.

I had lost Dad when I entered. A few minutes after the speech, I caught sight of him near the center of the room. He was standing near Squires and a group of people who seemed to be the center of attention. He motioned me to come over. I did, and he said he wanted me to meet Ephraim Squires.

To my eternal surprise, the stem-winding orator was not Ephraim Squires. I was introduced to a short, wiry, almost grotesque-looking individual. He was not much over five-six or -seven. He had a head much too large for the size of him, heavy shoulders and arms, a disproportionately long body, and ridiculously short legs. He was a black man. The kinky hair, heavy black mustache, wide nose, and thick lips indicated that. Yet, his complexion was fair. He was what used to be called a "high yeller." Indeed, he was yellow. He seemed afflicted with a permanent case of jaundice. His voice, as he acknowledged my presence and introduced me to the two women on either side of him, was weak and breathy, even raspy. He then ignored me and stepped back a pace to enter into an intense conversation with Dad. I observed him. He was a singularly ugly man. His eyes were extremely large, almost bulbous, and of such a pale blue they were gray, almost colorless. They seemed more like two pale holes in his head. The massiveness of the cranium, the sallow complexion, the high cheekbones and hollow cheeks marred by a bluish beard no razor could remove. . . I could only think of him as grotesque, some form of hideous gnome. Yet, I was drawn to him.

Perhaps it was his ugliness. There was a form of hideous animal magnetism about him. Even his smile, wide with a great many uneven, yellowish teeth, did nothing to relieve his ugliness. Yet, he seemed very relaxed, self-confident, assured.

"So what do you think?"

It was the girl on his right, to my left as I faced him. She was in her early or mid-twenties and almost unrelievedly plain. Her complexion was dark for a white girl and marred by the scars of earlier acne. A pronounced line of dark hair, almost a moustache, graced the line of her thin lips. Her eyes were brown and rather listless. Her hair was mouse-colored and worn in an unflattering style, short, straight, with bangs that met her eyebrows. She wore a tan sweater that revealed no evidence of breasts. There was absolutely no feature about her to recommend her.

"I'm sorry," I said. "I wasn't listening."

She repeated her question. "What do you think?" There was a mocking irony to her voice.

"Of what?"

She smirked. "My, you are a phony. Of anything. Of me. I'm the ugliest, plainest creature you ever saw. And she's the loveliest."

I followed her gaze to the girl on my right. Luscious was the only word for her, almost jet black hair falling in soft waves to her shoulders, the whitest, clearest skin I'd ever seen, big eyes of the darkest blue, almost violet, full red lips. She was very dramatic in a black sweater and skirt. The ripeness of her figure was obvious.

"She's gorgeous, isn't she? You like Gloria, don't you?"

I was annoyed by her. "Do you always tell people what they think?"

She smiled, rather bitterly, and shrugged. "Gloria turns everybody on. Luscious. That's what she is."

I didn't like having my mind read by her.

"I actually meant Ephraim. What do you think of him?"

I looked at him again talking with Dad. "Very interesting," I said.

"What a noncommittal phony. Are you ever honest? Why don't you say he's the ugliest, most repulsive creature you've ever seen?"

I looked at her but said nothing. God, how I detested her.

"But you better believe he's a real man, all man. None like him."

"With her?" I motioned toward the luscious Gloria with my head.

"And me."

"Both of you are his women?"

She smirked again. "She's for show and I'm for go."

"And what is that supposed to mean?"

She shrugged again. "Maybe you'll be lucky and find out."

I was disgusted with her and hoped it

showed. I looked away. "Who's that?" I asked, motioning toward the handsome black man who'd spoken.

"You really don't know anything, do you?"

My anger flared. "Look, Miss—Miss whatever-your-name-is . . ."

"Edna. Eddie. I look like a boy. I even have a boy's name."

"Okay, Edna. If you want to put me down, be my guest. I don't give a shit."

Her laugh was mocking. "Oh, my, but you do," she said. "His name is Samuel Daniel Cooper, the Reverend Samuel Daniel Cooper, Jr., known to his many admirers as Sam Dan."

I had heard of him, of course, Sam Dan Cooper, the new hope of the blacks, successor to Martin Luther King, Jr.

"He's a powerful speaker," I said.

"Oh, yes, Sam has a great mouth." She gave her characteristic shrug. "Words and music."

"And what does that mean?"

"It means Sam has a great voice and speaks the words Ephraim gives him very well."

Father spoke to me. "David, I've invited Ephraim and his friends out tomorrow."

"It's been a hard week. It will be good to relax."

"How nice," I said.

Mother was angry, particularly when she learned it was to include a late afternoon swim, cocktails, and buffet. She complained of the short notice, that she didn't know these people, and she hated surprises. Dad tried to smooth things over, but he knew he was wrong. I didn't want these people in the house either, and I must admit I did nothing to give Mother an attractive picture of them.

Our guests were seven: Ephraim Squires and his two girlfriends, Edna and the luscious Gloria; Sam Dan Cooper and his wife, Violetta, a very handsome, statuesque black woman with a beautiful *cafe con leche* complexion. There were two husky, goon bodyguards, both black, both morose. Neither swam, nor did they say much. They just stood around with bulges under their suit jackets. One was called Edward. I've forgotten the other one.

Mother took an instant and intense dislike to Squires, and the more he tried to ingratiate himself to her, the more she disliked him. When he appeared in his swim trunks and jumped in the pool to thrash around inexpertly, Mother whispered to me that he looked like a yellow ape. "I'll bet he pees in the pool, too." She refused to swim or even change into her suit. Her official explanation was that she had to prepare drinks and hors d'oeuvres. Dad and I both knew better. To me, she said, "He's already undressed me with his eyes. I'm not going to encourage him."

Everyone else, except for the two goons, swam. I guess there was no place to hide the guns in a swimsuit. Gloria was positively eye-stopping in a skimpy bikini. Violetta was indeed a handsome woman, I decided, proof that black is beautiful! Her wet skin shone like smoky crystal. After a short swim, she changed into a very dignified African dress with a scarf around her head. Quite beautiful and, on her, appropriate. I tried to talk to her, but it was difficult. She was either shy, diffident, or not very bright. Sam Dan was very muscular, swam very well, and enjoyed it. He changed back into his black suit, which was his trademark, and thereafter was very attentive to the free booze. His glass was forever empty, and he occupied himself with filling it. I had a chance to talk briefly with Gloria when she reappeared in an obvious and decollete cocktail dress. She said she was a sociologist and wanted to help mankind. I felt sure she could. She spent most of the evening dazzling Father. Squires paired off with Mother, who couldn't be rude to him, although he kept finding ways to touch her hand or arm or put his hand in the small of her back. I was stuck for most of the evening with Edna, who seemed militant about making herself as dowdy looking as possible and in being as rude and antagonistic to me as she could.

[At this point David asked Morrison if he really wanted to know all this detail. Morrison insisted he did. He found it fascinating, he said.]

I asked her what she meant by show and go?

She shrugged in the manner I'd both come to get used to and to loathe. "It's not hard to figure. Gloria's show. She's beautiful. She's got big tits.

She turns everybody on. But in bed she's a dud, just a thing to look at and play with. I'm go. I got a great ass, and I know how to use it. And I like it. I can fuck all night. I may be the best fuck in the world. She turns him on. He plays with her while I fuck the hell out of him."

I said it was a little hard to imagine.

"Come over to the motel later. You can watch. He's horny as hell the way he's pawing that—" Her mouth started to form a word that was either "blond" or "bitch" or maybe both. But she didn't say it. Instead she caught herself and said, after a slight hesitation, "—your mother."

"You were wise to mind your tongue."

Another shrug. "What you don't know is, Gloria is God's joke."

I played straight man and asked what that meant.

"Gloria is beautiful but lousy in bed. It's the ugly, hairy ones like Ephraim and me that can really do it. God's joke on the human race. Everybody lusting after the gorgeous people, while all the time it's the ones like me that are really good. God's laughing his head off." She laughed in a strange bitter way. "You're God's joke, too, blond, handsome Adonis. But I bet you stink in bed."

I was stung by her ridicule. Oh, how I hated her.

I looked at her. Very quietly, I said, "Pray God, you never find out."

"You sonofabitch," she said.

187

The only interesting conversation of the evening resulted from my asking Squires—I kept trying to rescue Mother from him all evening—why he was called Sam Adams. His explanation was detailed and given with considerable immodesty.

"I am a student of the American Revolution. It was the first successful revolution in the western world, the prototype for all others that followed. The French and Bolshevik and Chinese revolutions were merely an imitation.

"Think about the American Revolution. There never should have been one. The Colonials were basically English, loyal to crown and country. They had been singularly well-treated by the English government, left largely alone, allowed to develop as they pleased. They had a large measure of self-government and economic prosperity. The grievances that led to the revolution weren't anything really, more alleged than fact—a little taxation, some customs duties, the quartering of a handful of troops. None were serious, and even these were subject to change by appeal to the British Parliament. There should never have been a revolution and would never have been one except for Samuel Adams."

He paused, savoring having the floor. I looked over at Dad. He seemed spellbound, a rapt expression of pride on his face. Squires rasped on.

"I'm pleased when people compare me to Sam Adams. He was the first and probably the best

188

revolutionary in the world. Just think how the history of the world would be different had there been no Sam Adams. I am a student of Sam Adams. I know all about Sam Adams. He is my hero. I copy him in every way I can.

"Like me, Sam Adams wasn't much to look at. Like me, he was no orator. He had a thin, quavering voice. But, also like me, Sam Adams was a master organizer and supreme propagandist. Almost singlehandedly he united the colonies and started the Revolution. Think of what he did. Just think. There were thirteen jealous, divided colonies strung along the East Coast. The distances were immense for those days. The only means of transportation was by sailing ship or horseback or stagecoach over nearly impassable roads. There was no radio or telegraph. The only means of communication was by word of mouth or letter. To send a simple message could take weeks. Think of what he did. My task is simple compared to his. I jet from city to city. I pick up the telephone. I send a wire. What he did is not to be believed."

"And what was that?" To the others, Mother's question was just a question from an interested person. I could detect a tinge of mockery and derision in it, however.

"Adams did several things more or less at the same time. On one hand he organized a whole extralegal revolutionary government. He had committees of correspondence to maintain communication between the colonies. He organized

189

committees of safety to protect the revolution-
ists. There were the minutemen, the Continental
Congress. All of this was a revolutionary government working outside the regular government. In many places it was the *de facto*
government. At the same time, Adams worked
within the system. He kept constant pressure on
the government, petitions, speeches, protest after
protest, the famed rabble in the streets. When
the British reacted to his pressure, he was
ready—the Boston Massacre, the Boston Tea
Party. All was by design. When the British
reacted with the Coercive Acts, Adams used it
to bring the revolution closer.

"You see, Adams was also the world's first
master propagandist. He didn't try to argue
with the British. He understood that revolution
is emotion. He developed symbols—the Liberty
Bell, the Liberty Tree, many others. There were
freedom songs, stirring ones. There were slogans
galore, "Give Me Liberty or Give Me Death,"
"No Taxation without Representation." He had
fiery speakers like James Otis, Joseph Warren,
and Patrick Henry to stir up the Sons of Liberty.
The rum flowed like water. Every man was
made to feel important. The British were the enemy. Liberty was all that mattered. The rabble
was sent out in the streets to make another incident that brought the revolution ever closer."

"And that's what you're doing?" Mother again.

"In so far as I can, yes. Our situation is
much different from two hundred years ago. We

are spread over a much larger area; yet communication and transportation are so much easier,
as I've said, that I don't have as serious a problem here as Adams did. We also have an advantage in that our grievances are very real. So
many different people are so oppressed in so
many different ways that there is no problem
convincing anyone of that. On the other hand,
we are not facing an absentee government an
ocean away. Our oppressors are right here, very
much among us, and extremely powerful and
ruthless. Adams had an easier task. He could
point to the British as the enemy and work for a
simple goal of driving them out. Our enemy is
our whole economic and political system. The
corporations and the government they control
oppress us. It is much harder to work toward
that much bigger goal and to unite so many
diverse groups behind a common cause."

"And you are doing it?"

"Very well, I think." He smiled and looked
at Sam Dan Cooper. "The bell of liberty still
rings in America."

"And your new order or whatever you call it.
What will it be like?" I had never heard
Mother be so militant in an argument. She usually sat quietly, knitting or something, saying
very little. She obviously disliked Squires very
much to pursue him like this.

He smiled. It struck me as condescending.

"I doubt if there is time tonight to go into all
that. Clearly, the economic system is morally

bankrupt. There is no hope of reforming it. Total destruction is the only hope for better distribution of the nation's wealth. Unfortunately—I say that because I wish it were not so—the political system is now indivisibly linked to the economic system. It must go too, the Constitution with all its merits, Congress, courts—all must go."

"You speak of destruction. What do you replace it with?"

Another condescending smile. "My dear lady, the task of the revolutionary is revolution. First things first."

"I see." Her voice had taken on a hard edge. "Tell me, Mr. Squires, when you blow up this country, what will happen to me, my home, the way I live?"

He looked at Father. "We hope not to blow up anything—although I sometimes wonder if that will ever be possible. But we are trying. In any event, Mrs. Callahan, I'm sure a beautiful lady like you will always manage in any society. Besides, your husband is one of our strongest supporters."

The party wore on, seemingly endlessly. Mother was inwardly boiling with rage. I knew it, Dad knew it. I'm not sure whether the others knew. Mother is very good at concealing her feelings. She smiled more and talked more than usual. Perhaps people meeting her for the first time would mistake this for cordiality.

Father and I were to drive them to the New Englander Motel in two cars. We were all invited to join them for a drink there. Mother refused. Dad said he wouldn't be able to stay. He went off first in the Mercedes with Squires, Gloria, Edna, and the two bodyguards. I remained behind while the Reverend Samuel Daniel Cooper, now quite drunk, had a nightcap. He had two—one for each of his heads, I guess. Mercifully, I then got him out to the car. I was driving away as Dad returned home.

I had not intended to go into the motel, but the new great hope of the black people was now staggering so badly Violetta couldn't handle him. I put his arm around my shoulders and, with the help of Violetta, guided him to their rooms on the second floor. The door opened on a sight that almost made me drop Cooper in a heap on the floor. The three of them were naked. Edna lay on her back on the couch, her hips writhing, moaning, "Make him good, Glor, oh, make him good." The other two were embracing. He looked even more grotesque with his short bandy legs. She was kissing him passionately while he pawed her breasts and hindy. He bent over and mouthed her breasts while Edna kept up her refrain to "make him good" and to "hurry, hurry." Squires had the biggest, most disgusting prick I had ever seen. I didn't know any were that big. Then Gloria dropped to her knees and massaged and sucked it like a grotesque lollipop. "Hurry, hurry, I can't wait. Oh, please . . ." Squires finally gave into Edna's pleadings and mounted her. He pumped away hard while she moaned and screamed and screwed her hips like a hula dancer in a frenzy. Gloria was not out of it yet. Somehow she laid back against the couch and positioned her head and shoulders between Squires and Edna, so he could kiss her and slaver her breasts while screwing the hell out of Edna. I turned to leave—and saw Violetta undressed and heading toward the couch. I'm sure I swore as I left.

"My career as a revolutionist ended right there—or would have if you hadn't gotten me back into this."

"I'm sure you'll see worse things before you die."

"Oh, I know a lot of people wouldn't be bothered by it. They'd think it sexy. I just can't. Blame it on Mother. She's a real lady. I've too much respect for her, for all women, to see any degrade themselves as those two women did."

"You're right, of course. We need to hold on to as much human decency and dignity as we can. Fortunately, we have a President of the highest moral example. Not a breath of scandal in him or his family. And believe me, the Democrats have tried to find it." [Pause.] "And that was the night your father died?"

"Yes."

"Did he seem ill that evening?"

"No. He was fine."

"I always thought Brendan's death a little

strange. Oh, I know he had put on weight, but he was only fifty-three. To die in his sleep that way . . ."

"The coroner said it was a heart attack."

"I'm sure it was his heart, but I always figured there must have been something to overexcite him. Did he and your mother have a fight?"

"No."

"Are you sure?"

[David laughed. It is easy for me to say there was an uneasy quality to it, for, of course, I know he is lying.]

"They were both in bed when I got home. I don't know what happened. But Mother never said there was anything unusual."

"Oh, well, it is of no importance now. Go on about Squires."

"There isn't much to tell. I've seen him briefly a couple of times. Three to be exact. I've told you about those. Do you want to hear it again?"

"No, I guess not."

"He does not accept me. I am not my father. I'm a—"

"You told me that the last time. Tell me what you make of Squires?"

"What I make of Squires? In what way do you mean?"

"As a revolutionary. Is he one? Is he Sam Adams?"

"As he defines Sam Adams, I suppose he is. I just don't know if his appraisal of Sam Adams is correct or not. I haven't made a study of the subject. I'm really not interested, you know. I can tell you that Dad took him seriously. Dad believed that Sam Adams bit. He liked Squires and believed in his revolution—if it was nonviolent."

"And what do you think? Is he a revolutionary?"

"Christ, I don't know. I'm not the one to ask. I detest the creature."

"Well, stop detesting him for a moment. You've seen enough of him to form an objective opinion of him and what he is doing. That's what I need from you."

[David sighed.] "There is no question—the man is an organizer, and he is a propagandist. He's got a natural gift for it. There is no doubt he has done something no one else has been able to do—unite all the dissidents and disaffected. He's surrounded himself with the damndest collection of have-nots and way-outs you've ever seen. He's found the key to uniting all these people. Dad explained it to me once. The trouble with dissent in America has always been that there was so much of it. The Constitution positively guarantees it, free speech, free press, and all that. Anybody with an ax to grind is free to do it. So every minute somebody, more likely an organized group, is protesting some injustice or other, appealing for support, marching in the streets to have their own way."

"As I've said many times, we have anarchy, not democracy in America."

"And because there is so much, nobody pays any attention—except to themselves. The gay libbers want something different from the women's libbers, who want something different from the welfare mothers and the elderly and the young and mental patients and convicts and blacks and Indians and Jews and Bulgarians and Lower Slobovians—it is endless. As Father put it, the establishment exploited the division among the dissidents to maintain the status quo. The big thing Squires has done—like him or not you have to give the bastard credit—is to unite the dissent. 'Unity Amid Diversity.' That's his slogan. He's given the whole protest movement a focus. He has all these terribly unlikely people embracing each other, brothers and sisters united for liberty—and all that crap."

"And afterwards?"

"Disaster, of course. They'll tear each other to shreds."

"Does Squires know that?"

"I've never heard him say it, but I'm sure he does. Squires is no dummy. He's fomenting a revolution. He's destroying. I don't think he gives a damn what happens later."

[There is a pause of almost a half minute. Morrison was apparently thinking.]

"That's all very interesting. There is no doubt that Squires is the leader of this movement or whatever you call it. He's in charge. And he's damn good at it. We must never sell him short. He is one guy never to be underestimated. What I really want to know is whether he is violent?"

"Personally?"

"I want to know if he will lead these people of his into violence."

"Wow. That's tough. I don't know. There are a lot of people around him who want violence. He's got a goon squad. They're tough, and they have guns. I assume they'd rather use them than not."

"But Squires personally?"

"That's what I don't know. I've never seen him with a gun in his hands. I've never heard him tell anyone to get rough. On the contrary, I've heard him urge everyone to cool it. 'Don't make waves' is his expression. Everybody knows what it means. In all his speeches and letters, he tells everyone to protest, to hold rallies, marches, demonstrations, wave the flag, drink that liberty slop—and make lots of noise. I think he's smart enough to realize that he's in no position to challenge the government. He's too weak. What he wants is to win respectability. He wants to widen the base of his support, try to get at least some of the middle class on his side. He can't do that if he looks like a loser, if he's foolish and bizarre. Everyone will start to laugh at him, and the movement will collapse."

"Is that working?"

"In a way, yes. He uses Sam Dan Cooper as a front man. I may know him as a simpleton and a secret drunk, but the public doesn't. Using the words Squires puts in his mouth, Cooper is a spellbinder, the best since Martin Luther King, Jr. Cooper has got the blacks stirred up. And because Cooper is a preacher and respectable, the black middle class has joined the movement. The same with the women. That bitch Edna and a couple of others have been able to bring in the respectable women's libbers. That's part of Squires's genius. He offers something that means all things to all people. Who doesn't like liberty and freedom?"

"And who isn't oppressed in some way?"

"Precisely."

[Another long pause by Morrison.] "So I gather you don't think Squires is violent by nature."

"I guess I don't. I think he knows that's what the establishment—if that's what we are—wants. He's too smart to do it."

"Do you think he might secretly want to be violent, slit a few throats, that sort of thing?"

"Lord, I don't know. He might. Anyone in his position might like to. But Squires is a heady guy. He—"

"Can he be *made* violent?"

"Made violent? By whom?"

"By anyone. Could there be some action, some incident, that would shove him into violence?"

"Now you've really got me. I couldn't guess. You know, Uncle Richard, I really don't know the guy very well. I don't know anything about his background. You need some kind of deep psychological study, and I couldn't even begin to do one. I just now realized I don't know how old he is."

"Forty-two."

"That old. I would have said he was younger."

"He's forty-two, born in Worcester, Massachusetts. His real name was James Brown, of all things, and his parents are both high school teachers, very respectable, very middle class. He was educated at Amherst and got a law degree from Harvard. For the last ten years, or until he turned full time revolutionary, he lived and practiced law in the Roxbury district of Boston. He was not a bad criminal lawyer, lots of public defender cases, that sort of thing. His wife and two children, aged ten and eleven, still live in Roxbury."

"Wife and two children!"

"My information is that he is quite devoted to them, sends money, visits every week or two."

[David gasped and made several expressions of disbelief and amazement.]

"I'm afraid, David, that underneath your fiery revolutionary lies a humdrum, middle-class soul."

"I just don't believe it."

"Why not? That's the history of most revolutionaries. Lenin and Trotsky were both upper middle class. Hitler was a corporal, after all. Our hero Sam Adams was a Boston Adams. Squires is of the mold."

"How did you find out all this?"

"Private detectives, although I'm sure the FBI knows more. We just don't want to use any government sources if we can help it, as I explained to you."

"But if you knew all about him, why ask me?"

"Because I don't know all about him. I wanted your opinion. I still want it. Can he be made violent?"

"I don't know. I can't tell you any more than that."

"I understand. I'd rather have an honest I don't know than a wrong guess. We're just going to have to try and find out. We'll put a little pressure on him and see how he reacts. I'll be back to you in a couple of days with instructions."

"You're going?"

"Yes. Been here too long already."

[There are various rustles and sounds indicating Morrison and David went to the door of the apartment. Then there are last words, fainter, harder to hear from the far end of the room.]

"Uncle Richard, are you afraid of Squires' becoming violent?"

[Morrison laughed.] "My boy, I'm afraid of his *not* becoming violent."

[There is the sound of the door opening and closing.]

The poetic in me wants to say of that first summer—everything in my life is marked in relation to my thirteenth birthday—was the best of summers and the worst of summers. In truth, it was neither. It was far from the best. Nor, in the eons of summers I spent while in school, was it a particularly bad one. What it was was important. I learned a great deal that summer. I became what I am that summer.

As my mother predicted, and I guess I sort of anticipated, my sexuality came roaring back in a couple of days. It was terrible. There was a ferocity, yes, a savagery to my desire for her. I knew pain to look at her. To see her emerging from the pool, dripping, toweling off her legs and arms and thighs and torso—torture. If she wore pants or a sweater, indeed anything, the curves of her body—torment. Even if she wore a long skirt and prim blouse, the sight of her loveliness wounded me. The sound of her voice, the sweet pungence of her perfume, the touch of her hand, were my private hell. If she were gone and Dad was busy and I was alone in the house, I'd go to her room and touch her clothes and bury my face in their softness and fragrance. If I made her a drink, I secretly squeezed the glass that her hand had held. My sight dwelled on where our ecstasy had been, the sauna, the sofa. To lie in my bed, remembering, was a bitter-sweet agony.

The jealousy was worse. If he touched her or kissed her—heavens, if he even looked at her or spoke to her—it was as if I were being stabbed. My heart throbbed, my muscles contorted with desires that were both murderous and suicidal. To think of what they were doing while I lay awake, numb and rigid, in my bed was a fantasy of imponderable violence and masochism.

My mother felt it, too. I know she did. I could see it in her now chronic tension. I could see it in her eyes, both in her avoidance of looking at me and in the pain and concern they showed during those few fleeting moments when we were alone in the house. We had to kiss and touch. It would have been unnatural had we not. Questions would have been asked. But it was hard—to use a mild word—to be mother and child when our bodies ached to be lovers. She did stop coming to my bath. Partly, it was now inappropriate at my age. Mostly, neither of us could have stood it. I'm sure there would have been the most godawful splashing.

She persisted in coming to tuck me in. It was the only sweetness on most days, our only real time together, filled with secrets and whispers and commiseration.

"It's so *awful*, David."

"I know."

"I want you so. Sometimes I don't think I can stand it."

"I know. You can."

"I'm so afraid of doing something foolish."

"I know. You won't. I'll help you."

She caressed my face. "Oh, David. Sometimes I think you're five million years old. I couldn't make it without you." She kissed me passionately, deeply. "It is hard for you, too."

"Yes."

She reached under the covers. "Let me do it for you."

I'd always take her hand away. "No. Not unless we can do it together. It's no easier for you."

"But it *would* be easier for me, knowing you—"

"No."

She kissed me again. "Oh, my darling, does it help to know how much I want you, need you?"

"Yes. . . . But he wants you, too. He has you. Anytime he wants."

"God, darling, God. Don't do that. Don't be jealous."

"I'm sorry."

"If you only knew how much I want you, always, constantly. It never goes away."

"Yes."

"There's no one like you. Never, never, is it like it is with you. There's no comparison. None at all."

"Yes."

"I have to let him touch me, David. I have to do it. Don't you understand? I have to. It's a duty. I must for both of us."

"Yes."

"I can barely stand it as it is. Don't torture me by being jealous. I can't stand it if you are. I'll shatter into a million pieces."

"I'm sorry. I won't be jealous. I promise."

I think it was my protectiveness of my mother that saved me, saved us. I remember very clearly thinking out the problem and realizing exactly what I had to do. I couldn't go on this way. She couldn't either. I had to survive. We had to survive. It was up to me. I learned rather quickly—if not easily—what to do and how to do it.

I learned to concentrate. Those first few weeks taught me that. I learned that the mind was a thing to be turned on and off. I could think certain things, or I could not think certain things. I could see, or I could not see. Hearing was a sense to be controlled. Feelings were objects, to be used or not to be used. I came to realize that my torture was self-torture, a product of self-pity. I had to forget myself and think of others. Of her. If we were going to survive, it had to be so. A sort of numbness, an automation overcame me. I did what had to be done, what was required. What I wanted or needed or felt was of no importance. I learned to live out my days, doing what was necessary, yet living for a moment that could be mine, however rare. And its rarity made it more precious, its sweetness more in my regard.

I know I should not interject. I should just let David Callahan tell his story, but I cannot resist a comment. I do not always like David Callahan. He is not a very nice person. He does terrible things. Yet at this moment in his narrative, I am nearly overwhelmed with pity for him. I'm sure he exaggerates. What he says is not always so. He puts himself in a most favorable light. Yet, all that aside, I am stung by what he is saying. In that cauldron of emotions into which he was thrust, and really not by his own doing, he reacted, out of a need for survival, with an incredible maturity. What he thinks and understands and does cannot be believed of a person aged thirteen. What he does possesses a native wisdom that exceeds the capacity of most self-actualizing adults. Yet, that in itself is debilitating. He is crippled emotionally and intellectually by the very acts that seem to save him. And that is why I have come to despise Carla Callahan. I truly cannot muster any pity for her. In her lust, she did it to him. And in his love, he reached out to save her, maiming himself as he did so.

* * *

I had already concluded by the time my father arrived home on the Monday evening following my thirteenth birthday that I had to

206

spend as much time with him as possible. I perhaps did not think in those terms at that time, but in effect I felt I had to shield my mother and myself from him with a curtain of seeming affection. I had to talk to him. I had to spend as much time with him as was possible and suitable. My performance the night he returned—and that is what it was, a performance, a role, a gigantic deception, a do-or-die battle of wits—was calculated toward that end. I was conning my father. In the ensuing days and weeks, under the onslaught of my own sexuality and jealousy, it all began to unravel. I would be swimming with him and all the while be observing her beside the pool. I would be playing catch or frisbee with him but secretly be watching her at a window. I would talk with him in the evening but be conscious always of her presence, her odor, her femininity, her sexuality reaching across the space that separated us. I'd jog with him on the beach and think of her and ache to be with her.

He knew. He had to know. Oh, he couldn't know what I was thinking, but he had to know I wasn't really involved with him and what we were doing. He said as much. Several times. "You know we don't have to do this, son." Or, "Son, if there's something else you'd rather do . . ." I'd protest. I'd insist we go on being together. But he knew. And there was a precedent for it. I'd always spent a lot of time with my mother. I'd always made it clear that I adored her, even preferred her. My father had long accepted this without jealousy, without rancor. He sometimes commented on how close my mother and I were. He thought it wonderful for mother and son to be so close. That wasn't happening now. Mother and I were cast into a dual role that neither of us could play. We weren't being that close anymore. Even if no one knew or guessed the truth, it was still obvious that son and mother were growing apart. Even a numbskull of a Freudian psychologist, knowing nothing of the truth, could have offered a reason. I seemed to be preferring my father. That's what I was trying to seem to have happened. Yet it wasn't working. My inner rage, my jealousy, was heading both Mother and me straight for disaster.

I put my feelings in a box and wrapped it in colorful paper and tied a pretty ribbon around it and put it away on a shelf. I left my boxed feelings there, bringing it out only rarely, briefly, when all was safe. I forced my mind to think only of the moment, the precise thing I was doing, forgetting all else. In psychological terms, I learned later, I became task-oriented. I concentrated wholly on whatever I was doing with my father, the game we were playing, the sport, the conversation. I learned to force all other thoughts and feelings out of my mind. I refused to think of my mother, even to notice her. My desire, my wanton passion for her became a thing forbidden to enter my head, except at certain prescribed times. I concentrated wholly upon him, what we were doing together, what he was saying, what he wanted, what would please him. I consciously strove to enter his life in every way possible, to think as he did, so I could anticipate him and his every thought. Yet I learned not to intrude. He was busy, involved in his affairs. The fine tuning of our relationship was how involved in his affairs I could become, when and when not to leave him alone.

And it was not just with him. I learned that summer to control my own thoughts when I was alone. I forced myself not to think of her. I abandoned daydreams. I could make myself concentrate on a book or a television program. Wholly. It became a game. Concentration. I reveled in my power to control my mind. I could even think nothing at all.

My one luxury was at night. I'd abandon myself to her. Out came the box, the string untied, the wrapper removed. I relived all our precious moments together, every caress, every sensation, every motion, the smells of her femininity and our blended fluids, the wondrous sounds of her words, "Oh, my God!" while she shuddered beneath me. I released all that I had held in check that day. My eyes stung with the rapture of memories and the pain of my unrequitedness.

It worked. For a long time, I never told Mother what I was doing. I don't know why. I guess the wondrous effects of concentration were my private exercise. She knew what I was doing in the sense of being with my father, conning him. She was lavish in her praise of my virtuosity, grateful for our retreat from the abyss. Yet she never knew how I did it. Father didn't know anything. He basked in my attentions and my affections. Over and over he said how sorry he was that I was going away in September.

The secret to my con of my father was politics. It was his passion. There were times when, I'm sure, my mother and I were subsidiary to whatever political problems or machinations he was working on. My con was therefore very simple. I concentrated on politics. I read the *New York Times* and *Washington Post*, both of which he had delivered, the *New Republic*, *Nation*, *Atlantic*, *New Yorker*, and a half dozen other magazines he subscribed to. I watched the television news and specials, generally with him. It was duck soup to get him talking. I'd make a comment, ask a question, say I didn't understand something. Off he would go, delighted to have an audience. The only difficulty was ending the conversation. Sometimes it would go on half the afternoon, through dinner, and into the evening. At first he would express reservations about my interest. "Are you sure you want to know all this?" My assurances, my concentrated attention, allayed his doubts. Halfway through that summer and for years thereafter, he became a man overjoyed at having a son who shared his interest in politics.

My father was away a lot that summer, but mostly by the day. He'd go to his office over the bank in Westport or to New York. Even if he went to Washington, he'd leave early in the morning and take the shuttle back to New York, arriving home late. Everytime he went to Washington, Mother and I would pray for the phone to ring—he was staying over. It happened exactly three times, weeks apart.

With him gone only for the day, there wasn't much Mother and I could do, except crave each other and commiserate. Mrs. Riordan was there. I tried to suggest we could go upstairs and lock the door. Mother wouldn't. And there was no time in the evenings. We didn't know when he was coming home. Many times there would have been time, lots of time, but how were we to know? The only real opportunities were those occasional days he left early for Washington. The first morning in the silent house was an ecstatic surcease from longing. It was the first time since my birthday weekend. In three hours I don't believe a word was spoken. There was neither breath nor time to be wasted on them. The second such morning Mother had just started her period. I wanted to. She wouldn't. My mother would do just about anything sexually, but she drew the line at that. It was revolting, she said. The third time, Mrs. Riordan came early and caught us in the middle of it. Oh, I don't mean she actually caught us. She came into the house. Mother heard her in the kitchen. "Oh, Lord, how long has she been here?" She frantically wiped herself, sneaked down the hall to her room, dressed, and appeared downstairs with some excuse. But she had been badly frightened. She would never chance a morning again.

So that summer Mother and I had a morning in mid-June, a night in early July, another in late July, three days in late August. I can still remember the dates. I remember every time with my mother. June 18, July 5, July 24, August 26, 27, 28. We tried one other time. One evening Mother announced we were going shopping in New York the next day. I had outgrown everything. I needed clothes for school. She told me nothing else. She wanted to surprise me. We took the train in early. We shopped all morning and into the early afternoon. She seemed very excited as we bought a great array of items. Some things she had sent out; yet she seemed to keep a number of packages to carry, more than she usually did. Early in the afternoon, she took me to a hotel, a small one, quiet, not very well-known. I don't remember the name of it or where it was, but we walked from Saks. It couldn't have been far. She went to the desk clerk. She wanted a room for a few hours. She and her son had been shopping. We wanted to leave our parcels, rest, and freshen up before going to the theater that evening. Would we be staying the night? No, we'd be returning to Connecticut. She paid in advance.

In the elevator I said I could have done that.

"I know. But I thought this best."

"Did you give our real names?"

"Yes, if I'm Mrs. Frank Lindstrom of Noroton Heights and you're Ernest Lindstrom."

We walked down the hallway toward our room. I felt the heat of anticipation in my loins. Breathing became difficult. I opened the door. We went inside. The door was closed and locked. We stood there. The room was old, dreary, somehow sad, in its plastic cheapness.

"I can't, David. I want you so. I've planned this for days. But not here. I can't. I'm sorry."

"I know."

We left. We hadn't even set down our packages. We went home on an early train.

And so it was a summer in which Mother and I saw a lot of each other, but to no good end, if that is not too vulgar a pun. We resolved—I remember the discussion very well—to make as enjoyable as possible our time together. If we couldn't do what we wanted to do, we'd try to enjoy what we had to do. We swam and rode, the usual things. We shopped and went out to lunch a lot. I enjoyed being out with my mother. She always made me feel that I was the most important person in the world, her date, her beau, her lover. She gave me the certainty that she enjoyed my company and did not want to do anything else but be with me. If I were in a situation I didn't know what to do, I'd ask and she'd tell me. If I did the wrong thing, she'd tell me without accusation or faultfinding. If it was a difficult situation, she'd steer me out of it. I rarely felt awkward or clumsy or inept when I was out with my mother.

"I tried very hard not to love you, David." [There was a pause, the sound of a deep sigh.] "Let's say I tried, not very hard, I guess, certainly unsuccessfully."

"Because of our relationship?"

"Yes—well, no, not really. It was very complicated." [Pause.] "It's hard to explain. Our being mother and son—"

"Are we really mother and son? Could there be no mistake?"

"None. I am your mother, your natural mother. You were born between these legs, from this body. You are my son, my only child—my most beloved son."

[There is a long pause. There are sounds on the tape, but I cannot detect what they are doing.]

"Go on. I want to hear. You were saying how you felt about our relationship."

"Yes. I was frightened by it, terrified that your father, others would find out. It would have been a disaster—in every way a disaster. I had no way of knowing what your father might do if he ever found out. He may not show it, but he has a violent temper. It's the Irish in him, I suppose, the red hair. I was afraid he might harm you, even kill you in a rage. Myself, too.

So, in a way the—our relationship, mother and son, was . . . I was always conscious of it. Yet, our being what we are never bothered me with you. It never stood between us. Did it you?"

"Never. It made it better."

"I worried about it before. Afterwards, I didn't—at least not very much. It's like being a virgin, or rather not being. You think about it and worry that some terrible thing will happen. After you've done it, you find it was nothing and wonder what you had been so afraid of."

"That doesn't sound very nice. It wasn't nothing to me. It was everything to me."

"Oh, David—"

"I'm only kidding, Mother. I know what you mean. Once you've committed some dreadful sin, you stop worrying about it. You fear the consequences, not the sin. There's a psychological basis for it. I studied it."

"All I know is that your being my son was not why I tried not to love you. I told myself it was ridiculous having my lover under the same roof. It was truly impossible. I told myself, over and over, there had to be something wrong with me. There I was, a twenty-eight-year-old woman, wanting, aching, yes, lusting after a thirteen-year-old boy. I told myself what I felt for you was just some kind of aberrated mother love. If I hadn't been your mother and you my son, I would never have gone to bed with you—or want to every waking moment. I looked at your friends. They were children. I wouldn't dream of sex with one of them. Why you? Okay, the sex was good. What you did to me, what I felt—wonderful. But I shouldn't be doing it with a child. That really bothered me, David; it really did. If I wanted sex—and I did want it—I should be having an affair with a grown man. There had to be something wrong with me that I lusted after a boy. It really bothered me. I seriously considered having an affair. I considered everyone I knew. I looked at men, appraising them. I'd heard of bored, sex-starved women doing it, consciously picking out a lover. Why not me? If I had a man, a real lover, maybe I'd forget how much I wanted you. Does that hurt for me to say that?"

"Yes. But I understand now. I couldn't have stood it if you'd told me then. I really believed you liked me, being with me."

"I did, darling, I did. That was what was so awful about it. It was just that I felt I shouldn't. There had to be something wrong with me that I did."

"So you took a lover."

"Yes—you. Only you. You were and are my only lover."

"You never took another man?"

"No, I couldn't." [Sigh.] "I had too much pride. I just couldn't reduce myself to it. And there were all the complications. I already had you to hide from your father. If there was another man or a succession of men and I had to keep him from both you and your father. Impossible." [Pause.] "Oh, darling, don't look at me that way. Let me finish. I was about to say I really didn't want another lover. I had you. You were the most glorious lover. You were all I wanted. Only you."

[There was a long silence.]

"Oh, God, how did we get into this? I'm saying it all wrong." [Pause. Heavy sigh.] "When I was with you, when we were making love, it never bothered me. You *have* to know that. It was just—sometimes, when we were out or you'd be talking with your father, you seemed so terribly young. This feeling of—"

"Cradle robbing."

"You're being beastly, David. Simply awful."

[He sighed.] "I'm sorry."

"And it only was at first. By the time you were sixteen and had filled out and matured, it had all gone away. We looked right together. I not only wanted to be with you, I was proud. You were so handsome. No one who didn't know us could believe we were mother and son."

"And now?"

"We have a problem again. Forty-year-old women aren't supposed to run around with twenty-four-year-old men. They may want to. But it doesn't look right."

"Who says?"

"I say."

"I mean who says you look forty?"

"But how much longer?"

That summer mother and I studied sex. I got books from the Westport and Pequot libraries. I bought, or she bought, all the likely looking paperbacks in Kleins or the Remarkable Book Shop. I started it. I simply wanted to learn all there was to know. I brought home the books and kept them in my room away from Father. He wouldn't have cared, I guess, but I just didn't want to talk with him about sex. He and I had had the customary "talk" about sex. It had been dreadful, my pretending ignorance. But I didn't hide the books from Mother. She saw what I was reading, said, "That's about the last thing you need to study" and joined in. It filled our time when Dad was gone for the day. We'd sit together downstairs or in my room reading and giggling and laughing at our wisecracks. She'd say, "Good heavens, I didn't know that," or some such comment, then read the passage aloud to me. Or I'd read to her. We talked about it, very openly, no shyness or reserve. "Does it really feel good when I do that?" I'd ask.

"Yes, but I like it better with you inside."

We read about all the positions, and she'd giggle in amazement. "I never would have believed." She pushed me back on the bed and entwined herself with me. We were both fully clothed. "Good heavens, it *would* work." She unwound herself and went back to the book. "Remember page 103. We have to try that."

Another time when we were reading together, I heard her gasp in amazement.

"What?"

"This." She read on, intense interest on her face. She turned the page and another.

"What is it?"

"Just a minute." She read on a moment. "This is a book supposedly written by the world's greatest madame."

"What's a madame?"

"You know, she runs a whorehouse—a brothel. She says the vagina is only a muscle and can be trained like any other muscle. You can make it tight and strong like any muscle. You can flex it." She went back a page or so and read again. "Isn't that something? She says there are women who can actually pull a man's penis inside them and then make him come without his ever moving a muscle. Amazing. She even gives exercises. You're supposed to practice with a pencil or pen or something small like that. You're supposed to work at gripping it so it doesn't fall out. Fantastic."

"Are you going to do that?"

She smiled. Great delight shown in her eyes. "You know me and exercises. But I'm not going to tell you. A woman should have her mysteries."

She reached her hand to my face. I buried my lips in her palm and kissed it passionately.

"Let's not read any more, David. I can't stand it."

The three days we had together at the end of August coincided with Mrs. Riordan's vacation. We were alone together for over eighty hours. There was great intensity, even urgency, to our lovemaking. We felt compelled both to make up for the summer's longing and to store away, like squirrels, treasures for the winter when I would be away. I secretly started to keep count of how many times we made love, but I lost track. Our lovemaking was not constant, although we tried to make it so. But we continually exhausted each other and aroused each other, frantic at the passing hours. But it was also great fun, and we laughed a lot as we practiced what we had learned from our summer's study. I remember page 103 was a delight.

* * *

I have read somewhere of the difficulty novelists have in portraying the passage of time. I understand that various devices—all terribly mysterious to me—are used to convey the elapse of weeks, months, and even years in the life of the progagonist. But even if I did know how to do this, it would not help me much. I simply do not know and have no way of finding out the length of time over which David recorded his reminiscences. The portion just reported may have taken him an hour or days. I don't know. Worse, I really have no firm knowledge of when the next episode occurred and thereby fits into this tale. I am guided by the fact that Morrison told David he would get back to him in a couple of days with instructions. Couple! That can mean anything from two days to two weeks. All I know for certain is that David did receive instructions from Morrison. He did not record the receipt of them. They may have come by mail or phone call. David may have visited Morrison elsewhere, or he just may not have bothered to record it. What exists is David's complaint about his efforts to carry out Morrison's commands.

* * *

There are times when I believe I must have committed some great evil in my life to have Ephraim Squires visited upon me. Left to his own devices, I suppose a shrink would read into that statement that I'm overcome with guilt about my relationship with my mother. Bullshit! I'm not. There isn't anything but beauty and true love in what we do—and I'm *not* protesting too much. But Ephraim Squires and that she-bitch Edna are too much. They are an affliction on the human race—on me.

I walked into the headquarters of the Liberty Party on K Street. Squires has sure used the money I've given him to buy a respectable front for his ragtag revolution. You walk in, fancy room, receptionists, lots of literature, flags, slogans, typewriters going, phones ringing. If you didn't know better, you'd believe it was a real political headquarters. And from Squires's standpoint a lot of people do believe it. Behind the reception area is another room where the goons hang out, coats off, shoulder holsters at the ready. There are a bunch of offices off this room, for Edna, Cooper, and others. Squires's office, big and luxurious, is at the far end of this room.

When I walked into this inner room—I don't know what else to call it—I was greeted with silence. There had been a lot of talking and some laughter. Bang, a curtain of silence fell. Everyone looked at me, then turned away. I heard a snicker or two; then the conversation picked up in hushed tones. I asked to see Squires. I was told he was busy. I said I'd wait. This earned a shrug. I went over to a chair in the corner and sat.

Almost an hour went by. Finally, Edna appeared. She stood in the middle of the room, maybe ten feet away from me, and said in a loud voice, "Well, if it isn't pretty boy, God's gift. What you doing here, boy?" She said it in mock black English.

I know I flushed. I couldn't help it. The damn female always makes me so mad. I know that's what she wanted, and it makes me madder that I can't help but react to please her. I said I wanted to see Squires.

Still in the phony accent, she said, "What you

want to see him about, boy? You want to give him some more of your daddy's money?"

Everyone was looking at us. I heard a loud snicker. "No," I said. "I have some information for him."

"In-for-ma-tion. I doubt if there is anything you can tell him that he hasn't already forgotten."

"That's for him to decide."

"Who says?" She pointed her finger at me and raised her voice. "You just watch your manner, boy. You watch how you talk to your betters." This earned her loud laughter. "I decide who gets to see Mister Squires. So you just tell me this big piece of in-for-ma-tion of yours."

"I'll tell only Squires."

"Mister Squires."

"Mister Squires."

"Then you sit on your ass there till it rots." Amid great laughter, she turned to walk back to her office.

"Edna," I called after her, "I know ridiculing me is the national sport to you—that and being Gloria's asshole—but—"

I'd gotten to her. She turned back to me, angry. "You just watch it."

"I have watched it."

"Damn you. I'll have your head pinched off."

"You go right ahead. I'm sure you could. But I'll tell you something first. Just because you're only half a woman. Half, hell. You're just an ass and nothing else. But if you do have any brain at

223

all and care about anything except being fucked, you better let me tell Squires what I know."

She stood there, her face the color of raw liver. She could have killed me if she'd had a gun. I was aware of a stirring among the goons in the room. She'd only have had to say one word.

"And what is it you know?"

Squires had come out of his office and was standing there in shirtsleeves, tie at half-mast. He looked like an ape in costume. "I'll tell you in your office—alone."

He shrugged and motioned to the door. "C'mon, Edna. Let's hear what our great benefactor has to say."

"I said alone."

"And I said for Edna to join us."

I gave it up and went inside. There was no point in arguing with him. I just wanted to get this job over with and get out of there.

He sat behind a big executive desk. With the wall paneling and leather chairs and executive phone, he could have passed for a business executive—if he didn't look so ghoulish. Edna stood beside him, still fuming. I sat down across the desk.

"You know, Squires," I said, "all this would be a lot easier if—" I started to say respect, but thought better of it. "You know I don't deserve this treatment."

"What treatment is that?" I could tell he

started to add the word "boy." Instead he smiled broadly, enjoying his joke.

"Go ahead," I said. "Have your fun."

"Sticks and stones. That sort of thing?"

"Squires, I can't believe you are so well off you don't need all the help you can get."

"Indeed, we need a lot of help. But you? Your few pennies? We can always get money."

"I'm sure of that. But I thought all this—" I motioned to encompass the whole fancy office, "—was a big drive for respectability. You're hardly going to get that if you persist in two-bit stickups and street muggings."

I'd angered him. I saw it in his eyes. "I'm not going to argue with you, Callahan. You ain't your old man. Him I liked, trusted, believed in. You—" He smiled broadly. "But then I'm sure you have your redeeming virtues. I'm sure that gorgeous mama of yours must love even you. But to me you are just a pipsqueak."

I was angry again. I know I showed it.

"What I want to know is what you come round here for. You don't think I believe you believe in us. I don't see you out in the street, getting dirty, walking your legs off, carrying a sign that comes to weigh a ton. I don't see you mixing with the real folks and people, trying to help them help themselves. Okay, so you're a poor little rich kid. I don't see you trying to make points for us among those rich, society folks. You're a phony, Callahan, a grade-triple-A, superlarge phony, and we don't need you

225

around here anymore. I don't like you annoying Edna. She's my girl. You just leave her alone. Right, darling?"

She said nothing, but looked self-righteous.

All I wanted was to get out of there. Nothing was going as I'd planned. It never did with Squires. I decided to do what Uncle Richard wanted and get the hell out into the fresh air.

"You've been infiltrated," I said.

"Like whom? Not by you I trust."

"Elderton." Leroy Elderton was a top gun in the revolution. I don't know what his job was supposed to be, but he was a confidant of Squires, a key lieutenant. I saw surprise register on both their faces. "He's an FBI informer. They know every thought you've ever had, every move you make before you even think of it."

"How do you know?" His voice was low. He was now serious.

"My friend, you've been too busy putting me down. You've been having your little fun and games. I'm a nothing, a pipsqueak. Just great fun. The only trouble is that you forget that I worked with my father a long time. I met most of the people he knew. Some of them don't consider me a pipsqueak."

"How come he never told me?"

"He didn't know. Nobody knew until just the other day. It was revealed—just say it was revealed. There are, believe it or not, misguided

226

saps in this town who want to help you. I was asked to get the information to you."

"Why you?"

"For obvious reasons. Slipping you secret information is hardly a move calculated to enhance a political career on the Hill."

He paused a moment, thinking. "I don't believe you."

I stood up. "Fine. Great. Marvelous. Splendid."

"Why would you tell me?"

"For two reasons. First, I was asked to. Second, I thought maybe—just maybe—there might be an end to this horseshit with me around here."

"Who asked you to tell me?"

"Sorry, Squires. No way."

"I don't believe you."

"Then don't."

[Edna] "He's lying, Ephraim. Elderton is no traitor."

"What makes you think you aren't infiltrated?"

[Squires] "Of course we are. Maybe half those people in that room out there are johns. But they don't really know anything."

"Elderton does."

"I don't believe he's a spy."

"And you believe the FBI is a bunch of dummies. They'd be content with listening to dummies who don't know anything."

He was silent, clearly affected by what I was saying.

227

"I don't have much respect for you, Squires, but I did think you were smart enough not to underestimate what you were up against."

I knew I had him.

"Feed Elderton some false information. I'll bet it ends up right in the Justice Department."

"Get the hell out of here, Callahan. I can't stand the smell."

I talked to Uncle Richard today. As prearranged, I phoned him from a public phone to another public phone. I told him what had happened with Squires. He seemed pleased. I suggested the FBI had better act on any information obtained from Elderton. He said he was way ahead of me.

I can dispense with my years at St. Albans rather quickly. There is no need for any long description of my five long years there. Indeed, it is impossible, for the years seem indistinguishable, one from the other, all equally disagreeable. We Americans do terrible things to our children. We drag out the years of schooling unconscionably. All that is taught in the upper six grades of school could be learned in a year, certainly not more than two and only then in the case of a serious student with a great thirst for knowledge. The subject matter is stretched out and padded. Great exercises in repetition are practiced. Not only is the same material taught over and over—consider the repetitions of Amer-

ican history, for example—but within a single
class, teachers instruct and discuss and drill—the
very word suggests they are dealing with block-
heads—then review and test and review the tests.
It is all silly and stupid and somehow dehuman-
izing. So much of the school years are wasted in
activities that have no reasonable relationship
to education—discussion, plays, stupid reports,
sports, homework, futilities of proving the student has done his studies, pep rallies, school
meetings, clubs, practices of bewildering vari-
eties, guest speakers, and a great deal of aimless
time killing. Clearly, what we call education is
a monstrously expensive babysitting operation,
a means of making jobs for teachers and peda-
gogical officials, as well as keeping young people
off the job market until their brains have rotted
and their enthusiasms atrophied.

St. Albans was an all-boys school—one of the
few left at that time—located in the Berkshires
near the village of Brookton, about two hours by
car from Westport. Brookton is a picture-post-
card village come to life, mostly a single street
lined with gracious white clapboard homes shel-
tered by giant sugar maples. There are a few
stores and shops, a couple of bars, and a restaurant. The principal landmark, other than the
school, is the historic Brookton Inn. It was fa-
vored by skiers, whose parties and affairs were
about the only surcease from the monotony of
the village. When I was there, St. Albans had
about fourteen hundred students, which about

equalled the population of the village. The school was run by the Jesuits, but half the faculty was laity.

My father wanted me to do well at St. Albans. I told him I would do my best. Mother and I talked about it in one of our last conversations before I left for school.

"Will you be all right?" Her concern was genuine.

I said I would.

"It'll be hard."

"Not you, too. Dad is always saying how hard it is. I'm no dummy. That school'll be duck soup."

"I don't mean the school. I mean—you know what I mean."

"Yes. But when is it ever easy?"

She squeezed my hand in both of hers. "Oh, David . . . what have we done to each other?"

We said nothing for a moment. Finally, I said, "I worry about you. You'll be alone with him. I won't be able to help you."

"I'll be all right. I've things to do. I've some new exercises I want to try. I'm going to work out a whole new program. I may take a class, flower arranging or something. Maybe painting." She smiled. "If I can quote someone, I'll be fine."

"These new exercises. Any particularly interesting ones?"

She smiled again. "Maybe. You'll have to be surprised."

I remember trembling a little. I wanted her so.

She gripped my hand tightly. She always had surprising strength for such a tiny person. "Oh, David . . . it won't be long. It's only two hours away. I can drive up once a week at least."

"Yes."

"I'll get a room at the Inn. If you can get away—who knows? We may see more of each other than we do now."

"It'll be like New York. You don't like hotels, remember?"

"It'll be different. Trust me."

"Mother."

"Yes."

"Don't come for a month."

"Really? Are you sure?"

"It'll take me that long to get the school under control."

"What do you mean?"

"I can't explain, but you'll see. My surprise."

She smiled. "Okay. I'll see you in October—when the leaves change. It'll be beautiful."

I remember regretting asking her to wait a month. It didn't take that long to figure out St. Albans.

From the first day, I applied what I had learned in dealing with my father. I concentrated wholly on whatever I had to do. I had my feelings tightly bound in the box in my mind, releasing them only at night in my bunk or during the times when I was with her. I lay there in the darkness tortured by the memory of her, counting the days or hours till she could come again. I'm sure my face was contorted with pain. I know I cried silent tears many times. But no one knew in the darkness. These feelings were never allowed out any other time.

I was probably the greatest student in the history of St. Albans. I'm sure the Jesuit fathers are still citing me as an example to poor, misguided unfortunates. I played every sport and excelled at them all. I disliked baseball, hated football, and royally detested basketball, but I forced myself to be the star of all three teams. I hated the sweat, the stinking locker rooms, the naked bodies, and filthy talk, but I added those feelings to my mental box and concentrated on whatever had to be done in the sport. I was big enough and fast enough. I was always athletic. Both Mother and Dad had seen to that. When I decided I had to fill my time doing something and concentrated on what there was to do, I became a schoolboy star. I batted four hundred something in baseball, set school records for receptions as tight end, and averaged over twenty points a game for four seasons as a forward in basketball. I ran the four-forty and eight-eighty in track. I was on the swim and tennis teams. I even made the ski team for two years before I gave it up.

I was a straight A student. I simply decided that what there was to learn and do in class was duck soup. All I had to do was concentrate. I did all the work required, then had time to read extra books and write reports. While other kids were fighting the work, bellyaching, and killing time, I had it all finished. A person who concentrates can do anything.

My biggest problems were social. I had always been a loner. I had never really played with other kids much, even when I was little. My mother was my companion and playmate. I never had a friend. When I arrived at St. Albans, I was stunned by how young everybody was. I felt like I was a million years old. I felt like an adult. Some terrible mistake had been made, and I was cast among children. I was appalled by the giggling and teasing and horsing around, the wild boasting and filthy language in which human speech was an exercise in repetition of the word "fuck," the lying and strutting, and the constant absorption in girls, girls, girls, boobies, tits, asses, and fucking, none of which any of them knew an iota about. It was like living in a cesspool, no, a child's toidy, stinking beyond comprehension, until I felt I would drown in the pure shit that is the mind of an eighth-grade American boy. It was all an implied insult to my mother. I was enraged, until I learned to put that in my box also.

I learned to participate in all this by seeming to. I'd hang around awhile, as little as possible, but just enough to seem almost one of the boys, or at least not too stuck up, smile, pretend to laugh, say a few words, go along with a stupid prank, and not snitch on those stupid enough to be caught. I refused to go along with their stupid masturbation, but managed to convey that I did or would. In time, the impression was gained that I was experienced with girls. I never discouraged it, but I also never said anything.

Yet, none of it would have worked had I not been a star athlete. If I had just been a good student, my aloofness, my silence, my lack of wholehearted participation, would have meant a dog's life for me, if a dog's life is one of unrelenting social misery. But I was bigger than most. I was the mainstay of any athletic endeavor. If I was not liked, I was needed and soon respected. Not being liked was fine with me. I detested them, everyone. I have not a single friend or even much more than a nodding acquaintance from my years at St. Albans.

I never had any problem with the teachers. I simply figured that if I could con my father, living under the same roof with my mother, I could con these people. I never broke the rules. I never made waves. I did all that was required, then more. I was a pedagological delight. I made everyone feel they had become educational wizards. Yet for social and personal reasons, I was careful not to pour it on too thick. To do so would have been to invite the label of asskisser. I remained aloof from the faculty too. I always kept myself distant from them. I didn't want to be friends with them either.

I had trouble with only one teacher, and not much at that. Mr. Snowden, who taught English lit and poetry, wanted to befriend me. He liked to talk. "Callahan," he might say, "I know you are the greatest thing to hit St. Albans since the founding, star athlete, student nonpareil, well-liked by all, a teacher's dream. Yet, I can't believe you are for real. Sometimes I think you are a machine, a robot. I keep telling myself that inside you somewhere there has got to be a real live boy who has real feelings, who makes mistakes, maybe even laughs and cries. Suppose that could be so?"

I consciously lifted a page from my mother. I said nothing. He said nothing either. He seemed comfortable with the silence. Damn him. I was in a subordinate position. I had to say something.

"I'm sorry, Mr. Snowden. I do the best I can."

He smiled a little and shook his head. "Okay, Callahan. I have no right to pry. But if you ever need to talk to someone about anything, I'll try to be available."

I never needed to talk—to him, the bastard.

When I look back on St. Albans, I realize I got the most out of it, a pretty decent prep education. But that was not my purpose. I didn't want it or need it or care about it. All I was doing at St. Albans was to try to manipulate others so I could spend as much time with my mother as possible. That wasn't much, but all my efforts gained a little, undoubtedly more than if I had stayed at home. My mother became bosom buddies—not literally of course—with Father O'Reilly, the headmaster. She smiled at him and charmed him and did him favors. She'd host a tea and greet the mothers of the boys as his hostess, which never ceased to amaze me. Mother is just not the type to hostess a ladies' tea. She even insists to this day that she was terribly fond of Father O'Reilly. All her support for the school gave her a valid excuse to spend extra days at Brookton. And she conspired with me to gain us time together. The star athlete could always be excused from a practice, the best pupil allowed to miss a few classes after Carla Callahan explained how important it was and how much she needed to take me with her. I came to live for the occasional afternoon, the infrequent evening, when we could steam the windows of our room at the Brookton Inn. There were even one or two times a year when Dad was away on a trip and she would find a way to get me out of school for the night. Looking back, I suppose there were a surprising number of times we stole a few hours or a day or two out of our lives. But it never really seemed like much at the time. Mostly, we had only a few minutes, an hour. We developed quite a collection of isolated parking spots and, after Mother lost her inhibitions about it, became surprisingly expert at doing it in the front seat of a TR or MG. Stolen moments. That's what they were. And I earned them on

the playing fields and in the insufferable class-
rooms of St. Albans.

* * *

As I listen to these tapes, I often wonder
what sort of person David Callahan might have
become had his mother kept her hands off of
him and had he been granted any chance at all of
developing normally. He had a good mind. Even
under these adverse conditions, he was a good
student. His knack for concentrating, for con-
trolling his thoughts, is the key to success at any
age and most remarkable in one so young. I cannot tell if he had a brilliant, creative mind. He
might have, had he ever taken a genuine interest
in anything other than lusting after his mother.
There are times in these tapes when I feel he is
rather creative. Once in awhile he is almost poetic in his choice of words, his imagery, his expression of his feelings. There is no hint that he
ever had any literary or poetic or dramatic
inclinations, but given a chance, it is not too far-
fetched to imagine that he might have contributed to the arts.

I can carry this analysis only so far from the
information on these tapes. I am certain, however, that David Callahan was a remarkable individual and had the potential to make some real
achievement. His stunted life and his death are a
total waste. He was rich, handsome, intelligent,
gifted, possessed of every opportunity—or po-

tential opportunity—our society can offer its young. Such a waste.

David Callahan's tapes pose a dilemma for me that is both moral and literary. I simply do not know how much of his sexual musings and assorted erotica to include. As far as I am personally concerned, any of it is too much. I find it disgusting and embarrassing. I am sure many people find it titillating. I'm sure there are publishers who will want more, more, more, and be greatly exercised that I have expunged a syllable. I suppose it is inevitable that these tapes or portions of them will be offered for sale by pornographers—whatever else they may call themselves—for the entertainment of the perverted and the obsessed. Everything I am or have ever stood for in my life cries out for me not to pander to the lascivious. I truly wish David Callahan had been a eunuch or, failing that, possessed a greater sense of privacy and decency in what he put on these tapes.

My problem is literary in that I do not know how much of this material to include. David Callahan might muse for an hour or more describing his mother's body, her appearance, the sensations he felt. He could become almost surgical in the descriptions of her anatomy and totally explicit in describing their carnal activities. He would apparently sit there in his apartment, lonely, frustrated, and engage in sexual fantasies. On occasion, he would become quite "lost" in these fantasies and quite sexually aroused. His voice would become dry. He would sigh, even moan a little. His voice would trail off until he was hard to hear or understand. At other times, he would turn braggart, expounding on his sexual prowess and hers.

How much of this do I include? I cannot believe the totality of it would interest any sane person. It becomes a stultifying bore. I have not had any literary experience of this sort. I want to preserve the integrity of David Callahan's confession. I want to permit him to show his feelings for his mother and hers for him, at least as he understood them. Their relationship is difficult to comprehend at best. It defies understanding. They called it love, but I hardly think it qualifies as that. If not love, what was it? An obsession, surely, but such a strange one. I confess that I do not know when I have given the reader a sufficient understanding of this tormented couple and the devastation they wreaked on themselves and our nation.

Another thing. David Callahan is dead. None of this will matter to him. But Carla Callahan Lampton is very much alive, our ubiquitous First Lady. I thoroughly detest her for who she is and what I know she has done, both personally and publicly, but I have no wish to engage in character assassination with this endeavor. She may not deserve it, but I would like to preserve my own sense of chivalry. Telling the truth does not mean pouring it on.

If this were an ordinary situation, I would

discuss my moral and literary problem with an editor or some friend experienced in this type of writing. I might even bring in an associate or ghost to help me. But for obvious reasons, I cannot discuss this project with anyone. I must work alone and do what I think best. I have decided, therefore, to include what follows. I have tried to eliminate my personal revulsion as best I can. I've minimized any concerns for the reputation of Carla Callahan Lampton, if any of it remains by this time. I have tried not to pander to titillation but to try to portray the relationship between David Callahan and his mother. It seems to me there is still one question unanswered about them. Why were they so obsessed over so prolonged a period? Granted the incest might have occurred. Granted they might have had a pronounced sexual attraction for each other. But why did it continue? The circumstances were certainly adverse. "Stolen moments" was the way he put it. They lived a monstrous and complicated lie. It must have been exhausting to maintain it. They lived in fear—she in terror—that Brendan Callahan would discover their secret. When David went off to college in Ohio after St. Albans, he and his mother were physically separated. It would seem natural, even inevitable, that their passion, however grand and obsessive it was, should have subsided with time. They should have worn it out physically. By all that is normal, they should have wearied of it emotionally. Some sense of self-preservation should have led one or both to break off the relationship and take another lover. Carla Callahan confessed she thought of it and even may have tried. Surely this should have occurred to her again, so hopeless was the situation.

Why this prolonged obsession? Why, why, why? I am far from certain there are any real answers on these tapes. I doubt very much that David and his mother knew the answers themselves, or indeed thought of the question. I will not speculate on the possible answers, although readers and those who may hear the actual tapes are free to think as they please. Merrill Lampton has not yet stamped out thought.

If the tapes do not offer a certain why to the obsession, they do provide an abundance of how. David Callahan gives no shortage of explicit examples of how he and his mother maintained their relationship at full flame for years. In my editing, I have tried to offer what seems to me to be the most informative and revelatory portions of his narrative. Again, I have juxtaposed his descriptions with her comments made in that unguarded evening in his apartment when he got her talking about their relationship. It begins with her.

* * *

"I traveled the road between Brookton and Westport so often I knew it by heart. I could have driven it in my sleep. I'm not sure I didn't some of the time. I remember one night in particular. We had had the whole afternoon and evening until you had to be back at ten. We didn't even stop to eat."

"I remember."

"I was exhausted. Every bone, every muscle, in my body ached. I can remember hardly being able to drag myself out of that Inn and get into the car. I'm sure people looked at me, wondering what I'd been doing. I don't know how I drove home. I remember I stopped for a coffee and brandy to stay awake."

[She laughed, softly, lightly.]

"Mercifully, your father was still out at a meeting when I got home. I had time to bathe and be in bed asleep when he got home."

"I guess I should be sorry for all the trouble I caused you. But I'm not. How about gratitude? I'm glad you always came to Brookton." [He laughed.] "And *at* Brookton."

"That's terrible. Awful. You always were awful. What did I used to call you?"

"Teenage satyr."

"That's right. You were a teenage satyr."

"You didn't seem to mind."

[Pause.] "We must be getting old, worn out. We never used to waste time talking like this."

I believe, I truly do, there has never been sex in the world like my mother and I do it. She used to say we had to be a couple of freaks. She may have been right. But if we are, then the whole world should be such freaks. The thing between us is that my mother has the capacity for unlimited orgasms. She didn't just have one or two or a few. She could apparently go on forever—still can. At least the only ending I've ever known to her was muscular exhaustion or the clock. If we've been apart for awhile, she'll come quickly at first, sort of in spasms, a whole cluster of orgasms racking her, very fast, one right after the other. That will subside, and nothing will happen for, I don't know, a minute or two, maybe more. Then it will start again. Then she is gone. She'll go over and over and over. There is no counting. And no apparent end except exhaustion or a muscle cramp. She used to worry about this at first. She'd say there had to be something wrong with her. I kept telling her it was wonderful, to enjoy it. I looked it up in books and read it to her. Apparently a small percentage of women can do this. It's natural to them. Unlimited orgasm may not be common, but it is hardly rare.

What is rare is someone who can do it like me. I believe a lot of women could experience prolonged pleasure if only they had someone to do it with. I have always been able to do it over and over. If I have not been with her for awhile, the first ejaculation comes out almost as a steady stream. There is a second one quickly, then a third, several, sometimes others spaced further and further apart. But even when there was not a drop of semen to be drained from me, I could still keep an erection—at least lots of times I could. I don't know how. Maybe it was concentration. No, her continually going under or over or beside or around me, her demanding with her body more and more, was endlessly exciting to me. And she had perfected the madame's exercises. Had she ever! There were times when she'd squeeze me so hard I'd cry out in pain and, I swear, other times when she'd hold me so tight it couldn't go down. If I failed, she'd keep me inside her and—I don't know how she did it—massage me and stroke my testicles with her hand until she had me back up and at her again. And there were other times when I'd get so mad at not being able to satisfy her. I'd be so weary; then a rage would overcome me. Frustration, I guess. Spent, absolutely dry, I'd bang away at her, angrily, savagely. Gasping for breath, I'd thrust at her like I had a sword and could cleave her in two. She loved it. She'd cry out in pain sometimes and come and come and come. Finally, I'd collapse in failure and roll off of her, exhausted. There was no end to her. I could never satisfy her. Never once.

"David, do you think I'm a nymphomaniac?"

"Heavens, no. That's a term everybody uses. I doubt if anyone knows what one is."

"Isn't it someone who can never get enough?"

"No. As I understand it, the nympho never really enjoys sex, yet sleeps with everything in sight trying to prove something. You don't do that."

"Then wanting it all the time, never being able to get enough is—"

"You're just a nice, normal, healthy girl."

"You aren't just saying that?"

" 'Course not." [He laughed.] "I'm not so sure how normal it is that I can't satisfy you."

"That's what I mean."

"That's my problem. Not yours."

"I don't want it to be a problem. Sometimes you get so angry you scare me. I think I ought to pretend. Ask you to stop."

"Don't you dare."

"I can't. It's the best part. It's like—oh, I can't say. Yes, I can. You know, fireworks. At the end they shoot up a whole big thundering shower of rockets, filling the whole sky. That's how it is."

"End with a bang."

"I don't like your language."

[He laughed.] "I meant the fireworks."

[There was a longish pause.]

"David, I worry sometimes. I seem to want it all the time. Oh, after I've been with you and we've done it a lot, I'm okay for a few days. Maybe a week or more. Then gradually it comes over me. I get like an animal, a caged animal, clawing at the bars, desperate to get out. That goes on forever. A couple of weeks at least. Then, if I don't have it, have you, the headaches start, blinding, excruciating headaches that drive me out of my mind. I think I'm going crazy."

"It's the tension. Migraine."

"There's nothing to do but go to bed and take drugs. You know how I hate to take drugs."

"I thought I was the cure."

"You are. That's what I mean. When I'm with you, you seem to blast the pain right out of me. Then I'm all right for a few days. There's got to be something wrong with me."

"No, there isn't. You just like sex."

[Another longish pause.]

"There's something I never told you about. I'm not very proud of it."

"Confession time."

"Oh, it's not what you think. I wanted you, nobody else." [A pause, as though she is struggling for words.] "When you were in college and so far away . . . weeks would go by before we could be together. I'd go wild with pain. I had to do something to prevent the headaches. I started masturbating. I'd lie in bed and come and come. I hated myself, but I had to do something."

"It's nothing to—"

"No, let me finish. I heard about water. I started doing that."

"What?"

"You lie in the tub and let the warm water run between your legs."

"Really? Did it work?"

"It worked. But it didn't help the headaches. Nothing did. Oh, God, I even bought a dildo. A fancy expandable one. I tried to use it. But I couldn't. It revolted me. I burned it before your father found it." [She sighed deeply.] "Nothing worked. Nothing ever works but you. I needed you. I always need you."

"Right now?"

"Yes."

The futility of trying to satisfy her lent a certain caste to our lovemaking. When she realized and accepted that she was insatiable, she began to teach me to hold off on my orgasms as long as I could. She taught me to hold off and hold off. She'd repeat, "Hold . . . hold . . . hold . . ." over and over while she shuddered in orgasm after orgasm. If we'd been apart for a long time, which was the usual circumstance, and my penis was just a rod of proud flesh, it was a form of exquisite torture for me to try to hold off while she writhed below or beside or on top of me. I couldn't do it for a long time. She'd laugh and hug me as I exploded into her in failure. But I learned. I learned not to think about or feel what was happening to me and to concentrate only on her, her motions, her orgasms, what she was doing. I learned to enjoy the suffering she imposed. Then, when her spasms of coming had begun to subside, she'd say, "Now," and I'd begin to thrust into her, bringing on a whole new series of cataclysms for her as I erupted into her again and again. She liked it that way. Still does. The best of all possible worlds she calls it. It is about the only way I can begin to keep up with her when we have only a short time together.

When there is more time, we can be very physical in our lovemaking. Despite her appearance, my mother is very strong and has tremendous stamina. At times our lovemaking is a physical contest, hard exertion, demanding, even brutal. There is sometimes great pain associated with what we do. It began the summer I was fifteen or sixteen. I don't remember for sure. Sixteen, I think. Dad was away. We had three days together. The first day was consumed in our pouring out and filling up of our passion. I remember awakening in the morning with that feeling of impenetrable loss that she was not there beside me. I arose and found her in her exercise room. She was in the midst of her floor exercises. She stopped in the middle of a split and looked up at me. "Now?" she said. It was that strange way of speaking again, part question, part negative.

"Yes."

"Mrs. Riordan—"

"Not at 6 a.m."

"Here?" The question-negative again.

"It's exercise.

It was—that day and many times since. We rolled all over that mat and onto the floor and against her equipment and ended up in the corner under her practice bar, panting and grunting, sweat shining on us. I can't imagine how we looked and sounded.

My mother is very limber, very acrobatic. She can do anything with her body, including some things that don't seem possible. We have made love, or tried to, in every conceivable position, standing up, sitting down, from the top, bottom, sideways, from behind. She does something to me—quite frequently, because I like it—I lie on my back, and she does the split on top of me. She takes me inside, squeezing me like a vise, her legs straight out on either side. She may bounce there a couple of times; then very slowly she will rise, pushing herself up with her feet and legs, almost to the end of my penis, twisting and turning her hips in a screwing motion, then come crashing down on top of me, to repeat the motions again and again. I try to hold off, but soon it is a choice between orgasm or exquisite death.

We do it with her standing on one foot, a standing split with her leg against my chest, her hands on my shoulders for balance. She moves her hips as I thrust into her, around and up and down, whatever pleases her. And it does. She likes that a lot. We even do it with her standing on her head. She'll do a handstand and somehow arch her body and split her legs till I can get into her. Or she'll begin sitting in my arms, her legs around my hips, me inside her, then fall backwards, my hands supporting her hips, until her hands are on the floor. She likes that too. It must have something to do with the blood rushing to the head. My mother can do anything with her body. From that position she can pull herself back into my arms if I can brace myself enough to hold her. Quickly she moves into another position, often keeping me inside as she does it. I sometimes wonder if I'm a lover or a partner. It is very tiring but so sexy. I can never look at gymnasts or acrobatic dancers without being turned on.

Sometimes we are almost brutal with each other. She likes to fight and wrestle and have me overpower her, as though I were raping her. I was guarded about it at first. I didn't really try until I discovered how much she likes it. She is very strong. It is not easy to grab hold of that writhing, twisting, struggling body and get her flat on her back on the floor or bed. Bending her arms and pinning her down spreadeagle is not too difficult, but getting her legs apart is something else. She struggles and fights as hard as she can. Sometimes while pinning her arms, I can force my knees between hers and break her open that way. Other times I release her arms, letting her hit me and push at me while I pry her open with my arms. It is very difficult that way. It takes all my strength. When I finally get her spreadeagled on the floor or the bed and am inside her thrusting, she still struggles and fights until at last her own eruption of orgasms takes the strength from her. When it is over, we lie there in each other's arms, our chests heaving in a search for air, mercifully exhausted.

Sometimes there is a lot of pain associated with our lovemaking. I mean more than just the pain of exertion. She tries not to, but sometimes she can't help scratching me or biting me. She is always sorry afterwards. I guess her marks, quite visible in the locker room at school, encouraged the notion that I had a girlfriend and was a man of the world. I denied that was what caused them—or said nothing—but I wasn't believed. Sometimes in the middle of my orgasm, she'll pinch my balls till I can't tell pain from pleasure. I know she wants me to hurt her. I can never ram her hard enough. She keeps asking for more and more, harder and harder. But I can't bring myself to hit or bruise or harm her body, even though I know she wants me to. The most I'll do is stick a couple of fingers up her rectum while she is coming. It drives her wild. She also does that to me, but I don't really like it.

Lovemaking between my mother and me is always an adventure. There is constant variety, innovation, imagination. I don't know what other couples do, but I cannot imagine there are many women in the world who have my mother's body and can do with it what she can. And what a faker and fraud she is. Everyone thinks of Carla Callahan as a goddess, beautiful, but icy cool, always poised and controlled. I overheard a man say once that she was gorgeous but probably lousy in bed. Probably a cold fish. Wouldn't want to mess her hair. Ha!

* * *

It is this passage that I tried to avoid putting in the book. I don't want to know all this. It is too perverted. It is too destructive even of the likes of Carla Callahan Lampton. Yet here it is, only somewhat expurgated. I suppose I don't need to comment on it, but I can't resist. Theirs was not love. It was not even sex between them. It was hardly pleasurable. They were doing anything but using their bodies to express affection, love, even passion. Their relationship had gone beyond even lust. They were two lost, forsaken human beings, punishing each other in most physical ways for the misery they had inflicted on each other. The piper was extracting a terrible price already.

* * *

I shouldn't have gone. I know that. But I couldn't help it. I detest Ephraim Squires, I truly do, but I just had to tell him I had nothing to do with his arrest. I had no way of knowing Elderton would be killed. I was just delivering a message—I wasn't fingering Squires.

I don't know why I had to tell him; I just did. Okay, it was a stupid thing to do, but how was I to know?

When I got to the courthouse, there was a large crowd filling the street outside. The cops were trying to hold them back but with no noticeable success. It seemed to me there weren't nearly enough cops on the scene. I pushed my way through the crowd, determined to get inside and talk to Squires. I had a hard time. The crowd was already big, and everyone seemed trying to push forward, too. A couple of times I thought I would be knocked down or get into a fight just trying to squeeze forward.

When I got to the front, I could see that part of the crowd was Squires's people, his men who had come to meet him. But they were far outnumbered. It seems it was lunch hour and hard hats from a nearby construction site had come en masse to see the excitement. I couldn't believe they would bring Squires out to face this. They did. He appeared at the doorway, flanked by two marshals. He stood there a moment. He looked very short and small. I saw bewilderment, consternation, then fear on his face. Then he saw me. His bravado returned. He smirked at me and raised his hand in the fuck-you gesture. He meant it for me, but the crowd misunderstood. An angry roar arose. I've never heard anything like it. There was no identifiable sound or words, nothing to describe other than a rising moan or roar. The hard hats surged forward, pushing the cops and Squires's men aside like toy soldiers, and seized Squires. I saw fists being raised and swung repeatedly, then a knot of men surge away, carrying Squires with them.

In the distance, I heard the sirens as police reinforcements came. I had to get out of there. But where? I ran into the courthouse, pushing my way through the crowd at the door, then went out another entrance and home. I wonder why Squires wasn't taken out the other door. I don't know what to do. Squires is probably dead. God, what is happening? What have I gotten myself into?

* * *

Carla Callahan visited her son, and he let his machine run. He told her about his meeting with Squires and is rewarded with appropriate, motherly sympathy. She reacted particularly to the threatening moment when, to her, it seemed Edna might have him killed. David also told of the abduction of Squires at the courthouse. He is very upset by all that has happened. "Uncle Richard" has gotten him into a first-class mess. He explains it in detail to her. To shorten this already too-long manuscript, I am eliminating these discussions, because essentially the same ground was covered again when Morrison came to the apartment to hear David's complaints.

* * *

"What seems to be the problem, David?"

"If you don't mind, I'd like to begin by reviewing what has happened."

"Of course. Go ahead."

"You asked me to see Squires and tell him Leroy Elderton was an FBI informer."

"And you did it superbly. You really put the burr under his saddle." [He laughed.] "If you can imagine Squires as a cowboy."

"Richard, I'm distressed because you put David in a position of danger. That woman, that Edna creature . . . she could have—"

"I had no way of knowing, Carla."

"Clearly, these are volatile people, disturbed. They'll do anything."

"I hardly think anything would have happened to David."

"Maybe not there. But what about later? Suppose they came here to kill him."

"Carla, you're being hysterical."

"You call it hysterical if I—"

"Both of you, please. I'm trying to make a point."

"I'm not arguing. I'm just trying—"

"Mother, please."

[She acquiesced. There was silence for a few moments. David continued.] "You asked me to tell Squires that Leroy Elderton was an FBI informer. I did. He didn't believe me. I told him to feed Elderton some false information as a test. I'm not sure what happened at that point. Do you know?"

"Yes. It wasn't very clever of Squires, but it worked. He led Elderton to believe—I assume no one else knew of it—that he planned a confrontation with police by staging one of his marches for liberty up Pennsylvania Avenue to the Capitol. There deliberately would be no parade permit. The cops would be forced to move in. There would be scuffles, the whole familiar scene. Elderton believed this and forwarded this information to the Justice Department. The riot police were out in force. Pennsylvania Avenue and the Capitol looked like a police convention. Squires, who had no intention of staging the march there, had Elderton dead to rights."

"An interesting choice of words, Uncle Richard. Elderton is dead."

"Squires had to kill him after that."

"You don't really believe that, do you? Oh, I know that's the official line, but it just isn't so. I haven't talked to Squires, but I have talked to some other people. They tell me—they *insist* Squires didn't have Elderton killed. And I believe them. Why would he?"

"Because he was a spy."

"That's just it; he wouldn't. Squires is too heady a guy. He'd neutralize Elderton, keep him from important information, but use him to feed the FBI phony stuff. Whatever Squires is, he is no fool. If Squires didn't kill Elderton, who did?"

"I'm sorry, but I'm not ready to admit that your friend didn't."

"He's not my friend."

"I meant nothing personal. It was just a manner of speaking. The FBI arrested Squires and his whole crowd. They believe he murdered Elderton—or one of them did at his bidding. They're certainly conducting an investigation along those lines. I don't know of any other suspects."

"That's just it. Squires was arrested and questioned. They couldn't hold him, so they—"

"There are laws to be observed, rules of evidence. It would have been better if Squires could have been kept in jail—for his own safety. But he had a jailhouse lawyer to get him out. I suppose he wishes he'd stayed in the cooler longer."

"Uncle Richard, there is something terribly funny about all this. For starters, it strikes me as strange that the FBI made such a hero out of Elderton. You certainly hadn't told me he was an actual agent. I thought he was just a paid informer. All this fuss over him, full military funeral attended by the President, statements of praise, condolences to the widow, a posthumous medal, a private college fund for his kids."

"I see nothing strange about it. Elderton was a fine man. I might say he proved in his life and courage what a black man can do if given a chance."

"That's almost a line from the President's TV speech. I'm sorry, but the whole thing bothers me. Ordinarily, the FBI wouldn't even admit it had infiltrated the Liberty Party, let alone make a martyr of one of its people. It's just strange."

"I think not."

"Look, Elderton is killed—not, I think, at Squires's orders. A great public fuss is made. The President praises Elderton. He is raised from FBI agent doing his job—hell, lots of agents have been killed with no mention of it at all—to national martyr. The attorney general says he has ordered the arrest of Squires as a prime suspect in the murder. The President makes a televised speech denouncing those who would destroy our country and what it stands for. He didn't mention Squires or the Liberty Party, but nobody needed a college education to figure who he was talking about."

"Yes, but—"

"Let me finish. All of a sudden, a lot of other people are in the act—marching, demonstrating, waving the flag, patriotic rallies. The moment Squires walks out of the grand jury room, he is seized by a mob, roughed up, and kidnapped. Where were the police then?"

"They were there. They couldn't handle it."

"They could handle a nonexistent march up Pennsylvania Avenue. I understand Squires was beaten up pretty bad. I hear they did a job on his face. I'm asking you, Uncle Richard; who are these people?"

"David, is it so bad that some Americans love their country? Want to protect the flag? Defend our way of life?"

"You don't need to ask, nor I to answer, questions like that."

"As far as I know, they are what are generally called patriotic groups—veterans, things like that."

"The far right."

"I suppose they are. Look, the President denounced their actions. He asked the country to abide by law and order. He has always stood for that. You know that."

"It is interesting that Lampton took to television to denounce the Liberty Party but only issued a statement through his press secretary urging law and order."

"He can't go on television every time—"

"And his statement seemed rather tame to me. I had an idea he ought to do it once more with feeling."

[There is a period of silence. David had gotten rather emotional. Morrison seemed to be hoping to cool him off.]

"What are you driving at, David? Say what you're thinking."

"Okay. You came here, sat in that very chair, and asked me to tell you all about Squires. You wanted to know what made him tick. You particularly wanted to know if he was violent by nature. I told you I didn't know, but I didn't think so. I thought by your questions you wanted to know how to keep him from *being* violent, but your remarks as you went out the door—you said something about being afraid of his *not* becoming violent. I wondered about it at the time. Then there is all this business with Elderton being murdered, Elderton martyred, a previously nonexistent "patriotic" mob, Squires beaten up—and not quite killed, mind you— that's very interesting, too, I think. A real mob would have finished him off while they had him. I'm just wondering if you haven't been orchestrating a gigantic scheme to make Squires violent."

[There is a very long pause. It lasted thirty-seven seconds.]

"Here's what I want you to do."

"You're not going to answer?"

"I want you to go to Squires and—"

"Go to Squires! You've got to be kidding. I'll never get on the same planet as Squires. I'm finished with him—*forever*. If that's what you hoped to accomplish, you succeeded brilliantly."

[Morrison laughed.] "I assure you I had no such purpose. And you aren't finished. You've just begun. Go to Squires and—"

"Uncle Richard, this is insane. You may think me a fool, but Squires sure isn't. If he didn't kill Elderton, he sure as hell knows it. It doesn't take much brains for him to figure that I told him about Elderton to get him into this whole mess. I set him up. That's what he'll think. Why shouldn't he? It's the plain truth. I did set him up for you."

"He'll think no such thing."

"Oh, c'mon, Uncle Richard. There's nothing else for him to think."

"He'll realize you are a real friend. You warned him about Elderton. Without you, he'd—"

"Excuse me, Uncle Richard, but you've got to be out of your mind."

"Son, I'm not used to being—"

"I'm sorry. It's just that I think I know Squires better than you do."

[Morrison paused.] "All right. Perhaps your difficulties have increased as a result of what has happened. It just couldn't be helped. But I think if you try, you'll be able to get to Squires again."

"I'm sorry, but no way."

"He doesn't have to like you. He doesn't have to trust you. I've told you from the beginning all he has to do is need you. All I want you to do is—"

"Uncle Richard, listen to me. Ephraim Squires and the Liberty Party have gone so far underground they'll never surface. I haven't the foggiest notion where to even begin to look for Squires."

"You asked me a question a moment ago which I didn't answer and am not about to answer. But I'll tell you this much. Driving Squires underground was part of our plan. He's right where we want him."

"And where is he?"

"I don't know. We honestly don't know. And we're looking. But you can find him. I know you can. He'll see you if only because he hates you."

"Richard!"

"Be still, Carla. No harm will come to David—if he does what I tell him. I promise you that."

[Carla Callahan muttered something indistinguishable in the background.]

"Get to Squires anyway you can. Offer him money, tons of it if you have to. Make him an offer he can't refuse. I don't care how you do it."

"So David can be killed?"

"No. They won't harm him. David, forget being a friend. Forget all that business of your being your father's son. It never worked anyway. From now on, you are to be a conduit, a messenger. That's all. Don't tell him whom you're representing. For Christ's sake, don't ever tell him that, but let him know that he needs you because you have contact with what he must now consider his enemies. Yeah, use that term, enemies. He's got to know there are people out to destroy him."

"And supposing by any stretch of the imagination this latest scheme of yours works—which I most surely doubt—what message am I to deliver?"

"No message. A question. Ask him what he wants."

"What he wants? You're kidding."

"No. What does he want? And, of course, I

want you to size him up, find out what he's thinking, going to do."

"Find out if he's now violent?"

"Yes, that too."

"What is it he's supposed to want?"

"I don't have an answer in mind. Just a question."

"Forgive me, Uncle Richard, but I think you always have an answer in mind. You've gone to too much trouble to only ask a question."

"Stop assuming, David. Just go see Squires."

[Morrison left. David, still very wrought up, left his machine running as he talked to his mother.]

"This is madness, Mother, unadulterated madness."

. [There is a pause. I can imagine David pacing the floor or waving his arms theatrically, but the tape doesn't reveal that. When Carla Callahan spoke, her voice was calm, controlled. She was obviously trying to soothe her son.]

"Richard is usually a very sensible person. I doubt if he is mad."

"Completely loony. But I'm not talking about him. I'm the one who's gone from his rocker. Just tell me what I'm doing mixed up in this thing? I don't give a damn about any of it."

"The President—"

"I couldn't care less if Merrill Lampton is elected dogcatcher. I care about you, and I care about me. I want us to be together. That's all I've ever wanted. I want us to live together and be happy. So what have I got? You're up in Connecticut doing God knows what."

"I'm all right, David."

"And I'm down here, groveling around this goddamn apartment, consumed with loneliness, pining away for you. I've spent my whole life wanting you. I've finally gotten to a time and age to have you, and what have I got? Ephraim Squires! God! Can you believe it? Ephraim Squires and his she-bitch Edna and some stupid, phony plot that even Don Quixote would have scoffed at. I must be crazy to go along with this. I must have—forgive me, Mother—blown my fucking lid."

[Pause, then a soothing voice.] "You're not crazy, darling."

"Let me ask you a question. A tough question. Do you think I ought to do this? You're my mother. You love me. Do you think I ought to do this?"

"I don't know, David. I really don't."

"Should I tell Uncle Richard to forget it? Should I turn in my badge as superspy, under-cover agent—what is it I am now?—messenger boy?"

[There is a pause marked by a heavy sigh from Carla Callahan.] "I don't know, David. I can't tell you what to do."

"Why not? You're my mother."

"Oh, David—"

"Should I pack up and go back to Connecticut?"

"David—"

"Should I be happy with you instead of so goddamn, fucking, miserable alone?"

[There is a long pause, lasting more than a half minute.]

"I understand, David. You're upset. I don't blame you. But being upset isn't going to solve anything. Let's try to calm down and talk about it sensibly."

[Half sigh, half words, David said, "All right." There is a sound which I imagine is his plopping into a chair.]

"You keep asking me to tell you what to do. I can't. It's your decision. You have to know how much I love you. How much I want to be with you. You can't doubt that."

"I know."

"But this has to be your decision. If you want to quit and come home to Westport, that's agreeable to me. I'll be thrilled to have you."

"You won't think me a quitter?"

"The thought will never enter my mind. But it obviously has yours."

"Yes. Shit, shit, shit, yes."

"David, you really don't have to swear so much."

"I know I don't. I'm sorry."

[Short pause.] "I don't like what you're doing either. It sounds dangerous. I couldn't bear it if anything happened to you. But . . ."

"But what?"

"I'm probably a silly, patriotic fool. But the

265

President asked you personally to help him. Richard says you're needed; you're the only one who can help him. I don't know. Richard is the only real friend we have. He has done so much for us. If you refused to help him now—well, I don't suppose it would matter very much. He'd understand, I'm sure."

"Oh, it would matter all right. If I'd refused in the beginning, he'd have found another boy. But right now—I've a feeling I'm vital to whatever wild-eyed scheme he's concocting. I think my quitting now would mean a surefire retirement for Merrill Lampton—not that I don't think that'll be the end result anyway." [He sighed.] "You're right, of course."

"I didn't say anything."

"Oh, I know, it's my decision."

"David, I am *not* twisting you around my little finger."

[He laughed a little.] "She said, protesting."

"David Callahan! I object—"

"All right, Mother. It is my decision, totally mine. There should be a decision about Lampton's third term in six months or so. I guess I can put up with it that long. But, Christ, forgive me if I feel like a sap being used this way."

"Would it help if I moved here?"

"Would it! I've been trying to get you down here for months."

"I've changed my mind."

"I thought you didn't like Washington."

"I don't. It's big and dirty and noisy and

266

full of blacks. The crime is enough to scare a person half to death. But if it'll make things easier for you, I'll come. I'll go back to Westport today. It'll take a couple of weeks to pack and close the house. Then I'll come—"

"God, Mother, it'll be heaven. You and I together again. I'll move some of my stuff out. You can have the other bedroom for your exercises and—"

"I don't mean *here*, darling."

"What do you mean?"

"I can't move in with you. This is much too small, David. It would never work. Richard wants you to have this place for your work, to meet people. I can't move into this apartment."

"But where?"

"I don't know. I'll have to find a house or apartment somewhere."

"For crissake."

"Don't be silly. I'll be around the corner. I'll be practically living with you. It's a whole lot better than having me in Westport. Stop frowning. Sometimes I think I spoiled you."

"You sure did spoil me. I'm spoiled for any other woman on the face of the earth."

"Oh, David, you make it sound so awful."

"I'm sorry. I really am. Look, I'm glad you'll be close, even if we're still apart. What time is it?" [He must have looked at his watch.] "We've got a couple of hours before you leave. You want dinner or what?"

"What."

His mother left, and David was again alone. But he was still worked up about his situation. He told his silently running tape about it.

* * *

If I've a shred of honesty in me, I'll admit that I never cared a damn about my father. He stood between me and Mother. He was a pain in my ass—a literal pain—that I had to fuss over and butter up to gain a few precious moments with her. I wished him dead. I truly did. Many times I wished it. And I lucked into his early death. Fifty-three and he has a heart attack. How lucky can I be? Yeah. Sure. How lucky am I?

More honesty. If I speak the truth, I'd admit I wish he wasn't dead. Oh, I don't want him around. But I would like him alive for ten minutes so I could talk to him about Lampton and Uncle Richard and this crazy scheme. He'd be appalled. He'd never let me do it. None of this would ever have happened if Dad were alive. Dad hated Merrill Lampton. He viewed him as a natural disaster. He had scoffed at him when he entered the primaries. He couldn't believe the G.O.P. was dumb enough to nominate him. He contributed heavily and worked hard to insure his defeat. When Lampton was elected, Dad reacted with stunned disbelief. I was away at St. Albans, but Mother told me that election night, or rather the next day when the results were confirmed, was one of the few times Dad ever knowingly, deliberately, got drunk.

Dad was quite irrational on the subject of Lampton. Even when I came home the next summer and Lampton had been in office six months or so, he was still railing at the election results. I can't remember any specific conversation; there were so many of them. Anything could set him off, an item in the *Times*, Lampton's image on the boob tube. "There he is. Old forty-four-point-two. The bastard. The forty-four-point-two percent bastard."

I can remember laughing and saying, "The way you feel about him, I would have thought he was a hundred percent bastard."

"He's a hundred percent nincompoop, that's what he is."

Father rarely mentioned his name but most often called him forty-four-point-two. I think he hoped it would catch on like "Tricky Dick" did for Nixon and "Bozo" for Ford. But it never did. Forty-four-point-two had been Lampton's election margin. Dad's refrain went something like this:

"Forty-four-point-two. The bastard won by forty-four-point-two of the vote. One of the most minority presidents in history. That goddamn bastard down in Texas did it. He siphoned off enough votes to give it to Lampton."

There was no arguing with Dad about the

subject. I can remember trying. "His electoral vote margin was quite large," I said once.

"We should have amended the Constitution long ago. The electoral college was a monstrosity from the outset—the one great mistake the founders made. They knew it was a mistake, but it was the only way to get a strong chief executive. So now we have that nineteenth-century mistake visited upon us in the form of Merrill Lampton. My God!"

I wasn't about to argue more. Dad was irrational and emotional about the President. Talk of Lampton hardly qualified as a political discussion. Dad was very emotional, very bitter, and his temper would flare. I quickly detected this and either ignored the subject, agreed with him, or at least did not argue with him. Uncle Richard either couldn't or wouldn't ignore the subject, and as a result their lifelong friendship was damaged. There were many arguments between them. It became a constant of their relationship. I remember one in particular. Uncle Richard had come out for the weekend. It was Saturday night, near Christmas, I think, because it was quite cold. We had a fire in the living room and sat there with brandy and coffee after dinner. Mother had had us all dress—amid complaints from Father. I suspect she hoped formal clothes would lead to more formal behavior between Dad and Uncle Richard. I remember her very well. She wore a pale pink gown, very soft and clingy. She looked particularly tiny and lovely, and I wished we could be alone. I could tell she did too. I thought maybe she'd come to my room that night. Not hardly, with Uncle Richard there.

All evening long there had been tension in the air. It was like waiting for the other shoe. Dad dropped it finally. "Well, Dick, have you seen old forty-four-point-two's latest?"

Uncle Richard smiled. With his square face and wide mouth, that could be quite a process. Most people were charmed by it. Father wasn't. "I assume you mean the President?"

"Who else? Your boy. Old forty-four-point-two."

"Don't you think you're wearing that joke a little thin, Brendan? He was duly elected—all quite constitutional."

"So was Hitler." Dad bit off the words and spat them at his best friend.

Uncle Richard stirred in his chair. I could see a slight flush come to his face. "I doubt if anyone—except you in your irrationality—thinks Merrill Lampton is Adolf Hitler. Tell me, Brendan, why do you hate him so?"

Mother said, "I doubt if Brendan hates him."

"But I do; I truly do. I hate the unprincipled bastard."

"I wish you'd find another word, dear."

"Carla, there are times when it is an accurate description. Oh, I'm sure he had parents. But bastard is the only way to describe his character.

271

Why do I hate him? I hate him for what he is. I hate him for what he's doing to this country."

"Okay. Fair enough. Let's take them one at a time. What is he that is so hateful to you? Most people consider him a decent, upstanding, God-fearing citizen. There has never been a breath of scandal about him. He had a wife for over twenty-five years, raised a family. I know for a fact that his grief at her death was genuine. He is at least a President who sets a good moral example—unlike some of your recent Democrats, I might say. So why is he so awful? Why do you hate him?"

Father had been waving his hand, as if trying to fan a breeze to blow Uncle Richard away. "My God, what stupidity. Has government in the United States been reduced to bedroom morality? Lampton is a good President because he's chaste—if he's chaste. Kennedy was bad because he engaged in bedroom athletics. My God! What absurdity. By that measurement Hitler was a saint. Children loved him. He made an honest woman out of Eva Braun before he died. What a saintly, Christian human being."

"That's nasty. A corruption of what I meant. A man's personal life is—"

"You want to know why I hate him? Because he's unprincipled. He has never stood for anything in his life but himself. He has no ideas of his own. No philosophy motivates him. He's an opportunist. He's the great me, the great I am.

Expediency is his god. He'll do whatever is required at the moment to benefit himself."

Uncle Richard laughed. "That's nonsense, Brendan, and you know it. Merrill Lampton has a consistent public record. His views are well known. They have been consistent for years, as governor of California, as United States senator, as President. Just because you don't agree with them, just because you don't like them, don't call him unprincipled, an opportunist."

That was, of course, true. Father knew it. He looked at Uncle Richard in undisguised disgust and sat down. Uncle Richard, smelling triumph, was not about to let up. "Merrill Lampton has been a true conservative. You may not like it, but his record speaks for itself. He has been for the free-enterprise system, for self-reliance, for self-determination, for minimal government interference in the lives of people, for law and order, for protection of people and property, for a strong national defense, for adherence to the principles that made this country great. He's against—"

"I know, the reverse of all the aforementioned. Please, spare me his campaign speeches. You're right. I was wrong. It was Nixon who was unprincipled and an opportunist. I'm afraid it is hard for men of my generation to forget that bastard. Yes, Lampton is principled. He is consistent. He is consistent in running this country to ruin."

Uncle Richard laughed.

"You ask why I hate him. Okay, I don't know. I admit it. I have a gut reaction. I see him or hear him, and I have the overwhelming sense of being in the presence of evil. Oh, I hear the words. But they are empty. He takes ordinary words, phrases we all cherish, and they come out twisted, evil. The man scares me. Frightens me to death. That's all I can tell you."

"That's some progress at least. You now admit you have no reason to hate him. You've just some kind of emotional thing. You don't like the way he parts his hair or something. Okay. I'm glad to have that straight. Now tell me how precisely he is ruining the country."

"For crissake. You and I've had this argument so many times—"

"Tell me, where is the ruin? He's balancing the budget, holding down inflation; profits are up. Is that ruination? Maybe not you, but some people call it good business. He's developed a sensible energy program. He's put the damned bureaucrats on the leash, cut their cherished spending programs, and started putting this country back on the road to sanity. The criminals are being locked up. The judges are stopping their coddling. People can start to go out at night again. Americans are starting to live honest, sober, hardworking, self-reliant lives again. And you call it ruin."

Now Father laughed, a false scoffing, guttural snicker. "Nine percent unemployment, inflation almost that high, and you call it prosperity.

Don't you have any idea how people live? You have to make four bucks an hour to barely rise out of poverty. There are millions of people in this country, in cities and out in the sticks, who barely have enough to eat. They can't afford to get sick. They have no hope anymore of owning a home, sending their kids to college. We have become a nation of haves and have-nots. And believe me, Dick, the nots are beginning to outnumber the haves. The whole thing is going to blow one of these days."

"Heavens, you've been saying—"

"Just one minute more. It's been going on for years. We've neglected the poor, the black, the young, the unemployed. Instead of jobs and opportunity, we've given them lectures on self-reliance." He tried to imitate Merrill Lampton. "I stand for what made this country great. For crissake, the frontier has been gone for a century. To tell people to work at nonexistent jobs, to tell them to shift for themselves when earnings after taxes barely put food on the table and buy rat poison and roach killer—I tell you it's an invitation to revolution. The history of the world tells us—"

"That's what you want, isn't it?"

"No, it isn't what I want or you want. That's what you don't understand. The revolution is already here. They just haven't held it yet. I can't stop it. You can't stop it." He pointed at me. "David can't stop it. Lampton can't even stop it—now. But I can tell you every time he opens his mouth to offer a pious platitude instead of providing butter, every time he offers a cushy couple of billions to his friends—energy program, indeed. Handout to the oil companies is more like it. Everything the man does makes it worse."

"Nonsense."

Father actually wasn't shouting. But it seemed like it. "No, Dick, it isn't nonsense. It's fact. Lampton had better buy a lot of guns. He'll need them. He'd better start filling the sandbags. He'll need lots of them."

He pointed his finger at Uncle Richard. "Lampton isn't dumb. He knows this. He's got the FBI and the CIA. He's even got his own goons, à la Nixon. He knows what's going on better than I do. Sometimes I think he wants it. Sometimes I think he wants the country to burn."

"You've lost your mind, Brendan. Your hate—"

"Maybe. Maybe. And another thing. I'm beginning to wonder about you. I've known you almost my entire life. You're my best friend. Let me ask you. What the hell are you up to? Lampton's your boy. You discovered him. You made him President. You are his brain trust. You're anything but dumb. You gotta know what I'm talking about. This country is facing a serious threat of revolution. Do you want—"

"I know nothing of the kind. All I know is I've been hearing talk of revolution ever since I can remember. We had the Weathermen, the

Minutemen, the SDS, the Yippies, the—what were they called, the Patty Hearst thing—the Symbionese Liberation Army. We had Charles Manson. Remember him? We had women's libbers, men's lib, gay liberation, every kind of goddamn freak, queer, lazy, shiftless crook, bomber, terrorist known to man. We've been blown up, bombed, shot at and threatened. The country's still here. Better than ever. What's so damned different about your particular set of revolutionaries?" He snarled the last word.

"I'll tell you what's different. They learned from just what you're talking about. They've gotten smart. They figured out a simple thing. There has only ever been one successful revolution in this country. These people are starting to use the same technique."

"What revolution?"

"I thought you might ask that. Everybody forgets. Dear old forty-four-point-two talks about it all the time, but doesn't remember it. *The* Revolution, 1776 and all that. These people have studied Sam Adams and Patrick Henry. Adams is their hero. They're following his pattern. They're getting organized. They're communicating. They're burying their differences in favor of a common cause. I tell you, Dick, it scares me to death. These people are prepared to fight. I spend almost my every waking moment trying to convince them they don't have to. But I wouldn't bet a nickel that the guns don't start one of these days."

277

"We'll be ready for them if they do. Better believe it."

Dad stood up. He looked at Uncle Richard and shook his head, very slowly, very sadly. "That's exactly what I'm afraid of. You're no better than they." He walked out of the room and didn't come back.

"I often wondered if you and Dad—if your friendship suffered by your disagreements over the President."

[Richard Morrison laughed.] "No, not on my part at least. Nothing could damage my affection for your father. And I don't think he changed toward me. If we talked about business or personal things, he was still my good friend." [He laughed again.] "It was just the President he couldn't stand. It was serious at the time—or must have seemed so to you. Brendan and I had disagreed on everything political and economic for years, our whole lives. This was the worst disagreement. He took it personally that I supported Lampton, liked him, worked for him. But our friendship wasn't damaged over it. The most that happened was we stopped talking about it."

"Unless you did ruin your friendship."

"I suppose. Your father was irrational about the President. No doubt of that. But he was right—we now know—about the revolutionary groups. I should have listened to him earlier."

"I thought you had."

"Yes, later. But not at first."

[Pause.] "Well, I'm glad to know you and Dad remained friends."

"Of course. I simply knew him too well to be bothered by his tirades against Lampton. I knew even then it wasn't all Lampton. Something was bothering your father, something personal. I didn't know what—still don't. He seemed to take his anger out on poor Merrill. Didn't you notice that?"

"No."

"I did. I've often wondered what was bothering him. Don't suppose you had any idea?"

"None."

My father was terribly proud of my success at St. Albans. He enjoyed going to the school, seeing me play, being the father of the star athlete and outstanding student. I did not always enjoy having him there. There were only occasional weekends when Mother and I could have time together. I lived for these. Most were ruined because Dad came along. I used to think it a cruel fate, a twisted irony— A week or two had gone by without my being with her. I was tortured by desire. I knew she was coming. I could barely restrain my anticipation. Then to have him show up with her unexpectedly. Cruel.

Much of my senior year was consumed with the choice of the college I was to attend. I was much sought after by colleges and universities. I lost count of how many letters and invitations and personal visits from campus representatives I received—or rather Dad did, for I put him in charge of it all. I hated it. He adored it. All of the Ivy League schools considered me one of their own, New England prep school and all that. Most of the Eastern colleges sought me, all three military academies, which was a joke, and a great many of the traditional football and sports universities, Penn State, all the Big Ten schools, even some from the Far West and South. I remember Notre Dame made a big pitch for me. The football coach virtually drooled at having a real fighting Irish named Callahan on his team.

All of that was dispensed with rather quickly. I simply said I didn't want to be a jock. I had done it at St. Albans. I'd been good at it. But I had never really enjoyed it. I might play football at college, then I might not. I didn't want to have to. I didn't want to be caught in some kind of athletic pressure cooker. Win or else. I wanted to go to some college where sports were deemphasized. If I played, I wanted it to be fun. In fact, I wanted to give up team sports. I wanted to concentrate on tennis and golf. They were useful. What good was football after college? I might run some track to stay in shape. But I didn't think I'd play football and basketball in college.

"I'm just not a jock." I remember saying that.

I was a little surprised at his reaction. He

beamed and got moist-eyed, put his hand on my arm, and squeezed hard. To my mother he said, "Isn't our boy something?"

"I've always told him he was something else." I saw her nearly imperceptible smile.

We were at dinner in the Brookton Inn. It was a warm, antiquey, very colonial room. A large log fire sizzled and crackled at the end of the room. Dad wore a turtleneck sweater and a heavy tweed jacket. I remember he looked too warm. His face was flushed. Mother looked radiant, although I can't remember what she wore. Probably white or blue. She usually did. She seemed tense. We both wished he'd just go away for a couple of hours. But I also suspect she was tense because she knew what was coming. They had talked this over on the way to St. Albans.

"I thought you'd mind, be disappointed."

"At your not playing college football? Heavens, no. Why should I mind?"

"I thought—well, you sent me here. You wanted all these sports."

"I did, true. I wanted you to have the experience, the rough and tumble, the comradeship, the exercise. Look at yourself, son. You've filled out, put on weight. You're confident, sure of yourself. You're in good physical shape." He laughed. "We have a beautiful boy, Carla."

She smiled. "Brendan, you're embarrassing him."

He wasn't and she knew it. But it was something to say.

"But you've had it, the sports. You did it. You were good at it. Now it's time to go on to something else." He paused. "You know, son, what I'm most pleased about are your grades. Your teachers, Father O'Reilly, all say you are the best student ever to go to St. Albans."

"You surprise me." I meant it.

"That I want you to be a student? I'm the one who's surprised—that you know me so little. I don't want my son to be an empty-headed jock. I want my son to be able to think and to care. There's a great big world out there. We need people who care about what is happening—to people, the world—and are able to do something about it." He smiled. "Here I am, making a speech."

"It's all right, Dad." Then I added, "I agree with you." I'm not sure I should have said that. I doubt if I meant it. I certainly did not come equipped with his sense of social consciousness. I didn't really like people. I sure didn't care about their problems. And hang the world. All I cared about was that blue-eyed loveliness across the table from me.

"So where do you want to go to college?"

I said I didn't know. I hadn't thought about it.

"Good. Take your time. With your grades, you've the whole world to choose from."

We ate a moment or two in silence. I had a feeling of tension. I could feel it arcing off my mother toward me.

"I would like, son, to make a couple of suggestions."

I tried to laugh. "I know all about your suggestions."

He laughed a little too. "What else can I call them? They're not commands. I'm not going to make you do anything. How can I?"

"Wishes?"

"Okay, wishes. I wish—I think you should go away to school." He said the words very fast, as though they were something distasteful and he wanted to spit them out quickly.

I laughed. "I didn't know we had a college in Westport."

"I'm serious, son. This is hard for me. I want you to go far away to college."

I looked at him. I tried to keep my gaze level. Curiosity was what I hoped I was registering. "How far?"

"Far enough so you can't come home every week—so we can't see you so often."

I knew I must not even glance at her. I didn't need to. I could feel what she thought. I could feel her fear. I kept my eyes on his. Then I looked down at my plate. I could hear the fire and feel its heat. I could hear a conversation at a table behind me. They suddenly seemed to be talking very loudly. They had no sense of privacy.

"Why?" I said.

"Dammit, David. This isn't very easy. It

283

sounds like I'm dispatching you somewhere. Getting rid of you."

"Aren't you?"

"No, no." He was very distressed. He couldn't seem to say what he wanted to. He sighed. "I'm trying to do what's best for you. Look, when I was your age, I was a lot like you. Son of wealthy parents. At home a lot. I even lived in the same house you do. When I was eighteen, I went to Yale. Four years. It was a great mistake. I never got away. I was home every weekend. I kept my old friends. I never had a chance to be away, be alone, develop in my own way. I was always under the influence of the family. It was a huge mistake."

I felt very calm, almost disembodied. My voice seemed to be someone else's. "Is that the only reason?"

I couldn't be sure. Did I imagine a hesitation?

"Yes."

"Am I too close to you?" I finally looked at Mother. The blue pools were very wide and dark and deep. "To her? Am I a mama's boy?"

"Don't be silly, son."

"Then why send me away again?"

"I told you. It's best for—" He tried to laugh. "Oh, forget it. It was just an idea. I'm spoiling our evening with it."

"What do you think, Mother? Should I go away to college—far away?"

She didn't answer. She just looked at me. I was unaware of her even blinking.

"I'm sorry. I really am." He was trying to jolly it up. "Have you developed a taste for brandy yet?"

I knew I shouldn't keep looking at her. Not with him there. But I couldn't seem to stop. Very levelly I said, "I think you're right, Dad. I'll look at some colleges further away."

I don't know why I did it. Not then. Not now. I didn't have to go. I could have told him anything. I could have said Yale or Harvard or Princeton were the finest schools in the world. It was better to get the best education and not worry about my character. I could have stayed close to home. We could have continued as we had at St. Albans. She knew it. We had a terrible fight over it. It was a month or six weeks later. I had been writing away to colleges for catalogs and applications: Notre Dame, Chicago, Berkeley, many of them. She had come up to Brookton and brought them. Getting her son out of class to talk about college was easy. We were in our room at the Inn. I knew she was angry. She hadn't said a word since picking me up at school. In our room, she took off her coat, reached in her handbag, pulled out the handful of catalogs, and threw them on the bed. They lay there accusingly.

"Are you so tired of me?" It was more accusation than question, said with more anger than self-pity or self-righteousness.

I said nothing.

"You'd better answer me, David." She did not raise her voice; she never raised her voice, but her anger was a coiled spring in the words she uttered.

"No."

"No what?"

"No, I'm not so tired. I'm not tired of you at all."

She pointed. "Then why these? Why are you so determined to get away from me?"

"I'm not. Dad wants it."

"And you always do what your father wants." It was not a question. It was mockery.

"No."

"Then *why*? Tell me. Just *why* are you doing this to me?"

"I can't. I don't know. It just seems the thing to do. I don't know why. I never know anything—"

"You know how to make me want you. I ache for you. What am I supposed to do? Become a nun?"

The thought was so ridiculous, I laughed. It was a mistake. She became angrier.

"Have you got a girl?"

I don't know what I said or did. The whole idea was so ridiculous. I suppose I smiled or laughed or something.

"Answer me. Have you got some little piece on the side? A nice young, sweet, understanding

piece of ass? Something better than me? Some
piece of trash you can really fuck?"

Her anger, her language, was so out of character I was stunned. But she misunderstood my
silence. She slapped me, right in the face. It
stung. She had hit me hard.

"Who is she? The bitch." She hit me again.
"How many times does she come for you?" And
she began to hit me with both hands, as hard as
she could, as if each blow was a punishment for
every time she imagined the nonexistent girl
had an orgasm with me. My face burned. I
grabbed her wrists to stop her. We struggled. I
could hardly hold her. Finally, she stopped resist-
ing. She stood there a moment, her eyes wide in
horror at what she had done and said. Very
slowly a moan escaped her, and she collapsed on
the bed, her body convulsing with sobs. It was
the only time I ever saw her cry like that.

I didn't know what to do. I stood there a
moment; then I sat on the edge of the bed and
put my hand on her back. She felt very tiny,
very fragile. I didn't know how to comfort her.
After a time, I said, "Mother. There's no one
but you. Never has been. Never can be." She
continued sobbing. Very slowly, unsure of what
I was saying, I began to speak of all she was to
me, all the treasures she offered me. "No one
knows this. Until now it was my secret. I lay
awake at night, every night, thinking of you,
your soft creamy skin beneath my hands, the
hard muscle underneath. Who would have a

body like yours? Who would have breasts as soft as yours? Whose would fill my hands so perfectly? Who would have that hollow in your thigh? Whose waist would be so tiny? Whose ribs so fragile? Who could take me so far inside and grip me so tightly? Who would shudder beneath me as you do?"

I guess I went on for a long time, talking of all we had done together. I got very passionate. I had never wanted her so much, or so it seemed at the time.

"I don't ever want to leave you."

She turned on the bed to face me. Her tears were rivulets on her face. Her eyes were red, swollen.

"Then why are you doing it? Why are you going away?"

"I'm not. Not really. It'll be just more distance. He's right—but not for the reasons he thinks. We're too close. You're there. I'm here. We're going to run out of luck. Sometime, when we least expect it. It's not me he'll harm. It's you. I worry for you." I stood up. I suppose I paced the room. "I do worry, you know. I do. Sometimes I think he suspects us, knows."

"He doesn't. I know he doesn't."

"All right. But he will, if I stay here. Oh, not here at St. Albans maybe. But if I'm in college and you drive up every week or weekend. He's no fool." I turned and stood over her, looking down at her. "We aren't as careful as we used to be. We're taking chances. Today is a risk. Right now. How many times can you go out shopping?"

"He's away. He doesn't know."

"What if he comes back and you're not there. Oh, Mother, don't you see? I've got to go away. Change the pattern. Allay his suspicions, if he has any. Reassure him. Make it different, safer." I sat down beside her. "You do see, don't you?"

"Then you're doing it for me?"

I smiled. "It's hardly for myself. I don't like to suffer that much."

By spring I had narrowed down my choices, filled out applications, and been accepted. I don't really know why I chose Hinsdale College in Ohio. I don't even remember where I heard of it. Someone on the St. Albans faculty, I suppose. It was a small school, supposedly very good academically. There was an intercollegiate sports program, but nobody seemed to care whether Hinsdale won or lost. It was as good a school as any. I guess my decision was based on location. It was far enough away to be distant. Yet close enough not to be on the moon. The interstate highways were nearby. It looked like an eight-hour drive or so. There were airports nearby. Mother and I could manage, at least once in awhile. I didn't even visit the place before I accepted.

I told them at dinner during my spring vacation from St. Albans. It was late April, beginning to turn warm. It was one of Mother's nights she had us all dress for dinner.

"I've decided on a college." I tried to say it casually. "Yes?" Mother's voice was expectant.

"Hinsdale. Hinsdale College. It's in Ohio, not far from Cleveland."

There was an expression in her eyes like she had been wounded. But she smiled and said something about its being nice.

Dad was pleased, particularly after I told him about its academic standing, deemphasized sports. I said I thought I'd like the intensive system. I explained how it worked, one course at a time. We talked about it, the college, what I'd study, all that.

Dinner was over and the coffee and brandy drunk when mother spoke. There was an edge to her voice. It wasn't exactly anger. More determination.

"There is something I want to say, Brendan. I'd like you to listen."

"Of course, dear." He gave her full attention.

"I have not interfered, Brendan. You wanted to send David away to Massachusetts. I said nothing. Now you want him to go away to Ohio."

"That's his choice."

"Oh, yes, maybe Ohio is, but you're the one who suggested he go farther away. All right, so be it. I'll not protest. But he's now almost eighteen. My son, my beautiful boy. He'll go off to college. I'll hardly get to see him. Then it'll be graduate school, God knows where, and a job and—" She hesitated on the next word as though it were hard to say. "—and marriage. I hardly get to see him now. Soon he'll be gone for good. I feel I'll never have seen him or known him or enjoyed him."

She had obviously rehearsed her speech well. It was a very convincing exposition of injured motherhood.

"Oh, Carla, we'll see lots of him."

"Just listen to me. No, we won't. He's going. He's almost gone from me now. I want—no, I demand, Brendan, that you give me one summer—just one summer out of my whole life with my son. I want to take him to Europe this summer." There was a touch of bitterness in her voice as she said, "Then you can have him. You can send him away if you want."

Father banged the table. "Carla, you're right. We'll all go to Europe this summer."

"No. Not you. Me. I'm selfish. I want my son all to myself. If you go, you and he will talk politics all the time. What fun is that?" She reached out and took my hand. "I want David and me to see the sights together. He can be my escort, my boyfriend." She laughed. "We'll be lovers—for one beautiful summer."

I was shocked when she said the word. I hoped I didn't blush. She laughed again, rather flirtatiously. "You're embarrassed. You don't want to be seen in Europe with your mother."

"Don't be silly. I'd adore being your—your boyfriend."

"And what about me? What am I supposed to do all summer?"

"It'll serve you right. All the days you've left me alone for years."

And so Mother and I went to Europe. If I were poetic, I might say—and so there came to pass the best of all possible summers. We poured over travel brochures, made elaborate plans, and then discarded them all. Most were for Father's benefit anyhow. We both knew how *we* were going to spend the summer, and it wasn't about to be looking at stained-glass windows and marveling at Rembrandts and El Grecos. We had our own marvels to perform.

We spent it in sunny climes, Spain, the Riviera, Italy. We intended to go to Yugoslavia and Greece, but we never made it. We flew from New York to Malaga. We had reservations at the Pez Espada in Torremolinos and drove there in a taxi. She took one look at its stilted ornateness and said no. We drove along the coast road until she spotted a small, flower-covered hotel near Fuengirola. We stayed there and a dozen other hotels on the Costa del Sol. All were small, intimate she called them, quiet, native, and near a beach. She adored Spain and hated to leave. But we had to. After a month we took the ferry to Marseilles then drove to the Riviera. Finally, we flew to Rome. It was the only large city we visited, and only for one day. We finished our trip at Sorrento and Capri. She adored Italy, too. She adored everything.

It was *our* summer. She kept saying that. And yet I think it was truly *her* summer. Mother was thirty-three, but no one would have believed it. She was at the height of her beauty. She glowed with health. Her energy was boundless. She was positively radiant. It was the only time in her life she ever truly surrendered her inhibitions. She did entirely what she wanted to do and when she wanted to do it. There was no husband, no one she knew. There was no need to maintain appearances. It was as though she had escaped to another world where no one knew her. She became entirely different, thoroughly uninhibited. She laughed a great deal—almost constantly, it seemed to me—and giggled and did silly things. She felt no restraints that summer.

Mother discovered that summer she had a gift for languages. She picked up Spanish amazingly well and learned quite a bit of French and Italian, at least as it was spoken on the streets. She adored doing anything native. She toured the markets, nibbling fruit and buying vegetables we never ate or clothes or souvenirs we seldom wore or kept. She adored the tiny restaurants and bars. In Spain, simply her presence in a bar in the evening would turn the men on. Their machismo would reach epidemic proportions. Some fellow would start the rhythm, clapping hands, clacking spoons. Someone would begin to sing. Mother would join in, slapping the table, clapping her hands with the beat, her body swaying. Soon she would be on the floor with me and others doing her version of the flamenco. The Spaniards—Italians, too—would go wild. More than once I feared a fight over her. But she always controlled it, because she'd never let a single one touch her, except me, not even her hand while dancing.

I could not blame the men for wanting her, for Mother was almost entirely sensuous that summer. And when she wasn't sensuous, she was lascivious. Her appearance, her expression, her every action that summer, conveyed to anyone with eyes to see that she was a wanton, a seminal vessel, probably totally depraved. And the impression was the measure of the fact. I think she thought of nothing else. She wanted it all the time, and there was no refusing her. Because we had time and were always together, there were not so many long, exhausting sessions. Instead, there was frequency. We made love every day, several times a day, many times a day. We'd be in our room, having coffee or wine, suddenly I'd be aware of her looking at me. "Again?" I'd say. She'd smile or nod or just take my hand. We'd be standing on the balcony looking at the sunset over the sea. Her hand would touch me. A few caresses. We were back on the bed. There were days we couldn't seem to get out of the hotel room. She'd see me watching her dress or combing her hair. The effort would be abandoned. I'd step from the shower. She'd be standing there waiting for me. If we were out on the street, at dinner, in a cafe, she'd take my hand or put her hand on my leg—or worse. It was the signal to go home. Neither of us had to say it.

We abandoned clothes in our room. They were an encumbrance, a waste of time to be always coming off. She virtually abandoned them on the street. She bought several outrageous French bikinis and wore them on the street, apparently unmindful of the cars she stopped or the people who stared. She relished her body, how it looked, what she could do with it. She went topless at St. Tropez. We went there only because she wanted to do it. We'd run together on various beaches, her breasts bobbing and dipping, hardly contained by her bikini. People would stare. Italian and Spanish men would even applaud and call to her in praise. She even got a little suntan that summer, the only one in her life. She was scared to death of freckles but couldn't help herself—and she didn't freckle. She bought every sexy outfit she could find. On the Riviera, it was sexy elegance. The night we gambled at Monte Carlo, she was dressed to the nines—or maybe undressed. Salome's last veil I called it. She called me John all evening. Or she would go out in the most outrageous getups. I remember one day in Spain. We tried repeatedly to leave the room. Each time one or the other of us would want to do it again. She had dressed three or four times. We would get to the door, once into the hallway. We'd stop, look at each other, and laugh. It was our joke for the day. Finally, late in the afternoon, after siesta, she got up to again dress. We *had* to go out this time. She reached for her panties and dress, threw them down in mock disgust, and put on my T-shirt. It was not a new one, very thin. Her nipples were the topography of the front. The shirt barely covered her naked bottom. She looked at herself in the mirror. "Yeah, that'll do."

"That?" I said.

"That. C'mon."

We went out on the street. It was in Fuengirola, maybe Marbella. We walked arms around each other, stopped to look in shops that lined the *paseo*.

"We seem to be attracting a lot of attention," I said. "Don't suppose it's you, do you?"

"It's you, darling, not me. But I know what to do about it." She broke from me and ran across the sand into the water. She came back with the T-shirt wet. It clung to her like wet tissue paper. Her pink nipples were clearly visible. "Is that better?" she said. We ate in a sidewalk café and went to Spanish bars that evening, her still in that getup. She drank a lot of wine and got a little smashed. She enjoyed the music thoroughly and danced a great deal. The bar was jammed. I thought the Spanish men were going to reenact the Spanish Civil War over her. When we finally left after midnight and were walking home, she wanted to do it there in the street. I said she had to be kidding. I'd take her home.

"No. Now. Here."

"The *Guardia*. They don't like—"

"If you won't do it, maybe they will."

She pulled the shirt off and stood there naked in the street. I grabbed her and pulled her into the darkness of an alley. We did it standing there in the alley. She declared she wanted to do her exercises, which meant a standing split and upside down. When I finally got her back to the room, my back was scraped from the rough stucco of the building I'd leaned against.

I remember times like this particularly; yet mostly we were very tender, very romantic, very much in love. We walked in the moonlight and listened to sweet music and laughed and enjoyed each other and our bodies. The summer nights of Spain were filled with the sweet odor of a flower, *La Dama de la Noche*, the lady of the evening. I called her that. My lady of the evening.

"You don't like the morning?"

We laughed. We could laugh and love at the same time.

"And noon," I said, extending the joke. "And siestas and teatime and dinner hour and happy hour and—"

"Quarter to two, and three-fifteen, and twenty minutes to four—"

We laughed ourselves silly.

"You poor, poor dear." She patted my face and tried to make a cooing sound. "I'm wearing you out, you poor thing."

"Who's complaining?"

"You'll get off the plane a poor, shrunken, wasted figure. Old before your time."

"And you'll bound off the plane full of health and vigor."

It was our joke.

It wasn't really a joke, but we made it one. I did become very tired. I have no great memory of sleeping that summer, although I'm sure we did. We both instinctively felt there was no time to waste on sleep. Both of us were constantly waking each other. I suppose it was a summer of cat naps. I did become tired. I couldn't keep up with her. She was sympathetic. "You want to rest?" she said once.

"I've got all winter for that."

She became very ingenious at arousing me. I'd lie there spent. She'd put on an act with clothes, dressing and undressing and parading around, for she knew that excited me. Or we'd simply talk, lying in each other's arms. She'd ask me what I liked about her body and get me talking about it. Or she'd tell me or show me what she liked about mine. Sometimes she'd tickle me and roughhouse with me. Once she poured wine all over me and began to lick it off. Once she put lipstick all over my penis "so I'd be pretty." I protested. She said she'd take it off—and did. She wanted to shave me—all over. Would I shave her? We did, then let it all grow back.

We tried not to think of Father and going

home. But we had to a little. He was dispensed with in occasional picture postcards and a dutiful weekly phone call. One overseas phone call came in August just as we were making love late one afternoon. She was scissoring me, as we had come to call her doing the split on top of me. Hardly losing a movement, she bent forward and reached the phone.

"Yes, operator. This is she."

She began to rise on me, gripping me tight, but pulsatingly.

"Why hello, dear. How are you?"

She swiveled her hips as she rose.

"Oh, we're fine. Having a wonderful time. Getting lots of rest—and sun."

At the word "sun" she had reached the end of me. She gave a particularly hard twist of her hips.

"You should see my tan. You won't believe it."

She remained at the end, swiveling her hips from side to side as hard as she could. I writhed in sweet agony.

"I'm sorry, Brendan. He went out. He'll be sorry to have missed you."

At "sorry," she plunged down on me. The bed creaked loudly.

"That? Some street noise. The window's open. They have a lot of donkey carts here. Make a fearful racket."

She was rising on me again, as before, a pulsating grip, swiveling her hips.

"Oh, soon, I think. He'll be coming soon. Very soon."

And as she punctuated her words with a savage twist of her hips, I came, and she plunged down on me, as hard as she could, and rose and down, and rose and down, and rose and down . . .

"Yes, I'm fine. Love it here—"

Her eyes began to close. Her mouth stayed open.

". . . Just a minute . . . Here he is now. He just came in."

She could barely say the words as she handed me the phone.

"Hi, Dad, just got in."

Both hands now free, she leaned on my chest and began to revolve her hips savagely. She arched her back and rubbed her pelvis hard against me.

He wanted to know if I was having a good time. "Marvelous," I said. "Truly wonderful. But we miss you."

Her mouth was open, framing the words, "Oh, my God." Her breath came in gasps.

"I'm not really sure when we're coming home."

He said he was lonely. Felt like a bachelor.

Her whole body writhed and shuddered, over and over, as she moved against me. It seemed forever that she came.

"Why, yes. I could ask her."

I was starting to come again. Oh, lord, what could I do?

"She must be in the bathroom. Hold on a minute."

I held the receiver at arm's length while we both shuddered in simultaneous orgasm.

She recovered first and took the phone.

"What's the date, dear? I lose all track of time."

I tried to move out from under her, but she wouldn't let me. She held me tight and began to scissor me again, holding my shrinking penis inside her.

"I want to stay till the first of September. . . . Yes, dear, I know you're lonely. . . . I'm sorry. . . . But this is the one gorgeous summer of my life . . ."

Somehow, the knowledge of summer's end, plus what she was doing, aroused me. I was hard again. The stirring in my loins began again, far away.

"Don't spoil it, Brendan. . . . I deserve this. I'm not asking much. . . . Yes, dear, I know; I miss you, too."

Pulsating. Swiveling.

"You are a dear. Much too good to me . . . what? Yes, I love you too, dear. . . . Goodbye."

To me she said, "Hang up the damn phone."

We stayed till the fifteenth of September, flew home from Rome, and had a single day to spare before I had to leave for college. Our last night in Capri we had dinner in a small café, drank wine, and felt sad and mellow.

"Will there be trouble for staying this long?"

She shrugged. "Not much, I hope. It'll work out." She smiled and took my hand. "Let's not talk about it. Our last night. Let's enjoy."

"Yes."

"Three full months alone with you. The one true summer of my life." Her smile was wan, her voice a little bitter. "To think my whole life was reduced to a single summer." She brightened immediately. "But what a summer."

"Can't you leave him, Mother?"

"That doesn't make much sense. Divorce your father? Marry you?"

"No, not marriage, of course. But we could live together. Sons live with their mothers all the time. Nobody thinks anything of it."

"Divorce your father? Live with you?"

"Yes. Why not?"

"Money."

"He'd have to make a settlement."

"About two cents a year."

"Who cares about money? We can—"

"Live on love? David, it's impossible."

"Why is it impossible?"

"We'd never get away with it, that's all. Never. So don't think about it."

"But why?"

"Because I'm married to your father. For better or worse. I'm not going to divorce him. I'll never get divorced. Never. We'll just have to make the best of it."

"Was that the real you that summer?"

[She laughed.] "I should hope not. Running around the streets nude—or practically."

"I thought you were beautiful."

"You would." [She laughed again.] "Look at me now. I think you're a nudist at heart."

"Only with some people."

[Long pause.]

"I try not to think of it."

"That summer? Why? I remember everything about it. It was the most wonderful summer of my life."

"That's just it. When you get to be—my age—"

"Thirty-nine."

"Don't remind me. At my age you begin to think of what might have been, if what you wanted was right, if you had been so smart, if maybe, just maybe . . ."

"I thought only men did that. The grass is greener, if only, all that nonsense."

"Women, too. This woman anyhow."

"And what would you have been?"

[She laughed lightly.] "That's my secret. A woman must have—"

"Oh, yes, mystery."

"It's hard enough to have any with you."

"A gymnast."

"No, I'd rather enjoy it. I wouldn't want to have to do it."

"A dancer of some kind. Ballet, maybe."

"Same."

"Hmm. A movie star. Every girl wants to be a movie star."

[She laughed.]

"A great international beauty. A femme fatale. A jet setter. A—what's her name—Jackie Kennedy. Rich, beautiful—or she was—style setter, photo in all the papers. Carla Callahan today wore . . . Carla Callahan today was seen. . . . Is that it?"

[Long silence.]

"You're not going to tell me."

"A woman has her—"

"—mysteries. How awful."

I went to see Mother's new house in Georgetown. It is not unlike our place in Westport, only on smaller grounds. I can't imagine what she is going to do with all that space. She was there meeting with an insufferable array of decorators. I imagine all this must be making a significant dent in Father's money.

Uncle Richard was there. Two things developed. He didn't think it too wise, just now, for me to be seen at Mother's house. People would talk. I'd begin to be noticed. I wanted to argue with him. What was I? Some kind of pariah from my own mother? But I said nothing. What's the use?

The other thing he said was to hurry up and see Squires. "Too much time is slipping by," he said. *He* thinks too much time is passing. Christ, I feel like my whole life is slipping through my fingers like sand. Mother is less than a mile away, moving into a house that I'm forbidden to visit. What a crazy world! Crazy, crazy. Mad, mad, mad. [Scornfully, he tried to sing a few bars of "It's a mad, mad, mad world," but he didn't know the words.] Hurry up and see Squires. God, there's nothing I'd like to do more. But Squires doesn't exist. If he's alive—and I'm not positive he is—he cannot be found. I talk to people who know him, but I can't learn a thing. One guy said today, "Callahan, I'd kill you for what you did, only you ain't worth it. It would only give your friends a chance to bust us and rough us up some more. But if I can't kill you, I can tell you to get the hell out of here and stink up some other place." Nice. Grand. I even went up to Boston to hunt Squires. I thought maybe he was hiding out with his wife in Roxbury. He may be, but it isn't where he used to live. The house is empty, all gone. Hurry up and talk to Squires. He's got to be kidding. Hurry up and find a needle—no, find a haystack with a needle in it.

My four years at Hinsdale were a total waste. I got nothing out of them. I suppose it might be said I got nothing out of them because I contributed nothing. But truly, what is there to be gotten from a liberal arts education? A smattering of knowledge? A love of learning more? Maybe, but that can be found a lot better and quicker. No, a college education is merely a dreadfully expensive and wasteful way to postpone life. All it offers is a largely worthless sheepskin as a badge that a person stood the course.

I was not at Hinsdale as at St. Albans. I simply didn't care. I seemed afflicted with terminal ennui. I slept a lot, ate, drank beer, watched a lot of television out of boredom. Periodically, I'd rouse myself, concentrate and do well in a course just to prove I could, but even then I didn't care.

I majored in political science, not out of any particular conviction, but simply out of the need to major in something. Actually, I enjoyed a couple of psychology courses more. I thought what I learned was nonsense, but there was at least some fun in recognizing the nonsense. Father was very pleased that I studied political science. That was one reason I did it. In truth, I felt I learned more about politics and government from him and his friends than all the courses taught by Professor Jenson.

Sports was a problem. In succession, the football, basketball, baseball, and track coaches discovered my record at St. Albans. There was a lot of pressure right from the beginning. "We've a great quarterback, Callahan. A real arm. Strong. Accurate. With you at end, we can sweep the conference." I said no. "Where's your spirit, Callahan? We need you." I said no. My would-be teammates talked to me in the dorm. "Callahan, why don't you try? We need you." I said no. The president of the college even made a trip East to talk to Dad. He came out. I said no. He put his arm around my shoulder. I must say he understood. As a result of all the pressure, I never played any sport at Hinsdale. I played a lot of golf and tennis. But I didn't try for the team. I played a lot of fooling-around touch football and frisbee and baseball. I enjoyed it. It killed time. Hinsdale needed a lot of time killed.

My biggest activity was meeting Mother. I'd drive six hours east to Stroudsburg, Pennsylvania, in the Poconos. Sometimes I'd leave early in the morning. Most often I'd drive at night, check into one of several motels, sleep a little, and wait for her to arrive at eleven or twelve the next morning. It was about a three-hour trip for her. We'd have the afternoon together. She'd leave about four to get home as if she had been shopping somewhere. I made that trip across Interstate 80 to Stroudsburg so often I knew every seam in the concrete. I came to hate it, just a level, double ribbon, a helix of mind-bending boredom. I tried not to, but I couldn't seem to help counting the mile markers, all three hundred of them across Pennsylvania, easily the largest, dullest state in the union.

Mother and I changed over those years. She began to have her terrible headaches. She'd appear in the motel room, her eyes shielded behind heavy dark glasses, the skin chalky white and stretched across her face, dizzy, weak from pain and fatigue. Her first orgasm would be very difficult. Sometimes I didn't think she'd ever make it. I'm not sure she enjoyed it when she did. It would be savage in its intensity. It seemed to wrack her with physical pain. She'd cry out and writhe and shudder and gouge my back till the blood ran. Each successive one would be easier; yet the whole four or five hours would be a frantic time of violent orgasmic activity. She seemed to need it so badly. It was as though I were giving her a fix to last the weeks until we were together again. Occasionally, she would spend the night when Father was away. By the second day she would be all right. It would be fun and experimental again. But that was not often.

It was worse during vacations when I was at home. She started coming to my room at night, once, then again, always unannounced, never very often. The risk was stupendous. I know how she did it. In the wee hours, two or three in the morning, she'd leave her bed. She'd leave the door to her room, and mine, ajar so as to minimize the noise of lock against latch. She'd pad down the hall past my father's room, her bare feet noiseless on the rug. I'd know she was there by her hand on my mouth for silence. There'd be a rustle of her nightgown being discarded. I'd glimpse her body in the starlight or occasional moonlight from my window. Then she'd be in bed beside me. We made love in the simplest possible way and in total silence, no whispers, very little movement, no moans or gasps, almost holding our breaths. Only the repeated shuddering told of what our bodies felt. Then she'd leave me as silently as she came, her lips having brushed mine in thanks. I thought then, and still do, that in our silence our lovemaking was never sweeter.

I lost my virginity at Hinsdale. Ha! Ain't that a laugh? Her name was Barbara—Barbara Kingsley. She was sort of the campus catch. Every small college, I suppose, has a girl everyone slavers over. She was tall, five-eight or -nine I guess, and statuesque with large breasts that made the rest of her look slenderer than she really was. Barbara was quite a big girl, a hundred and forty pounds and not fat. She dressed rather dramatically, lots of turtleneck sweaters, very formfitting, skirts and boots. She could get away with it because of her size and her posture. She carried herself well. Her posture was the most attractive thing about her. I had noticed her. She was in a class with me. But she didn't really do anything to me. Too big. Too much of her. No subtlety. Something. I was probably the only man on campus to have that opinion. A date with her was much coveted. There was much speculation about her in the dormitory. Her interest in the theater—she was in a couple of campus plays and hung around the stage a lot—only fueled her sexpot reputation. And she was very liberal politically. She was active in campus politics, always passing petitions for this and that. Several guys in the dorm regularly declared her a great lay. She was supposed to be very proud of her tits and liked them sucked on. I listened but said nothing. My dormmates reminded me of St. Albans. Older, but still kids.

She called to me across the campus. It was the fall of my senior year, I think. I stopped. She ran up to me, her breasts bobbing as she ran. She wore a dark orange sweater, brown shirt, and boots. It enhanced her long brown hair and brown eyes. She did look nice, running toward me. She wanted to invite me to a dance some weeks hence. It was "Sadie Hawkins Day." The girls turn, she said. Women's lib. No boy could refuse. I did. I never committed myself to anything. There were lots of reasons for this, but mostly I never knew when Mother might decide to fly to Ohio for a weekend or phone for me to meet her in Stroudsburg. Besides, the last thing I wanted was a date. And with her.

"You can't refuse. I'll pick you up at eight."

"I thought boys asked girls."

"Not on Sadie Hawkins Day."

I believe I thought something like fuck Sadie Hawkins and her day. My language, at least the language I thought, deteriorated during college. Instead, I protested that I just couldn't. I was flattered. Maybe some other time.

"Oh, no, you don't. You have to."

I sighed in total exasperation. I didn't want to be mean to her. Yet—

"Really—Barbara, isn't it?"

310

"You know damn good and well it is—David."

"Okay, that's phony. I'm sorry. Look, there are all kinds of guys dying to go out with you. You can have the whole campus—"

"Except you, right?"

"That's right. Why me?"

She laughed and tossed her hair away from the side of her face. "David Callahan, it is a statistical fact you've never had a date on this campus. You are the most gorgeous hunk of man in this godforsaken place. Yet, you never date. No one has known you to ever look at a girl with the slightest interest. You disappear regularly in your car for days at a time. You are too mysterious. I've appointed myself in charge of solving you."

Being asked to the dance by Barbara Kingsley made me a bit of a hero on campus, a status I would gladly have relinquished.

She came for me at my room in the dorm, and we went to the dance. She wore a long white gown that completely covered her; yet it was very formfitting and sexy. I thought she had style, if only she weren't so big and obvious.

The dance was a disaster, dim lights, lots of crepe paper, ghastly punch, dreadful music from a college band. She danced very close, rubbing herself up against me. I was more or less stunned by how big she was. In heels, she was almost as tall as I. Her waist seemed huge, her hips heavy. Mother was so tiny. I was dumbfounded by the sheer dimensions of her. She kept pushing against me. I couldn't seem to do much about it. Nor could I stop her from blowing in my ear and licking it with her tongue. I'd done that long ago with Mother in the den. Somehow it didn't seem very sexy now.

After awhile, she said, "I see your roommate's here. Let's go to your room. I'll meet you there. I'm going to the little girl's first."

I really didn't believe it, but I didn't know what to do. I went to my room and waited. I felt very guilty. I was being unfaithful. But I forced it out of my mind. I'd never had another girl. It was time. This one was supposed to be a lot of woman. I tried to think of her sexually. The sheer size of her. Maybe.

Somehow I didn't want to face undressing in front of her, buttons, studs, socks, all the paraphernalia of a tux. If she didn't come, I'd just go to bed. When she knocked softly on the door, I answered it naked.

"Well. You don't waste much time."

"Isn't this what you wanted?"

I took her coat and threw it across the chair.

"Shall I unzip you?"

"Kiss me a little first."

I took her in my arms. I just couldn't get over the size of her, the *size* of her, all of her pressed against my chest, not having to lean down to kiss her.

"I feel like you're measuring me, not kissing me."

"I'm sorry." I tried to kiss her better. Her mouth was warm and moist, not much else.

"Do you have a tongue?"

We did that for awhile. She ran her hand down my back, felt my buttocks. Her hand was cool, strangely small on my penis.

"Yes," she said.

"Yes, what?"

"Yes to both of your questions."

I tried to think what I'd asked. Then, I unzipped her. She stepped out of her dress and unharnessed her bra. She stood there in her panties.

I guess this was supposed to be the second coming. This was what turned all the boys on. Barbara Kingsley's boobs. They were massive, pendulous, with strangely small nipples, very hard.

I looked at her a moment.

"You like?"

I didn't say anything. I was a little awe-struck, I suppose. All this was only supposed to exist in magazines.

"Lie down."

I complied. She sat on the edge of the bed and smothered my face in her breasts. So this was what the boys liked. She was very adept at moving them around. She seemed to like it. She moaned in pleasure.

I pushed her away.

"Some one—Steinbeck, I think—once wrote

that the seat of procreation isn't in the mammaries. Take off your damn pants."

She seemed startled but did and lay on the bed on her back. I climbed on her, still unable to fathom how big she was. She wasn't really fat, but there was just so much flesh on her bones. She spread her thighs. There was no hollow. I went in her. I wasn't the first; yet she was surprisingly tight. She moaned as I began to thrust into her, but she didn't move. In awhile I said, "Don't you ever come?"

"I can't. You come. I like it."

"For crissake." I rolled off of her. She was surprised, hurt. "Don't you ever come?"

"I told you I can't."

"Never? How many guys have you had?"

She looked like she was going to cry.

"How many?" I said. "I'm not the first. How many?"

"A couple."

"For crissake, every girl knows how many. How many?"

"Ten."

"I'm the tenth?"

"Eleventh."

"You've never had an orgasm?"

"Not that way."

I shook my head and started to laugh. "Unbelievable."

She began to cry then and started to get up. I pulled her back on the bed.

"I'm not laughing at you. At them. They

crawl on you and squirt and call it sex. It's not your fault."

Very patiently I started to arouse her. She truly did like to have her nipples played with. She became very passionate. It was hard to get her to come. It took a long time. Position was the problem. Finally figured out she had to be on top. She was so heavy I thought I'd smother. It seemed to take her forever. But she made it. I did too, timing it to come just after her, although that was a bit of luck. It wasn't bad, and she cried a little.

"Why are you crying?"

"It was so wonderful. I never thought I could. I thought there was something wrong with me." She cried harder. "I'm so glad . . . so glad."

"Do you want to do it again?"

She laughed amid her tears. "No, no, I couldn't stand it."

She wanted to go back to the dance. I said that was stupid. She said we had to. People would talk. I swore.

She wanted to be my girl. I wouldn't. I told her I couldn't. It wasn't possible. I never explained why. I went out with her a little. We talked. I fucked her from time to time. It wasn't lovemaking. She got to be pretty good at it. I liked the way her long hair fell in my face. People called her my girl. She wasn't.

"Can't you love me, David?"

"No."

"Why, for God's sake? This is awful. Tell me what I do wrong."

"Nothing. You're fine. It's me, that's all."

"I love you so, David." She put my hand on her breast. "So much. In every way. There's no one since you. You're the only one who's ever . . . what's wrong with me?"

"Nothing. You're kind, generous—too generous. I like you. I like to talk to you. You're fun. You're company. You laugh. I just can't love you."

It was inevitable that she and Mother meet. Mother and I were walking near the campus. Actually, we were on our way to the car to go to the motel. Barbara called to me, ran up. I executed the introductions.

I don't know whether I don't remember what was said then and afterwards or whether I remember too much. The words are a jumble in my mind.

"Lord, your mother is gorgeous."

"Is that the girl you're fucking?"

"She's so young."

"Don't deny it. I know you are."

"She could be your sister."

"Yes, I am."

"Are you sure she's your mother?"

"You like those big tits. Shoves them right in your face."

"Yes, she's beautiful."

"I'm so happy to meet David's friends."

"It isn't that way, Mother. It just happened, that's all."

"And you like it?"

"You've got to be the best-looking mother I've ever seen."

"She does it."

"You're very sweet, dear."

"You're not being fair. I'm not the only one—"

"How often?"

"Is she a good mother?"

"I told you—that's different. He's your father."

"She's a wonderful mother."

"Once in awhile. A few times. I'm sorry. What can I say?"

"She sure is beautiful."

"Is she better than me?"

"Can I go to your place some time?"

"Not in your league. No comparison. Please stop it."

"No."

Dad was away a lot the summer I came home from college. He was gone for days at a time, and during one period of several weeks, he was home hardly at all. He'd fly in, stay a couple of days, and then leave again. Mother and I had a lot of time together. We made love a great deal, so much so that it lost its urgency. We had time to just enjoy being together and to talk a lot. Mother wanted to talk about Barbara. I didn't.

"Why not?"

"Why don't you talk about you and Dad?"

"Because it'll cause you pain. You'll be jealous."

"Okay, there's your answer."

"But I have to do it with your father. As little as possible, I might add. You didn't have to do it with her."

I remember sighing. Such logic. "What do you want to know?" I said.

It was late at night. We were lying in each other's arms in my room. There was a full moon, and its light bathed both our bodies. Suddenly she sat up and tucked her legs under her. She was very beautiful in the moonlight. I thought of the statue of the little mermaid in Copenhagen.

"Why did you pick her?"

"I didn't. She picked me. There was a dance where the girls invite the boys. She invited me."

"And you went."

"I couldn't get out of it very well. I tried, but there was no way short of making an ass of myself." I was already annoyed at this third degree. "Look, at school you got to go along with some things, or you're an absolute outcast. Then the problem's impossible."

She didn't say anything.

"We went to the dance. She was sexy. She wanted to go to my room. We did. That's all there was to it."

"Hardly all. Was she good?"

"No. She didn't know how."

She laughed at that. It sounded spiteful. "And you taught her?"

"Yes."

"Then she was good."

I sighed. "Oh, shit."

"Don't swear."

"I've heard you."

"I gather she was good. You kept going back for more and more."

Oh, Christ. "Mother. Barbara isn't—wasn't a very sexy person. She wanted to do it once in awhile. She enjoyed it. That's all there was to it."

"How many others?"

"Girls? Just her."

"Did you love her?"

"Of course not."

"Then why'd you go out with her?"

"Oh, Lord, I was lonely. I liked her. She was comfortable to be with." I sighed. "It was something to do, that's all."

"Did you like her big tits?"

"Could you use another word?"

"Boobies, breasts. What word do you like?"

"Not particularly. You can't do anything with them. I'm not a child anymore." I sat up, facing her in the moonlight. I put my hands on her shoulders, then reached down and cupped one of her breasts. "You're being silly, awfully silly."

"Did she love you?"

"She said so. I guess she did."

I saw her smile. "I can't blame her for that. She's got good taste." She held my hand against her breast. "It's just—when you get to be thirty-seven—you worry about younger—"

"Very silly." I pulled her down on the bed.

I guess the conversation did some good, for Mother seemed to be over her jealousy of Barbara. She was not mentioned very often, but when she was, Mother spoke of her almost affectionately. I remember once—it might have been that summer—Dad was kidding me at the dinner table—at least it was supposed to be kidding—that I never brought a girl home.

"Half the fun of being a father is getting to meet those sweet young things his son brings home."

I said something about not daring to bring them around him.

Mother said, "David had a girl in Ohio. I met her. Very lovely, very sweet."

Dad brightened immediately. "Really?"

"And very built. You'd have adored her, Brendan."

Dad wanted me to invite her for a visit. I lied and said I might sometime. But I won't. There is no point in ever seeing Barbara again. But I do think of her sometimes. She truly did love me. I think of her as very young, yet very womanly somehow, very soft, fleshy, comfortable, natural, elemental, a woman of the earth. We talked, although I don't remember what about. Yet, sometimes we didn't talk. We were just together in silence. I liked being with her. She was comfortable. I did like her—a lot. Making love to her—I mean sex with her—was strangely satisfying. She just enjoyed it. Or maybe she just enjoyed my enjoying her enjoying it. She'd lie in my arms, great inconceivable mounds of her. I felt very relaxed. All very strange, really. No great feats of orgasm. She'd come and I'd come; then we'd lie there, very relaxed, somehow satisfied. Very strange. I used to kid her about being so big. I'd tell her there was too much of her. She was gross.

"More than you know how to love anyway," she said once.

I'd tell her I was sorry. I liked her, but I couldn't love her. I was sorry.

The last time I saw her she said, "Your problem, David Callahan, is that you really do love me. You either don't know it or won't admit it."

"That's not so."

"Okay, so it isn't so. What *is* so is you made a woman out of me—a real live woman."

"A whole lot of woman. I'm glad."

"I don't know if *I* am. Now the problem is to find a man who—" she gestured toward her breasts, "—thinks—"

"The seat of procreation—"

"Exactly. I guess I'll just have to wait for you."

"Barbara, don't."

"Okay, okay. You've given me enough warnings. We'll see what happens."

Nothing happened. She went home to some town in the Los Angeles area. She has written a couple of times. I taught her how to live. She's determined to live life to the fullest, to get involved in important things that are larger than herself. She wants to make some mark on the world. Crap! Sounds like Dad. I never answered either letter.

I talked to Sam Dan Cooper tonight. He is apparently the only leader of the Liberty Party not in hiding. Even Lampton can't touch the latest savior of the black folks. I saw he was making a speech here in Washington. I went. There were undercover cops and agents all over the place, so he made one of his less inflamatory speeches. Lots of talk of unity and liberty. It had one meaning to the audience but couldn't lead to his arrest under the Freedom of Information Act. Very cleverly done. I detected Ephraim Squires's hand.

I shoved my way forward after the meeting and virtually forced Cooper to talk to me.

"I know what you want," he said, "but it's impossible. He won't see you. He doesn't trust you. Can you blame him?"

"No. But he doesn't understand. It wasn't my doing."

Cooper smiled. "Whatever you say, man."

"Doesn't he need money?"

"Bread is always welcome."

"Okay then."

"Give it to me. I'll see that he gets it."

I laughed. "And I don't trust you, Dan." On impulse, desperate for anything, I said, "I'll give it to Edna."

"How much?"

I had intended twenty-five or fifty thousand. I didn't want this chance—if it was a chance—to slip away. "Hundred grand," I said.

He arched his eyebrows and walked away.

* * *

It is probably a matter of no importance—I can always take this out when I edit the manuscript of the book—but a man came to the door a little while ago. He said he was from the British Office of Immigration. He wanted to check my passport. I left him standing in the foyer while I got it. All very routine, he said. And it seemed so. But I'm bothered by one thing. He said he was checking on the status of those registered with the American embassy. Quite a number of them, he said. All routine. Quite thankless. Trouble is I never bothered, quite deliberately, to register with the American embassy. I don't like registering with anything I don't have to, particularly now. It is, as I say, probably nothing, but still it seems strange.

Today was some kind of day. I'm not sure I want very many like it. It began with a phone call a little after eleven this morning. A male voice said, "Callahan?"

"Yes."

"O'Briens. One P.M. Be there."

O'Briens is a large, popular, and busy watering hole off Sixteenth Street in downtown Washington. At one in the afternoon it was a mob scene. I had no idea whom I was to see there, but I had hopes. I saw Edna in a booth with two black goons. As I approached, she spoke to them and they left. I sat down.

"If it isn't pretty boy," she said. "God's joke."

I said nothing.

"You've been making lots of noise about seeing someone."

"I've been trying to."

"Well, stop. You aren't going to."

"Why?"

"You know why."

"It wasn't my fault. I didn't know it was going to happen. I was suckered."

"And the sun rose in the west."

"Believe me, I had no idea they were going to kill the agent."

"Who're they?"

"I can't tell you."

She shrugged, the same as always. "At least you admit it was they."

She looked terrible, more sallow than ever, her complexion more pockmarked, her clothing particularly illfitting.

"Do you want a drink?"

"I don't drink."

"May I have one?"

She shrugged.

I ordered. There had to be some way to get through to her. I felt this was my only chance. "How is he?"

"As well as can be expected."

Damn her. "How's Gloria?"

"You're way out of date. Gloria is long gone. She bored him. They all do, but me. Gloria was succeeded by Alicia. Now gone too. Now it's—" She smiled. "Big tits. Great big tits. Turns him on."

"And that turns you on?"

She shrugged. "Why not? Where's the money?"

I had in mind demanding to see Squires before I gave it to her. But at that moment my drink came. In that process I had an impulse.

"Did anybody ever fuck you just for yourself?"

She laughed. "Who'd you have in mind? You? God's joke?"

"I'm awful sick of that."

"What?"

"That God's joke crap."

"Aren't you, pretty boy?"

"No, I'm not." I was quite angry at her taunting. "At least I wouldn't have to suck somebody else's tit while fucking you."

I saw her flush a little. "You wouldn't be able to get it up."

"Try me."

She smiled, a scornful smile. "I wouldn't want to hurt you, pretty boy. I'd bust your balls."

"You do talk a lot."

"Where's the money?"

"It'll cost you."

She laughed. "You mean it, don't you?"

I started to get up. "Let's go to my place."

"Not on your life."

"Where?"

She started to say something, then stopped. She looked at me intently. "I believe you mean it." She shrugged. "Oh, well, it'll be fun to see pretty boy flop. The great lover. Ha. Go across to the Statler. Get a room. I'll meet you there."

"Not on *your* life. You're coming with me. Tell your pals to wait."

We went into the hotel. I got a room, and we went to it. We were hardly inside when she disrobed. She had a very bad figure and wanted to flaunt it at me. She was very thin and bony with square shoulders and hardly any breasts. She should have been a boy. About her only redeeming feature was good legs. They were very thin.

I saw the hollow between the muscles of her thighs.

"I tried to tell you. Let's see you get it up, pretty boy."

"Do you want a drink or something?"

She laughed, scornfully again. "I knew you wouldn't be able to."

I touched the hollow in her thigh. I felt her tremble slightly. "I like that," I said.

Quickly I got out of my clothes.

"At least you're pretty to look at. That's something." She looked at my limp penis. "And nothing else."

I kissed her. She might have been wood. "You don't make it very easy," I said.

"Why should I?"

I truly was filled with panic. I had to do something. I had to concentrate. I sat on the edge of the bed, pulled her to me, and mouthed her breasts. "The boobs don't matter, Edna. It's the nipples." I caressed her thighs and hips and bottom and felt her trembling, a little, then more and more. Her arousal aroused me.

"You son of a bitch."

"Lie down."

"I'll fix you. I'll bust your balls."

The circular motion of her hips was apparently involuntary when she was aroused. And when I went in her, it was like being thrust into a hot wheel revolving around me. For a second I thought I'd come. But I'd had long practice, years of practice. I thought of Mother and silently repeated to myself, "Hold . . . hold . . . hold . . ."

"You son of a bitch. You goddamn . . . s.o.b. . . ."

Her motion increased. Hold . . . hold . . .

Then it stopped, as she shuddered and jerked in her orgasm "You bastard . . . you fucking bastard . . ." she said, over and over. I knew I had her. I had won. I kept thrusting into her, again and again, holding off and holding off. Slowly her hips started their revolutions. Faster and faster, while her mouth streamed out obscenities. Then moans. Again she came.

A third time. And a fourth.

"Come, you fucking bastard. Goddamn you, come."

I wouldn't. She tried to pull away from me. I held her arms and banged away at her. I felt her strength ebbing. She was moaning. Almost crying. "God. Please. Come."

"Say now."

"Oh, God, anything—now."

"Am I God's joke?"

"Oh, Lord, please . . ."

I pushed faster into her. "Am I?"

"Oh, no, no—please."

"Say now."

"Oh, God—NOW!"

And I came, repeatedly, again and again. I had no idea what my record was, but I was determined to break it. And it wasn't passion I squirted into her. It was venom, my hatred for her, for Squires, for all of them, for my situation, my goddamn beastly fucking, miserable, shitty situation. My rage was boundless. Again and again, time and again, I banged at her with all my might, and she, spreadeageld on the bed, was compelled into orgasm after orgasm. When it was over, I got off of her, went to my coat, and got the packet of money and threw it on the bed beside her. "Tell Squires that's from God's joke."

She lay on the bed a long time, then slowly got up, went in the bathroom, then came out and dressed. She left the money on the bed. At the door she said, "I can't take it. Not now. I'll see that you give it to him."

"Edna, you're more beautiful than you think." She said nothing. "You turned me on. Just you. Just yourself."

She stood at the door, her hand on the knob, and looked at me a long moment. I could not read her expression, except that she looked softer, less pugnacious. "Where'd you learn to do that?"

"What?"

"Hold off like that. Come late."

"From someone."

"She's a lucky lady." She smiled. The scorn was gone as she said, "See ya—pretty boy."

* * *

329

I have twice had visitors today, and I perceive that I am in a very serious situation. This morning two inspectors for the general post office came to the door. They wanted to see my television license, they said. Just a routine check. It was raining, and I had to invite them in. They stood in the doorway while I retrieved my license and showed that the tax on my set was paid up to date. Unfortunately, my work table with tape recorder, this manuscript, and other associated papers were in plain view. The tapes themselves are filed in a cardboard box. Hopefully, they did not see them.

I was not unduly alarmed by this visit, although it was the first time in all my years in England that anyone had ever asked for my license. I'm also certain my tax status could have been obtained at the post office. Such a visit could have hardly been necessary.

The midafternoon visitation was more alarming. When the bell rang, I hurriedly looked out the window. Two men at the door, a telephone company lorry out front. Hurriedly, I shoved the box of tapes out of sight behind the sofa, then spread some blank pages on top of my manuscript and transcription. When I opened the door, one of the men said he had come to give me a new telephone.

"I really don't need one," I said. "It works fine."

"I know, sir, but this is a new model. We're discontinuing the old one."

I tried to act impatient. "I really can't be bothered," I said and tried to close the door.

"Truly sorry, sir, but it's orders." They quite insistently pushed their way inside. "It'll only take a moment."

There was no way to stop them. While the one man went about replacing the telephone, the other seemed inordinately interested in my work table.

"You writing a book, sir?"

"You're an American, aren't you?"

"Me? Heavens, no."

"Your accent sounds American."

He laughed. "Oh, that. I lived in Canada awhile. Guess some of it rubbed off."

I hardly believed that.

"What's your book about, sir—if you don't mind my asking."

"I'm writing a monograph about my adventures with the African pygmies. I spent some time there years ago."

"Really? That should be interesting." He showed no willingness to pursue the fascinating topic. "Mighty nice tape recorder you got there." He peered at it closely.

"Yes. I recorded some of the African languages while I was there."

The replacement of the phone was finished, and they left. It had all been plausible, and yet I am concerned, yes, frightened. Still, I tell myself there is no way they could have traced David's tapes to me. It just isn't possible.

I have worried about this for some time, and I've reached the following conclusions. I had better think of a safe place to hide these tapes and all these materials when I'm not working on them. More importantly, I'd better work night and day and finish this book. When it's done, I'm going to take a long trip to the South Seas. I'm tired of this English winter. The chill is terrible.

More than two weeks passed before David saw Ephraim Squires. He recorded his thoughts almost daily. I have telescoped these in the interests of readability and what I now concede is speed.

* * *

I sometimes think I am living my whole life in the future. It seems to me I've always been looking forward to, waiting for, something that is *going* to happen, maybe, someday, hopefully, with luck in the future—the end of a school term, being alone with Mother for a few days, a few hours. Here she is ensconced in an overpriced home not more than a mile away. I sit here, waiting for the phone to ring, to hear her voice saying she will be right over. It is always her choice now. Gone are those happy days when she was there whenever I wanted her. I want her all the time now, more than ever before.

She has changed. It is so subtle that some-

332

times I'm not sure of what I perceive. She is more elegant in her dress now. Her fur coat or a fur wrap is more in evidence. The clothes are more expensive, more formal, less casual. She takes more pains with her makeup. She is more beautiful than ever, but it is more studied. It is hard to describe, but she seems more turned on. She is already being talked about as the new hostess with the mostest. Her "small but brilliant" parties have made the society pages. She is the "beautiful Georgetown hostess" and the "gorgeous blonde widow twice seen at White House parties." She seems to enjoy the celebrity status, the best tables, the courteous greeting from the headwaiters, the stir she creates. She has changed.

She visits me here once a week, occasionally twice. We make love. But it's different, or do I imagine? Sometimes it seems to me that it is more for me and less for her. She asks me to hold off less and sometimes not at all. She seems more easily satisfied, more ready to quit. I asked her about it. She laughed and said after all she wasn't as young as she used to be. It makes sense. I believe it is so. I also believe that once I'm done with this Squires thing and have moved in with her, ours will be a good life together. She constantly says so. I do believe it.

Squires. I had about despaired of seeing him. My afternoon as stud for Edna must have been wasted. For two weeks, I'd hung around the apartment, hardly daring to go out for fear the phone would ring or someone would come to the door. Finally, sick of it, I went out to dinner a few blocks from here. As I was walking home a little after ten, a car pulled up to the curb, and I was told to get in. I did. I saw only that it was a compact car with three men already inside when tape was slapped over my eyes and plugs thrust into my ears. I could feel what must have been dark glasses being fastened over my taped eyes. Unable to see, hardly able to hear, I had to rely on feeling. I tried to remain calm and concentrate, but the route was impossible to follow. We seemed to stay in town. There were many turns, many stops, for what must have been lights. It was very circuitous and seemed to go on forever. If the intent was to give me a ride, to lose me, it worked. When the car finally stopped and I was pulled out, another seige of walking began, in and out of buildings, up and down stairs and elevators, through passageways. Finally we went through a series of doors. I was pushed into a chair. The glasses came off, my ears were unplugged. The tape was painfully ripped from my eyes, and I was in blinding light.

Actually, the room was not that brightly lit. It was just that my eyes were having trouble adjusting to light again. In a few moments, I was able to see that I was in a basement room, windowless and low ceilinged. There was an array of pipes and heating or air conditioning ducts. There were perhaps a dozen men in the room.

Several carried rifles or shotguns. I saw at least two submachine guns. Squires sat at a small table, facing me. Perhaps a half dozen feet separated us. It was about the only empty space in the small room. Edna was standing to his left. She wore another drab brown sweater and skirt. She was looking at me. It seemed to me her features had softened. I saw no signs of her old baiting of me.

"Edna tells me you're a pretty good stud."

Squires had changed, radically so. He now had a long, vivid scar running down the right side of his face from the temple to his chin. There was an apparently permanent angry purple welt under his left eye. He looked ghastly. I'd heard he had been beaten badly. I had no idea it was this bad.

"I'm sorry," I said. Involuntarily my hand touched my own cheek as if I were touching his scar.

"It don't matter, Callahan. You were just doing your job."

"No, I wasn't. I had no idea."

He laughed. The cruelty which had been done to his face seemed to affect his voice, his laugh, his artificial, distorted smile, his whole personality.

"You're a lousy liar, Callahan."

"I'm not lying."

"Okay, you're the epitome of truth. But the fact remains you told me about the FBI guy. He got himself killed—but not by any of us. Your boys—"

"They're not my boys."

"Excuse me, federal agents—" He snarled the words, making them drip with ridicule. "—tried to pin it on me. They knew they couldn't. But it gave them a chance to hand me over—what the hell. You know all about it. I saw you there."

"I told you. I didn't know. I was used as much as you."

He forced a smile. "It don't matter none, Callahan. I never was much to look at."

I wondered why he was trying to fake ghetto talk. He was too educated to be any good at it.

"Like I said before. Edna thinks you're a pretty good stud."

I said nothing. Her face was expressionless.

"Would you like to give us a little demonstration of your technique?" He and several of his men laughed at that. "You wouldn't? Too bad. I might have learned something. Never can tell." More laughter. "Now Edna has her talents. I'll admit that. She's got a rubber ass. But I got me a new number. Somethin' else. You better believe it." He looked around. "Where'd she go? Where's big tits?"

Somebody said she'd run out of the room suddenly.

"What she do that for? Go get her. I want to show her to my friend, Mister Callahan."

Someone left the room to find her.

"She's gonna be our new Miss Liberty. We

got her all fixed up, waitin' for you to get here. We're gonna take her picture and use it to inspire all our troops."

A door opened behind me and I heard steps.

"Here she is now. Miss Liberty herself. A little applause, boys."

There was enthusiastic handclapping and cheering. She stood to his right wearing a black raincoat.

"What you got that coat on for, honey? Take it off. I want Mr Callahan here to see your costume."

She said no and seemed to beg him with her eyes. But he reached up and started to rip off her coat. Reluctantly she removed it. She was nude to the waist. Her large and beautiful breasts had been painted in concentric circles of red, white, and blue. She wore the flag draped around her as a skirt. She carried small American flags in each hand. She tried to cover her breasts with these.

"Wave the flag, honey. Show him how you wave the flag."

She waved the flag.

It was Barbara Kingsley.

"Wave the flag higher, honey." As she did so, he pawed at her breasts, smearing the paint that had been on her nipples.

What can I say? How can I possibly describe the look in her tear-filled eyes? Impenetrable shame. I don't know how else to say it. And her shame was no more than mine, sitting there, watching her being humiliated, doing nothing to save her. He kept on pawing her breasts; then he pulled her closer to him and mouthed them, the paint making a garish streak on his face.

"I'll bet you never saw a set like those, eh, Callahan?" Finally, he released her. "Well, no matter. Did you bring the money?"

"I didn't know I was being brought here. I hardly carry that much money around on the streets."

He laughed. "Come the revolution, there will be no more crime on the streets." He laughed harder. "'Course, nobody will need that much money. Well, no matter. We got plenty of money. Exactly what do you want to see me about so bad, Callahan, bad enough to try to bribe me with a hundred grand?"

I forced myself not to look at Barbara and to concentrate on his face. It was to me now the most sadistic I had ever seen.

"I came to ask you what you want. What you need."

"Christ, Callahan, are you still trying to play that revolutionary benefactor bit? That was your old man. You're not even a wart on his ass."

I was consumed with rage at him. Yet I knew I had to control it.

"I'll not shit you, Squires. I'd love to see you dead. I'll do nothing to help you. I come from your enemies. I am their emissary. I am to ask you what you want?"

He laughed, or was it a snarl? "Now that's a

new twist. What do I want? What do you mean, what do I want?"

"I don't know."

"Do you mean peace terms, surrender?"

"I don't know."

He laughed again. "You sure are some hot-shot emissary, Callahan. You don't know nothing."

I said nothing. He seemed to think for a moment.

"Okay, Callahan. This is crazy, but I'll go along. What I want is guns. Lots of guns—and ammunition." He leaned back in his chair and jerked a rifle out of one of his men's hands. "I don't mean pea shooters like these. We got these. I mean real guns—recoilless rifles, mortar, bazookas, antitank guns, antiaircraft missiles. The whole works, ammunition, everything. Explosives. Lots of explosives. It's gonna be war. This country's gonna burn." He slammed the rifle down on the table. "Mr. Emissary, you tell your people that."

I felt I was looking at both a madman and the personification of evil.

"All right. How do I get in touch with you?"

He laughed. "You mean you're gonna give me guns?"

"I doubt that very much. But you'll get some kind of an answer."

"Okay, I'll go along with the gag. It won't

hurt for them to know I mean business. You got a week. Same time, same station."

"Do we have to go through all this rigamarole of getting lost in downtown Washington?"

"Good thinking. It just wastes gas. Edna will call you. She's practically your girlfriend anyhow." He thought that very funny. "Now get him out of here."

As the tape was going over my eyes, I heard him say, "How's your society mama, Callahan? Suppose she'd like a crack as Miss Liberty?"

I feel intractable sadness, irrevocable loss. I've had several drinks and will have several more, but I know they won't help. All will probably be better in the morning when I phone Uncle Richard. I'm just tired, emotionally empty. On that drive here from their hideout, sitting in the back seat of the car, unseeing, unhearing, I was consumed with rage. If I could only have gotten my hands on Squires, I would have happily, joyfully, choked the last snickering breath out of him. I would have choked him until that evil, leering face turned to pulp in my hands. In the darkness I had an indelible vision of Barbara forced to stand there, half naked, her eyes filled with tears, looking at me while he pawed and mouthed her breasts for all to see. I could kill him, and I will. Somehow, I don't care what it takes, I've got to get her out of there.

Now I find it hard to believe it really was her. How did she get there? Was she abducted, drugged, forced to join them against her will? I don't know. Did she change somehow? Did she fall for that revolutionary bullshit and join them? Does she like that sexual humiliation? Was she crying only because I saw her? Oh, God. It's all my fault. I know it is. She loved me. She truly did. And I couldn't love her. How could I? Even now if by some means I could get her out of there, what would I do with her? Marry her? Can I love her now? Take her home, take her anywhere away from Squires and that obscene place? But how can I? What can I do?

You're beautiful, Callahan—a beautiful mess. You can't even make the simplest decision. You are a blob of jelly—a jellyfish tossed on the waves of circumstance. And what beach will you end up on to dry and die in the sun? Oh, lord, you are full of shit. David Callahan, big blob of shit.

I have spent nearly a year running after lame-brained, so-called revolutionaries. I have been abducted, threatened, ridiculed, scorned, and humiliated. I have even fucked a woman I thoroughly detest. Why? I don't have to do this. I'm young, intelligent, educated. I have plenty of money. I don't ever have to work in my whole life. So what am I doing, wallowing in all this filth? I'm supposed to be saving my country. I'm supposedly making some great noble contribution by keeping Merrill Lampton in the White House. And that is the original harebrained scheme if one ever existed. There isn't a prayer. And who cares whether he does? All I care about is an end to this, going back to Connecticut, and living with Mother. Uncle Richard can go hang his schemes. Tomorrow— today, really—I tell him I finished my job. I just resigned.

Lord, it's late. I got to go to bed.

[There is no break in the tape, but obviously David turned off his machine and then some- time later—I don't know how long—came back to it.]

I can't sleep. I lie there. All I can think about is Squires with Barbara. The mere thought of him touching her, mouthing her breasts while he fucks Edna. It fills me with loathing and hatred. Squires. He has brought nothing but evil and pain into my life—and death. It was Squires who really killed Father. No, I killed him. I know I did. But, goddamn it, if there had been no Squires, it would never have happened. If Squires had not existed. If Dad hadn't known him. If Dad hadn't invited him to the house. If Squires hadn't been putting on his disgusting exhibition with Edna and Gloria. I might have stayed awhile. The fight might have been over by the time I arrived home. I wouldn't have heard it. If I hadn't heard—oh, Christ, if, if, if.

I heard them fighting as I came through the door from the garage. Both were shouting. The mere sound of it shocked me. They rarely fought and never shouted. Mother just wouldn't do it. Now she was screaming at the top of her lungs. Her voice sometimes broke, inadequate for the air she tried to force through it.

"How could you bring them here? Scum. That's what they are."

"They're human beings—just like you and me."

"They're human maggots; that's what they are. Filth. *Filth*. Goons standing around with guns. In my house. This very room. How could you?"

"They didn't have guns."

I heard her laugh scornfully. "I suppose those were slingshots bulging under their arms. How could you? Don't you dare ever bring anybody like that here again."

"Who in the hell are you to tell me what to do, you . . . you . . . ." He never finished saying what name he had in mind.

I stood in the kitchen, listening. I felt paralyzed. I didn't know what to do, leave them be or try to stop it.

"That beast. How could you bring that creepy bastard here? Plotting revolution, here, in my house, trying to destroy me, while you sit there approving it, adoring the filthy creep."

He stuttered in rage, but managed to say, "What makes you so high and mighty? Who the hell do you think you are?"

"Someone who knows shit when she sees it. That's what he is, shit, shit, shit."

"You ought to. You were in the goddamn gutter when I—"

I heard her slap him.

"Don't you hit me."

"Stop it. You're hurting me."

That's when I burst into the room, consumed with rage. They were in the living room. His face was red, and he had her by the shoulders, shaking her. I lunged at him and pushed him away, hard. "Take your hands off her." He stood there glaring at her and me, his face still livid with rage.

Mother, now with an ally, wouldn't let it be. "Your creepy friend. Your savior of the masses. Leering at me all evening. Pawing me. He wanted me to go to the motel with him. How do you like that?"

Father stammered. Nothing would come out except, "So what?"

I joined in. "It would have been grand." I told them what I'd seen, Squires slobbering over Gloria while fucking Edna. I used those words and worse.

Mother still wouldn't let it go. "Now, *now*, what do you think of your fine revolutionary creep? Tell me just what?"

Father tried to laugh, but it came out a dry rasp, deep in his throat. "You two should talk."

Dead silence.

Mother's voice was icy cold. "Exactly what do you mean by that?"

"It's too late for righteous indignation, Carla.

344

I know about you two. Mother and son. For Christ's sake. I've always known about it. I've tried everything—"

"You bastard. You unmitigated bastard."

"Oh, sure, deny it. Go ahead. I can't prove it. The last thing I want is to prove it. But I know. I've always known. So don't either of you talk to me about motel rooms. Don't give me that leering and pawing horseshit. Don't give me your goody-goody righteousness. Just spare me your phony virtue, your high and mighty horseshit, Carla."

I remember the three of us standing there in silence. I have no recollection of how she looked or how he looked. I remember only saying, "I'll be leaving in the morning," and going to my room.

I wish I didn't remember what happened next. I wish some kind of Freudian blockage had occurred so the memory of that night would be forever suppressed from my consciousness. But I do remember. Everything. And I suppose I have to tell it.

I got in bed but couldn't sleep. I lay there, quite rigid, hardly moving. The waning moon rose outside my window and bathed my bed in pearly light. I had no idea of the passage of time, other than the rising of the moon. Somehow I couldn't move, turn my head, and look at the clock.

I remember being consumed with hatred for him. I concocted the most diabolical plots to do away with him so I could possess my mother. I'd sneak into his room and plunge a knife through his heart, then make it look like burglars. I had no knife, no gun. I'd strangle him. I could feel his rubbery throat in my hands, Mother in the doorway to her room, laughing, telling me to go on.

In time, this nonsense ended, and I began to think more clearly. I'd leave in the morning. Uncle Richard would help me get a job in Washington. He was a friend of the President. I'd get a job in the White House, maybe Congress, somewhere. It wouldn't be hard. I'd set up an apartment in Washington. Mother would come and live with me. She'd have to. She couldn't stay with Dad now. Oh, it would be good. I'd have a job, my own money. I'd be free of him, my own man. I'd have her every night. We'd sleep together. No one would ever know. It would be wonderful, heaven. Practically married. When I was thirty, I'd come into grandmother's trust. There'd be plenty of money. Screw him. I went over it again and again, what I'd say, what she'd say, the helpless expression on his face, what would happen, how wonderful it would be to be free.

I don't know what possessed her. She said later she had to talk to me. I don't know. I guess so. Maybe she was just lonely and afraid. The oiled latch was almost silent as she turned it. She stepped inside my room and carefully closed the door, leaving it slightly ajar so as not to risk the noise of the latch again. Noiselessly she came to the side of my bed. She wore a pale blue nightgown. The skin on her arms and shoulders was almost luminescent in the moonlight. As she always did, she bent over to put her hand on my mouth. I reached up and took it to show I was awake. She bent over and put her lips against my ear. More breath than sound she said, "Don't leave me."

I pulled her down to sit on the bed beside me. Into her ear I breathed, "Never." I kissed her. She was all warm soft sweetness. I had never felt such passion. Her skin was alive in my hands. I had never wanted her so much. I felt her breast through the nightgown, her waist. She twisted her mouth from mine and breathed "no" into my ear. I kissed her again. Oh, how I wanted her. I felt her tension leaving her. Her "no" had become a helpless yes. I took her nightgown off and my pajamas, and she was in bed beside me, our naked bodies one in the moonlight. I had always liked the sweetness of this silent lovemaking in the forbidden night. I caressed and kissed her, and she began to come almost as soon as I entered her, but in total silence, only her trembling and shuddering showed her passion, shuddering, shuddering, again, shuddering.

I heard the choking even before the light went on. I pulled out of her and rose to my knees on the bed. He stood in the open doorway in his pajamas, horrid striped ones, I remember. He was red in the face, gasping, clutching his chest. He tried to speak. More rattle than voice he said, "You shits . . . have you no . . ." I leaped to the floor in front of my bed, terrified, yet so filled with rage I was ready to kill if he took one more step. He moaned. He turned blue. He clutched his chest as if to drive his hand through it, then doubled up with pain. "Die, you bastard," I screamed. "Die! Die! Die!" I'm sure I laughed, as in slow motion—it seemed to take forever—he slowly, slowly, collapsed to the floor, while I screamed over and over, "Die! Die! Die!" and called him every name I could think of.

When he was silent and unmoving on the floor, I looked at Mother. She was on her knees on the bed, her mouth open with an unuttered scream, her eyes wide with horror. "The son of a bitch is dead," I said.

"You don't know that," she said and tried to go to him.

I stopped her. "Good, then the bastard can watch." And I raped her, again and again. She fought me at first and cried out her quite justified horror, but I overpowered her. I'd had lots of practice. While my father lay on the floor dead or dying, I raped my mother, again and again, and I made her come too. Did I ever make her come, swearing and screaming at me as she did so.

I'm not very proud of it, but that's what I did.

After awhile I dressed in my pajamas and

went to him. He was dead. I dragged him back to his room and with her help got him back into his bed. "We'd better keep the lights out," I said.

We sat in the dark downstairs. She trembled as I held her.

"I'm sorry," I said. "I shouldn't have done that."

"It's all right. I understand."

"I couldn't help myself. Can you forgive me?"

"I said I understood."

"Did I hurt you?"

"I'm all right."

Our voices sounded very small in the empty, darkened house.

"Will we get away with it?"

"There's nothing to get away with."

"The police . . ."

"The cops won't even come. He died of a heart attack, in his sleep, in his bed."

"Oh, David . . . David . . . it's like we killed him. It's like—"

"It's not. He had a heart attack. Don't ever think anything else. I won't let you."

She was better in the morning. Daylight, the bright sun seemed to take the chill from the house. I checked everything. There was nothing to see. Then I called the doctor. He came and pronounced Father dead. Mother had no difficulty being a bereaved widow. She has never

349

spoken of Father's death since, nor have I, until this moment.

* * *

Was it murder? Legally, probably not. Death was from natural causes. No blow was struck, no shot fired. Yet I cannot help but feel that if the full facts were laid out before a jury in a fair trial, some sort of conviction would have been obtained. For they did kill him, as surely as if they'd thrust a knife into his heart. In a way they did just that. Brendan Callahan was an essentially decent person, perhaps the only one in this ill-fated cast. He loved his wife. He loved his son. He knew, or at least strongly suspected, the incest between them. He knew he was being cuckolded by his wife and son under his own roof, virtually under his own eyes. The anger he must have felt can only be guessed. Yet for years he tried to save them both from themselves. He must have spent years trying to convince himself that it either wasn't true or would go away in time. If he were just silent, his family would not be destroyed. At the same time, I suspect, he tried to impede the obsession. He sent his son away to school. He tried to get him involved in political affairs. Anything to make a man out of his son.

I often think of Brendan Callahan. To know for years of the incestuous relationship between your wife and your son and to say nothing is an act of supreme maturity, courage, and love. I doubt if very many men could do it. I'm sure I couldn't. That in a moment of rage, goaded by his wife and son, he blurted the truth he had been holding within him for years is only human.

I believe it was murder, and I so accuse Carla Callahan Lampton, the only surviving member of this trio. She seduced her son on his thirteenth birthday. She maintained the incest, indeed acted like a jealous bitch when he showed signs of breaking away from her. I also believe she knew her husband was aware of the incestuous cuckolding. She could not help but know, yet kept that knowledge from her son to maintain the illicit sex. I believe she most certainly knew the likely repercussions of her conduct that evening, if she did not indeed plan it. She was a woman of almost complete self-control. The events at that party hardly justified her rage. For years, she had avoided just this sort of scene with her husband. Why that night?

Her going to her son's room that night, of all nights, was an act of premeditated murder. She must have known her husband was unlikely to sleep on such a night. Yet she padded down the hallway to her son's room. If she had wanted to talk to him about his threat to leave in the morning—as she led him to believe—she could have simply turned the lights on and begun a conversation with him. It could have been heard by her husband. The situation between the three of them was not irreconcilable. A few denials and apologies could have papered over the rift, at least as well as it had been for years. No, she went attired in her nightdress, bent on sex. She pretended to resist. It had to appear he was seducing her. The guilt had to be shifted to her son.

I believe Carla Callahan Lampton hoped her husband would enter that room to discover them. I believe she intended for her son to kill his father that night. And he did. "Die! Die! Die!" he shouted at him as the heart attack, surely a lucky convenience, saved him from the task. It was murder, premeditated by Carla Callahan Lampton, as surely as it is possible for one human being to take the life of another.

David knew this, deep in his soul. He would try very hard, but the knowledge was something he was not totally successful in repressing.

* * *

I had never realized before what a ghastly ritual death is in the United States. Mother had wanted to keep the funeral small and private, but there was no way to do it. Uncle Richard insisted on staying with us to help with the arrangements. He was in the way, being in the house; yet his aid was invaluable.

If the services could have been restricted to the family, that would have been quite a production. There was Aunt Maureen and Uncle Edgar to contend with. She was a blob of blubber compared to mother's quiet dignity. Then there was a vast assortment of aunts and uncles, nieces and nephews, and cousins I hardly knew existed. And all of Dad's friends insisted on paying their respects at the funeral home. Many came from New York, Washington, and around the country. All had to make appropriate expressions of sympathy and say a few words in praise of Dad. The funeral was delayed a day just so everyone could get their licks in at the funeral home. Even Squires and his entourage stayed over an extra day to visit the dead. He seemed genuinely grieved and spoke of a great loss. I wondered if he knew he was the real cause of it all. The telegrams and letters came in a flood and were weeks in being answered. The phone had to be taken off the hook.

I don't know what I felt—other than a desire to have this fiasco ended. I tried a couple of times to tell myself that I felt a genuine grief for my father's death, but if I did feel it, it was lost in the incessant expressions of "What a pity" and "Such a loss." The real truth is that I was more worried than anything, worried about Mother and me. I had wanted him dead. Wanted it for years. Wanted to have Mother all to myself, to live with her almost as man and wife, to love her without lies and deceit. Now that I at last had her, I was afraid that Father and the manner of his death would come between us. I saw a lot of her during the funeral.

353

We sat or stood together, accepting condolences. Yet we were never alone during those days. She seemed very wan, very tired, drawn, obviously not herself. She was an enigma. I had never seen her thus and could not tell what she was thinking. Her grief truly did seem genuine, and I realized there was a great deal about her relationship with Father that I had not known. Would his death change her? Would our love never be the same again? Would I never have what I'd hoped so long to gain by his death? I began to realize over those endless days that I felt very strange with her and didn't know how to act. Was I to be her son or her husband? I had always been a son. How did a husband act? How did she want me to act? By the day of the funeral, I was in knots of worry.

After the funeral she dismissed everyone, Aunt Maureen and Uncle Edgar, the priest, even Mrs. Riordan. Over Uncle Richard's objections, Mother insisted that he go back to New York. "I'll be all right," she said. "David's here. We need to be alone." It was late in the afternoon when she finally got him out the door and into a cab. He wouldn't let me run him to the station.

Her hand on the knob, she sagged against the door to the now empty house. Her eyes were closed, and she looked very tired. "What a ghastly, ghastly mess," she said. "It's finally over." She rested there a moment, then said, "Make me a martini, will you? A pitcher of them. A whole bucketful."

She followed me into the living room, and I made the martinis. I gave her one, and she drained it. I poured another.

I didn't know what to say. "Good?" I tried.

"Very."

I didn't know what else to say.

She professed how much she needed the drink.

I agreed with her.

I looked at her, and she looked at me. The silence was dreadful. The distance between us was infinite.

Suddenly she laughed. "I feel like a bride on my wedding night. And you sure act like a groom. Why don't you try kissing me?"

I did, hungrily.

"Oh, David . . ." she said and put her hand on my cheek.

My voice seemed to tremble as I spoke the truth. "I don't know if I'm your son or your husband."

She smiled. "Try lover."

"Now?"

"Now."

We walked upstairs, carrying our drinks. At the landing I started for my room and she for hers. She stopped, smiled, and said, "Come on." It was only the second time I'd ever made love to her in her room. It seemed to symbolize our new relationship. In the open doorway she said, "I want you to come here anytime you want me." After we made love, quite passionate love as I remember, we went back downstairs and had some dinner from the refrigerator. Later, we went back upstairs to her room, and I watched her bathe and prepare for bed. I spent the whole night with her in bed. During it, she asked me if I wanted to move into Father's room. I said I'd better not. It wouldn't look right. Actually, I knew I wouldn't be able to stand it.

Mother tried very hard during the next few weeks to establish our new relationship. She was very sweet to me and considerate. She seemed to defer to me as often as she could. What did I think? What did I want to do? What did I want her to wear? She made a great effort to be as glamorous and sexy looking as possible, at least when we were alone in the evening. A certain amount of bereavement was still necessary for Mrs. Riordan's benefit. She worked especially hard at her exercises, saying she was going to have to keep her figure now, couldn't have me running off with a younger woman. As if I would. We made love a lot, at least every night. And it was sweet, because the sense of urgency, of stolen moments, of cheating, were gone. We were much more relaxed about it, for both of us knew we had the rest of our lives to enjoy it.

I kept telling myself that I'd never been happier in my life, that living with Mother was all I'd ever hoped it would be. Yet I was strangely unhappy and a trifle depressed. I had such a feeling of him and his presence. I was glad to sleep in her room and to avoid the night and its memories in mine. It was no big deal. I wasn't acting out an Edgar Allan Poe story or anything like that. I just couldn't quite forget him.

She sensed my unhappiness and several times asked me what the matter was. About the third or fourth time, she wasn't about to be put off by my smiling denials. I decided to tell her what was at least partially the truth.

"All right, I am a little unhappy. Nothing to do with you. You're wonderful. It's just that I've got to do something with my life. Get a job maybe. I can't spend my days here with you, no matter how silken your arms."

She said she understood. She suggested I talk to Uncle Richard.

I told Uncle Richard a bit more than I had told her. I told him that prior to Father's death I had been thinking of getting a job in Washington. It seemed an even better idea now. I had to get going on some kind of a career. I could set up an apartment in Washington and take Mother in with me. It would do us both good to get out of the house in Westport. He thought it a good idea. He promised to make a few inquiries and get back to me. Lord, did he ever get back to me. I've got a little job for you, son. I want you to hang around with the man who helped kill your father, fuck his women, live like a hermit in Washington, and stay away from the only person you've ever loved and wanted in your life so Merrill Lampton, your friend and mine, our beloved President, savior of our nation from the socialist hordes, can have another term as President. You'll do that little thing for me, won't you, son? Oh, sure. I'm dumb, a brainless blob of shit; I'll do anything you want me to. Christ, Callahan, go to bed. On second thought, it's already dawn. Why not a shower and a cup of coffee?

* * *

I have received a notice from Her Majesty's Inland Revenue Service asking me to appear in London two day's hence for a routine audit of my tax accounts. I am not fooled. My tax accounts are perfectly in order. This is just a transparent ruse to get me out of the house so it can be searched. I am appalled that the British government would cooperate with the Americans in this endeavor, but I suppose the Americans said I was some sort of desperate fugitive from justice. I could protest to the British government, but how can I?

All of this is terribly upsetting. I must make some decision on what to do. I feel some sort of net is closing around me. God, what long arms Merrill Lampton has. But I can't waste time thinking about my problems. I must continue this work as rapidly as possible.

Richard Morrison, accompanied by Carla Callahan, came to David's apartment to hear his report. It was all recorded.

* * *

"I didn't know you were bringing Mother. I don't think this is something she will want to hear. At least I don't want her to."

"If you can figure a way for her *not* to come, I wish you'd let me know."

"You didn't have to tell her you were coming here."

"I'm just as involved in this as you are, David. I feel the President has commissioned us both."

[He sighed.] "Whatever you want. But just be glad you weren't there last night."

[He then told them what had happened the night before, much as he had already set it down on tape. He had just described the humiliation of Barbara Kingsley, when Carla Callahan interrupted.]

"That awful girl. Allowing herself—"

"She wasn't *allowing* herself. She tried to stop it. She was embarrassed. There were tears in her eyes."

"Still, she must have allowed them to dress her up before you came. When she saw a decent person there, she was embarrassed and left the room. It's entirely her own doing. I have no sympathy for her."

"Mother—" [He hesitated, sighed.] "Mother, the girl was Barbara Kingsley."

[There was a prolonged silence. Obviously, the name had surprised Carla Callahan.]

"Oh, David. I'm so sorry."

[More silence.]

"Who's Barbara Kingsley?"

"She's a friend of David's from college. He was very fond of her at one time."

"I *am* sorry, David. That must have been hard for you."

"Really, Richard. How can you let David do a thing like that? Not only did he see a friend humiliated, he was in great danger himself. Those are desperate men. They might have beaten him up. He could have been killed. How could you let him go there?"

"I didn't know, Carla."

"You know now. I don't want him ever to go there again. Do you hear me, Richard? I mean it."

[He sighed.] "All right, Carla." [To David.] "What did you find out?"

"They want war. They want to fight the whole United States government, the Army, the Navy, the Air Force, *and* the United States Marines, not to forget the Coast Guard. They want weapons. And by weapons they don't mean pea shooters, as they call them. They don't want to go bang bang. They want to go boom boom. They want artillery, missiles, mortars, rockets, recoilless rifles, antitank guns, not to mention hand grenades, dynamite, high explosives, and anything else they can blow up the whole country with. If you have a spare A-bomb lying around, they'll gladly use that."

[Morrison laughed.] "Good. Perfect."

"I hope you're being facetious."

"I'm not. I'm perfectly serious. Their shopping list is a bit long, but we'll have to see they get some items on it."

"You're kidding!"

"Good heavens, no. This is what we've all been working toward for over a year. We've gone to a lot of pains to make them mad enough to fight. Now we have to give them something to fight with."

"My God. I can't believe what I hear. You *want* to arm them. You intend for them to blow up the country. You *want* people to be killed."

"Don't be silly. They aren't going to blow up the country. They are going to make a lot of threats and noise and in the end hurt only themselves."

"My God! You are either a damned fool or the world's champion optimist."

[Morrison's voice took on an edge.] "I assure you I'm neither. I know, and the President knows, exactly what we're doing."

"And that is?"

"We want to give them just enough weapons so they *feel* powerful. We want a lot of bluster from them, a few threats. We want a situation that *seems* dangerous."

[There was a pause in the conversation. It seems David was trying to gain control of himself. When he spoke, it was with a quieter, less angry tone.]

"Uncle Richard, I don't mean to be disrespectful, but the way you're talking is very dangerous. I know these people. Ephraim Squires has a scar from here to here. He's an angry, bitter man, very volatile. You give him a few weapons, and, believe me, he'll use them. Will he ever!"

"I'm sure there's some truth to what you say, but—"

"I want out. Right now."

[A pause, quite prolonged.]

"I hope you don't mean that, David. The simple truth is you are the one indispensable person—outside of the President, of course. All we hope to accomplish depends upon you. If you drop out, we'll have President Houston Walker next year. I hope that thought scares you as much as it does me, and you'll reconsider."

"Uncle Richard, this is no damn fun for me. I feel like a social outcast. Hell, I can't even visit my mother in her own home."

"That's only for a little while, David. We're all making some sacrifice in our personal lives."

"For what? So Lampton can stay on as President?"

"That's right. I think it a worthy goal, I might say even noble. Your contribution is indispensable."

"Okay, if I'm suddenly an indispensable man—which I doubt—then I have a right to know what I'm indispensable to. What is your plan?"

"David, it's better if you don't know."

"I think it's better if I quit."

[Pause.]

"Richard, I think David should know. You and the President got him—and me—involved in this. He has a right to share your confidence. It's only fair."

[Morrison sighed deeply. When he spoke, it was with resignation; yet there was a conspiratorial tone to his voice.]

"I told you before. If we are to have any chance of keeping Merrill Lampton in office—and, in my opinion, saving the country—we must have some kind of national emergency that will require calling off the election in November."

"And Squires's revolution is to be the emergency. Uncle Richard, forgive me if I'm rude, but you've got to be kidding. The United States elected presidents in the middle of the Vietnam War, Korean War, World War II, World War I, the Civil War. Need I go on? And a couple of those were fair-sized emergencies. You haven't a prayer. There's no emergency that could stop an election in this country."

"I wouldn't bet on that, David. You're forgetting your history. In the disputed election of 1876—"

"That again."

"Yes. It was probably the greatest political crisis this country ever faced. No probably. It

363

was. And it was a planned crisis, an engineered crisis."

"You told me that. The *New York Times* . . ."

"So I did. The point is that Grant was almost kept in office past his term. We intend to see that Merrill Lampton is."

"You'll never get an election canceled."

"Maybe not. But if the election is held amid such turmoil and threats, if it obviously is not a fair election, then Lampton will have to remain in office until a proper election can be held."

"You mean you'd give guns to maniacs just to keep Lampton in office?"

"I would and more. Houston Walker will be a worse disaster than anything I can dream up."

[There is a long pause.]

"Aren't you forgetting something, Uncle Richard? A little organization known as the United States Congress? An organization very much controlled by the Democrats? You don't think Congress will allow Lampton to pull off such a stunt, even if he gets a chance to."

[Morrison laughed.] "That must not have been a very good college you went to. You sure didn't learn any American history. Congress will be neutralized. Merrill Lampton will do just as Lincoln did—Abraham Lincoln no less. At the start of the Civil War, Congress wasn't in session. They were back home enjoying their tail and mint juleps. Lincoln did what was necessary to fight the war. He ordered up troops. He spent money. He ordered war materials. He did what had to be done. Then he waited for Congress to show up and ratify what he'd done. It wasn't legal. Congress didn't like it. But Congress had no choice. It'll be the same now." [*He laughed.*] "You better believe Congress will adjourn before the election."

[David made a sound, half sigh, part snort.] "Forgive me, it's still a harebrained idea. It'll never work."

"Okay, so it doesn't work. No harm done."

"But you've given guns to Squires."

"Just a few. Enough to give him courage to come out in the open. Then we'll mow him down and be rid of him and his kind once and for all." [He paused for effect.] "I have an idea you might like that."

[Prolonged silence.]

"What arrangement do you have to get back to Squires?"

"Edna, one of his girls—the ugly one, Mother—is to get in touch with me next week."

"All right. Tell her to tell Squires we'll give him some weapons."

"They'll want to know what and when."

"String them along. Let them believe he gets what he wants. As for the when, we have to time this very carefully. Timing is everything. Just tell him it will take some time. Meanwhile, he should get some transport and a secure place to hide the stuff. Don't shake your head at me, David. I know what I'm doing. Oh, yes, make some arrangement so you can get in touch with

them. That's vital. There will be very short notice on all this."

[Again, David's mother remained behind to
talk after Morrison left.]

"David, you look so depressed."

[Long silence.]

"I am depressed. And I'm angry. But what I
really am is stupid. I'm depressed because I'm
stupid, and I'm angry because I'm stupid.
Worst of all, I don't seem to be able to stop
being stupid."

"That's silly, darling. Talk to me about it."

"I might as well. There's never been anyone
else I can talk to. In my whole life there's been
only you. That's my real problem, isn't it? I
love you. I've always loved you. I always will
love you."

"Oh, darling. You don't need to say all that. I
know it. I share it. You are the most wonderful
lover in the world."

"Let me finish. All I want is to be with you.
I don't care where. I'll live in Georgetown
with you. I'll happily go back to Westport. I'll
live in a grass hut, any place."

"I doubt if I'm the grass-hut type."

"I'm serious, Mother."

"I know. I'm sorry."

"All I want is you. So what am I doing as
some kind of superspy? Look, I have the
greatest respect for Uncle Richard. And I'm
fond of him. I don't call him Uncle for nothing. But, lord— He's got a harebrained scheme.

Call off the election. Jesus Christ, how stupid can you get? And to give guns to Squires? You want to know what that is? Murder. Pure and simple murder."

"Richard says—"

"I know what he *says*. I heard him."

"—only a few guns."

"Great, just great. Squires already has a few. You mean a few more, don't you?"

"I'm no expert, David. I simply don't know."

[Long silence.]

"Mother, I'm going to be very honest. Deep in my soul, down where I live, I don't want to do this. I have the strongest feeling I should get out of this right now. But I also have the feeling you want me to go on. Do you?"

"David, I don't want you to do anything dangerous. . . . I don't want you to ever go back there, to that place, his headquarters or whatever it was. I don't want anything to happen to you. . . . David, this is hard. I don't know what I feel myself. . . . God, David . . . look, the President said it's important. He seems to be counting on us. Maybe, if you just saw this woman again, Edna. Give her Richard's message. Maybe that'll be the end of it."

"Do you know how I finally got to see Squires?"

"How could I?"

"I fucked Edna. I know you don't like that word, but it's the only word to express it. Love it hardly was. She'd always ridiculed me. I was pretty boy, God's joke, nice to look at but unable to do it. Squires was supposed to be a real man with his big cock. I showed her. I showed her I didn't need any other dame to turn me on like Squires. I fucked her. I fucked her till she begged for mercy."

"Good! I'm glad you showed her, the bitch."

"Really! I'm stunned. You're not angry?"

"No. As you say, it wasn't love or even sex. It was—just a job. I'm glad you defended yourself."

[He laughed.] "My word. Who'd have believed it?"

[She laughed, too.] "I don't think it's strange at all."

"She wanted to know where I learned to hold off."

"And you told her?"

"Hardly."

"Would you like some more practice?"

"What I'd like is that girl I used to know. The one I could never quite satisfy."

"She's not far away."

When Edna phoned this afternoon, she said exactly two words, four syllables, "Eight eleven." I tried to say something to her. I wanted to tell her it was safe to come to my place. She'd hung up.

Eight eleven. It figured to be a room number at the Statler. It was. She opened the door. She wore the same mousy-looking attire and was as always militantly unfeminine. I saw no signs of her angry arrogance. She looked rather wan, tired, and nervous. After standing there, near the door, for a moment, she said, so quietly I could barely hear her, "Will you do it again?"

I asked what.

"Fuck me."

I smiled. "No, but I'll make love to you."

She trembled slightly, then smiled, very wanly. "I'll probably be thrown out of the revolution for saying it, but thank you for putting it that way. Look, I can get fucked any time I want. Far more than I want, really."

"I know."

"I'm good at it."

"Yes."

"But you were different. Oh, I know you were mad. I know you were proving something. But you still made me feel like a woman. Maybe I was just a little special."

I said nothing.

"I liked it—feeling like a woman. I have to know if you meant it."

"You don't give a fellow much chance to romance you."

"You would have?"

"Yes. I intended to." It was a lie, but what could I do?

"How?"

"By ordering us a drink." I moved toward the phone.

"I told you I don't drink."

"But what would you drink if you did?"

"Don't please. I don't want it to be alcohol. I've had that—lots. I want it to be real."

I laughed. "You sure do make it hard for the preliminaries. Okay, let's assume we are undressed." I began to take off my pants. She also undressed, far faster than I. When she was there before me, scrawny and bony in her nakedness, I said, "I'll tell you what I told you before. You are more beautiful than you think. You have nice legs, particularly beautiful thighs. I like that hollow." I touched it. "Very partial to that hollow. And you are very talented with your hips. When you start to move them— see, you're starting now—it is positively tormenting. Yes. Yes. But the best thing is the way you respond. It turns me on."

She took my hands from her and knelt before me and caressed me, very lovingly, very expertly. I lifted her to her feet and kissed her. In a moment she spoke in my ear. "I don't want you holding off. It's not natural. I want you to come as you want to. It'll be enough for me."

Afterwards, she lay on the pillow, tears rolling down her cheeks. Very softly she said, "Thank you. I'll remember it always."

"Why don't you leave him?" I asked.

"Because I love him, and he loves me."

"You're kidding."

"No. We're two of a kind. Two lost souls. We need each other."

"He has other women turn him on while he
370

screws you. You live in constant humiliation. That's not love."

"I don't want to talk about it anymore."

She was silent for a time, then asked, "Was I good?"

"Very."

"As good as the other?"

"Who?"

"The one who has you hold off."

"And I don't want to talk about that."

"She's very selfish. Any woman that has a man make love like that is very selfish. She's all out for herself. She doesn't really love you."

"You're dead wrong. And I still don't want to talk about it."

Again we were silent for a time.

"Edna, I'd like to have you help me do something."

"Do we have to talk business already?"

"It's not business. It's personal. I'd like to get Barbara out of there."

"Barbara Kingsley? You know her?"

"We were in college together."

She sat up in bed and looked down at me. "Well, I'll be. So you're the one. What a small world."

"Isn't it."

"I'll be damned. She told me there was a guy. Not that she needed to. She's carrying a torch big enough to light the world. So you're the one. Do you love her?"

"No. But I can't stand her being humiliated that way."

"That was nothing. She and Ephraim cooked it up. He said there was some society guy coming in. He wanted to shock you and dreamed up that Miss Liberty gag. She didn't know it was you. I figured something was wrong when she ran out of the room as soon as you were brought in."

"I still want her out of there."

"So you *are* in love with her."

"No, I'm not. But I'm fond of her. I can't have her hurt this way."

"She volunteered. She can walk out any time she wants to. We all can. All you got to do is send a message. Baby, I love you. I want to live with you."

"I don't want to live with her. I just want her out of there."

"Then forget it. I know Barbara. She's the best of all the girls Ephraim's had. She's in love with you—really in love. And I know why—now. You made her feel like a woman, a real woman. God knows why she doubts her femininity, built like she is. But she does. There's no accounting for it. I'll do you a favor. I'll explain it to you. You got two choices: either love her and live with her or leave her alone. She's finding her own way—just like all of us. She'll be fine. She's better off without you."

"But I can't bear the thought—his pawing her and screwing you."

"You really are mixed up. You obviously screwed her while you loved somebody else—the selfish lady, I suspect. What's the difference?"

I was beginning to be angry. "And what side of your mouth are you talking out of? You wanted it to be natural with me. Is that what you call it between you, Squires, and her?"

She shrugged. "I'll tell her what you said and bring you an answer. Who knows? Maybe she'll call you."

"I think I know how to get her out of there. Squires said he wanted guns. Tell him he'll get them—if I get Barbara out of there. Guns for Barbara. Even he'll admit it's a good deal."

"When and where?"

"I'll have to let you know. It'll be soon. Squires is to have transport ready and a place to hide the stuff."

"No problem."

"I'll need a safe number to call you."

She gave me a phone number. It was to an automatic answering device. I was to say the words "eight eleven." She'd call me.

* * *

I have fled the Cotswolds. I tried to make it look as natural as possible. I'm sure my every move is being watched. I waited till the day I was supposed to appear at Inland Revenue in London. I carried a briefcase, which would look like it contained my financial records, and

a piece of luggage appropriate for an overnight stay in London. At least I hoped it looked
appropriate, for it was rather large. Into both
pieces I stuffed all I need to carry on this
work: the tape recorder, tapes, transcript, this
manuscript. The suitcase with the recording
machine was very heavy. It was hard to walk to
the rail station so as to make it appear to weigh
much less.

I didn't know what to do. I didn't know
whether I was being followed or not, but I
couldn't risk believing I wasn't. On the train to
London, I decided to lift a page from this book
and try to lose anyone following me. I have
spent the whole afternoon and evening moving
about London. I went directly to the Inland
Revenue office, as though I intended to keep the
appointment. I took the elevator to the proper
floor. I was encouraged by being alone in the
lift. Then I walked down a couple of flights
and wandered around the building, gradually
making my way back to the street some time
later by another exit. I quickly hailed a cab and
had him drive around London, then another cab,
then the tube and a bus and a tube and cab. I
don't know how many times I changed or
where I went or how much money I spent. I
suppose I had the greatest possible tour of London, but I wasn't enjoying it very much. I believe I lost anyone who tried to follow me. But
I'm not sure. I don't know anything about this

spy business—except to believe they—Lampton's
people—are far more clever than I.

About ten-thirty in the evening I ended up
in the Kilburn district of London. It's hardly
Mayfair, but it is what I need. I walked
around aimlessly for almost an hour, then took
these rooms. Rooms? Ha! It is just a sleazy one-
room bedsitter, but it will do at least until I finish this book. When I have all this in someone
else's hands, perhaps I'll be safe then. I've got to
work, work, work. I've got to finish this as
quickly as possible.

On my travels today I did figure out one
thing. I had wondered how they found me out.
Of all the people in the world who might have
David Callahan's tapes, how did they hit on me?
I don't believe he told anyone. I certainly have
not. Yet they came to my place unerringly. How
did they know? Then I realized my mistake.
The bloody tape recorder. They traced anyone
who had bought or rented one of the infernal
gadgets. God, how clever they are! I can only
hope now that I've given them the slip. The
Kilburn is full of fugitives. IRA bombers have
hid out here for years. Surely one unemployed
American college professor can go unnoticed
here. But I have to hurry.

Morrison again returns to David's apartment
in Washington.

* * *

"I have a message for you from the President. He asked me to give you this."

"The President?"

"No one else. I don't even know what he's written."

[The sounds on the tape are suggestive of a letter being torn open, although I'd never have guessed it without the accompanying conversation.]

"Shall I read it to you?"

"If you don't mind. I'd like to hear what he says."

"It's in his own handwriting. It says, 'Dear David: Richard has told me of the excellent work you have done and of the risks you've taken and of the personal sacrifices you've made. I can only tell you how grateful I am. I regret that for awhile longer I cannot see you and thank you personally. I look forward to that day with anticipation. Until then, may I remind you that some of our greatest patriots worked for the good of the nation, unsung and unheralded. I look forward to being able to tell the world what you have accomplished. Until then, please accept my humble thanks as a token.' That's very nice, Uncle Richard. Did you ask him to write that?"

"I merely suggested you might like some communication from him. The words are entirely his—and from the heart, I can tell you."

"Yes. Very nice. May I keep it?"

"I'm afraid not. He asked me to burn it personally. You understand."

[There are sounds that I know to be Richard Morrison burning this important evidence against Merrill Lampton. When I first heard it, and even as I listen again, I swear I can smell the paper burning. I almost weep that David was unable to keep this written evidence of Lampton's role in the plot. But these are clever, careful people. How well I know.]

"I just thought you might like to know the President is aware of what you're doing and appreciates it. He understands how hard it is for you."

"Yes. I'll write him a note expressing my thanks. You can give it to him."

"No. We don't want anything in writing that isn't absolutely essential. This isn't going to be another Watergate. We want no memos, reports, nothing to shred. Above all, we want no goddamn tape recorders. God, what asses Nixon and his crowd were. I'll tell Merrill personally how much you appreciated his letter. Okay?"

"If you think that best."

[Morrison's tone brightened.] "Have you heard the news?"

"About what?"

"The primaries, of course."

"Houston Walker's winning in a walk. Or is that too bad a pun?"

"Not that. That was expected. I mean the write-in vote for the President. He almost won the Republican primaries in Ohio, California, and New Jersey yesterday, and he's not even a candidate. He can't legally serve even if elected. It's something, I tell you. Merrill Lampton is the most popular President this country ever had. The people love him and want him."

"Forgive me, Uncle Richard, but I detect your fine hand in the write-in campaign."

"Certainly, I've encouraged it. But I never expected such success. This is a tremendous outpouring of affection for the President."

"And that helps your plan?"

[Morrison chuckled.] "It doesn't hurt it. Not one bit. Now to business. This is the message I want you to give to Squires."

[There is a pause. David is obviously reading a paper handed him by Morrison.]

"I thought you didn't want to put anything in writing."

"I said as little as possible. We thought of having you memorize all this and tell it to Squires. I'm sure you could do it all right, but I'm equally sure Squires would garble it somehow. We decided to put it in writing to avoid any mistakes. We've gone to considerable pains to insure that the paper and the typewriter can't be traced. It's all right. Don't worry about it."

[Another pause. David was apparently reading.]

"It's just columns of numbers and letters. What is it? Some kind of code? Squires will never understand this."

"You're to explain it to him. It's very simple really. The first column of numbers is dates. The second column is the zip code, giving the origin and destination of arms shipments. The third column, the letters, are the abbreviations of the railroad. The last column is the number of the freight cars carrying the stuff. I assume he'll be able to do the rest."

[A rather long pause. I can almost feel David's bewilderment.]

"I don't get it."

"What don't you get? These are dates and places of arms shipments. I assume he'll be able to knock off a train. I didn't want to spell it out anymore for fear this paper falls into the wrong hands. As it is now, anyone reading this information would never be able to figure out what it means."

"I know all that. What I mean is—hell, you don't mean to say the army ships its weapons by railroad car? On a regular freight train?"

"Of course. Always has. A lot of it goes by truck, even barge. But we just thought a freight derailment would be easier than a truck hijacking."

"I just don't believe it. You mean there are no guards on these shipments? No convoy? Just a regular train?"

"Well, of course. The United States is the largest maker of munitions in the world. You don't see any convoys of trucks with tanks and soldiers, do you? The stuff is moved from the manufacturer to the military just like any other merchandise." [He laughed.] "It might as well be toilet paper or baby rattles. The trick is to know the time and place of the shipment."

"And the weapons are all assembled?"

"Yes, or virtually so. I'm sure Squires has enough exservicemen among his goons to solve any problems."

"They don't ship the triggers separate?"

[Morrison laughed again.] "Your lack of knowledge of weapons is boundless. No problem. Don't worry about it."

"I thought Squires might."

"The only problem he'll have is that the ammunition is shipped separately. Some of those shipments are weapons. Others are the ammunition. That's why he needs transport, to get the ammo together with the guns."

"Sounds grisly."

"Don't worry about it. We know what we're doing."

"Where'd this information come from? The army?"

"There's really no reason for you to know, David. There really isn't. But if you'll remember, I told you we were trying to do this without using bureaucrats. We don't want any leaks."

"So private munitions makers supplied this?"

[Silence. Morrison did not reply.]

"I don't know anything about it. Is this a lot of shipments in a short period of time?"

"You're smart, David. You're going to go places for us when this is over. Let's just say some effort went into providing a proper shopping list for Mr. Squires."

[A very long silence.]

"All right. I'll see he gets this."

"I'd say good, except I expected you to protest. The last time we talked you were much against doing this."

"And that's why you arranged the note from the President."

"I thought you might need some encouragement."

"I said I appreciated it."

"Is that why you aren't protesting? Did the President's letter mean that much to you?"

"I said it was nice of him. But in honesty, I have another reason."

"And that is?"

"Barbara. Barbara Kingsley. The girl I know. I'm arranging a swap. Squires gets his guns. I get Barbara out of there."

[Morrison's voice grew hard.] "I don't like that. I don't like it one bit."

"I'm sorry, Uncle Richard. I know I disappoint you. But the truth is that I don't give a damn about Merrill Lampton and this whole wild-eyed scheme to keep him in office—a scheme that hasn't a prayer of working anyhow. I just realized recently, too, that I don't really care what you're doing to the country. So you want to arm Squires. You want a lot of shooting

381

and dying. Okay, so be it. I don't give a damn any more. I want to live my own life. I want to be happy. I want to do what is important to *me*. Barbara Kingsley is—or was—important to me. I'm going to do what I can for her."

"You're in love with her?"

"I'm not in love with her. But she's a nice girl. I care what happens to her."

"What happens if Squires says no to your deal? Where are we then?"

"He won't. You better believe he wants the guns more than he wants her. She's nothing to him. He'll find another girl next week anyway. But guns. You sure fixed it so he wants to fight."

[Morrison sighed.] "David, can't you leave love out of it? It's a complication. Emotions always complicate things. Can't you just give the message to Squires and let it go at that?"

"You could. I can't. On second thought, you're no different from me. You're so emotional about Merrill Lampton being President, it's not to be believed."

[Morrison laughed.] "I guess you got me there." [He sighed.] "All right. Do what you must. I guess your motives don't matter. It's results that count."

"I assure you you'll get more results than even you want."

"Let's hope so. Oh, yes, one more thing. Tell Squires that if he doesn't act on this information, that's it. He gets no other chances. This is a one-strike ball game."

"In other words, you want his little revolution to start before the election. What if he doesn't?"

"He will. We'll see to that."

"What if he figures the election of Houston Walker will solve his problem? Walker is already talking about appeasing Squires. Sometimes I think Walker is more of a Squires than Squires."

"And that's why he'll never be President. Just get the damn message to Squires. Today if possible."

Another exciting evening in the life of David Callahan, boy spy. Christ, what a fuck-up you are, Callahan. It all began with my placing the call to Edna. The blasted machine. "This is an automatic answering service. When you hear the tone, please leave your message." [David said it in a falsetto imitation of a female voice.] Tone. "Eight eleven." I stand there like a fool, holding the receiver like I expect the damn machine to say thanks or something. Who in the hell ever invented these blasted impersonal gadgets?

Then I decided to call Mother. If I can't see her when I want, I ought to be able to talk to her on the telephone. This is supposed to be a secure phone here. I rang her unlisted number. "This is Mrs. Callahan's phone. She is out, but will return your call. When you hear the tone, please leave your name and number." I stood there stupefied. She had put in one of these phone gadgets, too. I couldn't believe it. I stood there holding the phone, then banged the receiver down. I thought about calling back and leaving some kind of crazy message, like, this is your son, David; remember him, the one who wants to hold your body and caress you and send you into flights of orgasm? But I thought better of it. Somebody else might hear the tape.

About six o'clock Edna returned my call. I asked her if she wanted to meet at the same place. She said no, she'd better not. I asked if Squires was jealous. She didn't answer. We had difficulty deciding where else to meet. She wouldn't come here. Finally, she agreed to allow me to pick her up in my car. I picked her up outside the bus station about seven, and we drove aimlessly, ending up in College Park, Maryland. We had hamburgers and coffee in a Hot Shoppes drive-in.

"I talked to Barbara. I've never seen anyone so gone as she is on you."

"Did you tell her about us?"

"Does it matter to you? I thought you didn't love her."

"I don't."

"I didn't tell her all the gory details. But she knows. If it makes you feel better, I don't think it matters to her."

I asked if she'd told Barbara I was getting her out of there.

"She said, 'To what?' "

"And what's that supposed to mean?"

"My friend, you aren't the only one who can issue ultimatums. If you love her and want her, she'll crawl out of there on her hands and knees. But if you don't—" She let one of her shrugs finish the sentence.

"I thought I made it clear. I just want her out of there."

"My friend, it's her life. You can't run it for her—unless you want to make her part of yours. Do you?"

God, how was I supposed to answer that? I suppose I should have lied, said yes, I love her, yes, I want her to move in with me, yes, I want to marry her, yes, I can't live without her, anything to get her out of there. But, I blew it. Callahan the fuck-up. I figured my swap for the guns would work.

"Tell Squires, no Barbara, no guns."

She laughed. "You really are dumb, pretty boy."

"That again."

"I'm not riding you. It's the simple truth. Ephraim doesn't care about Barbara. He'd give you a dozen Barbaras if it would get him one cap pistol. But he doesn't believe you. Why should he? Where in hell are you going to get the sort of guns we need? He doesn't believe you can, and I don't either. You're trying some big grandstand play for a girl you insist you don't love. Pretty boy, you haven't even gotten into the ball game, yet." She hesitated. "It's very simple. Even you can figure it out. Guns first. Then Barbara—if she wants to see you."

I said it was no deal. I was no fool. If Squires got the guns, he'd never let Barbara go. He'd keep her just to spite me.

"Then let's drive back into the city. I've things to do."

"Like fuck Squires while he paws—"

"What else?" She laughed. "My, you do like to suffer, don't you?"

I'd been had. I knew it. "What am I supposed to do? Give Squires everything he wants, then hope he gives me the little I want?"

"That's the way it looks."

I swore. I don't remember the words, but Mother would have chastised me. I handed her the piece of paper and took some time to explain it to her. "I'm to tell you, if Squires doesn't follow through on this, there'll be no other chance."

"I don't think this piece of paper will impress Ephraim much. But if there are guns there, we'll get them."

"There are guns."

"Who're you working for, David?"

"You'd never believe it. I'm a little green man from Mars. How about the Russians? The Chinese? I got it, the Arabs. They got all the money in the world."

"Okay. I shouldn't have asked."

"And I suppose I shouldn't ask if Squires will honor the bargain."

She never said another blessed word on the return trip to Washington.

When I got back to the apartment, I felt lousy. That hamburger was lying in my stomach like a rock. I poured a brandy, but it didn't help. I decided to call Mother again.

"Mrs. Callahan's residence." It was a male voice, very impersonal.

"Who in the hell are you?"

"This is Mrs. Callahan's residence."

"You already said that. I asked who you are?"

"This is Stanton, sir, the butler."

"Butler! Since when does she have a butler?"

"I'm with the catering service, sir."

"Catering service? What's going on over there."

I heard a mumble of voices on the other end, then an officious voice, very hard, came on. "Who is this calling?"

"Who in the hell is this answering?"

"All I can tell you is that this is Mrs. Callahan's residence."

"For crissake. A bunch of parrots."

"Who shall I say is calling?"

"For crissake, it's her *son* calling." I shouted the word. I know I did.

"Mrs. Callahan is with guests and cannot be disturbed. I'll see she gets the message."

"You gotta be kidding."

He hung up the phone. Godalmighty. I can't

even call her on the phone. This is too damn much.

* * *

Carla Callahan came to his apartment. I assume the next day.

* * *

"I'm sorry, David. I would have come to the phone if I'd known it was you. But the Secret Service man didn't tell me till later."

"Secret Service man!"

"I'm sorry. I thought I'd told you."

"Oh, come on, Mother. I haven't seen or talked to you in over a week."

"I had a small dinner party. The President did me the honor of attending. It was to be very quiet. No one was to know he was there. But everywhere the President goes, the Secret Service—"

"I know all that. So you're entertaining the President now. My!"

"He works very hard. He needs a little relaxation. Richard thought . . . I'm sure I mentioned it to you."

"You didn't mention it at all. In fact, you hardly ever say anything to me anymore."

[Long silence, almost a half minute.]

"Let's not quarrel, darling. Please." [There is

a sound, a rustle. Perhaps she arose from the chair and went to him.] "I'd rather make love."

"I thought you'd given that up."

"My, you are in a sullen mood. I know how to fix that."

[More silence on the tape.] "You're trembling."

"Lord, I want you."

"Then have me."

[There is a noisy, particularly passionate episode, which I see no point in describing here. Afterwards they talk. He tells her how wonderful she is.]

"You too, darling. The ultimate lover."

"Is that all I am? Your lover?"

"You're my son. I can't make you more."

"Okay. It was a dumb question. I've been asking a lot of dumb questions lately."

"Like what?"

"I don't want to talk about it. I want to talk about happy things. I've delivered Uncle Richard's message to Squires. As near as I can figure, my job is over. Let's pack up and go back to Westport."

"Wonderful, darling. We'll go soon."

"Soon? We'll go now. Tomorrow. I'll phone Uncle Richard."

"You are silly. I've several engagements. Merrill wants me to—"

"Merrill is it?"

"The President. He has a first name."

389

"My, you're chummy with him. What is it he wants?"

"There's a state dinner for the president of Brazil next week. He's invited me, that's all."

"Well, hang the president of Brazil."

"How can I?"

[There is a brief silence, followed by the sounds of a telephone receiver being picked up and a number dialed.]

"Mr. Morrison, please . . . Yes, this is David Callahan. . . . I see. When do you expect him? Tell him to call me as soon as he can. Goodbye."

"I thought you weren't to call him at his office."

"There are too damn many things I'm not supposed to do."

"Darling, will you stop it. You're getting all worked up again. Lie down. Let's—"

"Mother, you'd better get dressed. Go find the various presidents you're associating with these days."

"David. Don't be so beastly."

"I mean it, Mother. I want to be alone for awhile. I'm getting so I like it."

*　*　*

Carla Callahan returned to David's apartment, accompanied by Morrison. I have the impression it was the same day, perhaps in the evening.

"I'm sorry I called you at your office."

"I am, too. But no harm done—this once. My secretary assumed you were calling on some family matter. But let's not have it again, okay?"

"Yes. I'm sorry."

[Carla Callahan spoke, her voice bright, artificially so, it seems to me.] "Why don't we all have a drink? I could use one."

"One super martini coming right up. Scotch and ice for you?"

"Please."

[There are the familiar tinkling, clinking sounds of drinks being made. Over them Morrison speaks.]

"So you got the message to our friend Squires?"

"I gave it to Edna. I assume she'll give it to him."

"Could there be a problem?"

"No. Squires has already read it, I'm sure."

"And gone into action I trust. David, you've done splendidly, just splendidly. There's no way I can tell you."

[The sounds of drink making ended. From the silences, the pace of the conversation, I assume they were drinking.]

"Very good, darling. You learned your lessons well."

"All my lessons, I trust."

"Every one of them."

"You were a good teacher."

"I don't know what all that is supposed to mean, but as long as you two do."

"It means David makes the world's greatest martini."

[Pause.]

"I assume my job is now over."

"Yes—well, practically."

"Then I can leave here, go back to Westport?"

[Morrison hesitated, cleared his throat.] "Look, we've baited the trap for Squires. I'd like you to wait a few days to make sure he takes the bait. Will you do that?"

"Yes. I've something else I have to do."

"Oh, yes, the girl. Did he make the swap you wanted?"

"That's just it, he didn't."

"What girl? Barbara? What are you talking about?"

"David wanted to get his girl out of—"

"She's not my girl."

"Well, you wanted to swap the guns for her."

"That's true. But she's not my girl."

"David, you are silly. I think you protest too much. I don't care if—"

"Did he accept the deal?"

"No. That's just it."

"What is?"

"Squires doesn't believe he's going to get any guns from me. If he does, then there's a chance he'll release Barbara."

"Oh, David, I hope so for your sake."

"And that's why you're willing to hang on a few days more?"

"Yes."

"What will you do with her? Bring her here?"

"No."

"I know. She can have the house in Westport for a few days."

"No. You and I are going there—at least I hope we are."

"Well, what are you going to do with her?"

"I don't know. I'm just going to get her away from Squires. Maybe I'll give her some money and send her back to California."

"It strikes me, son, you've gone to a lot of trouble just to send your girl away again."

"She's not my—oh, never mind. I don't want to talk about it anymore."

"My goodness, Carla. These lovestruck young people." [Loud laughter from Morrison.] "I do believe we've gotten David's goat."

[There is some more conversation, which I am omitting for the sake of moving this task along more rapidly. Then Morrison left.]

"Would you like me to spend the night? Or are you expecting Barbara?"

"Are we going to fight again?"

[She laughed lightly.] "Don't be so sensitive, darling. I was only asking a question. I thought—"

"I'm not expecting her."

"So do you want me to spend the night?"

"What do you think?"

"David, *please*. Don't be so beastly."

"I'm sorry. I truly am. I'm sorry for the nasty things I said this afternoon. I didn't mean any of them."

"I know you didn't."

"I'm just not myself. It's this ridiculous spy nonsense, the tension, the waiting around."

"I know, darling. You needn't explain. Pour me another drink."

"Of course."

[Her voice raised a little as he moved across the room to the bar.] "I'm sorry, too, David. I didn't mean to make it sound like I didn't want to go to Westport with you."

"Then you will go?"

"This very minute if you want." [She laughed lightly, coquettishly.] "Hurry up and finish your drink. We left something unfinished this afternoon."

* * *

I have tried to tell myself that I have been imagining a plot against me, that I've gone to all this trouble for nothing. Perhaps all this cloak-and-dagger business of David Callahan's was affecting my mind. Today I called a friend in the Cotswolds from a pay phone. I have confirmed that I am not imagining things. My friend reports that my cottage has been ransacked, literally torn apart on the insides. He said it looked like whoever did it was searching for something. He wanted to know what it could be? I told him I couldn't explain it to him and suggested he never reveal that he received a call from me.

As a result of this, I decided to get rid of as much stuff as I can. I have spent two days going over this manuscript with a pencil. I know it is in bad shape. There are misspellings, poor constructions, some really awful writing. But I haven't time to do it all over. And I should have the manuscript typed. There isn't time for that either. And who could I trust to type it? I've decided to send what I've written so far to a publisher, along with the tapes I've used. This will lessen my burden and perhaps insure that at least this much of this story gets published. The rest of the story is pretty familiar anyhow. Someone else could finish it.

The problem has been, what publisher? By rights I should make the rounds of publishers, seeking the one who is right for such a book, most likely to appreciate it and make the most of it. But I haven't time. I can't risk being seen, let alone talking about all this with strangers. I am left with no choice, save one. I'm sending this to the only publisher I know. It isn't the right publisher, I know. It's a textbook house, much too scholarly for this sort of thing. But they have published a couple of my monographs in collections of readings on government. They at least know who I am. I'll just have to hope they publish it or give it to someone who will. But what a disappointment! I was so looking forward to showing this to people, playing the tapes, telling them the story. I wanted to see the utter disbelief in their faces. Now it's going off in a plain brown wrapper, no return address. Isn't that an irony? It's how it all began. But maybe my mind will be easier, and I can finish the remainder of this quickly.

David began a whole series of frequent transmissions that I feel I must, in the interest of brevity, attenuate. At one point he says, "It's strange to know something no one else knows, then watch it happen, waiting for the rest of the world to learn what you know." But the world was slow in learning. In mounting frustration, David recorded whole radio and television newscasts, none with a word about the stolen arms shipments. He rushed out to buy daily newspapers but found no mention. His bewilderment, his frustration, his impatience in waiting is clearly demonstrated on the tapes.

Finally, he found a small news item on the inside pages of the *Washington Post*. He read it aloud, swearing as he did so. It was just a mention of a train derailment near Elkton, Maryland. When he read the item into the tape recorder, it was as if he were telling a confidant what fools there were in the world. The next day, apparently, the *New York Times*, carried three separate small items, grouped together, of derailments in Colorado and Illinois, as well as the one in Maryland.

I am, of course, guessing, but it must have been a day or, more likely, two later that the *Times* carried a speculative piece linking the derailments together. It seems to me that I recall reading the article in the *International Herald Tribune* at the time, but that may be my memory playing tricks on me. David read the piece into his tape recorder. *Times* reporters had visited all three train crashes. All the derailments were apparently deliberate. In one crash, that in Illinois, a member of the train crew had been knocked in the head by someone. He was already dazed and could not give a description. The *Times* reported that apparently the contents of selected freight cars had been stolen, but the reporters were unable to learn the nature of the stolen goods. The *Times* piece ended with speculation that the three train wrecks were so similar as to raise suspicion. Both the Department of Transportation and the army were said to be investigating. The entry of the military into the investigation was particularly noted.

David had a great many derogatory comments about the stupidity of reporters. He was quite scornful of the careful wordage of the *Times* article.

Still, nothing happened. In frequent, I imagine almost daily, transmissions, David expressed his mounting irritation over the inactivity. I have the clear impression of a man pacing his apartment waiting for something, almost anything, to happen. He was trapped. He couldn't take his mother and leave Washington because he was committed to waiting for Barbara to get in touch with him. He had tried to make a deal. He had arranged for Squires to get guns. Was he going to use them? Did he indeed have them? Finally, he prevailed on Morrison to visit him.

* * *

"I think you can understand, David. I haven't much time just now."

"Dammit, I just want to know if he has the weapons."

[Morrison chuckled.] "Relax, son. Don't worry so much. You'll get your girl."

"Christ—"

[Another chuckle.] "Yes, my boy, Squires has his weapons."

"Then what's he doing with them?"

"I'm afraid we posed a bit of a logistics problem for him. The army is making it a bit difficult for him to move them around. Seems the army wants its weapons back."

"Can't you do something?"

"We are—as best we can. But you must understand; we can't call off the military entirely. It wouldn't look right."

[There is a pause. When David breaks it, his voice expresses both consternation and ridicule.]

"I don't get you. I don't get you at all. You've concocted this little scheme. You've spent all this money, all this effort, trying to keep your boy in the White House. It is now almost the middle of October. The campaign is in full swing. Houston Walker is attracting crowds suitable for the second coming. Your boy, whatsisname—"

"Strange how few people seem to know his name. Edmund J. Lamb, distinguished governor of Pennsylvania."

"Oh, yes, Sacrificial Lamb."

"I have never thought that nickname in very good taste."

"Maybe, but it's accurate. Walker is going to win. It'll be a rout. If Squires has your guns, he obviously is too smart to use them."

"He'll use them."

"He'd better hurry up. Has it ever occurred to you, Uncle Richard, that your whole scheme is about to blow up in your kisser?"

"It has occurred to me, of course. But I assure you it won't happen."

"Aren't you a *little* worried?"

[Morrison hesitated.] "I'll admit I had thought Squires would start his revolution before this. Everything is a little closer than I might like. But don't panic yet. I'm not."

[David snorted.] "Your calmness amazes me."

[Laughter from Morrison.] "When you reach my age, you learn to take things as they come. I assure you, we are taking steps right now to insure that Mr. Squires acts."

"Like what?"

"For one thing, I suggest you watch your television about a week from now. The President will be making a speech."

"A speech!"

"Quite an important one."

* * *

I suppose I should reproduce the whole speech here, but it is so familiar I hate to waste the time. Lampton admitted that a series of train robberies had occurred—seven in all—and that a substantial quantity of military arms had been stolen. He had reason to believe the robberies had been the concerted work of subversives bent on the violent overthrow of the government. He intended to use his full powers as commander-in-chief to track down the subversives and recover the stolen weapons. While he was President, he would not see harm come to this great nation. He asked the people to remain calm and to go about their affairs normally. In a few days one of two fine Americans, Edmund Lamb for the Republicans or Houston Walker for the Democrats, would be elected to the office he now held. He intended to use all the powers of his office to see that one of them was elected in an orderly fashion and that the winner was sworn in next January 20th as President of the world's oldest democracy. He intended to turn over the reins of government to his chosen successor just as it had occurred for over two hundred years. He asked the people to be patient and helpful as police and military units searched for the stolen weapons. He asked the public to lend whatever assistance they could by reporting any suspicious movements of trucks or cargo.

One of the reasons I have had to describe the speech and not report it verbatim is that the doorbell rang in the middle of it. David answered and admitted Barbara Kingsley. I have had monstrous difficulty transcribing their conversation, for David left the television on with the President droning away during the first part of his conversation with Barbara. I was immensely relieved when he finally turned the bloody set off. I have done the best I can to piece together their conversation. Some of my difficulty, it must be realized, stems from the fact the door to David's apartment must be one of the furthest points from the microphone, while the TV set is much closer. Too, as I discovered when the television was switched off, both were apparently choked with emotion. I had never heard Barbara's voice before. I can only say it was young and feminine, contrasting with Carla Callahan's breathy, more mature voice. But David was clearly emotional. He seemed almost unable to speak. His voice cracked a couple of times.

* * *

"David."

"Barbara! I didn't think you'd come."

"You should have known better. I came as soon as Edna told me."

"God, Barbara, I—Lord, I'm speechless. I don't know what to say."

[She laughed, girlishly it seemed to me.] "You can start by inviting me in."

"I'm sorry. Here, let me take your bag."

[She obviously entered. There is a click of the door latch.]

"What a nice place. You live here by yourself?"

"Yes."

"You cook and everything?"

"I don't cook much, I'm afraid."

"You poor man. Doesn't your mother—"

"She lives in Georgetown."

[She laughed again.] "She didn't look like the sort who likes to cook."

[Perhaps I'm eccentric, but this particular exchange both amazes and delights me. What a remarkable, genuine, unaffected girl she is. Her instant concern is for him and his eating habits.

402

Here is a tremendously emotional situation. David is full of it and can hardly speak. She enters and comments on his interior decoration. Amazing. I do swear women are better in such situations than men. A man will confront his problem and charge at it. A woman will try to ignore the problem and find something else, some aspect of nest building, to interest her. Of course, in this situation, Barbara doesn't know she has a problem.]

"Barbara."

"It's really me—or is it I? You don't have to keep saying my name."

"I don't know what to say."

"Then kiss me. I've wanted you to for such a long time."

[There is a prolonged silence, marked by the voice of the President: "While I remain in this high office, no hoodlums, no gangsters, no subversives will destroy our society, our institutions, this great land God has bestowed upon us. I will use all the powers of my office to—"]

"Oh, darling."

"Are you all right?"

"I'm fine. Why?"

"You seem thinner. You've lost weight."

"I thought you were measuring me. What's wrong?"

"Barbara, I just—"

"That time with Ephraim? I was mortified. I wanted to die when I saw it was you. It was

403

just a gag. I went along. I had to, really. Ephraim said he wanted to shock somebody. I had no idea it was you. I'm so sorry. I truly am."

"Barbara, it's—"

"Don't make more of it than it was. I was never his girl. There's never been—"

"Barbara—"

"—anyone but you. You do believe me?"

"I don't care about Squires. I'm just glad you're out of there. I don't want you ever to go back."

"Don't worry. I'll never leave you out of my sight again."

[There is a pause and finally silence as David—or perhaps it was she—turned off the TV set. She apparently was inspecting the apartment.]

"Oh, you have two bedrooms. Won't need that one. And a king-size bed." [She giggled.] "We won't need all of that."

[Silence.]

"You never used to be so slow. You were always trying to get me in bed. What does a girl— There *is* something wrong, isn't there?"

"Barbara, I—"

"For God's sake, quit stammering. Say what you want to say."

"Barbara— Oh, lord, all right. This is no place for you."

"Why not? There's plenty of room. We'll—"

"You can't stay here, that's all."

"You mean— No, it can't be. Edna said you loved me. You wanted me to come live with you."

"Barbara, I—"

"She brought me here herself. The last thing she said was 'Be happy. Enjoy.' Is this some kind of joke?"

"It's no joke. I'll tell you what. You can stay here. Mother and I are going up to Connecticut. You can stay here while—"

"Your mother! You're going off with your mother!"

"Yes. We'll be gone a couple of weeks anyway. You can have this place until—"

"I don't want your damn place until—until never. I want you. You mean to tell me you're still . . . there's still someone else?"

"Barbara, I—"

"Just tell me, please, who it is. Your mother? It can't be your mother. You aren't a mama's boy. I couldn't have made that mistake."

"I always told you not to love me."

"Why the hell did you send for me?"

"I had to get you out of there. I couldn't stand Squires—"

"At least I know where I stand with him. It's no damn never-never land; I can't love you; there's someone else . . . it's enough to make a girl weep—only I'm not going to shed any more tears over you, David Callahan. I'm going back to where I'm needed."

"I need you, Barbara."

"For what? For the same thing Squires does? To turn you on for some other bitch. You're no better than he is. But at least he's honest about it."

"Barbara, put down your suitcase. Don't do this. Isn't it enough that I care for you, that I'm fond of you?"

"I've seen more affection for pet dogs. God, what a dirty trick you are."

"Can't you understand, I—"

"What a dirty, dirty, filthy trick."

"Edna shouldn't have told you I—"

"You're damn right she shouldn't have. But, you see, she cares more about me than you do. She wanted me to be happy. But she didn't figure on that celebrated iceberg, David Callahan."

"Does it have to be this way?"

"No, it doesn't have to be this way at all. All you have to do is say, 'Barbara, I love you.' No, you don't even have to say that. All you have to do is take me in your arms and mean it."

[There is a prolonged silence.]

"Does it help if I say I want to. I really do. I just can't, that's all."

"And I can't stay here. Goodbye, David."

"Where'll you go? Not back to Squires."

"Goodbye, David."

* * *

There is the sound of the door closing, followed by minutes of silence before the tape ran out. I'm a little surprised he didn't say something. I would have expected him to run after her or shout something after her or even stand there and recriminate with himself. But I guess his silence is far more eloquent. I believe I should emulate him. I had intended to make some comments about Carla Callahan and the evil she wrought, but I guess I don't really need to.

There must have been something about the mechanical action of changing the tape that brought David out of his near catatonic state. He began to speak, apparently as soon as the new tape was put on.

* * *

I tried. I really tried. But what can I do? If she wants Squires, she can have him. If she wants him slavering over her while he fucks another woman, if she's that kind of girl, then good riddance. I never did care much about her. I told her that. I told her and told her. She has no right to demand of me. She's too damn possessive. Good riddance, Callahan. For once you handled something well. She's gone. It's over. Now Mother and I can go to Westport and be happy.

[There is the sound of David picking up the phone and dialing.]

"Mother. I'm free at last. Now we can go

to . . . what? Barbara was here. I was talking to her . . . I guess I heard something. I thought it was thunder. . . . What? . . . Are you all right? . . ."

[Carla Callahan obviously told her son on the phone what had happened while he was with Barbara. The Liberty Party, under the direction of Ephraim Squires, had launched a blow for freedom right in the middle of Lampton's speech. Mortar, recoilless rifle and rocket shells had fallen indiscriminately on Washington. The west portico of the Capitol was hit by one of the early rounds. Another round landed in the rose garden of the White House, shattering many windows. Several government buildings, including the Justice Department, State Department, NASA, and the National Archives took direct hits in the early shelling. All of this occurred right on television, apparently just after David turned off his set. When the round hit the rose garden, Lampton jumped out of his seat. "What the fuck is that?" he said. There was a mumble of voices. He sat down and tried to go on; then two Secret Service men came on camera and led him away. The television screen went blank for a few moments; then an announcer came on with a confused report of the shelling. This piece of film is now a classic and has been shown many times on BBC as the beginning of the end of American democracy. David, knowing nothing of all this, listened in amazement to his mother's version of these events.]

"But it can't be . . . Squires wouldn't fire at the Capitol. . . . All right, all right, I believe you. Do you know what that means? Uncle Richard and that madman in the White House, do they know what they've done? . . . Look, don't get excited. I'll be right over. . . . No, don't answer the door. I'll be there in a minute. . . . Oh, God, she's hung up.

* * *

David must have run out the door to find his mother. I have no idea how long he was gone, but I gather a considerable length of time.

* * *

Lord, she's gone. I couldn't find her. I broke into her house and went all through it. She wasn't there. I waited awhile, hoping she'd come back, but she never did. I knew it was silly, but I just had to find her. I ran around town like an idiot looking for her, and I had no idea where she'd gone. God, what devastation. The Capitol's been hit twice, the White House once. Pennsylvania Avenue and Constitution Avenue look like a battleground. I guess that's what they are. Damn Squires. Damn him, damn him, damn him. How could he? Fires everywhere. And every time the firemen arrive, a car careens by spraying machine-gun bullets.

[He turned up the volume on his radio.]

"The nation's capital is under some kind of attack by terrorists. The President has proclaimed martial law. The army has taken charge. All military personnel are ordered to report to their bases immediately. Troops are being sent from Fort Meade, Fort Belvoir, and Fort Myers. Yes, we have just received word that elements of the 82nd Airborne Division have landed at Andrews Air Force Base and are on their way into the city. And we have an unconfirmed report of a guerilla attack on Fort Meade, Maryland. There is a report more weapons and ammunition were stolen, but this is unconfirmed. I repeat, this is unconfirmed. And this just in. Lieutenant General Burton Burroughs, commander of the Second Army, has imposed an immediate curfew. All persons other than military personnel are to remain in their homes until further notice. Any unauthorized persons out on the street will be arrested immediately. To repeat, some form of major attack has been made on the city by— This just in. The Associated Press reports that shells and rockets have struck New York, Chicago, and Los Angeles. Government buildings seem to be the major targets. The source of these attacks, as here in Washington, is unknown, but they are believed linked to the recent series of train derailments."

[David sat up the rest of the night listening to the radio, all of which is heard on the tape.

There are other sounds on the tape, all difficult to distinguish. From time to time, he swears and curses various people, including Squires, Morrison, Lampton, and himself. Once or twice he rails at himself for what he has done. There are other sounds indicating that he is drinking heavily. All in all it is an extraordinary tape. The man who helped put the guns in the hands of revolutionaries hearing the effects of his work.]

"The sun has now risen on a scene of unbelievable devastation in this city. The Capitol, the White House, are damaged, along with the Justice Department, State Department, National Archives, NASA, Agriculture, Commerce, and the Supreme Court buildings. The top of the Washington Monument has been sheered off. Several rounds struck the Pentagon, and fires are still raging there. We have no reliable reports of casualties, but apparently they are heavy. President Lampton, who was addressing the nation at the time the attack was launched, was taken to the White House bomb shelter and is reportedly directing counter guerilla activities from there. Members of his cabinet and other senior officials have joined him in the war room. Men from the Second Army are patrolling the streets with tanks and armored personnel carriers. Other military units are reportedly landing by the minute at Andrews Air Force Base, as well as National Airport, Dulles Airport, and

Baltimore's Friendship Airport, all of which have been closed to regular traffic. With daylight, gunfire has ended in the city, but it was a night of thunderous explosions and rattling machine guns as guerillas launched an apparent all-out attack and beleaguered police and troops fought back as best they could. We will stay on the air here until—"

* * *

David ran out of his apartment, saying, "Curfew or no curfew, I'm going to find Mother." He left both his tape recorder and radio playing. The radio continues running on the tape for over an hour before it is finally shut off. The background noise associated with David's apartment continues awhile longer on the tape; then it too was shut off. When I first heard the tape, I assumed David had returned and turned the switches. The last tape proves I was in error. It is later in the day when David begins it.

* * *

The fat is in the fire now. I am in deep trouble. I went out this morning to find Mother. I went to her house. She wasn't there. I waited awhile, trying to figure out where she might be. I thought maybe Squires had kidnapped her, although I couldn't think why he would. I thought of hunting Squires, but realized that was impossible. The best thing for me to do was go back to my place and wait there until I got some word. If only Mother and I had gone to Westport last week.

It took some time to get back to my place. I had to dodge a couple of army patrols. I had no papers, and I just didn't have in mind being arrested. When I arrived, Uncle Richard was there.

"Uncle Richard. How'd you get in?"

"I set you up in this place. I've always kept a key."

"I'm glad you're here. Do you know where Mother is? I've been hunting her. I'm worried sick about her."

"She's safe. She's with the President. He sent a car for her as soon as the shelling began."

"The President! What's she doing with him?"

"I could explain it to you, but we have more important things to discuss just now." [Morrison's voice sounded very sober, very serious.]

"Well, I don't. Where is my mother?"

"When I came into your apartment, the radio was playing loudly. In an effort to shut it off, I discovered your tape recording device— there, in the panel behind your bar. There is no need for you to close the panel door. It won't hide anything any more. I'm afraid I have a weakness of curiosity. I wondered what other contraptions you have here. I'm afraid I found your microphone hidden in the vase of artificial flowers on the coffee table. I had always thought it a particularly unsightly decoration."

"So—"

"So I don't blame you for looking pale, David. Might I say guilty? I played your tape."

"There's nothing on it. Just the radio broadcasts. I thought it of historic importance. I wanted to—"

"We had another man, a President actually, who was big on history. He wanted to preserve his every word on tape—damn him. I told you I didn't like tape recorders. I trusted your good sense not to do anything like this."

"There's no harm. Just a radio broadcast."

"I'm afraid it's a bit more. You recorded yourself talking to your mother on the phone. In that conversation you made a reference to me and 'that madman in the White House.'"

"I was frightened and angry. It meant nothing."

"I fear it meant a great deal, son. Someone could read a great deal into it."

"All right. No problem. I'll destroy the tape. I only wanted the radio broadcasts. I'm sure they'll be a dime a dozen when this is over."

"What else have you recorded?"

"What do you mean?"

"I think you know what I mean. You have that microphone over there in the bouquet of flowers. We sat there most times when we talked. Indeed, it is about the only place to sit in this room, except at the dinner table. And I assume your microphone would pick up even there. David, I must assume you recorded my conversations with you. I cannot permit that. I want your tapes, all of them you have."

[There is a short pause. It is obvious that David is backed into a corner.]

"At your wish, Uncle Richard, I spent a great deal of time here by myself. I was lonely. I recorded a lot of thoughts and remembrances about myself and about my mother and father. They are too personal for me to allow anyone to hear them. I wouldn't even let my mother listen to them."

"What are you going to do with these tapes?"

"I don't know. I haven't thought about it. I guess I'll throw them away some day."

"Did you or did you not record my conversations here in this room."

[No answer from David. Morrison raised his voice.]

"Answer my question, young man. This instant."

[David hesitated, but only briefly.] "All right, I did. Yes, I recorded your every word here. I did it deliberately. You hatched your little harebrained scheme. You gave guns to Squires. Have you been out in the city? I have. It looks like a battleground. The Capitol is—"

"It couldn't be helped. It will be repaired. I want those tapes, David."

"Look, I'm the one out on the limb. I'm the exposed one. There are five hundred people in Squires's organization who can point the finger at me—*me*, not you, not the President. It's David Callahan that gets thrown to the wolves. Me! Well, I don't have any yen for the firing squad or whatever they do to traitors these days. I made those tapes to protect myself, and I intend to keep them."

"I can't allow that. We'll provide you all the protection you need."

"Oh, sure, the protection of the grave. When your little scheme blows up—"

"It's not blowing up. It is succeeding brilliantly."

"—and the whistle is blown on me, I'm as good as dead. You'd never let me go to a trial. I know too much."

"Don't be silly. You're practically a son to me. Nothing will happen to you. I want those tapes, and I want them now."

"No chance."

"All right. If you won't give them to me, let's destroy them now, right here. We can use the sink to build a fire."

"No. I'm keeping them."

[Morrison softened his voice. He tried a new tactic.] "I know this has been hard for you, son. It has been a strain. Both your mother and I have worried about you."

"You have, have you?"

416

"You've been childish and petulant. We've done everything possible to humor you."

"So that's it. Anything to keep dumb old David on the job."

"That's not—oh, hell, why not the truth. You've been erratic lately. I've been afraid of your doing something foolish. I came here to see for myself. And I was right, *you stupid fool!*" [Morrison's voice was now thoroughly menacing.] "I want those tapes. *Now!*"

[David laughed.] "Uncle Richard, you are a big man, but I don't think you're much of a match for me."

[There is a long silence punctuated by deep sighs from Morrison.] "My son, you are being foolish. I don't want any harm to come to you. But what can I do? Yes, there's one thing. Perhaps your mother can talk some sense into you."

And so I sit here, awaiting Mother's arrival to talk some sense into me. Lord, I wish she of all people didn't know of these tapes. She'll have a fit. It's going to be awful. But I'm not going to give them up. They're all I got. I know that now. If I give up the tapes, I'm practically dead. I've hidden them. No one will find them.

* * *

I have moved again. This afternoon I went to the post to mail the latest installment to the publisher. As I was returning, I saw them, across the street and down the block, two men entering a rooming house. I ducked into a doorway until they went into the building; then I came here, quickly packed, and fled out the rear. I hailed a cab and came here a few blocks away.

It is strange how you know them. Being a fugitive must heighten a person's senses. They could have been just two well-dressed men doing anything, building inspectors or something. But I know they were after me. They were too well-dressed. Their clothes were obviously American. Funny, I never would have noticed that before. There were bulges under their jackets. Oh, I don't know how I know. I just know.

I hope no one saw me. I've grown a full beard and taken to wearing a wide-brimmed hat, but I'm sure I'd be recognized. Fugitives always are, aren't they? I hope I've gotten away. I hope I've gained a little more time to finish this—and to get away myself. I want to get away. I want to live. David Callahan's confession has changed me. I feel I've wasted my whole life in the vanity of diffidence. I've studied obscure subjects that no one cared about, believing my erudition made them important. I've spent years as an expatriate. The Cotswolds have been my home. I even considered taking out British citizenship. I told myself over and over I didn't care what was happening in the United States. But I do care—now. David Callahan has made me care. I want to live. I want to go back home. I'll get there somehow. I want to fight Lampton and Morrison. I want to help restore democracy to my country. If I must die, I don't want it to be in a bedsitter in London. I want my life to have meant something. If give it I must, I want it to have gone for some purpose. I want to go home and fight.

David Callahan's mother came to visit him.

* * *

"David, what is this about tapes?"

"I'm sure Uncle Richard has given you a generous account."

"Have you been making tapes?"

[Sigh.] "Yes, I've made some tapes. I can't deny it."

"Of what?"

"I merely recorded some private thoughts to kill the time while you've been entertaining your various presidents. What were you doing with Lampton last night?"

"Richard said you recorded his private conversations with you—you're using them to blackmail him?"

"I am not blackmailing him. I simply wanted to protect myself—and you—when this whole foolish scheme blows up—and I do mean when, not if."

"How could you? Nothing of this must ever be known."

"But it will be, don't you see? Houston Walker's going to be elected President in a few days. There'll be an end to this shooting. Squires will make peace with Walker. The whole thing will come out, and I'll be the one they hang it on. And you're not out of it either, you know. I did it for both of us."

"You're so stupid, David. So *stupid*. You don't even know what's going on. Listen to me. Give up those tapes. They'll kill you for them."

"I doubt that. Uncle Richard—"

"He can't stop them. You're as good as dead unless you give me those tapes this instant."

"No."

"Don't be so stupid, David. Can't you hear what I'm saying."

"No."

"Why won't you give them up? Why are they so important? You didn't record our conversations. . . . My God, you didn't; you couldn't. How could you? You bastard. How could you do this to me? Is nothing sacred? You wouldn't even speak of what we've done."

"No one will know."

"Yes, they will. Richard may have already heard something. He seemed funny today. I want those tapes. I demand them—*now!*"

[Pause.]

"David, if you don't give me those tapes, I swear to God I'll kill you myself."

[He laughed.] "My, you're vicious."

"I mean it, David. As much as I love you, I'd kill you rather than have a word of what we've done come out."

"Then you'd never find the tapes. I've hidden them well."

[She slapped him. It is a sharp crack on the tape.] "You monster." [Again she slapped him.] "You *monster*. I won't let you destroy me this way. I won't. I want those damn tapes. Do you hear me?" [Her words, all screamed at him, are punctuated by the sounds of her repeated slapping.] "Let go of my arms. *Let go of me*. You're hurting me—"

[Then she cried, quite hard, convulsively. It went on for more than a half minute.]

"Don't cry, Mother. For God's sake, don't cry."

[Through her sobs, she said:] "I can't help it."

"I can't stand it when you cry."

[She seemed to sob harder, yet managed to get out a few words.] "I can't believe it . . . After all I've done for you . . . After all we've meant to each other . . . You'd do this to me . . ."

[Deep sigh from David.] "All right, Mother, all right."

"You'd destroy me this way . . ."

"I never intended for you to know the tapes even existed—for anyone to know. I'd never hurt you in any way, you know that. I don't give a damn about the lousy tapes. I'll destroy them."

421

"Oh, David—"

"I shouldn't have made them. I was a fool."

[Her sobbing ended, but her voice was still broken, if brighter.] "Oh, darling. I knew you couldn't mean it."

"Wait here. I'll get the tapes. We'll burn them."

"Yes, yes, I'll wait."

[David speaks from further away, apparently near the door.] "But I'd like to ask something of you."

"Anything."

"Let's go immediately to Westport. I'm worried sick about you here. We'll be safe there."

[He moved closer to the microphone.]

"You will go with me, won't you?"

[He is apparently all the way back to the coffee table.]

"Won't you?"

[Sigh.] "I can't, David. I just can't."

"You have something to do? Okay, we'll go tomorrow. We'll get a pass out of the city. We can drive—"

"Not today, David, not tomorrow." [Sigh.] "I'm afraid never."

"What the hell does that mean?"

"I don't know how to tell you this."

"Tell me what?"

"The President has asked me to marry him. I've said I would."

"Marry the President!"

"He wanted to tell you himself. I said it would be better if I—"

"Marry Lampton! Why he's so *old*."

[She laughed, lightly, perhaps artificially.] "He's not old, David. He's almost the same age as your father would be."

"Marry that bastard? For crissake. What are you going to do for sex? . . . So you've done it with him. How was it? Tell me, Mother, how's the President of the United States in the sack?"

[Silence.]

"Does he turn you on? Answer me, dammit."

"He's a very vigorous man."

"Is he now. Well, if you aren't something. Do you love him?"

[Silence.]

"Goddammit, answer me."

"I'm fond of him. He needs me."

"Sure, he needs his cunt."

"Watch your language, David. You're going too far."

"I'm going too far. God, you must be kidding. Why do you want him?"

"What woman wouldn't?"

"I can think of thousands, millions. Why? Because he's the President? You want to be the First Lady? Big White House wedding and all that?"

"It's to be a quiet ceremony. A big wedding wouldn't be appropriate now. We'll just have the Chief Justice marry us, then make a public announcement."

"The Chief Justice no less. How touching." [He made a sound that was both snort and sneer.] "Well, you better get at it soon. You've only got till January 20 to be First Lady."

"It'll be much longer."

"And what makes you think so? What makes you know so much?"

"I know, that's all." [She paused.] "We see no reason to wait. The wedding's the day after tomorrow." [Another pause.] "I hope you'll come." [She tried to sound gay, but her attempt was brittle, forced.] "I hope you'll give your mother away—make her happy."

"Jesus Christ, you got your fucking gall."

[There are a variety of sounds, apparently David stomping about, pouring a drink. He can be heard to swear repeatedly.]

"Dammit, Mother. I thought that we . . . I thought we were going to live together . . ."

"David, I—"

"I thought you loved me. I thought you wanted me. I thought you meant it all."

"I did, David, I did."

"But not anymore. Is that it?"

[Silence.]

"Mother, why? Just tell me why. You owe me that much."

"I'm forty years old, David. You're twenty-five. I can't live with you."

"It doesn't matter. You don't look forty."

"But I do. I've wrinkles under this makeup.

For all my exercises, my skin is no longer tight. Look at my hands. Look at them. Senile spots already. What a ghastly name. Senile spots. I have to wear gloves."

"It doesn't matter, Mother. You're the most beautiful—"

"And in five years, ten, twenty?"

"It won't matter. You must know how much I love you."

"It won't work, David. It's obscene for me to be seen with you."

"It's never bothered you before."

"Oh, yes, it has. It's bothered me for a long time. I need an older man, someone more appropriate to my age."

"Crap. What about sex? What about your headaches? I can tell your skull is splitting right now."

"I'll get used to it. I'll have to."

"If you think I'm going to sneak around on the side . . ."

"I don't. You and I must never do it again."

[David forced a laugh.] "You're kidding yourself, Mother. I just won't let you do it. I'll stop you from this nonsense somehow."

"God, David, what have I done to you? Can't you understand? Can't you grow up? It's all over between us—the sex, I mean. It has been over for a long time. We've got to be a proper mother and son from now on."

"What do you mean—it's been over for a long time?"

"It's not like it used to be, David. It couldn't stay that way."

"How long?"

[She sighed and muttered her frustration under her breath.] "David, everything changed the night your father died. I tried not to let it. God knows I tried. But I couldn't help it. I changed. We changed. Everything changed."

"What sort of change?"

"Oh, I can't explain it very well. When Brendan died, I was free, free to live my own life—or I should have been. But I wasn't. I—"

"You were stuck with me."

"Oh, lord, that's not the way to put it."

"But it amounts to the same thing."

"I wanted to live my own life. I was young, rich. I still had my looks. I wanted to—"

"And I held you back."

"Sort of—yes. You had your plans. You wanted something—I came to realize what you wanted wasn't what I—David, it was like being married again. I'd gone from a demanding husband to an even more demanding son. Is that so awful to say? Does the truth hurt too much?"

"Not at all, Mother. I feel just jolly. Tell me, what were we doing in the bedroom? When was the last time? Last week? And a couple of days before that? You were faking? You've been faking all these times?"

"You know I haven't."

"*How* do I know it? I've been too demanding. I'm a millstone. It seems to me that at least a few times, you—"

"I've wanted you, David."

"Oh, sure, my son the stud."

[Silence.]

"David Callahan—gigolo."

"Don't be so childish."

"What have you been up to? My God, you don't mean— You couldn't."

"You're wrong, David."

"Am I? You and Uncle Richard cooked this thing up from the beginning. I can hear it now. 'Richard, help me find something for David to do.' 'Sure, Carla. I'll get him involved in my plot to take over the country.' "

"It wasn't that way."

"Maybe not exactly that way. But you were in there on the bed, making your little contribution to keeping your husband-to-be in the White House, weren't you? *Weren't you?* 'Don't be so upset, David. Lie back down.' God, what a fool I've been. I wondered why Morrison brought you here all the time. Now I know."

"David, it's—"

"God, that's awful, Mother. Ghastly."

[Silence.]

"You used me. You *used* me. And all the time—"

[A prolonged silence.]

"Get out, Mother. Go to your stud in the White House."

"David, darling, I've always loved you. I only wanted you to live your own life."

"So you could have yours. I asked you once what you wanted to be. You wouldn't answer. Now I know. Mrs. Lampton, gorgeous First Lady. God, did you want it bad."

"David, I—"

"Uncle Richard, dear, old, kindly, fatherly Uncle Richard always said you were a remarkable woman. Always got what you wanted. Okay, so you got it. So just go, go to him. Please, just go. I want to try to salvage something of my life."

[Silence. Eighteen seconds.]

"I said go. Make it one last act of mercy for me."

"I want the tapes, David."

"Oh, yes, the tapes. The good old tapes."

"*I want those tapes.*"

"Is there never to be an end to your wanting?"

"Listen, David. They'll kill you to get them. I know they will."

"And with your encouragement."

"I won't be able to prevent it."

"And I'll die if I hand them over."

"No, you won't. Merrill's going to stay on as President. He's grateful to you. You can have anything—"

"All I want is for you to leave."

"God, David, *listen* to me."

[The voices are further away from the microphone.]

"Stop pushing me and listen."

"Goodbye, Mother—forever."

"David, listen—"

[The door slams. There is frantic ringing of the doorbell and knocking on the door. David says nothing and apparently does nothing. In a minute or so the noise stops. The silence, winding on the tape, is dreadful. Finally, David speaks, his voice wan, weak, very sad. He may be crying.]

Father. I'm sorry I killed you. You tried to warn me. I wouldn't listen. Dad, I wish you were here. What would you have me do? There must be some way I can undo what I've done.

God, that's awful. You hated him while he was alive, and now you want to talk to him. What a meathead you are, Callahan. Get control of yourself. You've got to think. You've got to do something.

[There is a short period of silence.]

Yes. I know what Dad would have me do.

[He dialed a phone number.]

"Call eight eleven. Call eight eleven. As soon as possible. It's vital. A matter of life and death."

[He hung up the phone.]

She's got to call. She's just got to. I've got to get to Squires. I've got to tell him he's being used, just as I was. I've got to tell him to stop the fighting. If he does, Walker will be President. Lampton's scheme will blow up in his face. I'll tell the truth. Yes. It isn't too late. But just call me, Edna. And soon. I've got to get to Squires.

Got to think. What if she doesn't call? Maybe she won't get my message. Got to think. Got to have a backup plan. The tapes. Mother's right. They'll kill me for those tapes. Got to think.

Okay. The tapes. Nobody'll find them where they are now. But what good is it if no one finds them? Lampton and Morrison, aided and abetted by the silken arms of my dear mother, get away with it. Not if I can help it. I've got to blow the whistle on them. Just got to. I'll go somewhere, take the tapes, put it all down—No, they'll hunt me down wherever I go. Got to get these tapes somewhere for safekeeping. But *to* someone, someone who'll know what to do with them if anything happens to me. Yes, someone. Who? Who? Think, you dummy. You haven't been thinking for years. It's not too late to start. Who? Who?

[There follow several minutes of silence, then the words: "Bonnie Blue Bell." This is the name of the Inn associated with Hinsdale College. There is another period of silence; then David uttered his devious signal that he was sending the tapes to me, a signal so obscure I almost didn't get it: "There are many aspects to this, but I think there are more factors."]

Now you're getting some place, Callahan. You've got a plan, two plans. That's two more than you've had in your whole life. Try a third. Barbara. What a fool I've been. I've got to find Barbara. Got to. If only the blasted phone would ring.

[There is such a long period of silence on the tape that I thought David's transmissions had all ended with those words. Finally, near the end of the reel, the phone rings.]

"Edna. I thought you'd never call. Just a second. Hold it just a second."

[I'm eternally grateful—I think the world will be, too—that David thought to clamp on a phone jack so both sides of the phone conversation could be recorded.]

"Okay, Edna. I'm so glad you called."

"Don't know why I did. It's an awful risk. What's so vital?"

"Edna, I got to get to Squires."

"No way."

"I got to, Edna. I got to tell him to stop—"

"Pretty boy, I said there is no way. It's the truth. What you want just can't be done."

"O, lord. Okay. Then you tell him for me. Can you?"

"Yes."

"Tell him I'm blowing the whistle. Tell him it's all been a huge plot to keep Lampton in the White House. Tell him the guns were given to him just so he'd fight. Tell him if he stops fighting the whole scheme will collapse."

"He knew that. He just wanted free guns. Besides, he can't stop it. He gave out the guns. God knows where they are. Everyone's freelancing."

"Squires doesn't have control?"

"Only generally. We're after the government buildings, the banks, that sort of—"

"Edna, he's got to find a way to stop it. All of this has been a big plan to get the election called off. Lampton figures if there is a lot of turmoil and the election results are questioned, he'll stay on as President until a new election is held. It's a crazy scheme, but that's what he's up to. If Squires will stop the fighting, the election will go on, and Houston Walker is sure to win. Squires will be able to make a deal with him."

"Pretty boy, where you been?"

"What do you mean? I've been here."

"Haven't you heard? Haven't you got your radio or TV on?"

"No. What haven't I heard?"

"Houston Walker's been murdered. That other guy, too—Lamb. They're saying we did it, but we didn't. Your boys did it."

"Oh, God, *no*!"

"You're right about no election."

"Edna, no. I never dreamed they'd do that."

"They did, pretty boy. You're in with a rough crowd. We've no choice but to fight."

"You do, Edna, you do."

"Maybe, but I'm not the one to stop it. I
432

don't think anyone can. I got to go, David. See you, come the revolution."

"Edna, wait. Where's Barbara? I got to see her. I've been a fool."

"You can say that again. I tried to help you, but there's no accounting for a jerk like you."

"Where is she? I got to find her."

"I don't know. I really don't. David, I'm sorry, but I have to go."

[There is a click of the receiver being hung up.]

Publisher's Note

This is the last material received from Professor Grayson. If there were more, or whether he intended to write more, is not known.

Recently the following item appeared in the *Times*:

> The body recovered from the Thames near Gravesend yesterday has been identified as that of Cornelius Walter Grayson, American political scientist and author, who has been living in Gloucestershire for some years. An investigation is being conducted into the cause of his death.

OFFSHORE
by
Gary Brandner

Santa Marta was a peaceful little resort on the California coast. One morning, an offshore drilling rig, owned by California Oil International (Caloil), appeared in the clear, blue water of the channel, taking everyone by surprise. Angry at the intrusion and afraid for the environment, the people of Santa Marta banded together to stop Caloil.

It was Big Oil versus small town, but for the men and women involved it meant much more—the conflict unleashed the fury of their hidden desires and all-consuming ambitions . . . and irrevocably changed their lives.

Joe Deitrich was the young, ambitious mayor of Santa Marta, with his eye on the governor's mansion in Sacramento and even the White House itself. But if he mishandled the Caloil situation, his political future would end right there in Santa Marta. . . .

Cheryl Solomon was a reporter covering the Santa Marta story for her magazine. At first, it was just another assignment. Bright and attractive, she was good at her job and had never allowed anything to interfere with her work. But suddenly she found herself falling in love with Joe Deitrich and she didn't know what to do. . . .

Wesley Traveller was the president of Caloil, and if anything went wrong in Santa Marta it would cost him his job. But he did not get to be president by merely allowing events to take their course. There were ways to control events, and Traveller knew them all. . . .

The following are edited excerpts from this new novel, currently available wherever paperbacks are sold.

This was the first time he had made it with Melody Heath. She wasn't the greatest lay in the world, but there was a satisfaction in scoring with the daughter of the richest man in town. Maybe he'd bang her once more before sending her home. Up at her fancy school she probably didn't get much good humping. From the way she threw her ass around and squealed, Max could tell that she liked what he did to her.

He went up the ladder through the forward hatch and onto the deck. He edged along the seaward side, where he'd heard the tapping. The fog was thinning now, and when he looked down into the water he could make out a round, orange object, partly submerged and bobbing against the boat.

"What the fuck?" he muttered, and pulled a boathook from its brackets on the cabin bulkhead. He dipped the hook into the water and brought up the orange object. It was a plastic hardhat, the type worn by construction workers. On the front in heavy black letters was printed CALOIL, the logo for California Oil International, one of the leading independent oil companies on the coast.

Gripping the hardhat, Max peered out across the channel, squinting to see through the lifting mist. At first it was just a vertical shadow looming out of the water, like an enormous fish with one digit pointing to the sky and giving him the finger. The breeze freshened suddenly, stirring the fog, and Max Barone saw what the thing was.

"Jesus Fucking Christ, an oil rig!"

Melody Heath came up on deck. She had put on her jeans and sweatshirt. "What is it! What's the matter?"

Max pointed out across the water. "That's what's the matter."

The sun was breaking through now, and the squat

black barge could be seen clearly. It had a raised plat-form at one end and the steel-girder tower of an oil derrick at the other.

"An oil well?" Melody said. "In our channel?"

"It's an offshore drilling rig," Max corrected. "And it sure as hell is in our channel. The bastards must have sneaked it out there during the night."

"They can't do that, can they?"

Max continued to glower at the barge, not listening to the girl. "They move right in and take over. They'll turn this channel into a sewer."

"Isn't there anything we can do?" Melody said.

"I'll call Joe Deitrich. He's supposed to be our mayor; we'll let him start earning his salary."

*　　*　　*

In the upstairs bedroom of their red-roofed Spanish-style house. Erica Deitrich lay awake next to her hus-band. She looked over at his profile, the clean, square features relaxed now in sleep. . . .

The telephone on the bedside table rang. Quickly, Erica reached for it on the first ring so it would not wake Joe, but he had heard it anyway.

Erica put her hand over the mouthpiece. "It's Max Barone down at the marina. Shall I tell him to call back?"

"No, I'll take it."

Erica lifted up the base of the telephone and set it on the bed between them. Joe took the receiver from her hand.

"Hello, Max." He listened for several seconds, frown-ing. "There's a *what* in the channel? The hell you say. Hang on a minute."

While Erica watched curiously, he walked across the bedroom and pulled open the draperies in front of the glass doors leading to the balcony. He slid the doors apart and stepped outside.

Shading his eyes, Joe looked down the hillside, across the Coast Highway, down to the beach and the channel beyond. "I'll be a son of a bitch," he muttered.

"What is it?" Erica called from the bedroom.

"Come and have a look."

There, halfway out in the channel, rode the drilling barge with its stark-black derrick.

"What is it?" Erica said.

"According to Max, it's an offshore oil-drilling rig."

"What's it doing out there?"

"That's what Max wants to know. I guess I'd better go down and find out."

Erica stayed out on the balcony looking across the town at the oil barge. It seemed so out of place there on the sparkling blue water.

"I want to go with you," Erica said.

Joe hesitated. "What for?"

"Because I'm concerned about what happens in our city."

Joe continued to look at her, saying nothing.

"If I have to have a reason, let's say I want to be there on behalf of the women of Santa Marta."

"Honey, that's the job I was elected to do—represent *all* the people." Joe's tone was warm and reasonable. On his lips was the boyish smile that won votes from people who didn't even know to what party he belonged. The smile that some very important people said would take him next to the governor's mansion in Sacramento.

Erica did not smile as she met his gaze. "Joe, I'd like to go."

His tone chilled half a degree. "Not this time. I'll tell you all about it when I get back."

* * *

Police Chief Homer Lantz had been up for an hour when he got Joe Deitrich's call. Homer, an early riser since childhood, at fifty-seven still needed no more than five hours sleep a night, and could get by with even less.

This morning Lantz was servicing his personal collection of handguns until Ruth woke up. He had just finished cleaning a Colt Police Python with a six-inch barrel and was starting to tear down an S&W Combat Magnum. It had been a long time since Homer Lantz had fired a gun in anger, but when the need arose, he wanted to be prepared.

438

When the telephone rang, his tone was crisp. "Lantz speaking." The mayor told him about the oil rig in the channel and asked if Lantz could pick him up.

"I'll be there in five minutes, Joe," he said.

Yawning. Ruth Lantz came out of the bedroom. She was a tall, gray-haired woman whose figure had settled over the years.

"Who was that?" she said.

"The mayor. He wants a ride down to the marina. Something's going on down there."

Lantz gave his wife a quick kiss and walked out to the blue and white Plymouth Fury, one-half of the Santa Marta police fleet. He got in and started the engine. It was one of the powerful 74s, built before the stringent air-pollution regulations that choked the life out of an automobile.

When the police car pulled into the parking lot adjacent to the marina, a small group of Santa Marta citizens gathered out on the dock. In the center of the crowd was Max Barone, talking and gesturing angrily out over the channel. Lantz parked the car, and he and Deitrich walked out to join the others.

"Well, there it is." Barone said, as the mayor and police chief reached the group. "Big as life and twice as ugly."

Deitrich looked out at the barge. From this closer perspective, it was indeed ugly. "Do you know anything about it, Max?" he asked.

"I know the thing must have been towed in during the night. That kind of barge don't run on its own power."

The people standing around murmured their agreement. There was an angry undertone that Deitrich did not like.

"Let's not get excited until we have the facts," he said. "Do you know who owns the rig, Max?"

Without comment, Barone handed him the orange Caloil hardhat. Deitrich recalled that when the leasing moratorium ended the year before Caloil had been the high bidder for offshore tracts in the Santa Marta Channel.

"Caloil has the leases, all right," Deitrich said thoughtfully, "but there's been no go-ahead for drilling operations."

"We can't just sit here and let Caloil take over the town," said Barone.

"Nobody is taking over anything, Max," Deitrich said patiently. "Let's find out just what's going on. Have you got a boat available to run us out there, Max?"

"We can use the Glasstron Sixteen-footer," Barone said, pointing to a sleek red and white outboard at the end of the dock.

"Want me to come along, Joe?" said Lantz. His fingers brushed against the leather holster. "No telling what kind of a reception you'll get."

Deitrich pointed at the Police Python. "Glad to have you come, Homer, but keep that thing buttoned up."

"Whatever you say, Joe," the chief said. He fell in step with Deitrich and they followed Max Barone out to the slip where the outboard was moored.

*   *   *

Back on board the *Pacific Star,* the Caloil executives watched the outboard move away from them toward the mainland.

With his eyes still on the boat in the distance, Traveller shook his head. "This mayor is no dummy. There was no way he was going to sign anything without checking out the angles. Putting pressure on him now would get us nothing but hostility. If we can get Deitrich to come over to our side on his own, we'll be in a lot stronger position."

"Whatever you say, Wes. I know how much depends on this operation."

No you don't, thought Wesley Traveller. For Phil Quarles it was just another legal problem. For the president of Caloil, the outcome of the Santa Marta project would decide his future. He was prepared to do anything to ensure that it did not fail. Anything.